For Kris, Scott, and Steven, who make us proud every day.

Art Zimmerman

THE LETTER

AUSTIN MACAULEY PUBLISHERS™

LONDON * CAMBRIDGE * NEW YORK * SHARJAH

Ordering Information
Quantity sales: Special discounts are available on quantity purchases by corporations, associations, and others. For details, contact the publisher at the address below.

Publisher's Cataloging-in-Publication data
Zimmerman, Art
The Letter

ISBN 9798889101826 (Paperback)
ISBN 9798889101833 (ePub e-book)

Library of Congress Control Number: 2023920570

www.austinmacauley.com/us

First Published 2024
Austin Macauley Publishers LLC
40 Wall Street, 33rd Floor, Suite 3302
New York, NY 10005
USA

mail-usa@austinmacauley.com
+1 (646) 5125767

Windfall

A piece of unexpected good fortune, typically one that involves receiving a large amount of money.

I can resist everything but temptation.
Oscar Wilde

Prologue

You don't know me, but I urge you to read the contents of this letter very carefully. I am prepared to deposit $250,000 in an offshore numbered account in your name if you precisely follow my detailed instructions.

Do not copy this letter. After you finish reading it, do not share it with anyone under any circumstances. If you do, your life expectancy will be significantly shortened. If you discuss this letter with your family, friends, police, or anyone else, same result. Trust me, I'll know. For your own good, do not test me. Think of this as a once-in-a-lifetime opportunity.

One week from this Monday morning, drive your own vehicle alone to the Bank of Charleston. Bring a briefcase or shoulder bag. A safety deposit box in your own name has been opened at the bank. The key to that safety deposit box is under the lamp in your bedroom.

In the safety deposit box, you will find a complete set of new credentials, including a driver's license with your photo, credit card, a new pre-paid cell phone, a map of Daufuskie Island, and $1,000 in cash.

Empty the entire contents of the box into your bag and leave the bank. Use the new driver's license and credit card to rent a car from Avis at the Charleston airport. A vehicle is reserved in your new name. Leave your own vehicle in the long-term parking lot. Back it into a parking space in the middle of a row and remove the license plate. Stick the plate into your bag and bring it with you. You'll need it later.

Drive the rental to Hilton Head Island and bring everything from the safety deposit box with you, including the cash, your license plate, and this letter. Also bring both cell phones. When you get to Hilton Head, turn off your old cell phone and leave it off. Then do not make any calls on your old cell phone or your new one. We'll know.

When you arrive on Hilton Head Island, check into the Heritage Hotel in Harbor Town with your new license and credit card. A reservation in that name has been made. When you get to your room, tear up this letter and flush it down the bathroom toilet.

On Tuesday morning, take the ten a.m. ferry from Harbor Town over to Daufuskie Island. Bring everything from the safety deposit box with you, including the two cell phones and license plate. Do not talk to anyone on the ferry.

When you arrive on Daufuskie, a car will be waiting to take you to Blaine Cottage, which is circled on the map. If anyone asks, you are visiting a friend. You will be met at Blaine Cottage by Mr. Jamison, who will give you your final set of instructions.

Do not deviate from any of these instructions. Remember, tell no one. Your future depends on it.

Part One
Tell No One

Chapter 1

August 2017

The fully-loaded Madison Maersk container ship was carrying eighteen-thousand twenty-foot-long shipping containers, as it slowly made its way through the Charleston Harbor and passed under the massive Ravenel Bridge over the Cooper River that connects Charleston and Mt. Pleasant, South Carolina. The Triple E class ship and twenty-man crew then headed to its assigned unloading dock at Port of Charleston's 400-acre Wando Welch Terminal.

The body was sprawled on one of the concrete truck lanes just outside the secondary entrance gates on the opposite side of the terminal.

The terminal's secondary gate complex is flanked by woods and located at the end of Shipping Lane, a short side street off Long Point Road, which leads to the main entrance gates. A cyclone security fence surrounding the port runs between the front and back entrance gates, which are a hundred yards apart from each other. When they're closed, the back gates are padlocked, and the small guard booth next to the gates is unmanned.

Shortly before ten a.m. on a typically hot and humid Monday morning in early August, former Army Ranger and veteran Mt. Pleasant Detective Steve Harris turned right onto Shipping Lane from Long Point and stopped next to a patrol car with its lights flashing. He showed his creds to the cop guarding the street entrance, drove to the other end, and parked next to two more cop cars and the coroner's van.

The senior Mt. Pleasant police officer on the scene was in his fifties and carried a few extra pounds since the day he saved Steve's life. Whenever they ran into each other, Steve's mind automatically flashed back seventeen years like it was yesterday.

He was a rookie cop riding on a routine patrol one evening with Sergeant Buddy Evans, his training officer. Just after dark, a call came over their police radio. A local resident out for a walk with his dog had called 911 on his cell to report hearing what sounded like two gunshots from inside his neighborhood drug store. Only three streets away, Buddy responded he was rolling to the scene. When they parked in front of the store, they put on their vests and drew their weapons. Seeing no one on the street, Buddy quietly ordered, "Boot, follow me in and stay behind me."

The lights were on, but they didn't see any customers. Buddy went in slowly with his weapon raised and called out, "Police!" No response. He pointed to Steve to go left before he headed right toward the pharmacy counter. Steve immediately went into full-alert mode like he was back on patrol in Iraq.

Two minutes later, he was still searching the store when Buddy called out, "Boot, over here." Behind the customer service counter was a middle-aged man on the floor lying in a puddle of blood with two holes in his now red and white lab coat.

Steve cautiously walked out of a side aisle and headed toward Buddy when he heard a scraping sound from somewhere behind him. His Ranger training kicked in, and he immediately dropped to one knee, a split second before a shot whizzed past his head. He rolled to his right and spun around to locate the threat, just in time to see a man's head explode a few feet in front of him. Before the crackhead could get off a second shot, Buddy fired two quick rounds into the man's face.

Steve walked over to his former mentor, and the two old friends shook hands. Buddy said, "How's it going, Steve? Haven't seen you around the shop much lately. Since the body over there was found outside the port security fence, it's in our jurisdiction. Chief told me he wanted our best senior detective to take the lead on this one, at least for now." He smiled and couldn't help adding, "Boot, that would be you."

Steve shook his head and laughed. "Morning Sarge. Chief also called me and told me to get right over here. Since the body is next to the port, I'm sure he'll also loop in the Port Authority, State Police, and Charleston County Sheriff, at least until we get a handle on what went down here. By the way, nice police work by your team on that jewelry store robbery. One of your leads is about to pay off."

Buddy said, "Judy Shuster, our newbie patrol officer, gets all the credit. She's the one who found something the dumb asses left behind in the store. Let me know when you arrest those clowns."

Steve looked over the scene and took charge. "What do you know so far?"

Buddy gave him a quick update. "A Mt. Pleasant resident called 911 from his SUV, a little before eight this morning after he spotted the body lying over there. The dispatcher called our department, and the alert went out on the radio. First cars on the scene blocked the entrance to Shipping Lane, and one of my guys confirmed the victim was definitely deceased. Since it was just outside the port, the Chief asked me to get out here and help the patrol guys secure the scene until you arrived. County Coroner showed up about forty-five minutes ago."

Steve looked around again and said, "Ask your guys to hang close until the crime scene boys get here. And have someone run some tape across the entire Shipping Lane entrance. Let's keep the street blocked off until my guys finish. Since the coroner is already here, I'll let you know when he plans to load up the body. Can't wait to hear his lecture since he got here before I did."

Well aware of the coroner's constipated disposition, Buddy replied with a grin, "That's our Bob. I'll have one of my patrol cars stay at the entrance and keep this street clear until the coroner and your team leave. There aren't any houses back here, mostly just woods. Doubt anybody saw anything, but I'll have a couple of my guys canvas the nearby businesses between Shipping Lane and Wando Park Blvd. Maybe we get lucky and someone saw or heard something. You need anything else, just holler."

"Thanks Buddy. I'll have our tech guys check for any tire tracks in that vacant lot I noticed next to the entrance. The dead guy and whoever killed him may have driven together and parked there. When I'm finished here, I'll get in touch with port security and review their surveillance tapes. Hopefully, the cameras picked something up. I'll also talk to the security guards at the main entrance, see if one of them noticed anything."

Buddy left to brief the cops on the scene, and Steve headed for the body. Crime scene tape was already stretched twenty feet in front of it across all four concrete lanes leading to the locked security gates that were closed that day. Steve pulled a pair of Tyvek booties over his size fourteens and gloved up before ducking his six-foot five-inch frame under the tape.

He approached a man kneeling next to a body that was lying near the left-hand security gate closest to the woods. Two muscular forearms poked out from a short-sleeved black shirt that matched the color of the dead man's hair. Below his worn cargo shorts were a pair of small, boat-shoed feet, no socks.

The victim was around five-eight with a hardened face that featured a thin half-moon scar along his right jawline down to his chin. His full head of long black hair was streaked with gray and covered his ears, completing a facial ensemble straight out of a low budget gangster movie that skipped the theaters and went straight to cable.

Charleston County Coroner Bob Jenkins was directing his forensic tech to take a few more close-up photos of the head. Jenkins was a small, thin man who looked ten years older than fifty-six. He had a long, thin nose, penetrating dark eyes, and lots of extra forehead that eventually reached a receding mane of long gray hair tied in a ponytail. In his white Tyvek coveralls, Steve thought he looked like a melting snowman.

The two men were good friends on and off the job and had worked several crime scenes together over the years since Steve made detective. They quickly fell into their familiar banter. Steve said, "Looks a lot like a dead body. Must be important to get you out here."

Bob looked up and deadpanned, "Morning Steve, or is it afternoon? Glad you could get here before lunch."

"Yeah, yeah, my bad. I was up in North Charleston on a Mt. Pleasant robbery case and took me a while to get around a traffic mess on 526 after a lumber truck dumped half its load early on the Wando Bridge. Don't mention it to the Chief. He told me to get my ass down here pronto. Anyway, I figured you'd already have the case wrapped up before I got here."

Bob returned fire. "Didn't think you were even allowed in North Charleston. But your uncanny powers of observation are still dead on. It is, in fact, a dead body. He was on his stomach before we turned him over for a look at his face. Hispanic male. Looks to be north of fifty but could be younger. One shot through and through the back and two more to the back of the head."

He pointed to an evidence bag. "Found this one shell casing under the body. No visible exit wounds from the head shots, so we should find those bullets in the body. No obvious defensive wounds. Based on the direction of the body, looks like the first shot was in the back as our dead man walking, or running, came out of those woods along the fence and fell right here. Killer made sure he stayed down with a double tap to the brain."

Steve couldn't resist one more taunt. "Strictly off the record, Bob, what do you think? Any chance this was a pro hit?"

"Just a hunch, and don't hold me to it, but he probably wasn't shot twice in the head by an amateur."

Back to business, Steve asked, "Any idea yet on time of death?"

"I'll confirm TOD when we get him back to the shop, but best guess right now is between five-thirty and six a.m. this morning, closer to six. We're almost ready to bag him and get him out of this heat before I end up lying next to him."

"Any ID?"

"No wallet, no car keys, empty pockets, nada. We'll run his prints through the system and see if we get anything. I'll call you with a prelim on the body, probably sometime tomorrow."

"Works for me, Bob. Crime scene guys are on the way. We'll search the entire area, including those woods along the security fence. Maybe find some footprints. We need to figure out how they both got here and why only one of them left. The shooter and maybe the vic, if they knew each other, could've parked in that vacant lot next to the Shipping Lane entrance."

As Bob turned back to the body, Steve said, "One last question. Who found him?"

The coroner pointed to a Pathfinder parked on the far corner of the street, just past the patrol cars. "Guy over there by that SUV. Said he missed his turn at Wando Park, came down here to turn around, and saw the body. Name is Terry Shaw. He was sure the man was dead. Shaw told Buddy he didn't touch anything, called 911 on his cell, and waited for the cavalry to arrive. Buddy has his contact info and asked him to hang around until you got here."

"OK, I'll talk to him before I cut him loose. If you get anything else, give me a shout."

Steve took another look around and walked over to the SUV. The middle-aged man leaning against the hood was holding a bottle of water and still looked shaken. He told Steve the same story he told Buddy and had nothing new to add. Steve thanked him and told him someone would be in touch if they needed anything else before sending him on his way.

As the crime scene techs began to arrive, Steve had a bad feeling things were going to get a lot more complicated. He had no idea how right he was.

Chapter 2

Steven Henry Harris was the oldest of four children and blessed with the genes to be a leader in whatever life had in store for him.

"Welcome to the world, Steve, you're late," his dad said with a big smile, when his son arrived on the scene a week later than expected after his wife Martha's difficult first pregnancy. Weighing in at just over eleven pounds and 23 inches long, he was already big for his age.

Raised in a military family, Steve's grandfather was decorated Marine Captain Walter Harris, a forward observer in the bloody battle of Iwo Jima. His job was to call in air strikes on the heavily armed enemy hunkered down in the mountains. He made it home from World War II a decorated hero.

Steve's father Henry was an army infantry platoon sergeant in Vietnam. Unlike his father, he came home to a nation in turmoil over the war with little fanfare. During his final battle, five of his men lost their lives when they were attacked from a hidden Viet Cong underground tunnel. Sergeant Henry Harris was wounded in the leg but survived the surprise attack after calling in air strikes. He was awarded a Purple Heart for his trouble.

Steve inherited his strict code of conduct from his grandfather and father that left no gray area between right and wrong. He would eventually follow them in the family business.

By the time he got to high school in Mt. Pleasant, Steve was the biggest kid in the class, already taller than his father. A man among boys, he was now over six feet tall and still growing. Despite his size and a quick temper he kept well hidden, everyone he met thought of him as a gentle giant with a ready smile. He was a good student and well-liked by his teachers. He also frustrated the school's athletic coaches by refusing to play any sports despite being a natural athlete. He told them he needed to concentrate on his grades to make sure he was the first one in his family to go to college. And he meant it.

To his fellow students, Steve Harris was a loyal friend, especially if one of those friends ever got in trouble. To his younger brother, two years behind him, and his two sisters still in elementary school, he was their protector as well as their big brother.

Two months after starting his final year of high school, Steve lost his best friend. The bad day started when the school principal came to his classroom and told the teacher Steve was needed in the office.

"What's going on?" he asked as they headed to the office.

"There was a phone call for you from your mom. She asked us to call her back as soon as you got to my office," replied the principal.

His brother Glen was already there. When the secretary saw Steve, she dialed the phone, waited for an answer, then handed it to him. "It's your mother."

"Hi Mom, it's me. What's up?" he asked cheerfully.

As soon as she spoke, he knew the news was not good. "Steven, your dad's been in a car accident," she sobbed. "He's in the hospital, and I'm here with him. Mr. Harvey next door is on his way to pick you and your brother up at school and bring you here. I've already told the principal, and he said he'd wait with you and Glen outside until he gets there. Mrs. Williams will pick up your sisters from Mt. Pleasant Elementary and bring them to her house."

His heart was now pounding. "Mom, is Dad going to be OK?"

"It's bad. He's in surgery. The doctors told me they're doing all they can for him. I'll meet you in the emergency room. I need to go." She hung up and left Steve staring at the phone in disbelief.

By the time he and Glen got to the hospital, they were too late. Their dad never made it off the operating table, and Arlington National Cemetery would welcome another hero before his time. Henry Harris was off that day from his security job after retiring from the army. On his way home from a quick trip to the local hardware store, his car was hit head on by a drunk driver who died at the scene.

Steve was devastated and struggled to come to terms with his new reality. Never again would he hear his father's voice telling him about life and leadership and family and the future.

He remembered his dad's words of advice back when he started high school. "Son, the most important promises you make in life are the ones you make to yourself. None of us knows how long we're gonna be on this planet, but as long as you're here, make the most of your opportunities. And if you ever fall short of an important goal, never give up. Just make sure the reason you fell short wasn't because you didn't do your very best."

Steve also realized he needed to adjust his plans after he graduated. With his dad gone and the family's finances now stretched to the limit, he knew college would have to wait and decided to join the army instead. He figured if he still wanted to get a college degree when he got out, he could always make that decision later.

After being promoted to Corporal and on a fast track to making Sergeant, he enrolled in the Army Ranger course. Despite the hardest physical and mental challenge of his life, two months later he was one of the few from his Ranger class to make it through. A month later, his unit was deployed to Iraq. Newly promoted Sergeant Steve Harris had found his calling, or at least he thought he had.

Until the second bad day of his life changed everything.

Two months before the end of his initial four-year army enlistment, Steve lost his brother Glen. He was killed by a stray bullet from a gang shootout on his way home after visiting some friends one evening. He'd been back home on a semester break from Virginia Tech, where he'd earned a full academic scholarship.

Despite an intensive police investigation, the shooter was never found. Steve had lost some good friends during his tour in Iraq, but nothing prepared him for his intense anger bordering on rage, along with the guilt he felt over the senseless death of the brother he couldn't protect while his killer walked the streets. He'd survived a war zone, but his little brother was dead. Glen was the smartest and kindest kid he ever knew and wouldn't hurt a fly.

Glen's killer was still at large during the final weeks of Steve's army career, and he made a life-changing decision. Instead of reenlisting, he left the army when his initial enlistment period ended and returned to his hometown to join the Mt. Pleasant Police Department.

That unexpected decision took the army by surprise, and his commanding officer did everything he could to talk him into staying. Steve was already a decorated hero after saving several soldiers when his platoon was ambushed during routine patrol in Iraq. The army needed leaders like him. But his mind was made up. His mother understood why, even if the army didn't. She knew in her heart Glen would too.

Steve Harris was in his seventeenth year with the Mt. Pleasant police department, the last ten as a homicide detective, when he was assigned to the port murder case. His relentless determination to never let a serious crime go unsolved on his watch had earned him the respect of every man and woman on the force.

That fierce resolve was about to be put to the toughest test of his career.

Chapter 3

August 2017

Emily Baker was always fast. Even on the playground in grade school, she easily outran the boys always chasing her to pull her ponytail. Growing up as an only child, she dreamed of following in her mother's footsteps and becoming a teacher. Until her parents, Jim and Mary Baker, died in a private plane crash that tuned Emily's world upside down just as she was about to start her junior year of high school.

They were flying across the state from Charleston to Greenville, South Carolina, for Jim's latest job interview. To save money, Jim's only bother offered to fly them in his small four-seater. Accident investigators eventually determined the crash was weather-related due to a severe thunderstorm between Columbia and Greenville. The plane went down in a stand of pine trees fifty miles from the Greenville airport. There were no survivors.

To make matters worse, her parents were struggling financially to make ends meet since her father lost his job at a failed start-up venture. Barely able to afford the rent on her mother's teacher salary, they were forced to cut back on expenses and canceled Jim's life insurance policy two months before the accident.

After the funeral, Emily moved in with her mother's older sister, Marie Parker. Her aunt was a widow and never remarried after her husband died of a sudden heart attack several years ago.

Joe Parker had been CEO of the highly successful software engineering company he founded. Marie was the primary beneficiary of her husband's estate, including a substantial life insurance policy. Shortly after his death, she moved into a new two-bedroom townhome on Daniel Island, the popular master-planned community situated between the Cooper and Wando Rivers. Running through the 4,000-acre island is I-526, a 20-mile auxiliary route of I-26 that loops around Charleston from West Ashley to Mt. Pleasant.

Emily had no other relatives or immediate family living in the Charleston area and was never very close to any of her grandparents. Her mother's parents lived on the West Coast, and her dad's parents retired early and moved to Arizona a few years ago. Emily had zero interest in moving to California or Arizona.

Since she was now living in a different school district, Marie helped her get approval from the Charleston County School District to attend Mt. Pleasant High School so she could at least be with her friends. Marie told the school board Emily would be able to use her dad's car to drive herself from Daniel Island to the high school. Her mom's old car had already been sold for peanuts.

Devastated by the loss of both parents, Emily constantly worried about how she would ever be able to afford college and realize her childhood dream. Despite the tragedy, she studied hard in high school and was an above average student. But it wasn't until she joined the high school track team that she was finally able to regain her balance.

She fell in love with running track. Her track coach was so impressed with her speed and work ethic, he told her she had the ability to get a track scholarship if she kept working hard and went for it. When she was offered an athletic scholarship to Clemson in her senior year, her dream of honoring her mother and becoming a teacher was reborn.

Emily excelled on the Clemson track team all four years, especially in her favorite event, the 5,000 meters. She graduated with honors and her coveted B.A. in Education. Returning home from Clemson for the final time, she moved back in with Aunt Marie. She couldn't wait to start her new job in August teaching fifth grade at Mt. Pleasant Elementary, the same school she attended as a young girl.

She didn't quite know how to broach the subject with her aunt about getting her own apartment until one evening over dinner to celebrate her new teaching job. She finally got up the courage to ask her, "What would you think about me getting my own place? Now that I'm starting my new teaching job in a couple months, I'll be able to afford it. Auntie, I think it's time I started making it on my own."

Marie smiled and held her gaze on Emily as she replied. "Emily dear, you know I'll always love you like my own daughter, and you're welcome to stay here as long as you want. It's been the joy of my life to watch you grow up and mature into a beautiful and responsible young woman these past few years. Your mom and dad would be so proud of you."

As a tear rolled down her cheek, Emily said, "I could never have gotten through losing them and finishing school without you always being there for me. I'm so grateful for all you've done. If it wasn't for you, I don't know what would've happened to me."

It was Marie's turn to dab her eyes. "Since you got home from Clemson, I've known you're more than ready to move on with your life. Of course, you have my blessing. As long as you promise to come to dinner once in a while."

Emily got up and gave Marie a long hug. "Thank you so much, Auntie. You know I wouldn't miss your lasagna for anything in the world."

They both laughed before Marie turned serious. "I know your finances are tight, so I'll take care of your first couple month's rent and your personal expenses until you get your first paycheck." Before Emily could object, Marie added, "Don't even think about arguing. It's settled."

Two weeks later, Emily found an affordable one-bedroom unit in the Anchor Apartments complex along Whipple Road in Mt. Pleasant, only a few miles from her new job. Emily signed the lease and her aunt co-signed. Marie also bought her some kitchen utensils and new furniture, including a couch and chairs for the living room, a dining set, and a new bed and dresser. Emily was finally ready to begin the next chapter in her life.

Even though her Clemson track days were behind her, she still ran nearly every morning. She loved the solitude of her early runs and was usually out the door by five a.m., well before most of the residents in her apartment complex even began waking up.

Every so often, she ran her favorite five-mile loop on the sidewalks from her apartment onto Whipple, then left down Long Point Road, which ended at the Port of Charleston entrance gates, before returning home. Even at her normal easy pace, she always made sure to finish those five-mile runs under thirty-five minutes with a sprint over the final quarter mile along Whipple back to her apartment.

After one of her early August morning runs to the port and back, Emily got her daily call from Aunt Marie to see how her run went and tell her niece to have a good day. Emily didn't mind Marie checking up on her. She knew her aunt missed having her around.

"Good morning sweetie, how was the run today?"

"Hi Auntie. The run was great, even in all this humidity. Just an easy five miles under 35 minutes."

"Well, you certainly aren't slowing down in your old age. I meant to ask you yesterday, why don't you invite that nice young man Richard you've been telling me about when you come for dinner on Friday?"

Emily smiled, well aware that her protective aunt was dying to meet him and check him out. "Sure, I'll ask him if he can come along. I think he gets back into town from a business trip to Chicago on Thursday. Hopefully, we can both come. See you then."

She had literally run into Richard Barnett a few weeks earlier at the finish line of a local 5K race after she blew past him with her trademark sprint over the last fifty yards. They hadn't seen each other since their Mt. Pleasant High School track days, and even then, they weren't in the same circle of friends. Richard had graduated from the University of South Carolina a year before Emily got her Clemson degree. He finished near the top of his class with a degree in Civil Engineering and joined the Charleston office of a major commercial construction firm.

"Nice finish," he said to her back as he crossed the finish line just behind her.

When Emily turned around and looked at him, she was both surprised and a little embarrassed. "Richard! Gosh, I didn't even recognize you. So sorry about that, I promise I wasn't trying to show you up. I was just locked in on the line."

Richard gave her a big smile and said, "Emily, you haven't changed a bit. Still as competitive as ever and still faster than me. We should catch up sometime, maybe have lunch or something."

"Love to," she smiled back. Since she wasn't seeing anyone special after she returned from Clemson, they exchanged cell numbers. Two days later they had lunch, followed by dinner the following week in downtown Charleston at Magnolia's for Richard's favorite shrimp and grits.

Emily was on a tight budget and glad Richard insisted on treating. Once they'd reconnected, their relationship quickly evolved from a few casual dates to talking on the phone every day to eventually something much more serious.

A week before the new school year began, Emily couldn't wait for her first day as a new teacher. She imagined she felt just like she did when she started first grade. Anxious and excited at the same time. She set up her classroom the way she'd always dreamed about it. On one wall, she put up a photo of each of her students that she got from their parents. In the middle of the pictures was a sign over a prominent empty space, to display a photo of her *Student of the Week.*

Soon after school started, her classroom walls were covered with colorful student artwork and class projects, along with her Classroom Rules and a pet turtle box in the back corner. On the blackboard every morning was her *Word of the Day*. On the first day of school, the word was *Marathon.*

Chapter 4

August 2017

Late morning on Tuesday, the day after the murdered body was found just outside the Port of Charleston's largest container terminal, Bob Jenkins called Steve with an update on the autopsy.

"I got some info on your dead guy. I'll email you a copy of my preliminary autopsy report, but no surprises. Cause of death was the two gunshots to the back of the head. Close range, probably four or five feet at most. Found both bullets from the head shots and sent them to ballistics. The shot in the back was through and through and not fatal. That bullet could be anywhere."

"Anything else?" Steve asked.

"I also found some fresh bruising on his chest and upper arms, almost like someone was repeatedly poking or punching him hard in the chest and grabbing his arms. Still waiting on the full tox screen from the lab. I'll also email you some photos of an identical tattoo on both upper arms. Looks like some kind of symbol, maybe a gang, but I don't recognize it. Could be something or nothing."

"Any change in your time of death estimate?"

"Body was lying in the heat before we got there, but TOD was still sometime between five a.m. and six a.m. yesterday morning, give or take a few minutes either way. Body was still fresh when I got there."

"Were you able to ID him?"

"We ran his prints and got a hit from the national database. Name is Jorge Rodriguez. Forty-eight, born in Mexico City and immigrated to the US in '95 at age twenty-two to live with his uncle Manny in Miami after his parents split. Became a US Citizen in 2008. Passport records show several trips between Miami and Mexico City between 2010 and 2015, nothing since."

"Any rap sheet?"

"He did some time in 2015 for possession when a Drug Enforcement Administration sniffer dog found a small amount of cocaine in the liner of his suitcase at the Miami airport after his last trip to Mexico City. DEA already had his prints in the system from a prior arrest."

"Where did you get that tidbit?"

"I talked to a DEA friend of mine over in Columbia, and he suggested we get in touch with Dale Hawkins, a DEA Special Agent in Miami. Hawkins heads up an international task force to track and intercept the drug cartel pipeline from South and Central America into Mexico and through our southern border before eventually reaching Florida. My guy says Hawkins is a bloodhound and has an encyclopedia of information about the major drug cartels, including the largest one operating in Miami. He's been with the DEA since graduating from the DEA Academy at Quantico twenty-two years ago. This guy knows all the cartel players."

"How can I reach him?"

"I called Hawkins earlier today, and he agreed to pull his file on Rodriguez. Sounded like a good guy on the phone and told me he'd lend us a hand any way he can. I'll text you his number, he's expecting your call."

"Thanks Bob, let me know if you turn up anything else."

As soon as he got the number, Steve wasted no time making the call. "Agent Hawkins, this is Mt. Pleasant Police Department Detective Steve Harris. Our County Coroner Bob Jenkins said he talked to you this morning. He told me you might be able to share some information about Jorge Rodriguez."

"Call me Dale, Detective," said Hawkins in a friendly voice. "How can I help you?"

Steve grinned and said, "Thanks Dale. My wife calls me Steve, at least most of the time, and that works for me. Bob said you have a file on Mr. Rodriguez. I'm calling to get any background on him you can share with us. Bob told me you guys arrested him back in 2015 for possession. Anything else you have on him would be much appreciated."

"Bob said you'd be in touch, so I dug out everything we have." Referring to the file in front of him, Dale gave Steve a quick summary on Rodriguez. "When he came to the US in '95, Jorge Rodriguez started working in Miami in his uncle Manny's construction company. Same last name. Manny Rodriguez did mostly residential remodeling stuff, kitchens, bathrooms, additions, deck replacements, that sort of thing. Jorge was basically a gopher and also took care of pickups and deliveries to his uncle's job sites. When Manny's business went under in 2014 after the bank canceled his credit line for too many late payments, Jorge got a job driving for a small local moving company called *Move It or Lose It* in South Florida."

"What were the circumstances around Jorge's drug arrest in 2015?" Steve asked.

"Pretty straightforward. We arrested him at the Miami airport after his last trip to Mexico City to visit some family members. At least that's what he told us. One of our dogs sniffed out a small amount of coke in his suitcase. We seized his passport, and he pled guilty to one count of possession. Second offense got him some jail time. When he got out of prison in early 2016, he was hired the same day as a delivery driver for Auto Warehouse, a retail auto parts company with six stores in South Florida, including Miami."

"How did he get a job so fast with a criminal record?"

"Here's where it gets interesting, Steve. Jorge was hired by the owner of Auto Warehouse, a Mr. Paul Franco. We've had him on our radar and think he may be involved with the Camino cartel's Florida drug operation. But so far, we've come up empty."

"What makes you say Franco is involved with the Camino cartel?"

"Most of our information is from one of our confidential informants. So far, we haven't been able to link Auto Warehouse with Camino, but we still believe there's a connection. We just haven't found it yet."

"How does that tie in with Jorge Rodriguez?"

"One of our DEA guys recognized Jorge from his arrest in 2015 when he showed up last year on one of our surveillance tapes of the Auto Warehouse parts storage facility in Miami. DEA had a tip that the Camino cartel might be using that warehouse as a distribution point. In early 2016, we started keeping tabs on Jorge, and also began taking a closer look at his trips to Mexico City before his arrest. We know the Camino organization is moving drugs from Mexico City to Florida."

"Anything turn up?"

"A month after we started watching Jorge last year, he dropped completely off the grid, and we lost him."

"Until he showed up dead in my backyard yesterday," said Steve. "What about his uncle, Manny Rodriguez?"

"After he lost his business in 2014, Manny was still doing some construction work, odd jobs he'd pick up here and there. We were able to trace him through his bank records and a credit card he managed to keep active until 2016. Shortly after we lost track of Jorge last year, Manny also disappeared around the same time. There's been no credit card use and no banking activity since, even though there's still over five hundred dollars in his checking account. He just vanished."

"Sounds like you think there's a drug connection between Manny and Jorge since they both dropped off your radar at the same time last year. Pretty big coincidence."

"You probably know how we feel about coincidences. Manny didn't have a passport and never traveled to Mexico City or anywhere else out of the country, at least as far as we can tell. But one of our theories is that Manny and Jorge worked together for several years in the Camino distribution network. We think Jorge may have been a Camino runner on his trips to Mexico City, and Manny coordinated the Miami end."

Steve said, "Until they both disappeared last year."

"That's right. Jorge surfaces in your town shot in the back of the head and, for all we know, Manny ended up as an alligator snack in the Everglades."

"Who's the top man these days in the Camino cartel's Miami operation?"

Dale explained the backstory. "His name is Joseph Camino. His father Carlos used to run the Camino cartel in Mexico. When Joseph was ready, Carlos sent his son to run the Camino operation in Miami several years ago. Joseph is the invisible man and keeps a very low profile. We've had an arrest warrant out for him on federal drug charges but haven't been able to find him. He's a ghost."

"You said Carlos Camino *used* to run the Camino cartel in Mexico. Where is he now?"

"Carlos died three years ago from a migraine bullet headache. We heard from one of our undercovers in Mexico that the rival Sanchez cartel believed Carlos was trying to move in on them, and Miguel Sanchez decided to give him a dirt nap."

"Sounds like you're back to square one on your end."

"We're still digging around Auto Warehouse to find a Camino link, especially since Jorge worked there when he got out of prison. We've now got an undercover working there. Meantime, do me a favor and give me a heads up if you turn anything up on your end. I'll also send you a copy of the file with everything we have on Jorge."

After exchanging email addresses and phone numbers, Steve said, "Dale, you've been a big help. We'll absolutely keep you in the loop. I'm going to email you a photo of the same tattoo on both of Jorge's upper arms, maybe they'll be familiar to you. I'll stay in touch."

The potential drug angle wasn't a big surprise to Steve given Jorge Rodriguez was apparently executed. Based on the information he just got from Hawkins, the involvement of a Miami drug cartel in his murder case was now a definite possibility.

He still had a lot of unanswered questions, starting with why Rodriguez was gunned down just outside the port.

Chapter 5

August 2018

Chuck Wilson was a burly 18-wheel truck driver with Popeye arms and an extra forty pounds, much of it from a large gut that made his belt invisible in the middle of his wide six-foot body. Now on the other side of fifty, his round stubbled face was dominated by two overgrown bushy eyebrows that almost met in the middle. On top was a thinning gray buzz cut. He also had a friendly smile for everyone he met.

He'd spent a lot of time on the road driving big rigs around the country ever since he got his commercial driver's license over twenty years ago. Whenever his distinctive raspy voice, laced with a heavy southern drawl, was heard on truck cab radios out on the interstates, his trucker buddies all knew it was Chucktown, that driver from Charleston.

A few months after turning fifty, Chuck was finally able to buy his own spacious tractor trailer sleeper cab, decked out with the latest bells and whistles and plenty of room for his XXL frame. Although the bank loan to buy the cab had set him back over a hundred grand with his cabin as collateral, he knew it was worth it. He spent a lot more time on the road than he did in the rundown family cabin he'd inherited in McClellanville, South Carolina.

Chuck was lucky he still owned the cabin. He'd enjoyed living alone and had been single most of his life, except for a brief period of wedded bliss two years ago with Carol. She was a thirty-five-year-old twice-divorced waitress he'd met at the Love's Truck Stop just outside of Atlanta. He chatted her up whenever he was driving through, and on one trip they became more than friends.

After a whirlwind romance that wasn't her first rodeo, they were married a month later. To no one's surprise, they didn't even get within shouting distance of their first anniversary before Carol filed for the marriage trifecta, her third divorce. Like a lot of Carol's decisions, marrying Chuck seemed like a good idea. Until it wasn't. Living in a tiny cabin in the woods in the middle of nowhere, with Chuck spending more time on the road than with her, wasn't exactly the fairy tale she envisioned. She'd had enough.

When he got home at the end of another long road trip, Carol was watching the end of another mindless TV rerun. This one was called *Pimp My Ride* about a couple of gearheads who tricked up campers, station wagons, and anything else on four wheels, with custom interiors. That day they were converting the back of a van by adding a bed, two captain's chairs, surround sound with some high-end TV and stereo equipment, and a mini bar. The inside walls were covered in faux sheepskin. *Livin' the Dream* was painted on the outside.

"Honey, I'm home," Chuck said with a wide smile as he pushed through the cabin front door.

"Honey, I'm gone," replied Carol matter-of-factly without getting up. She wanted nothing more to do with the cabin, or Chuck, and filed for divorce first thing on Monday morning. She told her lawyer to negotiate a settlement as quickly as possible and headed back to Atlanta.

Chuck took the collapse of his first, and probably last, marriage in stride. Fortunately, he'd wisely saved some money from his dad's life insurance policy as the sole beneficiary when he died a few years after his mom passed. Although the final divorce settlement put a dent in his retirement nest egg, at least Chuck still owned the cabin free and clear.

Truth was, he was much happier being married to his new Peterbilt sleeper cab, which allowed him to finally become his own boss as an independent trucker. Painted on both side doors of the imposing cab were the words *Chucktown Special* in fancy gold script. The *Pimp My Ride* boys would've been proud.

Chuck loved growing up in the small town of McClellanville, named by local villagers nearly two hundred years ago in honor of the McClellan family, the oldest settlers in the area. His parents bought the small two-bedroom cabin when they were married. Now it was a certified fixer-upper that barely survived the monster Hurricane Hugo almost thirty years earlier.

The old cabin sat on a wooded half-acre lot, including a small yard of mostly dirt with a few patches of indigenous weeds. Just inside the front door was a fairly spacious living room with a separate side door to a screened porch. The open plan kitchen was small, and the only bathroom was between two small bedrooms in the back. About the only thing he could afford to do the past few years was add a large gravel pad on the far side of the front yard to park his new sleeper cab.

For the past several months, Chuck was contracted by the Port of Charleston to transport standard twenty-foot shipping containers, from the port to warehouse facilities throughout the South and Midwest. Even though he enjoyed his home away from home in the new sleeper cab, Chuck was looking forward to a quiet weekend at the cabin with a case of beer, steaks on the grill, and a little summer fishing. Just what the doctor ordered.

Before he arrived at the cabin on this particular Friday, he stopped for some groceries at the small store in McClellanville, then swung by the local post office to pick up his mail. He'd decided to get to a P.O. Box several years ago so his mail didn't keep piling up in his rusty mailbox, now about to fall over, on the mile-long dirt road that led from Highway 17 back to the cabin.

He parked the *Chucktown Special* in the front yard and headed inside with his beer and groceries that included a huge sirloin and some bait. He cranked up the window air conditioner, popped the tab on his first cold one, and fired up the outdoor grill. When the steak was rare and the beans were hot, he grabbed another beer and was a happy man. After dinner, he settled into his favorite beat-up recliner that had seen better days but was too comfortable to take to the dump. It was also a perfect match with the worn-out couch.

As soon as it got dark, he shuffled into his bedroom and hit the sack. The plan was to be up bright and early on Saturday morning for some fishing. He still loved to fish along Jeremy Creek whenever he was home. As a young boy, he fished the creek and nearby Bulls Bay every chance he got.

Saturday morning around five a.m. he started the coffee maker. To catch the early tide, he wanted to have a line in the water by six. After a lighter than normal breakfast of three large biscuits loaded with ham and plenty of milk to wash it down, he grabbed his fishing gear and some bait and headed out the door.

He hoped Connor would be out fishing off the dock on the other side so he could find out what was biting and what they were biting on. Connor was a fourteen-year-old local kid who Chuck knew without a doubt was a bona fide fish whisperer. The kid had an almost mystical knack for catching fish any time of the year in any weather.

"Hey Connor, where's the fish?" Chuck hollered across the creek.

Connor yelled back his standard answer, "In the creek, Mr. Wilson."

"Anything biting yet?"

Connor proudly reached into his cooler and held up a large redfish. "The redfish are hungrier than a man on a diet. Got two nice ones already."

After an hour, Chuck still hadn't caught anything but enjoyed watching Connor reel in two more. By the time the tide stopped running a couple hours later, Chuck had only managed to snag one small redfish and a decent-sized flounder before heading back to the cabin. A perfect start to a beautiful day.

Whenever he was home for the weekend, Chuck made it a habit to eat at least once at T.W. Graham, his favorite local seafood restaurant on Pinkney Street. He always enjoyed sharing a few beers and swapping stories with some of the old-timers on Saturday nights. After checking the air pressure in his belly, he decided to walk to the restaurant from the cabin. It was only a mile, and he needed the exercise. His other option was to drive the junker pickup truck he kept parked behind the cabin, but he didn't want to risk getting stopped until he fixed the broken taillight.

"Hey Chucktown, where you back from?" George called from his table as soon as he saw his best friend lumber through the front door with sweat dripping down his face. George Cooper took early retirement several years ago from the old steel mill in Georgetown and had known Chuck since he was a boy.

"Hey Georgie, been out to Memphis for some of them fantastic ribs. Just got back yesterday and heading out again on Monday for Birmingham. Somebody's gotta work around here. Got room for one more?"

George waved him over, and Chuck turned with two fingers in the air and called over to Marge, who looked like she was performing a Cirque du Soleil balancing act with a large tray of food. She was in her mid-fifties with a full head of bright red hair and a permanent twinkle in her eyes.

Marge Mason had been a waitress at Graham's for over twenty-five years since she and Sam, her late husband, bought a vacant bungalow near the restaurant three years after Hugo. Fortunately, the mortgage was paid off before Sam's illness, and she was able to stay in the place she had come to love. Everyone in town was a friend of Marge.

"Margie, two cold ones, please, when you get a minute."

"Comin' right up, Chuck," she said as she glided by.

Chuck ordered the fresh redfish when Marge brought the beers. Probably end up with one of Connor's, he smiled to himself. Over dinner, he regaled

George with his latest road warrior stories before heading back to the cabin for an early bedtime.

He was wide awake by five a.m. on Sunday morning, well before the sun cleared the tall pine trees around the cabin. He soon got to work in the kitchen preparing his favorite big boy breakfast of a half dozen sausage links, three scrambled eggs, a heaping bowl of grits, and two oversized buttered biscuits. When he finished, he sank down into the recliner to look through the stack of mail he'd thrown on the warped coffee table in the living room on Friday. The small wooden table hadn't seen a drop of furniture polish in years.

Chuck was a junk mail junkie and loved to read through the monthly 'annual sale' flyers, direct mail coupon packets, occupant postcards touting 50% off for three days only, and summer clearance discount letters from one or two local car dealers. Since he had a P.O. Box, every piece of junk mail addressed to occupant was automatically stuffed into Chuck's box. He'd been on the road most of the past couple weeks and there was plenty of mail to keep him occupied.

Despite the stout monthly payment on his sleeper cab bank loan, he still loved window shopping from the comfort of his recliner for all the stuff he didn't need. A white envelope in the pile caught his eye. It looked too fancy to be an ordinary sales pitch. His name and address were typed on the front, including his P.O. Box number, but there was no return address and no postmark. Some kind of logo was on the back that didn't look familiar.

He carefully tore it open and began reading the formal typewritten letter inside. Chuck was an honest guy, but that kind of windfall would change anyone's life, especially his.

He thought about just chucking the letter and ignoring it. Except for the money. And especially the threat. He didn't scare easily, but it sounded real, and a shiver of fear began snaking down his spine.

Chapter 6

August 2018

John and Mandy Simpson were an attractive couple. They'd known each other since fifth grade and were sweethearts all through high school. Both were good athletes. John played on the football and baseball teams, and Mandy excelled as a guard on the girls' basketball team that lost the AAA state championship game by just two points in her senior year.

Their Charleston hometown had always been a popular tourist destination with its historic downtown, plenty of golf courses, world-class beaches on Isle of Palms, Sullivan's Island and Folly Beach, along with a generous helping of Southern charm. As more and more people began moving to Charleston in the nineties, residential construction exploded like weeds in an abandoned garden.

By the time they graduated from high school together, the housing boom in the entire Lowcountry region around Charleston had already been thriving for twenty years and showed no signs of slowing down. John had no trouble finding a construction job with a regional home builder. Mandy started working part-time as a salesclerk in a small retail clothing store while taking classes at Trident Tech, a local community college, for an Associate Degree in Accounting.

After getting her degree, Mandy found a full-time job in the accounting department of a small but growing local marketing company. The office was on the second floor of a renovated cigar factory in downtown Charleston on East Bay Street.

John and Mandy got married that summer. Money was tight and neither of their parents had much to spare but chipped in on a small 'wedding hall' for the ceremony and reception. The venue was an old addition attached to Garrett's Restaurant, located several miles north of Charleston on Highway 17 between Mt. Pleasant and Awendaw. The restaurant was owned by the Garrett family for three generations, and the locals knew the best southern fried chicken and fried everything else was on the menu.

The addition was basically a side room attached to the old restaurant over forty years ago. The décor was shabby chic without the chic. There was barely enough space for a small dance floor surrounded by a folding head table for the wedding party and six card tables covered with faded beige tablecloths for the few close friends they could afford to invite.

When the reception was over and everyone else left the restaurant, Mr. and Mrs. John Simpson hugged each other and stayed behind for one more dance by themselves. They'd never been happier and more in love. Life was good.

They were both making enough to move from John's parent's home into a small one-bedroom apartment in the rapidly growing town of Mt. Pleasant, just across the Cooper River from the city and only a few miles from the popular Isle of Palms beach. John and Mandy both wanted children but agreed to wait until they could afford a home of their own.

Shortly after Mandy started her new accounting job, John found a better paying opportunity at the Port of Charleston. Five years later, after paying off Mandy's college loan and saving as much as they could, they finally managed to scrape together a down payment on a new house.

The modest two-story, two-bed, one-and-a-half-bath starter was situated in the middle of a postage stamp lot in an older residential neighborhood north of the city. Off the back of the house was a tiny, shade-free concrete slab patio barely large enough for a grill and a small plastic table and chairs. The house was showing its age, but to John and Mandy, their new home was the Taj Mahal.

A few months after moving in, John arrived home late-afternoon after his six a.m. shift at the port and grabbed the mail from their box at the curb. He tossed it on the kitchen table and headed upstairs for a much-needed shower. The relentless August humidity was already in the red zone before the sun was even up when he left the house for work that morning in the dark.

Showered and changed, he felt like a new man and headed back downstairs to relax for an hour or so before Mandy got home from work. Tonight was spaghetti night, one of his favorites, and the hard work was already done. There were still two plastic containers of Mandy's special homemade sauce in the freezer, and he had taken one out to thaw before leaving for work that morning. They planned to take in a movie after dinner.

He set the table and settled into his favorite lounge chair to read the local morning *Post and Courier,* which was his afternoon paper since he was out the door so early every morning. He had spent that day with his dock crew unloading a Maersk container ship that had arrived overnight at the Wando Welch Terminal dock.

Before starting in on the paper, he grabbed the mail from the kitchen table and riffled through it. As usual, mostly junk, a couple bills and one of Mandy's celebrity magazines. There was also an expensive looking white envelope addressed to his attention in formal printed type. The envelope was hand-delivered with no postage mark and no return address. The top corner was stamped **Personal and Confidential** and on the bottom in bold type it read **Urgent for Your Eyes Only**.

About to toss it in the junk mail pile, he turned the envelope over. On the back flap were three fancy embossed letters *WSB* in bold script. All three letters were in a horizontal box. It looked like some kind of logo, but he didn't recognize it. Probably an invitation to another overpriced development with all the amenities of my dreams, he thought. Fat chance on our salaries.

Now curious about the envelope, he opened it and began reading a formal, undated, and unsigned typed letter. When he finished, all he could do was close his eyes and sit in stunned silence.

Chapter 7

August 2018

Emily loved everything about teaching and quickly settled into a routine. Her fifth-grade students loved her as much as she loved teaching them. She also had no trouble making friends with her fellow teachers and the school staff. She was happy to volunteer for the annual PTA fund-raiser, help decorate the sets for the holiday school play, and lend a hand with anything else whenever she was asked.

At the end of the school year, each of her students gave her a thank you card with a hand-written note just for her. One student wrote, "Miss Baker, you are the best teacher I ever had." She knew right then she was exactly where she was always meant to be.

Emily looked like a runner with her compact size and athletic body. Since returning home from Clemson, her signature long blonde ponytail and colorful hairbands soon made her easily recognized in the Charleston running community. In the past year, she often finished in the top three places in the local road races she entered, winning four of them. Richard entered the same races whenever he could fit them into his busy schedule and out-of-town business trips.

She continued running through the summer after her first year of teaching and was out the door for an early Saturday run in the August heat before school started back up in another week. Despite the forecast of a sweltering high in the mid-nineties and humidity to match, she planned to do a ten-mile run that morning while the temperature was still only in the eighties.

She had been gradually ramping up her weekly mileage to begin training for the full 26.2-mile Charleston Marathon in January, her first-ever long-distance race. When she asked Richard to enter the race with her, he told her he just didn't have the time to put in the training. In the end, he reluctantly agreed to run the Charleston Half Marathon held the same morning. Even though it was only half the distance, he joked that at least he'd be able to finish a race ahead of her for a change.

One her favorite running routes was down Long Point Road to Wando Park Blvd. and past some retail shops, an indoor sports complex, and a small publishing company. The sidewalk then ran along a quiet stretch of road with woods on her left. After three miles on Wando Park Blvd, she turned around in a picturesque new townhome neighborhood and returned on the same sidewalk back to Long Point and the final two miles to her apartment. When she got there, she checked her GPS watch. Ten miles in the heat in just over seventy minutes. I'll take it, she thought.

As she started walking on the path to her apartment building, she remembered she hadn't picked up yesterday's mail from the covered outdoor mailboxes for her building. After retrieving her mailbox key from the apartment, she returned to her mailbox and grabbed her mail.

Back in the kitchen, she opened a plain white business envelope that caught her attention. It had arrived in her mailbox with no postage and no return address. Stamped in bold type on the front were the words **Personal and Confidential** and **Urgent for Your Eyes Only**. On the back flap was a thin horizontal box surrounding the script letters *WSB*. She wondered how it got into her mailbox since it was locked except when the post office delivered the daily mail.

She removed a two-page letter addressed to her and began reading. Her hands were already shaking before got to the final line.

Do not deviate from any of these instructions. Remember, tell no one. Your future depends on it.

The letter was unsigned. After reading it again, she ran up to her bedroom. A safety deposit box key was under her bedside lamp. Confused and frightened, she sat down on the edge of her bed. She tried to make sense of it, but she had no idea who sent it and what they wanted.

She was only certain about one thing. *Somebody had been inside her apartment.*

Chapter 8

May 2017

Jamison Walters grew up on a multi-million-dollar estate in Miami, Florida. He didn't have any friends in high school or college that he considered close, just a lot of what he called 'acquaintances'. Although his fellow students thought he was friendly enough, Jamison mostly preferred his own company. He occasionally dated, but nothing became serious.

He'd heard the rumors growing up that Harrison Walters, his father, had made his fortune in the drug trade. Jamison never believed the stories. He admired his father's business success and always assumed he earned his wealth with hard work and smart financial decisions. At least until his parents disappeared.

Harrison and Charlotte Walters were sailing on their luxury yacht, named after Charlotte, from Miami Beach to Key West on a short pleasure trip in perfect weather. When the boat didn't return as expected the following weekend and repeated calls to Harrison's satellite phone went unanswered, the Coast Guard and Miami PD were alerted. After an extensive air and sea search, no trace of the boat or his parents had been found. The marina where his father always docked in Key West confirmed the boat never arrived.

Five days later, Harrison and Charlotte Walters were officially declared missing.

At the time of his parent's disappearance, Jamison had recently turned twenty-one and was an above-average student at Yale. He was just starting his final year when he got the news at school that his parents were missing. They hadn't returned from a sailing trip and couldn't be reached, despite all the high-tech communications equipment on the boat.

Jamison immediately returned home and was interviewed by the Miami police. He told them he had no idea where they were and hadn't talked to them since their sailboat left Miami. He loved his parents and refused to believe they had drowned. They had to be still on the sailboat, maybe they discovered a hidden cove someplace and decided to spend a few more days before sailing home. All the same, his dad should have called him or someone else by now.

"Did they mention where they were headed?" asked the Miami detective assigned to the case.

"About ten days ago, my father told me he and mom were planning to sail to Key West and return to Miami in a week. He said he had to be back in time for a big board meeting. Dad has been sailing most of his life and knows what he's doing on the water. When I didn't hear from them, I assumed Dad rescheduled his meeting, and he and Mom just took a few extra days to explore the Bahamas, which they've done often."

The detective switched gears. "Tell me about your father's business."

"He runs Walters International, a logistics company that specializes in imports and exports. I really don't know much about it, but he's always busy whenever I'm home. Since I started at Yale, I don't see either of my parents that often, just mainly around the holidays and over the summer. Last time I was home was a couple weeks before school started."

After answering a few more questions, Jamison finished the interview by repeating he had no idea where his parents were or why they hadn't called him. He told the detective they never talked on the phone much when he was at school.

A week later, one of his father's business associates, a man Jamison had met only once, paid him a visit at the family estate before he returned to Yale. A year earlier, the same man stopped by their house for a meeting with his father. All his father told him about the visitor was that he was the majority owner of Walters International.

That same man was now standing at the front door, and Jamison invited him in. He couldn't help but notice the man's perfectly tailored dark suit, starched white shirt, power silk tie, and expensive-looking shoes. He appeared trim and fit, around six-feet tall, without a hair out of place. Jamison guessed he was probably older than he looked.

"Good afternoon, sir, how can I help you?" greeted Jamison.

"Sorry about your parents, son, they were very nice people," the man said, a little too matter-of-factly and without an ounce of sympathy.

Before he could continue, Jamison interrupted him. "What do you mean, *were* nice people? The police told me they might still be out there, they just haven't been found yet."

"Just an educated guess since no one, including you, has heard from them since they went missing. I hope the police are right," the man said with zero conviction before abruptly changing the subject. "What do you plan to do when you graduate from Yale?"

"Honestly, I'm not sure. I was planning to join Dad in the business after graduation, but that won't be an option if something's happened to him. Right now, things are up in the air until I hear from him."

The man paused as if deep in thought, then handed Jamison a Walters International business card with the name Mr. Joseph and a private cell phone number on it. "Keep in touch and I'll do the same. I may have something that will interest you after you finish school next year." They shook hands and the man was out the door and into his chauffeured limo.

A month after his parents disappeared, Jamison reluctantly came to grips with the realization they were gone and would never be coming home. The man who had visited him after they went missing did stay in touch during his final year at Yale. After he graduated, the man made him an offer he couldn't refuse.

Jamison took the job.

Chapter 9

The Port of Charleston is ranked on the Top Ten list of largest ports in the United Stated based on cargo value, with over seventy-five billion dollars in imports and exports crossing its docks every year. The largest container terminal in the Port of Charleston's network is the Wando Welch Terminal in Mt. Pleasant, which handles nearly eighty percent of the port's annual container volume.

Every aspect of port security is tight for both truckers entering the port and the South Carolina Ports Authority employees working there. Security cameras are deployed throughout all Ports Authority facilities, including the security fences surrounding the port terminals.

Steve Harris needed to see the surveillance footage for Monday morning around the entire port security fence from five a.m. until seven a.m. He also wanted to review the security logs for every employee vehicle that entered or left and any transport trucks that entered or departed in the same two-hour window.

After getting the autopsy results from Bob Jenkins the morning after the body was discovered, he called Fred Waters, the number two man in the Wando Welch Terminal's security office. They'd known each other socially for several years, and enjoyed the occasional dinner together with their wives, who both volunteered at the East Cooper Community Outreach non-profit in Mt. Pleasant.

"Hey Fred, Steve Harris. I'm hoping you can help me with an investigation I'm handling."

"Hi Steve, assume you caught the dead body found outside our gates on Monday."

"Yeah, that's mine. Reason for my call is I need to see your security footage from Monday morning between five a.m. and seven a.m. around the main and secondary gate areas and along the security fence between them."

"Sure, no problem. But you should know somebody else already has that footage."

Before Fred could continue, Steve interrupted him. "Did you say somebody was already given a copy of Monday morning's perimeter surveillance footage? Who was it?"

"Not given, taken. Four of our Monday morning surveillance tapes were stolen, and we have no idea who took them. Fortunately, all of our surveillance footage is automatically backed up, so you can still see whatever was recorded during your time frame. My boss, Joe Cartwright, is beyond pissed and thinks it had to be someone who works here. We've already alerted the State Ports Authority about a possible mole, and they've started an immediate full-blown investigation."

Steve said, "Somebody was obviously very worried about what's on those tapes. How soon can I get a copy of the footage from all four cameras? I also need a list of any trucks and their drivers who logged in or out before seven a.m. yesterday, plus a list of all your employees who coded in or out of the gates during the same time frame."

"Can you meet me here at eight a.m. tomorrow? By then I can have copies of the footage and the main gate security logs for you."

"Fred, there's obviously a lot more going on here than I thought, especially if someone on the inside is involved. They must know the footage is backed up, so why take the risk of stealing the tapes?"

"Wish I knew. Hopefully, there will be some clues in the footage. I'll leave a pass for you at the employee entrance gate. See you tomorrow."

As soon as he hung up, Steve called veteran Mt. Pleasant Police Chief Jon Hartman, now in his twelfth year heading the department. After graduating from New York University, Hartman joined the NYPD and worked his way up from beat cop to Sergeant before being shot and nearly paralyzed during an armed robbery shootout that went sideways. Forced to take a desk job while rehabbing his severely injured hip and back for nearly a year, he excelled as an effective administrator and quickly earned the respect of his fellow rank and file police officers as a cop's cop.

Before he was cleared for active duty, he took a long-overdue vacation with his wife Maureen to a popular bed and breakfast in downtown Charleston. During a late lunch at a quaint restaurant near the old market, he ran into his former Captain, Mickey Delaney, who'd retired to the Lowcountry a few years earlier. After catching up on old times at dinner that evening, Mickey told him about an opening in the Mt. Pleasant Police Department for a new Chief.

Jon knew Maureen had wanted to move out of New York City for a long time, well before he was wounded on the job. Her parents were from Charleston, and she always dreamed about coming home. After talking about it well into the night, he decided to apply for the job. A month later, Jon and Maureen Hartman were headed south.

Steve updated Hartman on what he'd just learned about the missing surveillance tapes. He also mentioned he was meeting with Fred Waters at the port in the morning to get copies of the footage and the Monday morning security gate logs.

Hartman said, "Tell Fred we appreciate his help. I also need you back here this afternoon for a four p.m. press briefing with the locals. It will be a very short briefing, no details yet. Can you meet me at three-thirty to go over how we want to handle it?"

"You got it, Chief, see you then."

On Tuesday afternoon, Hartman and Steve briefed the local crime beat reporters. Other than mentioning that a man was found dead yesterday outside the port entrance, any other relevant details were on lockdown.

"Good afternoon," Hartman began. "Regarding the body found near the port yesterday morning, we're not at liberty to tell you much yet, including the name or a photo of the victim, pending notification of the family. Detective Steve Harris will be leading the investigation and will provide more details as they become available."

One of the local TV reporters asked, "Detective Harris, was the deceased a local resident?"

"We don't think so," Steve replied. "The most recent address we have for him is in Florida. We're still running down his background."

Another reporter called out, "How did he die?"

"At this early stage of the investigation, we don't have much to tell you yet. All I can say now is that he died under suspicious circumstances."

After a few more questions and a few more non-answers, Hartman ended the briefing. "Detective Harris will keep you informed as our investigation proceeds. Thank you."

The 'suspicious' death was briefly mentioned in the Tuesday evening local TV newscasts, and a small news story appeared in the Wednesday morning edition of the *Post and Courier*. Details were sparse.

John Simpson read the short article about the incident in Wednesday's paper. When one of his port co-workers asked him the next day if he'd heard about someone being found dead last Monday morning just outside the back security gates, John told him he saw something about it in the local section of yesterday's paper. Since there weren't any details in the article, he forgot about it.

Chapter 10

August 2018

Chuck was now officially scared.

He read the letter two more times before carefully checking the entire house to see if whoever was in the cabin had left any telltale signs. He found the safety deposit box key on his nightstand, but nothing was out of place, and nothing looked like it was missing. His laptop was still on the kitchen counter, right where he left it when he got home on Friday. He wondered if anyone tampered with it when he was fishing or at dinner yesterday?

He also worried someone might be watching him right now. He walked around the inside of the cabin again, looking for any hidden cameras, but couldn't find any. He always kept his cell phone with him in case he got a call about a pickup or delivery change, but he had no idea how they could track his calls. Although his own tech skills were pretty much limited to the on-off button, he had no doubt it could be done.

He grabbed another cold beer and went out to the screened porch to run through his options in his head. He had no clue what to do. One week from tomorrow would be a busy day if he followed all the instructions in the letter. He read it again. The quarter-million-dollar questions were what did they want and what would he need to do to get it?

His immediate concern was whether or not to call the port today and cancel his container pickup scheduled for early tomorrow. The trip was only down to Birmingham, and he needed the money for his next bank loan payment due in ten days. He decided to go since he could easily be back from Birmingham by Wednesday. There would still be plenty of time to get ready the following Monday if he decided to follow the instructions in the letter.

He got his laptop from the kitchen, powered it on, and returned to the porch. He clicked the file with his scheduled pickups and deliveries for the next few weeks.

On his way back from Birmingham, he had a pickup scheduled for Wednesday just outside of Atlanta. It was a flatbed load of heavy construction equipment for delivery to Greenville, a straight shot up I-85 from Atlanta. He was still waiting on his confirmation for another shipment he scheduled from Greenville back across the state to Charleston.

Chuck was nothing if not reliable and hated to cancel any trips, especially on such late notice. After thinking on it some more, he made his decision. He would pick up his scheduled container load from the port tomorrow and return directly home empty from Birmingham.

Canceling his return trip shipments from Atlanta and Greenville would put a dent in his income next week, but as long as he protected his steady port business, he felt could live with it until he found out what was going on.

He emailed his Atlanta and Greenville contacts and said he wouldn't be able to handle any shipments this week due to a family emergency. He apologized for the late notice and requested both contacts confirm receipt of his email. The last thing he wanted was burn any bridges. Besides, it really was a family emergency. It just happened to be his.

By mid-afternoon, he was too distracted to think about doing any more work around the cabin. He could fix the taillight on the pickup when he got back from Birmingham, in case he needed to use it the following Monday.

He was now at loose ends. He thought about driving over to his good friend George Cooper's place on the other side of town. But he worried if he talked about what was going on, whoever was behind this madness would somehow find out. Instead, he decided to clean up his cab and put on a load of wash.

He checked the rest of his driving schedule on the laptop and noticed he had another container pickup at the port a week from Monday, the day he was supposed to drive to Hilton Head. He was still on the fence to go or not go. He would make his decision when he got back from Birmingham.

He still couldn't figure out if the letter was fake or if his life might actually be in jeopardy. If the letter was real, he could pay off his sleeper cab with plenty to spare. Or be dead.

***

It took John Simpson a couple minutes for the letter to sink in. His immediate reaction was anger. Who sent it and what the hell did they want?

He read it again and forced himself to calm down. Think it through, he told himself. We could pay off the house with that kind of money. But who gives anybody $250,000 without a big string attached?

He didn't believe in fairy tales, but he did understand threats. The warning was clear. Don't involve anyone else. He had to find out if it was real or a scam before discussing it with Mandy. He almost threw it in the trash, but the possibility of a $250,000 windfall, as crazy as that sounded, was now stuck in his head.

He got up from his chair and hurried upstairs. There it was, a small key under the bedroom lamp, just like the letter said. Who are these people and how did they get in? The garage and front door were both locked when he got home. He checked the back door. Also locked.

He went around the house to make sure every window was latched. They were never opened in the summer with the air conditioning constantly on. All still latched from the inside. But he knew how easy it was to pick a lock if you knew how. Someone must have come in through the front or back door after Mandy left for work that morning.

The mail was usually delivered around lunchtime, so the intruder must have broken in after putting the letter in the mailbox with the rest of the mail before he got home. Anyone could've slipped the envelope into the mailbox without being noticed.

He thought about asking his neighbors if they happened to see anyone around his house that afternoon but thought better of it, at least for the time being. He still wanted to tell Mandy about it when she got home from work, but what if the threat was real? Would anything really happen to him, or her, if he told her about it? Or should he just call the police?

He read the letter again. *Remember, tell no one. Your future depends on it.*

Was it real or a hoax? He had a week from Monday to figure out what to do. For now, he decided not to discuss the letter with anyone, including Mandy. He put it back in the envelope, took it to the garage, and stuffed it at the bottom of his toolbox, where Mandy would never find it.

***

After Emily reread the letter, she still had trouble believing it. Who would go to all the trouble of threatening her in such detail? And someone offering her $250,000 was tempting but also sounded ludicrous. There was no way she could miss the first day of the new school year a week from Monday to go downtown, empty a bank safety deposit box, drive to the airport, switch her car for a rental, then drive to Hilton Head under an assumed name.

She didn't believe the carrot, but the stick was another matter. Three elephants stomped around in her head. *Is the threat real? Who sent the letter? What do they want from me?*

She had to decide whether to become Kathy Ritter or ignore the threat and the possibility of more money than she could earn in several years of teaching.

When she found the safety deposit box key under her bedroom lamp, she wasn't surprised. She knew whoever was behind this would make sure she found it. They must have somehow gotten into her apartment when she was on her ten-mile run that morning. The letter could've been placed in her mailbox any time after the mail was delivered on Friday. Nobody would even notice since the mailboxes were outside and could easily be opened by a pro.

Are they watching me now? She carefully checked the entire apartment for hidden cameras but didn't find any. If they were professionals with high-tech, miniaturized surveillance equipment, she knew they could hide cameras where she would never find them.

If the letter was real, a big if, she also assumed her cell phone and land line in the apartment were both being monitored. She started dialing Richard's cell phone but hung up before she finished punching in his number. She worried a call or text might put him in danger. Same problem if she contacted Aunt Marie. And if that was true, she couldn't call the police either. She had to decide for herself if the threat was real before she talked to anyone about it.

She had no idea what to do, so she jotted down some notes that might help her decide her next move.

- $250,000—Something illegal to get it?
- Tell someone—Will they find out?
- Go to police—Is threat real?
- Ignore letter—What will happen?
- Go to Hilton Head—Why?
- Disappear and hide—Could they find me?
- Follow instructions—Outcome unknown!

When she finished the list, she was no closer to any answers. She knew she might be in danger and needed help. Despite the warning, she still wanted to talk to someone about it. But who? And how?

Deep down she understood the reality of what she was facing, and not for the first time in her life. She was on her own.

Chapter 11

August 2018

On Wednesday morning, the week after the letters were delivered, Jamison got a cell call from his boss. After spending the past year handling routine assignments, he knew whenever the man called, it was important. Especially given Jamison's current project that he'd been working on for the past three months.

He answered immediately, "Yes boss."

"Mr. Jamison, update please."

"Yes sir. The letters were all delivered. Mr. Simpson read his on Friday afternoon and Miss Baker got to hers on Saturday morning. Mr. Wilson didn't go through his mail until Sunday. So far, none of them have been in contact with anyone about the letter."

"What's the status of the surveillance gear?"

"The cameras covering all their rooms, as well as the exteriors of their homes, front and back, are all working fine. We're also tracking all their calls. The cameras and trackers in their vehicles are also live. We've got all the monitors set up with round the clock coverage by our tech team. If any of them breaks any of the protocols in the letter, I'll inform you immediately, day or night."

"Excellent, Mr. Jamison. We still have five days until Monday, so make damn sure the team stays on their toes. When will you be leaving for Hilton Head?"

"Everything is arranged, sir. All three hotel reservations have been made at the Heritage Hotel on different floors as you instructed. I'll also make sure the ferry schedule is in everyone's room before they arrive. I plan to get to Hilton Head on Sunday afternoon and take the Monday morning ferry over to Daufuskie to get everything ready at Blaine Cottage. They should all get there by around eleven a.m. on Tuesday."

"Have you got the bank covered?"

"We have a man outside the bank watching the entrance, and our man inside the bank will be at his desk when the bank opens on Monday morning. All three safety deposit keys were found by our friends, right where we hid them. Everything you requested has been placed in their safety deposit boxes by our inside man."

"What about the airport parking lot and car rental area?"

"No problem, sir. We have two guys covering the long-term parking lot and another man near the Avis counter."

"Make sure the license plates on their personal vehicles have been removed," the boss ordered.

"Will do. Our drivers are standing by on Daufuskie to take our guests to Blaine Cottage."

"Check with Johnny and tell him to make sure our plane is at the Hilton Head Airport by early Monday afternoon."

"He said he'll be there. I'll reconfirm with him."

"Very good, Mr. Jamison. Sounds like you have everything in hand. Also be sure the audio equipment we discussed is all set up at the cottage before they arrive."

"All taken care of. We'll be ready for your call."

Before he hung up, the boss said, "One more thing. Call Mr. Davis and tell him to let us know if they mention the letter to anyone or make a copy. I don't want any surprises."

After the boss clicked off, Jamison went over all the details in his head one more time. He was confident he'd thought of everything. He then called Davis to make sure all three targets were following the instructions detailed in the letter.

Mark Davis was a computer genius who thought he could hack into anything. Until he got caught and was sentenced to a year in prison. He'd missed the sophisticated tracking software installed by a high-tech security firm in an insurance company's computer system. When he tried to hack into the company's mainframe, he was burned. The day he was released from prison, he was hired by Jamison's boss.

Mark answered his cell as soon as he saw the caller ID. "Jamison, what's up?"

"Need an update for the boss. What have our friends been up to?"

"We've been tracking them on our video monitors and audio feeds since the letters were delivered. Mr. Wilson was rattled but hasn't said anything to anyone. He picked up a container at the port on Monday morning and dropped it off in Birmingham. He got back to his cabin in McClellanville late yesterday evening. His emails show he canceled two other trips he had scheduled for later this week. Both cancellations were confirmed by email."

Mark continued, "Mr. Simpson hasn't said anything to his wife and hid the letter in his garage. He showed up at work on Monday morning and hasn't spoken to anyone about it."

"What about Miss Baker?" asked Jamison.

"She hasn't talked about it with her boyfriend Richard since she read the letter, but she's definitely on the fence. So far, she hasn't mentioned anything to him or her Aunt Marie, who she talks to every day. After her morning runs, she basically hangs around her apartment and reads. Her teaching job starts on Monday, and today she called the school to set up a meeting with the principal tomorrow."

"What did she say?"

"She made up a phony story about wanting to review some of her lesson plans for the new school year. We're assuming that was just an excuse to meet with the principal in person to tell her she won't be at school on Monday. We'll find out, but I don't trust her. If anyone's going to give us a problem, my money's on her."

"Thanks Mark, the next few days will be critical. Keep your team on full alert and call me if anything changes. If any of them gets cold feet or panics and says anything to anyone about next week, I need to inform the boss right away. And keep a close eye on Miss Baker. I'm not sure I trust her either."

Chapter 12

November 2017

Three months after the body of Jorge Rodriguez was found near the back gates of the port, Steve Harris was still knee-deep in the murder investigation. He was as determined as ever to solve the case, but so far had come up empty.

The stifling summer humidity was finally gone in early November when he sat down at the large conference room table in the Mt. Pleasant Police Department to review the case. Around the table with him were Chief Hartman, Rob Campbell, the South Carolina Ports Authority's Senior Security Investigator, and Joe Cartwright, Director of Security at the Wando Welch Terminal. Also attending the meeting at Steve's invitation was Miami DEA Agent Dale Hawkins.

After Steve introduced Dale to the group, Chief Hartman welcomed everyone. "Thank you all for coming. Help yourselves to the coffee and donuts. I know you're all busy, and Steve and I appreciate everyone making the time to be here. Dale, Steve has filled me in on your assistance in what has become a very complex investigation. Thanks for being here in person. Welcome to South Carolina."

Hartman looked over at Steve and continued. "Steve's been working on this case since day one and will give everyone an update and where we are on our end. I know Rob and Joe also have some new information to pass along as well. Dale will brief us on the progress of the DEA's investigation into the Camino drug cartel's activities that have a bearing on our case. Steve, please start us off."

Steve had his detailed case notes in front of him and got down to business. "Gentlemen, what started out as a basic murder investigation has grown into something much bigger. Here's what we know so far." He began with the discovery of the body near the back gates at the port and passed out copies of the coroner's final autopsy report.

"At the murder scene, we found what looked like fresh tire tracks in the empty lot next to the Shipping Lane entrance to the Wando terminal's back gates. Since that lot is mostly gravel, we were unable to get any usable tire impressions. Based on the surveillance footage from that morning, which I'll detail shortly, we suspect the shooter and our murder victim may have arrived together and parked there that morning."

Steve briefly glanced down at his notes. "A canvas of businesses on Long Point by Mt. Pleasant Sergeant Buddy Evans and his patrol officers on the scene turned up nothing. And since no one reported hearing any gunshots, the weapon was probably silenced. Ballistics showed the bullets from the two head shots were from a nine mil. If we find the gun, we should get a match. The initial shot to the vic's back was through and through, and we were unable to find that third bullet. However, under the body, we did find a shell casing with a partial print."

Joe Cartwright was fifty and looked forty. The former Clemson starting safety was a second team All-American and managed to keep his athletic six-two frame in top condition after a knee injury short-circuited an NFL career. His gym regimen would put men half his age to shame. He'd been the Wando Welch Terminal's top security guy for the past three years. He asked Steve, "What can you tell us about the victim?"

"Joe, thanks to Dale and his DEA team in Miami, the prints pulled from the body by County Coroner Bob Jenkins were a match to Jorge Rodriguez. According to Dale, he was suspected of working with Manny Rodriguez, his uncle, for the Camino cartel to transport drugs from Mexico City to Miami. Jorge also had a Camino tattoo on both arms. Your file folder includes a summary put together by Dale on both Jorge and Manny."

Steve glanced at Dale and said, "This might be a good place for Dale to jump in and share anything he can with us that will shed some light on what Jorge Rodriguez was doing in South Carolina, and why he might have been hanging around our largest container port."

Dale nodded and said, "First, I'd like to thank Steve for looping us in. As I told him earlier, one of our DEA undercover agents inside the Camino cartel has confirmed Jorge and Manny Rodriguez were part of the Camino drug pipeline from Mexico City to Miami."

"Any idea where Manny ended up?" Joe asked.

"A week after Jorge's body was found outside your port, his uncle Manny surfaced face down in a dumpster behind a Mexican restaurant in Miami. Two 9 mil to the back of the head, same as Jorge. We're guessing after Jorge was taken out, Manny became an expendable loose end."

Hartman asked, "What was Jorge Rodriguez doing up here in the first place?"

"Chief, we suspect he was most likely sent here by his Camino contact in Miami to coordinate the shipment of a specific container from South America that was offloaded at your Wando terminal that weekend. Fortunately, we had a tip from a CI who told us that container very possibly included a significant stash of cocaine hidden in the regular cargo. We alerted Mr. Cartwright at the port immediately and gave him the container number."

Joe Cartwright added, "That container was scheduled to be trucked out of the port on the same Monday morning Jorge was killed. As soon as we located it on the dock, we transferred it to our secure inspection building. A sniffer dog discovered the cocaine stashed in five boxes of textiles stacked in the front of the container."

Steve was curious about something and asked Dale, "How did the cartel find out the cocaine was confiscated that weekend?"

"We think someone on Camino's payroll, likely a port employee working in plain sight, heard that the cocaine was discovered and passed the word up the Camino food chain. Although the cocaine shipment was blown, we think Jorge was clueless and was still planning to ride with the driver of the truck hauling that container once it left the port. Our DEA working theory is that somebody in the Camino organization got pissed and decided Jorge was no longer needed and took him out of the loop."

Rob Campbell was the State Ports Authority's lead security investigator going on ten years and looking forward to retiring in another five. A fourth generation Charlestonian and proud of it with a native Charleston accent to match, he was a heavy-set short man with an intentionally bald head. His dry sense of humor and quick wit were legendary. Once when he was introduced to a guest he'd never met at a cocktail party, the guest wanted to impress Rob and told him he'd been living in Charleston for the last thirty years. Rob smiled and said in his distinctive Charleston drawl, "Welcome to Charleston."

Rob picked up the thread of Dale's comments. "We know someone on the inside stole four of our surveillance tapes of the perimeter footage from the morning Mr. Rodriguez was shot. Doesn't take a math wizard to add one plus one. Dollars to a dozen Krispy Kreme glazed, that same person also tipped off the cartel about the cocaine seizure. Unfortunately, our ongoing investigation has turned up zip so far."

Steve asked Dale, "Why do you think the shooter was a key player in the Camino camp?"

"Think about it. There was no reason to eliminate Jorge since he had nothing to do with the discovery of the cocaine in the container. We think the shooter came up from Miami to find out what happened, but Jorge had no idea the drugs on the container had been seized. In a fit of anger, we think the shooter lost his temper and took Jorge out when he tried to run. Jorge was basically a gopher who did what he was told. There was no reason a hit on him should've been ordered. Whoever shot him was likely someone high enough on the Camino organization chart that he didn't need permission."

The Chief said, "Steve, you and your team have been over the copies of the stolen footage that was backed up on the terminal's digital storage system. Let these guys know what you saw on the tapes that might have been important enough for them to be stolen?"

Steve commented while he played the surveillance video on the large screen in the front of the conference room. "At precisely five fifty-three a.m. on Monday, a tall male, as yet unidentified, put two shots into the head of a man lying face down on the concrete entrance area at the back security gates. The body was close to the woods near the left gate facing the port.

We weren't able to make out the shooter's face since he had a baseball cap pulled down to cover his face, and his back was toward the security camera. It was also still pretty dark, and the weapon was hidden from view. It's obvious from the video that the shooter was aware of the location of port's perimeter security cameras.

A second camera above the security fence between the main gates and the back gates shows the two men walking along the fence. But again, it was too dark to make out their faces. The taller man is wearing a black windbreaker, no doubt to hide his weapon. He's the shooter walking behind Jorge."

Steve took another sip of coffee before continuing his running commentary on the video. "The only other relevant footage was from one of the two cameras covering the perimeter fence from the main entrance. The shooter is clearly yelling at Jorge, whose back was up against the fence. From a comparison of

Jorge's height, which we know, we've estimated the shooter's height at around six feet-three inches."

He pointed to the screen for emphasis and explained what was now happening on the video. "Mr. Shooter and Jorge were initially seen here on the main entrance video footage facing Long Point Road at five twenty-one a.m. They're walking together from the direction of the Shipping Lane entrance before getting to the perimeter security fence on the right of the primary entrance gates. An argument started when they got to the security fence before the killer lost it. You can see him grabbing Jorge and shoving him along the fence toward the back gates. Jorge was found a couple hours later by a local resident who'd made a wrong turn onto Shipping Lane."

Steve paused the tape and asked the group, "Any questions so far?"

Rob said, "We're with you, keep going."

Steve looked up from his notes and said, "While we can't make it out clearly on the footage, we think the shooter shoved Jorge toward the back gates to get to their car so they wouldn't be seen by the cameras. That's when we think Jorge made a run for it, and the killer shot him in the back just as he reached the truck lanes at the back gates."

Steve next described the video segment showing the actual murder. "After Jorge face-plants on the concrete, the shooter fires two more into Jorge's head at close range and empties the dead man's pockets. When he can't find something near the body, probably the shell casing we found, he hurries along the woods toward Shipping Lane with his cap still pulled down and his back to the camera."

"He had to be parked close by," said Dale.

"We think he may have driven away from that vacant lot next to Shipping Lane. All we know is Mr. Shooter is muscular and about six-three. His age is basically a guess, but from what we could see on the video and the way he moved, we're estimating late-thirties or early-forties, give or take. Not much to go on."

When Steve finished summarizing the video, Joe Cartwright asked, "Did anything interesting pop up on the security gate logs you reviewed from that morning?"

"Nothing suspicious. I talked to a dock worker who passed by Jorge and the shooter in his car exactly when they were arguing along the security fence line, just before he went through the employee entrance gate for his early shift.

He said he didn't see anything. An independent trucker hauling a container from the port went through the exit gate at the same time, same result. He didn't notice anything unusual."

Steve started the tape again. "The only other thing of interest on the video footage of the entrance area is this young woman with a blond ponytail out for an early morning run. She has a clear view down along the security fence on the right side of the entrance gates, but we have no idea who she is. She runs around the main entrance area and slows down when she may have noticed the two men arguing only twenty feet or so from where she passes by them. She never stops and speeds again on the sidewalk next to Long Point until she's out of view."

Dale asked, "Has the security guard ever seen her before?"

"I talked to the guard on duty that morning. He told me he sometimes sees a young woman with a blond ponytail running past the main entrance gates very early in the morning. We haven't tracked her down yet, but Fred Waters has posted an extra security guard at the entrance so we can stop her the next time she shows up. We'll get her contact info, and I'll interview her about anything she might have seen the morning of the murder."

After another few minutes of discussion, Hartman ended the meeting. "Thank you all again for coming so we could update each other in person. Dale, Steve will continue to be your contact on our end. Please pass along our thanks to your boss as well. We still have a killer at large and probably a mole at the port. Let's all continue to coordinate any new information, day or night."

Steve drove Dale to the airport and talked about the case on the way. "Thanks for flying up here, I know you must have a lot on your plate. We appreciate you taking the time."

"Not a problem, Steve. Thanks for offering to loop me in on a video conference, but I wanted to meet you and the rest of the key people involved in your investigation in person. My primary interest is on the Camino cartel, and I welcome any new information I can get whenever or wherever their organization may be involved. These are bad people."

Steve said, "Whatever else we find or wherever our investigation takes us, I'll definitely keep you and the DEA informed. I have a strong feeling this won't be our last conversation."

Steve knew he needed a break in the case but had no idea where it might come from. As long as it takes, he told himself. But for the time being, his investigation was stuck in neutral.

Chapter 13

August 2018

Early on Monday morning, a week before he had to decide if he was going to follow the complex instructions in the letter, Chuck drove the *Chucktown Special* to the port for his scheduled Birmingham container pickup. He got to the port just after seven a.m. and logged in at the main entrance gate. He waved to the security guard and drove back to the container pickup area.

When his paperwork was completed, a 20-foot container on a flatbed trailer was hooked up to his cab. After a final inspection, he was ready to hit the road and head south. Before leaving the loading area, he checked his laptop for confirmations of his Atlanta and Greenville canceled pickups. He was glad to see the two emails confirming both cancellations.

Less than a mile out of the port on Long Point Road, he took the entrance lane to I-526 West. A few miles later, he got on the exit ramp to I-26 West. With interstate highways all the way, the seven-hour drive from the Wando Welch Terminal to Birmingham was a walk in the park.

During the drive, Chuck had time to get his thoughts together for the rest of the week. Along the way, he made up his mind and decided to follow the letter's instructions. He needed to find out what was going on and was too afraid to blow off the letter as a prank. He would find out for himself next Monday.

He slept in the cab on Monday night after dropping off the container, then headed back from Birmingham to McClellanville on Tuesday morning. Timmy, his mechanic friend in town, agreed to squeeze him in and fix the taillight on his old pickup on Wednesday afternoon.

He drove the pickup to the Walmart in Georgetown on Thursday and bought a few items, including a cheap briefcase and some new pants and shirts on sale for the upcoming trip down to Hilton Head.

Back home, he called Greg Stevens, his shipping contact at the port, to cancel his scheduled container pickup for next Monday. He hated making up lies, but he had no choice. His excuse was that he had to be out of town for a few days next week to take care of a personal family matter and planned to be back by the end of the week.

Friday morning, he went fishing at the creek, but by the time he got there, he knew he had missed the incoming tide when he didn't see Connor. He tried the flounder he'd thrown in the freezer last week for bait but didn't even get a nibble. His head just wasn't in it, and he finally walked back to the cabin for some lunch and a nap on the porch. Nothing left to do now but hang around and wait.

He woke up on Monday at four a.m. after a few hours of restless sleep. All he could think about was everything he had to do before driving to Hilton Head with a fake name in a rental car. He made some coffee and breakfast and read the letter again for what seemed like the hundredth time. At least he would get some answers soon.

By seven a.m., he was in his pickup for the forty-mile drive into downtown Charleston. He wasn't sure about the early morning downtown traffic when he got close to the city, but he figured he had plenty of time to be at the bank around the time it opened at nine a.m.

Built in 1817 and in continuous use as a bank ever since, the historic Bank of Charleston building is located on Broad Street, the oldest commercial street in the city. The two-story exterior features smooth, stucco-covered masonry walls, a gold leaf eagle on a prominent gable, and simple arched and rectangular window and door openings across the entire facade.

The key to the safety deposit box inside the bank was safely tucked in the top pocket of his new Walmart $9.99 work shirt. The letter was folded in the back pocket of his new tan khakis.

Just after nine a.m., he approached a friendly, middle-aged woman sitting behind the bank's customer service desk in an impressive lobby with elaborately carved details remaining from the original construction. "Is there someone who could help me get something from my safety deposit box?" Nervously, he added, "I have my key."

"Of course, sir, Mr. Gordon will help you as soon as he finishes up with another customer. May I have your name?"

Since his new fake credentials were still in the safety deposit box, he smiled and replied, "Chuck Wilson, ma'am."

After signing an access card and shaking hands with Ellis Gordon, one of the bank managers, he was escorted to his numbered box in the safety deposit box room. Gordon inserted a key into one of the two locks on the box, and Chuck inserted his own identical key into the second lock. Both keys were turned, and the door opened.

When Gordon left the room, Chuck withdrew the metal box inside and opened the lid to review the contents. Everything was there, just like the letter said. The photo driver's license and credit card were in the name of Paul Johnson. There was also a new cell phone, a map, and an envelope with ten one-hundred-dollar bills.

He emptied everything into his new briefcase and returned to the main lobby, thanked the woman at the customer service desk, and left the bank. Back on the sidewalk, he couldn't help staring at a pretty young woman with a long blond ponytail on her way in.

As he started walking quickly to his pickup parked in the bank's customer lot, he had a strong urge to turn around to see if anyone was following him. He half-expected to be arrested, but nothing happened. He was now sweating and sat motionless inside his truck with the a/c turned on high for several minutes to calm down before heading to the airport.

He had to drive up and down a few aisles before he found a spot in the middle of row TT and backed into a parking space in the airport's long-term lot. He dug a screwdriver out of his small overnight bag and made sure nobody was around before removing his license plate and putting it in his briefcase.

"Name please?" asked the agent at the Avis counter.

"Chu...Paul Johnson," he said, nearly slipping up.

"Driver's license and credit card, please."

He retrieved both from his briefcase and handed them to the rental agent, who inputted his information into the reservations computer and swiped the credit card. He signed Paul Johnson on the agreement after declining the insurance. The agent handed him back a copy of the rental agreement, along with the key for the rental and his new license and credit card.

She pointed and said, "Out this door to the right, Mr. Johnson. The Avis lot is down the sidewalk past Hertz. Your Tahoe is in space number seven. Do you need a map or any directions?"

"No ma'am, I'm fine."

"Have a safe trip," she said with a smile and waved over the next customer in line.

Fifteen minutes later, Chuck was on his way out of the airport and on his way to Hilton Head. The Monday morning traffic headed out of town was light and the drive would only take under three hours. When he got to the McDonald's on Highway 17 South, just before the I-95 entrance ramp, he gassed up and stopped in for two Big Macs, two XL fries and a large coke.

On Hilton Head, he entered the elegant lobby of the Heritage Hotel in Harbor Town on the south end of the island. He couldn't help but be impressed by the stately Southern charm of the old hotel. As he headed to the reservation desk, he practiced saying his new name in his head. Paul Johnson. Paul Johnson.

"Paul Johnson," he said confidently to a smiling, middle-aged reservation clerk dressed in her formal hotel uniform de jour. He handed her his new credit card.

"Good afternoon, Mr. Johnson. Welcome to the Heritage." She retrieved his key card and handed it to him. "Second floor, 217. Elevator is there on your left. Enjoy your stay. If there's anything you need, please don't hesitate to ask."

What he wanted to ask her was what the hell he was doing here. He thanked her instead and headed to the elevator with his new briefcase and the small overnighter he usually kept in his sleeper cab.

When he got to his room and locked the door, he noticed a ticket and ferry schedule for Daufuskie Island on the night stand next to the bed. The ten a.m. ferry left right from the Harbor Town Marina, a short walk from the hotel. Good, he thought, plenty of time for breakfast in the morning.

Exhausted from the stress and hardly any sleep the night before, after watching an old rerun of *Smokey and the Bandit*, his favorite movie, he flopped down on the bed to rest his eyes before heading down for some dinner. He never made it and fell into a deep sleep until three a.m. on Tuesday morning.

When he woke up and looked at the clock next to the bed, he groaned and lumbered to the bathroom. Back in bed, he was now wide awake. All he could think about was the ferry ride in a few hours and a meeting with someone named Mr. Jamison at Blaine Cottage on Daufuskie.

He jumped back out of bed when he suddenly remembered he was supposed to flush the letter. He pulled it from the pocket of his new shirt, tore it up and drowned it in the toilet. He was glad to finally be rid of it.

By four a.m., he still hadn't fallen back asleep and knew it would be impossible. He was also starving since he hadn't eaten since the Big Macs yesterday on the way to Hilton Head. He made some bad coffee in the room coffeemaker and started surfing the TV for something to watch until the restaurant opened at six. He found an old *Pimp My Ride* rerun. Too bad Carol isn't here to watch it with me, he muttered to himself.

At five a.m. he got in the shower, stayed under for fifteen minutes, then put on the other Walmart shirt he'd bought for the trip. He pulled on the same pair of khakis and went to the lobby to wait for the dining room to open.

After polishing off the last of the biggest breakfast he could find on the menu, along with three cups of coffee, he walked around Harbor Town to kill some time before heading over to the marina. All he brought with him was the briefcase and everything from the safety deposit box along with the license plate from his pickup and both cell phones, his and theirs. He had no idea when he'd be back from Daufuskie. He left the overnight bag in the room since it was booked for two nights.

At nine forty-five a.m. on Tuesday, he boarded the ten a.m. ferry for Daufuskie.

Chapter 14

August 2018

Mandy got home from work on Friday a little before six p.m. at the end of a busy week. It was ten days before John was supposed to be in Hilton Head, at least according to the letter. He got up from reading the paper and gave her a big hug.

He asked her, "How was your day, hon?"

"Very busy. The annual audit is in two weeks, and I've already been working on it for days. Mr. Carlton wants to review a preliminary report next week. How was yours?"

If only she knew, he thought, but instead replied, "Same old, same old. Finished unloading a ship late this morning, and the boss said I could knock off early this afternoon. Spaghetti sauce is on the stove. How about some wine?"

"Love some. Let me get into something more comfortable while you get the wine ready, I'm famished."

After a relaxing weekend and no mention of the letter, John was out the door before Mandy woke up on Monday morning for his six a.m. shift at the port. He decided to wait until Wednesday before asking his boss for the following Monday and Tuesday off to take care of some personal business.

"Everything alright, John?" asked Pete Lindstrom when he got around to asking his supervisor for a couple days off next week.

"Yeah, no big deal, Pete. I just need take care of some personal insurance stuff in Columbia on Monday. Mandy is swamped at work so I told her I'd see if I could get some time off to handle it. Plus, the brakes on my truck are almost shot, and the first appointment I could get was next Tuesday morning."

"Sure John, no problem. I'll call Larry. He's always looking for some extra hours."

"Thanks Pete, really appreciate it. Hate asking on such short notice, but I forgot Mandy is in the middle of preparing for her company's annual audit. She'll be swamped for the next two weeks." John breathed a sigh of relief when he returned to the dock.

On Friday evening over dinner, he told Mandy that Pete asked him to handle something for him on Monday in Columbia, and he would need to stay overnight.

"What does he want you to do?" she asked.

He had already rehearsed the lie in his head. "Pete asked if I could deliver some paperwork on Monday and attend an important SPA meeting for him on Tuesday morning. He told me he needs to be here to supervise the unloading of a new container ship on her maiden visit to the port. Never hurts to do a favor for the boss. I should be back by Tuesday afternoon before you get home from work."

Mandy grinned and said, "Well, if Pete asked you to do it, you could hardly say no. Besides, it's always a good idea to help out the boss before your next review."

At eight a.m. the following Monday, Mandy was ready to leave for work. He kissed her goodbye, told her not to work too hard, and said he'd take her out to dinner Tuesday when he got back from his trip. After she left, he retrieved the letter from his toolbox in the garage and put it at the bottom of his overnight bag. He left the envelope in the box.

Thirty minutes later, John Simpson, now Harold Masters, headed downtown for the Bank of Charleston. After picking up a faux leather briefcase at the Office Depot on Rivers Avenue, he got on I-26 East toward the city. Traffic was still heavy from the usual morning rush, and he didn't get to the bank parking lot until almost nine-fifteen.

In the bank lobby, he asked the security guard to direct him to customer service. The guard pointed to a desk next to the teller stations and said, "Mrs. Haskins will be able to help you."

After handing the signed access card for the box to her, she said, "Mr. Gordon will be right with you."

Gordon came out of his office and took John to the safety deposit box area. After opening the box, he made sure everything mentioned in the letter matched the contents of the box, including the $1,000 cash. He dumped everything into his new briefcase and left the bank.

When he got to the Charleston airport, after standing in a line for twenty minutes behind passengers renting cars from a flight that just landed, he rented the Tacoma pickup reserved in the name of Harold Masters at the Avis counter and started driving to Hilton Head.

Just past two p.m., he arrived at the Heritage Hotel and checked into room 302. He flipped on the TV to Fox News and ordered an early dinner from room service.

Tuesday morning, John had an early breakfast in the hotel dining room. Although they didn't know each other, he was sitting two tables away from Chuck. Before he got to the ferry dock, despite his nerves on edge, he couldn't resist walking past the iconic Harbor Town lighthouse to take a peek at the 18th green of the famous Harbor Town Golf Links. He'd only seen the course on TV when the annual PGA Heritage golf tournament was played there the week following the Masters every April.

Chapter 15

August 2018

Emily finally had a plan.

With no hope of figuring out whether the letter was real or not before next Monday, she knew she was going to have to make the trip to Hilton Head to find out. She really didn't want to miss the beginning of the new school year but convinced herself she had no choice. Her new students would just have to start the year with a substitute for a couple days.

The idea was simple if she could pull it off. If something went wrong and she wasn't back by next Tuesday, at least it would give whoever started looking for her the reason she was missing. The trick was how to do it without her watchers noticing.

After she read the letter on Saturday, she put it in the shoulder bag in her closet. She used the bag during the school year to carry her papers back and forth. The letter said she needed to bring a shoulder bag with her to the bank next Monday, so she decided to use the same bag.

On the following Wednesday, five days before the start of the new school year, she called Mt. Pleasant Elementary. She hoped the principal would be in all week to get ready for the opening of school on Monday.

When the receptionist put her call through, she said, "Hi Mrs. McCarthy, this is Emily Baker. I'm planning to come in tomorrow to bring some materials to my classroom and was wondering if you had a few minutes to meet with me."

"Emily, so nice to hear from you. Hope you had a good summer."

"I did, thank you. I got to spend some extra time with my aunt, and, of course, keep up with my running. I've decided to enter the Charleston Marathon in January."

"Emily, that's wonderful. Anything important you want to discuss?"

Emily hesitated. She didn't want to mention missing the first two days of the start of the new school year next week over the phone. "I just wanted to review a couple ideas I have for my new class. I also need to copy some lesson plans from last year that I'll bring with me."

"I'll be here all day, stop in whenever it's convenient for you. See you tomorrow, Emily."

Emily hung up and breathed a sigh of relief. So far, so good. All she had to do now was remove the letter from the white envelope and leave the letter in the shoulder bag without her watchers seeing her do it.

Since she had intentionally mentioned to her principal that she would be bringing some papers to copy at school, she went to the closet and left the light off. She quickly pulled out the letter from the envelope in her shoulder bag and put it at the bottom of some old lesson plans she kept in a box. She then put a stack of lesson plans with the letter into the shoulder bag.

Next, she folded two pages from one of the lesson plans, put them in the original white envelope in place of the letter, and put the envelope back in her bag. She carried the shoulder bag out of the closet to take downstairs for her meeting at school the next day.

The next step was crucial.

As she headed for the bedroom door, she stopped as if she just thought of something. She turned around and removed the distinctive white envelope from the bag, now with only an old lesson plan in it. She nonchalantly put the envelope on top of the dresser, then took the shoulder bag with the original letter in it and went downstairs. She put the bag on the small table by the front door with her car keys.

She hoped her acting job was convincing.

On Thursday morning, she took the shoulder bag to school for her meeting with Mary McCarthy. When she arrived, she poked her head into the principal's office to say hello and told her she just needed to copy some lesson plans and would be back to meet with her in a few minutes.

At her classroom desk, Emily wrote a personal note on a blank sheet of paper, addressed a school envelope to herself and added a stamp from the roll she kept in her desk drawer. Next, she removed the pile of original lesson plans from her shoulder bag and headed for the copier. The original of the letter was on the bottom of the pile.

At the school copier, she made copies of everything she had taken out of the bag, including the original two-page letter.

When she returned to her desk with the originals and copies of the lesson plans, along with the original and copy of the letter, she put the originals of the lesson plans and the letter back into her shoulder bag. She then spread all the copies she had just made on top of her desk, making sure to keep the copy of the letter hidden.

She pretended to sort the copies, then took the bottom two pages and folded the note she had just written around them, careful to keep the copy of the letter hidden from view. She inserted all three pages into the school envelope, sealed it, and put it in the shoulder bag.

She restacked the copied versions of the lesson plans, now without the copy of the letter, and put them on the side of her desk. When she was finished, she slung the bag back on her shoulder and headed for the principal's office.

"Good morning, Emily, nice to see you," greeted McCarthy. She was an attractive woman in her early fifties with a strong, confident voice and pleasant smile. Both her daughters were in college, and her husband was a successful Charleston attorney. Dressed casually in a pair of white cotton slacks and a light blue blouse, she got up and shook hands with Emily.

"Hi Mrs. McCarthy, good to see you as well. I wanted to see you in person to discuss a problem I have. My aunt is scheduled for some minor surgery next Monday, and she has no one else to take her to the hospital and stay with her. She'll need to stay overnight and can come home on Tuesday."

Emily was now in full sympathy mode. "I'm really sorry to spring this on you at the last minute, but I found out late yesterday that her surgery was rescheduled from tomorrow to Monday. I really don't know what to do."

"Emily, your family comes first, and I know how close you are to your aunt. By all means, be with her next week and we'll arrange for a substitute until you return to school next Wednesday. If you need more time, just let me know, it won't be a problem. I hope your aunt will be OK."

"Thank you so much, Mrs. McCarthy. Her doctor said it's a fairly routine procedure, and she should be good as new a few days after the surgery. Once I get her back home, she'll be fine."

"Did you also want to discuss anything about your lesson plans?"

"Actually, I found something I was looking for in my old plans I just copied. Thank you so much for understanding about next week. My aunt is so worried about me missing the first two days of school, but I know she'll be very relieved I'll be with her."

Moment of truth.

Before leaving, Emily said, "I need to drop off a letter in the mail to one of the parents from last year. I just wrote them a personal note to thank them for all their help, especially with our spring fundraiser. I'm also mailing them a copy of next year's fundraising schedule. Is there anything I can mail for you?"

"Thanks Emily, I actually need to mail a letter to the school district and was going to do it on my way home. If you're mailing something anyway, you can mail this for me as well."

McCarthy handed Emily an envelope and added, "Good luck with your aunt next week. We'll say a prayer for her and hold the fort until you get back."

Emily thanked her again before leaving. There was a mailbox on her way home, and she mailed both letters before returning to her apartment.

When she got back to the apartment, she took the shoulder bag upstairs. She took the white envelope from her dresser and put it in the bag. She then tossed the bag back into her closet for the trip next week.

She retrieved her mail from the outside mailbox on Saturday and felt a surge of adrenaline. The envelope she had mailed to herself on Thursday was there. She carefully pushed it to the back of the mailbox and returned to the apartment with the rest of the mail.

With so much on her mind, she really wanted to cancel her dinner date with Richard on Saturday evening at a new Italian restaurant in Mt. Pleasant. She reluctantly met him for dinner anyway, but before he had a chance to invite her back to his downtown apartment for a nightcap, she mentioned she was not feeling well and needed to make it an early night. She promised Richard a raincheck for the following weekend.

On Sunday morning, while packing for the trip to Hilton Head, she went into her closet. She left the light off again and quickly removed the lesson plan she had placed in the original white envelope. She replaced those two pages with the original copy of the letter, which was still at the bottom of the stack of lesson plans she'd copied at school.

She put the lesson plans back in the box in the corner of the closet and placed the original envelope and letter in her shoulder bag. She left the closet and put the shoulder bag next to her overnight bag on the side of her dresser.

The only thing now in the shoulder bag was the original letter and the white envelope it came in.

She'd done all she could, at least for now. She hoped it would work.

During an early dinner with Aunt Marie on Sunday afternoon, they chatted about the new school year, how Richard was doing, and her latest runs. When she got back to the apartment, she was exhausted and climbed into bed early. Thinking about all the possibilities of what might happen tomorrow kept her awake until she eventually fell into a restless sleep.

By six a.m. on Monday, she had already finished a long shower and padded downstairs, wearing only one of Richard's T-shirts, and started the coffee maker. After some peanut butter and a banana, her normal morning pre-run breakfast, she went back upstairs and dressed in a pair of jeans, a white blouse, and her favorite running shoes.

She left the apartment shortly before eight-thirty with her overnight bag and the shoulder bag with the letter that had started it all. After filling up with gas on Highway 17 South, she crossed over the Ravenel Bridge and took the East Bay Street exit into town.

Inside the bank, she signed the safety deposit box access card and handed it back to Mrs. Haskins at the customer service desk. A few minutes later, she shook hands with Mr. Gordon and walked with him to the safety deposit boxes.

As soon as Emily left the bank, Ellis Gordon made a call on his cell. "Sir, all three of your guests have now emptied their boxes and left the bank."

"Very good, Mr. Gordon," was all the man on the other end said before hanging up.

Emily carefully followed all the instructions in the letter and finally arrived at the Heritage Hotel on Hilton Head in her Toyota Camry Avis rental. She checked into room 120 as Kathy Ritter.

After an early dinner in the hotel dining room, she browsed a couple of the clothing shops around the Harbor Town Lighthouse area before heading back to the hotel. She rented *Sleepless in Seattle* on her room TV and nodded off before it was over.

Early Tuesday morning, she flushed the letter down the toilet and tossed the envelope in the bathroom trashcan. She showered, dressed, and ordered a light breakfast of oatmeal, fruit, orange juice, and coffee from room service before heading to the marina with only her shoulder bag to catch the ten a.m.

ferry. Her nerves were frayed knowing how desperate Richard and Aunt Marie would be by now to hear from her.

As she approached the ferry, she thought about turning around and going back home. But she knew she had to find out if the letter was real or just an elaborate prank. On the dock, she paused at the railing and closed her eyes. She took a deep took breath and imagined pushing herself to the finish line of her first marathon. A few minutes later, she walked on board.

Chapter 16

December 2017

Nearly four months after the body of Jorge Rodriguez was found at the port, all Steve Harris had to go on was a vague description of the killer and an even vaguer theory about why he was shot at the port. The port mole was also still a ghost despite the intense ongoing investigation by Rob Campbell and his State Ports Authority security team.

The murder investigation was going nowhere when Steve got his first break in early December. A couple weeks after the port security office posted an additional guard outside the port entrance, the runner with the blond ponytail was finally intercepted on one of her early runs. Her name was Emily Baker.

The security guard stopped her and asked if she'd be willing to talk to Mt. Pleasant Detective Steve Harris, who was investigating an incident at the port that took place in August. She said she'd be happy to help any way she could and left her contact information.

Steve called her early that evening. "Miss Baker, this is Detective Steve Harris. I was told you'd be willing to talk to me about an incident I'm investigating that happened last August as you were running around the port entrance. The date was Monday, August seventh."

Emily thought about the date for a moment before she said, "As a matter of fact, Detective Harris, that may have been the morning I did see something unusual near the port entrance on one of my early morning runs."

"Miss Baker, what exactly did you see?"

"I was running to the port from my apartment on Whipple Road. As I looped around the entrance, I saw two men having a heated argument a few yards down the security fence. I thought it was unusual for two men arguing along the fence at that time of the morning."

"Did you stop running to see what was going on?"

"Not really, I just slowed down to look at them since they were standing under a light pole. I couldn't hear anything they were saying, and I was past them pretty quickly. Then I just kept running back to my apartment."

"Did you get a look at their faces?"

"It was still pretty dark, but I did see their faces clearly. It all happened pretty fast."

"Anything else you may have noticed about the two men?"

"Well, the taller man was very angry and poked an older man in the chest, then pushed him up against the fence. Like I said, I was past them before I saw very much."

"Thank you, Miss Baker. You've been very helpful. Would you mind if I call you again if I have any more questions?"

"Sure, that would be fine. Can you tell me what this is all about?"

"Just a routine investigation, we're trying up some loose ends. Nothing to worry about. Thanks again for your time. Have a good evening."

Finally, some progress. If he could find a suspect, Emily Baker might be able to confirm his identity as the last man to see Jorge Rodriguez alive.

Chapter 17

Daufuskie Island, South Carolina, is five miles long and two and a half miles wide, situated three and a half miles from Hilton Head Island's Harbor Town Marina. Surrounded by Calibogue Sound, the Intracoastal Waterway, and the Atlantic Ocean, Daufuskie is accessible only by ferry, barge or private boat.

Although the island's full-time population is under a thousand residents, regular ferry service from Hilton Head has made Daufuskie a popular tourist destination, especially its Historic District and championship golf courses. Transportation on the island is mostly by golf carts and bicycles, along with a few regular vehicles owned mostly by residents to travel around the island.

At nine-thirty a.m. on Tuesday morning, tourists and a couple of permanent residents began arriving at the ferry docked at the Harbor Town Marina for the thirty-minute trip over to Daufuskie. After Chuck boarded, John got on a few minutes later. Emily was with the last group of passengers, making a total of twenty-two on board, before the ferry left promptly at ten a.m.

Remembering the instructions in the letter, Chuck, John, and Emily sat on the ferry's bench seats and spoke to no one. They still didn't know each other.

Emily was sitting on the same side as John, about three rows apart from each other. Chuck was seated on the other side of the aisle in the same row as Emily. When he glanced over at her, he thought she looked familiar, but couldn't place where he'd seen her.

About halfway to Daufuskie, the captain came on the intercom speaker. "Ladies and gentlemen, those of you on the right side have a great view of our porpoise escorts only a few yards off the bow. They usually like to show off by cutting back and forth across the front of the boat, so those of you on the left side should also get a chance to watch them play."

An elderly woman sitting next to Emily said to her, "They're absolutely beautiful. My sister told me about them after her last visit to Daufuskie, and I had to see them for myself. Have you been to the island before?"

"No ma'am, I'm just delivering some papers to a friend and then returning back to Harbor Town."

Emily tried to discourage any further conversation by looking out the open window, but the woman kept talking. "My name is Mabel, and. this is my first trip. I read in my travel magazine that it's a beautiful island with a very colorful history. Did you know that before the Civil War there were eleven plantations on Daufuskie Island?"

Before the history lesson could continue, Emily quickly replied, "I had no idea. Could you excuse me for a minute, Mabel? I need to use the rest room before we arrive."

"Certainly dear," the woman smiled and turned her attention back to the porpoise show.

When Emily got into the aisle and headed for the bathroom, Chuck looked up at her and tried again to remember where he'd seen her. Then it hit him. She was going into the Bank of Charleston yesterday morning as he was leaving. He was sure of it. Pretty sure. Except what would she be doing on the same ferry heading for Daufuskie Island? What are the odds? Must not be her. Can't possibly be her.

As the ferry neared the Daufuskie Island dock, John still couldn't believe he was here. Other than the money and the death threat, he'd rather be anyplace else than on this boat. He'd lied to his boss and lied to Mandy. Just thinking about it made him angry all over again.

Suddenly he remembered something. He forgot to remove the license plate from his car at the airport. Damn! Too late to worry about it now, it was stupid anyway. What was the point? I'll just have to put it back on tomorrow when I return the rental car, he thought. At least, I'll finally get some answers from this Jamison guy, whoever the hell he is.

The captain's voice broke his train of thought. "For your safety, please remain in your seats until the ferry has docked. We hope you enjoyed the ride. There are ferry schedules next to the gangway if anyone needs one. Thank you for riding with us today and enjoy your stay on Daufuskie."

Emily, Chuck, and John got up and made their way to the exit ramp separately. When they got to the end of the short walkway from the ferry onto the island, they saw three men who were built like NFL linebackers. Each man held a sign with one of their fake names on it.

Kathy Ritter. Paul Johnson. Harold Masters.

The drivers were spread several feet apart in front of a Lexus RX 350, a Land Rover, and a Ford Explorer. They quietly greeted each of their passengers by their new names and drove away from the dock separately, a few minutes apart from each other.

Emily's Land Rover was the last to leave. When the driver got off his cell phone, he said, "My apologies for the delay, Miss Ritter. I needed to confirm another pickup before dropping you at Blaine Cottage." He escorted her to the back seat and slowly headed for the cottage.

The three drivers took their pre-planned circuitous routes to the cottage so they would all arrive separately, five to ten minutes apart.

Nearly three miles drive from the ferry dock, Blaine Cottage was nestled among tall pine trees and flanked by two vacant lots in a secluded part of the island. Like all private residences on Daufuskie, the cottage blended into the native environment and was designed within the same architectural covenants established for the development of Hilton Head Island by real estate visionary Charles Fraser in 1956.

The Explorer arrived first and dropped Chuck off in front of the cottage. After a quick "Enjoy your stay," the driver was on the move before Chuck got to the front door. He knocked and was met by a young man who looked to be in his early twenties.

Jamison smiled and said, "Welcome to Blaine Cottage, Mr. Johnson. I'm Mr. Jamison. Thank you for coming. I know you have many questions about why you were asked to be here this morning and why all the cloak and dagger. As soon as our other two guests arrive, we'll get started. Meantime, please make yourself comfortable. There's coffee, tea, soft drinks, and bottled water in the kitchen, along with some sandwiches and snacks. Please help yourself."

"What other two guests?" asked Chuck.

"No need to be concerned, Mr. Johnson. Everything will be explained when we get started." Chuck shrugged and headed for the kitchen.

A few minutes later, there was a knock on the door. Jamison welcomed John with the same friendly greeting. John noticed the other man in the kitchen and remembered seeing him on the ferry.

John asked, "Who's he?"

"Mr. Masters, your questions will all be answered in due time. We're waiting for one more guest before we get started. Meantime, please make yourself comfortable."

Ten minutes later, Emily arrived. Her driver remained parked in front of the cottage. She was surprised how young the man who called himself Mr. Jamison looked when he greeted her at the door. He's around the same age as me, she thought. When she entered the living room, Chuck put down his second sandwich and said to her, "I think I saw you yesterday. Were you by any chance at the Bank of Charleston?"

Before she could reply, Jamison interrupted and said, "If you will all be patient, I'm expecting a call from the man who will explain why you're all here. Again, I know it's been a major inconvenience for each of you to get here, but I assure you he will explain everything. While we're waiting for his call, please put your old cell phones in the basket on the table next to the front door, along with the credit card from the safety deposit box, your hotel key card, rental car key, new cell phone, and the license plate you were asked to remove from your vehicle at the Charleston airport."

Before returning to living room, John said defiantly, "I don't have my plate. I forgot to take it off my car. Anyway, what was the point of bringing it here? This whole charade has gone on long enough, and I want some answers."

Jamison warned, "Mr. Masters, the instructions in the letter were explicit and were to be followed precisely. Do not make another mistake. Your next one could be your last."

After the reprimand, Jamison took John's license plate from his own briefcase and put it in the basket. All three guests put everything else their host had requested into the basket and returned to the living room. They sat back down in silence to wait for the call they all hoped would finally explain what they were doing here and what happens next.

Emily closed her eyes. After Jamison's threat to John, she knew there was no longer any doubt. She was in serious trouble and should never have come.

Chapter 18

March 2018

In early March, nearly seven months into his port murder investigation, his patience was wearing thin when Steve Harris got some good news. The murder weapon had turned up in Miami.

A man matching the general description of the port killer, based on the port security footage, was found unconscious in the parking lot of the Auto Warehouse parts facility in Miami by a passerby, who called 911. A few minutes before a Miami PD patrol car showed up, Dale got an urgent call from Doug Warren, his undercover agent at the warehouse.

Warren talked fast and said, "Boss, there's a guy unconscious in our warehouse parking lot. He's around the same height and build as the general description of your suspect in the Jorge Rodriguez murder at the Port of Charleston. Miami PD is pulling into the lot now, and EMS is right behind them. As soon as I heard all the commotion, I ran outside and took a quick peek at the guy before the cops showed up. May be nothing, but I thought you should know right away."

Dale called Miami Police Chief Gary Franks. "Chief Franks, this is Miami DEA Agent Dale Hawkins. We've had the Auto Warehouse building on West 18th under surveillance for several months based on a credible link to the Camino organization. Our undercover at the warehouse just called me about an unconscious man lying in the parking lot. He fits the basic description of a murder suspect at the Port of Charleston six months ago. My guy told me one of your patrol units just rolled up on scene."

"What's your interest in this guy, Agent Hawkins?" asked Franks.

"Chief, we were called in last August to assist local police and the South Carolina State Ports Authority in the murder investigation of a Camino cartel runner named Jorge Rodriguez, who was executed just outside their port. His prints were in our DEA database."

With no reaction yet from the Chief, Dale pressed on, "We shared what we had on Rodriguez with the local authorities up there. We also agreed to coordinate any new information generated here or there related to the Rodriguez murder. From the port surveillance video we were shown by their local detective handling the case, my undercover says the man in the parking lot fits the general description of the shooter, who we think could be a player in the Camino organization."

"What do you need?"

"If this guy has a weapon on him, specifically a nine mil, we'd like to see if that gun matches the bullets that were recovered at the Rodriguez murder scene. It's a long shot, but if the ballistics match, we may have our guy."

Dale added a warning. "If he is our guy, your officers need to know he's a potential serious threat. He should be put under twenty-four-hour guard at the hospital, preferably in handcuffs, until we can confirm if he's carrying the gun that may be our murder weapon. I'd also like to get his identity, especially if his prints are in the criminal database."

"Thanks for the heads up, Agent Hawkins, can't hurt to check it out. I'll talk to the officers who responded to the 911 call and find out if the guy has a gun on him. Give me your cell number, and I'll call you back in a few minutes."

Fifteen minutes later, Chief Franks called back. "Agent Hawkins, one of our officers on the scene confirmed the man was armed with a nine-millimeter Glock 19 in his waistband. I've alerted my men to hold him in custody at Miami General. Meantime, get your ballistics report to us ASAP. I'll have our Miami PD Detective Paul Owens get in touch with you as soon as I can reach him. He's one of our top guys and very familiar with the Camino organization and some of their serious players."

"Appreciate it, Chief, I know Paul. I think this parking lot guy could definitely be a Camino player, especially if he's the man we're looking for."

As soon as the call ended, Dale was on the phone with Steve. "We may have caught a break in your port murder case. A guy matching the basic description from the port surveillance video you showed us was just found unconscious in the parking lot of the Auto Warehouse building we've had under surveillance. He was armed with a nine mil Glock. Miami PD agreed to keep him under wraps at Miami General until we run his prints and determine if his gun is a match for the bullets recovered at your murder scene."

Steve couldn't hold back his excitement. "Fantastic news, Dale! I'll email you our ballistics report on the bullets right away. If we have a match, we're back in business. Let me know as soon as you get the ballistics comparison."

An hour later, Dale got a call from Paul Owens and filled him in on Steve's Port of Charleston murder investigation.

Owens said, "Thanks for the update, Dale. Just got a call from Chief Franks, appreciate the info on the guy from the Auto Warehouse parking lot. As soon as we know who he is, I'll let you know. We maintain a separate database here at the Miami PD on any members of the Camino cartel we've been able to identify. We'll see if we have anything on our parking lot man. Meantime, we're keeping him under guard at Miami General until he wakes up and we sort things out. I'd also like to touch base with Detective Harris up in South Carolina. If you have it, text me his cell number, and I'll be in touch as soon as I know more."

Owens called Steve and said, "Detective Harris, this is Miami PD Detective Paul Owens. I just got off the phone with a colleague of mine, DEA Agent Dale Hawkins. He told me he's been working with you on your port murder case. The link with your victim Jorge Rodriguez to the Camino cartel is interesting. My team here has been tracking the Camino organization for a long time."

Owens paused and said, "Hang on a second, Detective," He came back on the line less than a minute later. "Sorry about that, my Chief was calling me. I told him I was talking to you and would call him back with an update. My team is running the prints of the guy found at Auto Warehouse. We'll coordinate with Agent Hawkins when we get the results. He'll let you know as soon as we know. He told me his guys are handling the ballistics comparison of the man's gun with the bullets recovered at your murder scene. I'll keep him looped in on anything else of interest my team turns up that might be helpful to your murder investigation."

Steve preferred first names and said, "Thanks for reaching out, Paul. We've been getting nowhere on our end for the past few months, and this could the break we've been waiting for. I assume Dale told you we think our murder case is linked to a breach in our port security."

"Dale updated me on what happened up there with the stolen tapes, and it has Camino written all over it. These guys may be ruthless, but they're also smart."

The next day, Dale got the ballistics comparison back. After updating Owens, he called Steve. "Got an update for you. Our ballistics analysis has just confirmed the bullets found at your murder scene came from the Glock that was on the parking lot guy. We've logged the murder weapon into our Miami PD evidence locker. The only prints on the gun matched the suspect. He's regained consciousness, and we've arrested him on suspicion of murder."

"Thanks Dale, great news! Let me know when you name him. Meantime, I'll fill in everyone here, and we'll work on a game plan to coordinate our next steps."

The port murder case was back on track.

Chapter 19

Emily studied the other two men sitting in the living room. They didn't seem to know each other. The overweight older man with the gray buzzcut looked tired and nervous. The other man, who appeared to be around thirty, was clearly pissed off and had trouble hiding it. He looked like he was ready to bolt out the door any minute.

She had no idea who they were or what they were doing here with her, but she was certain all three of them got the same letter demanding they show up on Daufuskie Island today.

What still concerned her more than anything else was that Richard and Aunt Marie had no idea where she was. They would be worried sick if she didn't make contact soon. For now, she was at the mercy of this Mr. Jamison and whoever he was working for. The entire mess she put herself in still made absolutely no sense, but at least she wasn't alone.

Her thoughts were interrupted by a phone ringing in the living room. The sound was coming from a speaker on ceiling. Jamison pushed a button on a high-tech console mounted on a wall in the foyer and returned to the living room. He sat down and spoke in a normal voice. "Sir, your guests have arrived and are ready for your call."

A deep voice from the speaker on the ceiling said, "Thank you, Mr. Jamison. And welcome to our three guests. Miss Ritter, Mr. Johnson, and Mr. Masters. I know this has been an ordeal for each of you, my sincere apologies for the inconvenience. As I'm sure you've all guessed by now, each of you received the same letter. Until further notice, Mr. Jamison and I will continue to use your assigned names."

No one moved as ceiling man kept talking. "Thanks also for carefully following the instructions in the letter you each received. Except for the failure of Mr. Masters to bring us his license plate, which we had to retrieve ourselves.

Fair warning, I am a patient man, but I will not tolerate any further breaches of my instructions, including the new ones I will be explaining shortly."

Emily could see the same fear she felt in the eyes of the other two men after what the man in the ceiling just said. New instructions could only mean one thing. They would almost certainly not be returning home today. Despite the churning in her stomach, she did her best to remain calm and wait for the man to finish.

"Cards on the table," he continued. "I have a personal problem that involves all three of you. None of you has done anything wrong, but unfortunately, I need all three of you off the grid a while longer. If you cooperate with Mr. Jamison, no harm will come to you. For your own welfare, please don't try my patience. Failure to follow my instructions will not end well."

Ceiling man kept talking. "Each of you was given a thousand dollars in cash as a good faith gesture. As promised, I've also opened offshore accounts in each of your real names. Today, I'm depositing one hundred thousand dollars in each of those accounts. The remaining one hundred and fifty thousand will be deposited into your accounts when our business is concluded. You'll be given the account access information and security numbers at that time. For now, all I require is your complete cooperation."

John couldn't restrain himself any longer. In an angry voice, he said to the man who was running the show, "What more do you want from us? We've done what you asked. If we don't make contact with someone at home today, the police are bound to get involved."

The room went silent for a several seconds that seemed much longer before ceiling man spoke again. "Mr. Masters, you've already screwed up once, do not presume to threaten me. My patience with you is wearing very thin. The three men who drove each of you here are armed and waiting outside. Do not interrupt me again."

After another pause, he said each of his next five words very slow and very loud. "AM I CLEAR, MR. MASTERS?"

As if he had just been slapped, John quietly replied, "Whatever you say."

"Good, thank you Mr. Masters. Anyone else?"

When no one spoke, the man in charge said, "Mr. Jamison, I have to make a call and will be back in fifteen minutes. Our guests may use the bathrooms and help themselves to a sandwich and something to drink from the kitchen."

Dead silence. Emily was the first to stand up and speak. "Mr. Jamison, I need to use the bathroom."

"By all means, Miss Ritter, help yourself. There are two other bathrooms if Mr. Johnson or Mr. Masters needs to use them." Both men got up.

When Emily got to the bathroom and locked the door, she tried not to panic. If they wanted to get rid of us, they would have already done it by now, she reasoned. Right now, there was no choice but to hear what happens next.

A few minutes after everyone returned to the living room, ceiling man was back. "Here's what's going to happen. Each of you will be taken to a private dock not far from here by the same man who drove you from the ferry. A private boat will be waiting for your arrival. Mr. Jamison and my three men will accompany everyone together on the boat, which will return to Hilton Head.

Sometime this evening, Mr. Jamison will send a text to someone you know from your new cell phones to let them know you're safe and unhurt. As soon as the texts are sent, Mr. Jamison will dispose of the phones. When we arrive back on Hilton Head, all of you, including my men, will ride in two waiting SUVs to the Hilton Head Airport, where a private plane is on standby."

His parting shot was ominous. "Final warning. Do not try anything stupid. My men will not hesitate to use their weapons on anyone who tries to escape. Mr. Jamison will be flying with you and will share my final instructions once the plane is airborne. Have a good flight."

Emily's heart sank. She was outnumbered and being taken against her will by armed men to an unknown location. And she knew there was absolutely nothing she and the others could do about it, at least for the time being.

Chapter 20

May 2018

After nine months, the State Ports Authority investigation still hadn't identified the port mole who stole the security tapes recorded during the murder. Steve had no doubt that same person tipped off the Camino organization about the stash of cocaine seized in a container shortly after it arrived at the Wando Welch Terminal.

The name of the man found unconscious in the Auto Warehouse parking lot with the murder weapon back in March was identified as Al Robertson, forty-one years old and a long-time Miami resident. Robertson was married with three children and worked as a salesman for a Midwest packaging company. He told police he was on his way to meet a major sales prospect when he was mugged.

Robertson and his lawyer had insisted the gun was planted. In his statement, he claimed had never owned a gun, never even used a gun, and no idea where it came from.

Further investigation by the Miami PD turned up nothing. Robertson had no prior arrests, and his prints were not in the confidential Camino cartel files kept by both Paul Owens and Dale. There was also no record of any gun ever registered by Robertson.

Despite his claim of innocence, there was no visual confirmation of a planted gun since the CCTV camera overlooking the Auto Warehouse parking lot had been disabled for over a year. But when his alibi that he was in California on the day of the port murder was confirmed, the Miami PD had no choice but to release him from custody and drop the murder charge.

Dale and Steve were both convinced Robertson was targeted by the Camino cartel to shift his investigation away from the real shooter and get rid of the murder weapon at the same time. It was no coincidence Robertson had a similar build and age as the shooter seen on the port surveillance tapes.

All Steve ended up with was one more unproven link to Camino that led nowhere. He had the murder weapon, but no suspect and no fresh leads. His investigation had hit another wall and he was back to square one. As long as it takes, he reminded himself again.

Chapter 21

May 2018

The following week, Steve was in his office going over his notes for the umpteenth time when he decided to give Dale another call and pick his brains. "Hey Dale, just checking in to see how your Camino investigation is going. Hopefully, better than mine."

"Afraid not, Steve, what's up?"

"I got nothing since we lost our murder suspect. Our priority now is to find the mole who tipped off the cartel about the cocaine shipment we seized at the port. If we can find him or her, we think that could lead us to whoever took out Rodriguez."

"That would definitely help. We've got a full court press on every snitch we've got, but so far nothing useful has turned up. Our undercover man is still in place at Auto Warehouse."

"Anything new on Paul Franco, the Auto Warehouse owner?"

"We had our eye on him until he was found dead in the trunk of his car last month. No usable forensics, no shell casings, same type of weapon used in your port murder. Same MO. Double tap to the back of the head. Sound familiar?"

"Dale, these guys definitely take no prisoners. Sounds to me like somebody is getting nervous. Who was brought in to replace Franco?"

"Guy named Art Winston. We're still trying to get a line on him, but so far nothing unusual from our background checks. All we know is that Winston managed a plumbing supply company in Miami before he was hired. No priors and he's not in the system, but we're keeping tabs on him. With Franco's murder, there's not much doubt he became a Camino loose end for whatever reason and was taken off the board."

Steve reviewed where his own investigation stood. "I've lost count of how many times I've gone over the footage of the surveillance tapes that were stolen from the port. I'm convinced there's a specific reason those tapes were taken. Maybe to set up someone like Robertson for the port murder. Or they were worried about something else on those tapes. I just can't figure out what."

"Steve, there's got to be something else important on those tapes."

"The only thing useful we've gotten from the video, besides a sketchy description of the shooter, came from my interview with Emily Baker. She was the young woman seen in the video running around the port entrance that morning. When I interviewed her, she claimed she briefly saw the faces of the two men arguing along the security fence."

"Were you able to confirm one of the men she saw was Jorge?"

"I had a follow-up interview last week at her apartment and showed her a six-pack of photos. She immediately identified Jorge, no hesitation. If we ever get a suspect, I think Emily would also be able to confirm he was at the port with Jorge that morning. It's possible the cartel wanted to see if there were any potential witnesses on the video."

"You're probably right," Dale agreed. "We've reviewed the Camino files that Paul Owens maintains, along with our own files, to see if we could find anyone who might fit the shooter's general description based on what little we can see of him on the video footage. There are a couple possibilities, but with only basic height, weight, and age range, it's impossible to make any kind of positive ID."

"Anything would help at this point. Tell me about them," said Steve.

"One possible is a low-level gopher with an eye patch named Jimmy Winkel, aka Winky. The other possibility is someone who showed up a few months ago on some recent surveillance video of a meeting he had with someone we suspect is a high-level Camino operative. But we've never seen that mystery man again and have no idea who he is."

Steve had a thought. "What if I show the photos of those two guys to Emily? Maybe she'll recognize one of them as the guy who was arguing with Jorge at the port. It's a shot in the dark, but you never know."

"Can't hurt to give it a try. I'll email the two photos to you as soon as I can. Let me know if Miss Baker recognizes either one of them."

"Will do. Thanks again, Dale. Keep in touch and I'll do the same."

As soon as Steve got Dale's email with the two photos, he left a message on Emily's cell asking her to call him at her convenience.

She called back later the same afternoon. "This is Emily. I got your message that you wanted to see me. Is this still about what I saw at the port last August?"

"Hello, Miss Baker. Thanks for calling me back. I was wondering if I could stop by sometime tomorrow. I'd like to show you some more photos and see if you might recognize any of them."

"OK, sure, how about tomorrow morning at ten a.m. at my apartment? That will give me time to eat and get cleaned up from my run. Since the school year ended, I've been lazy and starting my morning runs a little later than usual."

"Perfect. I'll see you then, Miss Baker. Thank you."

After his meeting with Emily the next morning, Steve couldn't wait to break the news to Dale as soon as he left her apartment. "I just showed Emily Baker another six-pack of photos, including the two you sent me. She told me when she ran by the two men arguing that morning, the taller man turned around to watch her run by."

Still skeptical, Dale asked, "So, she got a good look at *both* men?"

"She told me she got a clear look at both their faces before she was past them. And she was certain one of the men in your photos is the taller man she saw with Jorge on the morning he was murdered."

Completely surprised by the unexpected turn of events, Dale replied, "I'll be damned, we've got him."

Chapter 22

The three armed drivers were waiting for them when they reached the bottom of the porch steps, with Jamison right behind. He said, "Please get back into the same vehicles you arrived in. I'll be riding with Miss Ritter. When we get to the boat dock, exit your car at once and get on the boat that will be waiting for us."

At a private dock along a sparsely used section of the island, an impressive Hatteras yacht was ready to board. Jamison led the way into the salon, followed by Emily, Chuck, and John. The drivers, now in security guard mode, boarded last. Two of them entered the salon holding a silenced Glock. The third driver remained outside on the stern.

After everyone was seated and the yacht got underway, Jamison explained, "When we get to the Skull Creek Marina on Hilton Head, there will be two Suburbans parked at the end of the dock. Each of you will be escorted separately to the vehicles by one of my armed men. Mr. Johnson and Mr. Masters will sit in the middle row of the first vehicle. Miss Ritter and I will ride in the second Suburban. My men are under orders to shoot if you try anything stupid. Trust me, you don't want to learn the hard way."

Before finishing his instructions, Jamison asked each of them if they understood the warning. When all three nodded they got the message, he said, "We'll drive to a private hanger at the Hilton Head Airport where a plane will be waiting for us. Remain in your vehicle until I talk to the pilot. I will then signal everyone to exit their vehicle and walk to the plane. Miss Ritter first, followed by Mr. Johnson and then Mr. Masters, single file. You three will board the plane first, followed by my men. I will board last."

John asked, "Where are we going?"

"Mr. Masters, as soon as we take off, I'll let you and everyone else know exactly where we're headed. Meantime, just do as you're told and no one will get hurt," Jamison warned.

The yacht eased into the Skull Creek Marina on Hilton Head and tied up. All three of them, especially John, knew their best chance of escape might be right here. He looked at Emily, and she slowly shook her head back and forth once. She'd already made the same mental calculation they'd all made. There was no longer any doubt what would happen if any of them made a run for it. This was not the time to find out.

Chuck and John slowly walked to the first Suburban and got in with their two minders. As soon as Emily, Jamison, and the third armed man were in the second SUV, one of the two men piloting the Hatteras untied the stern and bow lines and hopped back on board before the big yacht reversed into the channel and quickly left the marina.

The six-mile drive to the Hilton Head Airport took less than fifteen minutes. The two SUVs were driven to a private hanger where a Beechcraft King Air was parked. The twin-turboprop plane had room for eight passengers plus a pilot and co-pilot. The three captives were each seated a row apart on the right side of the plane, with their three bodyguards opposite them.

Before Jamison boarded the plane, he made two calls. The first was to Mark Davis, head of the cartel surveillance team. "Mark, I need an update."

"Everything is going as planned," he replied. "No problems getting into their homes this morning. Mr. Wilson has a nice sleeper cab parked in the yard, but his cabin is for shit. I packed a suitcase for each of them with some extra clothes, toiletries, and personal items. I got to the Heritage early this afternoon. The duplicate hotel key cards were right where you said they'd be."

"I put everything from their rooms into their personal carry bags, which are now in my car with their suitcases. I also removed all the surveillance equipment from each room and wiped them down. They're now all checked out of the hotel."

"Excellent Mark. Just leave their Avis rentals there, I have the keys. We're about to take off from the airport. Have you been to Blaine Cottage yet?"

"The cleaning team is sanitizing the cottage as we speak. I'll remove the SIM cards from their personal cell phones and flush them, along with their bogus drivers' licenses and credit cards. I'll dump their personal cell phones overboard on my ferry ride back to Hilton Head. I still have their burner phones as planned. Anything else you need?"

"Not right now. I assume you also removed all the surveillance cameras from their homes when you packed their clothes. We need to make sure there are absolutely no traces left behind. The cops are going to be all over this by tomorrow."

"All taken care of. I'm about to get the ferry back to Hilton Head, and I'll start driving to North Carolina as soon as I get off. Should take me about seven or eight hours to get to the beach house."

Jamison made his second call to the boss. "Everything is in order, sir. Just got off the phone with Mr. Davis, and he confirmed he's taken care of all the items we discussed. Our plane is ready to take off. No problems on my end. We'll all arrive at the house later this afternoon."

"Thank you, Mr. Jamison. Call me when our guests are in the nest."

Jamison boarded the plane and sat up front with the pilot. As soon as the door closed, they taxied to the runway and waited for clearance from the tower to take off. Jamison got on the intercom.

"Congratulations to our three guests for getting here safely. Rather than talk to you from the cabin over the engine noise, I'll update you from here in the cockpit as soon as we're in the air. Meantime, make sure your seatbelts are fastened for what will be a short flight."

When the plane leveled off, Jamison got back on the intercom. "Lady and gentlemen, thank you for flying with us today." The cabin remained silent. "We'll be landing at the Pinewood Airport on the Outer Banks of North Carolina. The flight will take about an hour. When we arrive, we'll follow the same drill as our arrival at the marina. Two Suburbans will take us to a private home on the beach, not far from the airport."

Pinewood Airport is situated a few miles north of the beach town of Duck on the Outer Banks, a two-hundred-mile stretch of peninsulas and barrier islands along the coastline of North Carolina and southeastern Virginia. The private airport is situated next to North Carolina Highway 12, the primary road running north and south along the coast.

As the plane approached the small airport from the south, Emily paid close attention to the coastline from her side of the plane to get a better idea of the landscape and any landmarks that stood out. She noticed a bridge to the mainland and then a small town as the plane made its final approach. The King

Air landed smoothly, using most of the airport's relatively short runway. The two Suburbans were waiting for them as soon as the plane's engines shut down.

Everyone got into their assigned vehicle in the same seating arrangements as the earlier drive from the marina to the airport on Hilton Head. In less than a mile north of the airport, on the Atlantic Ocean side of Highway 12, they turned into a curved driveway that ended at a large three-story house surrounded by tall pine trees on three sides. Situated along a secluded stretch of the Outer Banks coastline, the house was invisible from the road.

The modern three-story, seven-thousand square foot home was owned by hedge fund billionaire Wilver Renshaw, who built it ten years ago as a personal vacation retreat and upscale rental. The current summer rental rate was twenty-five thousand dollars a week. The exterior was painted white with dark green shutters matching the front door. The interior featured wide plank Brazilian hardwood floors throughout, including the eight oversized bedrooms, three on each of the two upper floors and two more on a main living level, each with its own ensuite bathroom.

Down the hall from the two bedrooms on the open plan first floor were a spacious chefs' kitchen, expansive living room that opened into a massive dining room with a floor to ceiling glass window facing the Atlantic, and a library room furnished with comfortable lounge chairs and a sectional. One wall featured floor to ceiling mahogany shelves filled with books.

Before entering the house, Jamison gave his three guests their marching orders. "Welcome to the Outer Banks. I will escort each of you to your assigned bedroom on the second floor. We've taken the liberty of packing some of your clothes and toiletries from your homes. The extra clothes, along with your overnight bags and anything else you left in your hotel rooms, will arrive later this evening. We've checked each of you out of the hotel. We'll take care of your rental cars.

Please keep in mind my security detail will be on duty twenty-four seven. One armed guard will be posted inside and outside at all times. Do not try anything foolish. There will be food and refreshments available in the dining room after we show you to your rooms. I'll join you there in thirty minutes for a briefing on your stay."

Emily asked, "How long do you plan to keep us here?"

"As long as necessary," Jamison snapped. "Everyone follow me."

Shortly after escorting his guests to their rooms, Jamison went back downstairs to wait for them in the dining room. Before he sat down, his cell phone vibrated with a text from an unknown number. The message sent a shockwave through his entire body.

Your parents are alive. You will hear from me. Do not reply or call this phone. Delete this message and DO NOT TELL YOUR BOSS.

Part Two
Missing

Chapter 23

September 1988–October 2016

When he started high school in the North Hills area of Pittsburgh, Billy Jones already knew he wanted to be a cop. His father and older brother Ron were both cops, and he planned to follow in their footsteps. But when his dad was so badly wounded in a drug bust gone bad that he had to be reassigned to permanent desk jockey status, Billy had second thoughts. The man he idolized his entire life was unable to cope with the change.

His father was a beat cop, not a paper-pusher, and began drinking heavily. Despite his family's encouragement, psychiatrist visits, and support from the entire department, especially his police chief, he couldn't turn the corner. Less than a year after being disabled, Billy's mother threatened to divorce him if he didn't stop drinking.

A month later, Francis Matthew Jones, dedicated family man, respected street cop, and now full-blown alcoholic suffering from severe depression, committed suicide with his own gun.

By his senior year of high school, Billy had finally shaken his feelings of guilt over his father's death. His mother and brother kept telling him it wasn't his fault, and eventually he was able to come to grips with the hard truth. There was nothing he could've done to save his father.

Money was tight, but he still wanted to get a college degree. His first choice was the University of Pittsburgh so he could commute from home and save money on room and board. On a Friday afternoon in early March, his mother handed him a long-awaited envelope from the admissions office of Pitt. When Billy hugged her and shared the good news, she told him with tears in her eyes, "Your dad would've been very proud of you today."

Soon after he started at Pitt, Billy decided to get some career advice from Charlie Jefferson, his dad's old partner and best friend on the force. In Charlie's living room, Billy told him he was thinking about applying to the

Pittsburgh Police Academy after graduation, but he wasn't as sure as he used to be since his father's death.

Charlie asked, "Have you thought about joining the army after you get your degree?"

"Not really. Ever since high school, I've always planned on becoming a cop."

Charlie knew he was still struggling with the memory of his father and gave Billy a new suggestion. "What about enlisting and becoming a Military Policeman. The army will train you, and you can stay in if you like it or get out after your initial enlistment period. Any police force in the country would hire an MP in a second."

Billy thanked him and promised to think about it.

One of Billy's favorite courses at Pitt was an elective in his junior year called *Introduction to Criminology* that included the basics of criminal investigation. A chance encounter in that class changed his life.

A pretty girl sitting next to him one day leaned over and asked him if he had an extra pen. She said hers ran out of ink. Billy glanced over at her, and his eyes locked on hers for an extra beat before leaning down and digging a spare pen out of his bag. She thanked him and returned to her class notes.

As they were leaving the classroom together, she said, "Thanks, you were a lifesaver. I just transferred from Auburn and hardly know anybody yet. I'm Molly, what's your name?"

"Billy Jones."

"Well, thanks again, Billy Jones," she said in her native southern accent before heading to another class. Molly Rankin grew up in Atlanta. Shortly after her parents got divorced, she enrolled at Pitt to live closer to her dad after he'd taken a new job in Pittsburgh.

Billy was so struck by Molly's smile and the most striking blue eyes he'd ever seen, he made sure to sit next to her again the next day. Before class started, Billy leaned over and whispered, "Molly, I have a serious question to ask you. Did your pen really run out of ink yesterday?"

Molly looked over at him with a sheepish grin and whispered, "Not exactly."

They began dating and quickly became inseparable. By the start of their senior year at Pitt, they had fallen hard for each other. The following spring, now in their final Pitt semester, Billy asked Molly to marry him. The wedding of Mr. and Mrs. William Robert Jones was celebrated that summer.

Billy and Molly returned from their honeymoon in Charleston and moved into Billy's family home with his mother and brother, who was still a bachelor. As soon as they were settled, he called Charlie Jefferson and told him he was taking his advice and enlisting in the army. Molly found a temporary job at a local bank downtown and stayed in Pittsburgh until Billy finished basic training.

He breezed through basic and began a four-month training course at the US Army Military Police School at Fort Leonard Wood in Missouri. After graduating as an MP, Billy got orders to report to the 3rd Military Police Group headquartered at Hunter Army Airfield in Savannah, Georgia.

Shortly after returning to Hunter from a deployment in Germany, he was summoned by his commanding officer. He wondered if it was about the assignment he'd requested. He stood at attention in front of the CO's desk. "At ease Sergeant Jones, take a seat," the Colonel began from behind his large, uncluttered desk as he picked up Billy's personnel file.

The Colonel looked straight at him. "Your military record is spotless, and your evaluations have been consistently high across the board. You have all the qualifications to become a Military Special Agent in the Army's Criminal Investigation Command, and I'm prepared to approve your request. This is a big decision, son. I want you to think about it again overnight and report back here at 0900 tomorrow before I put in your paperwork."

Billy stood and saluted. "Thank you, sir, 0900 tomorrow," he said as calmly as he could despite the urge to give the Colonel a high five.

Molly gave Billy a big hug after he recounted the meeting as soon as he got home that night. "I'm proud of you, hon, about time the army recognized how good you are."

After his CID training, Billy reported for duty at Hunter as a freshly minted Special Agent. He thrived on the job and over the next several years earned a well-deserved reputation as a thorough, diligent, and creative CID investigator. During his CID career, he had solved some complex missing persons cases.

Twenty years later and now qualified for an army pension, he began thinking it might be time for a change. Maybe settle down with Molly in one place, especially with the boys getting ready for college.

To celebrate his twenty-year milestone, Molly threw a party and invited their closest friends and some of his army buddies. When they were lying in bed that night after a more romantic celebration, Billy quietly asked her how she'd feel if he retired and started his own private investigation firm in Charleston.

"I'm still in my forties and ready for a new challenge. Steve Harris, an old army buddy I met back in basic training, is now a detective with the Mt. Pleasant Police Department. I reached out to him, and Steve invited us to come to Charleston and spend a weekend with him and his wife Janet to show us around. Steve told me they have plenty of room and to bring the boys."

She kissed him and didn't hesitate. "I love you, Billy Jones. And you know how much I love Charleston. If that's what you want and it will make you happy, me and the boys are all in."

He kissed her back. "Thanks Molly Jones, you have no idea how much that means to me."

Shortly after retiring, Billy and his family loved the house Steve thought might be perfect for them and moved to Charleston. When he found an affordable office space in an old, renovated cigar factory downtown on East Bay Street, *Jones Investigations* was open for business.

Chapter 24

By Tuesday morning, Marie Parker was worried sick. Something was very wrong. She hadn't heard from Emily since Sunday, despite numerous calls to her cell phone and several unanswered voice messages. She knew Emily should've already called by now, especially after her first day of the new school year.

She decided to call the school. When the receptionist answered, Marie said in a shaky voice, "Hello, my name is Marie Parker. My niece Emily Baker is one of your fifth-grade teachers, and I have an urgent message for her. I was unable to reach her this morning before school started. Can someone please check to see if she's in her classroom?"

"Miss Parker, since classes have already started, I'll be happy to leave her a message to call you at lunchtime."

In a panic, Marie said, "I'm sorry, but I really need to know if she's at school today."

"Please hold a minute, I'll connect you with our principal, Mrs. McCarthy."

McCarthy came on the line and said, "Miss Parker, this is Mary McCarthy, the school principal. How can I help you?"

"Mrs. McCarthy, I haven't heard from my niece Emily Baker since Sunday. I need to know if she came to school today."

Surprised by the question, McCarthy said, "Miss Parker, Emily was in last Thursday to see me and asked me if we could get a substitute teacher for yesterday and today. She told me she needed to take her aunt to the hospital yesterday for some minor surgery. She said she expected to be back in her classroom tomorrow."

Marie was shocked and frantically blurted, "I'm her only aunt, and I didn't have any surgery scheduled for yesterday! Emily wouldn't just make up a story like that without a very good reason. She's been like my own daughter. I'm sure you know her parents died just before she started high school. She's lived with me since the plane crash until she got her own apartment last year. We still talk on the phone almost every day. Mrs. McCarthy, I just know something is terribly wrong."

"Miss Parker, I believe you. Let's figure this out. Have you called her apartment?"

"Yes, and her cell phone. I've been calling her and leaving messages since last evening." Marie paused to steady herself before continuing, "I wanted to see how her first day went with her new class. When she didn't call me back last evening, I got worried. I called her boyfriend Richard, but he hasn't heard from her either. I called her again this morning, still no answer."

"Miss Parker, please try to stay calm. Here's what we'll do. I'll check with the other teachers to see if Emily mentioned anything to anyone. Meantime, you need to go to the Mt. Pleasant Police Department. Tell someone there your concerns and ask if you should file a missing person report."

Marie gave McCarthy her home and cell numbers in case one of the other teachers might know where Emily was. She doubted it but was grateful for the principal's help. Emily always told her how much she enjoyed working with her, and now she understood why.

At the Mt. Pleasant PD headquarters building, after explaining the situation to the police officer behind a glass partition in the lobby, Marie was escorted to a small conference room to meet with Hank Reed, one of the detectives on duty. She was still frantic and told him why she wanted to file a missing person report.

Reed said, "I understand your concern, Miss Parker, but it's been less than forty-eight hours since you last talked to her. Is it possible she just didn't mention to you where she'd be?"

"Detective Reed, I'm the closest thing Emily has to family. She would never leave me in the dark, especially after the first day of school. What worries me most is that she told Mary McCarthy, her school principal, that the reason she wouldn't be at school yesterday and today was to take me to the hospital for some minor surgery. Emily would never make up a story like that unless she was in trouble."

"OK, Miss Parker, I understand, but let's not get ahead of ourselves. Let me do some checking around, including the local hospitals. I'll also talk to

Mary McCarthy and visit Miss Baker's apartment building. Maybe one of her neighbors knows something about her whereabouts. I'll also need her cell phone number. Do you have a key to the apartment?"

Marie's stress level went up another notch as she gave him the number. "Yes, I'll go there right now to make sure she's not there. What if she fell or something? God forbid if she's hurt!"

Before she rushed out the door, Reed handed her his card. "What's your niece's apartment number? I'll drive over there myself and find out if anyone has seen or talked to her. If she doesn't make contact with you by this afternoon, call me and we'll open an official missing persons investigation."

After leaving the police department, Marie raced to Emily's apartment to make sure she wasn't there. On the way, she cried out to herself, "Where are you, Emily?"

***

Mandy Simpson was furious. When she got home from work on Tuesday, John was still not back from Columbia. She hadn't spoken to him since Sunday and left a message Monday evening on his unanswered cell. When he didn't call back, she just assumed he was busy with whatever he was handling for Pete Lindstrom, his supervisor at the port.

She called his cell again, still no answer. "Where in the hell are you, John?" she said out loud. In her phone contacts was the number John had given her for Pete's cell in case something important ever came up and couldn't reach John on the dock.

"Mr. Lindstrom, sorry to bother you. This is Mandy Simpson, John's wife. Have you heard from him today?"

"Hi Mandy. Sorry, he's not here. Last week John asked me if he could have off yesterday and today. He said he had to take care of some personal insurance business in Columbia yesterday, and today he had an appointment to get the brakes on his car fixed. I'm expecting him tomorrow morning."

Mandy had trouble processing what she'd just heard. "Mr. Lindstrom, something's going on that I don't understand. John told me you asked him to attend a State Ports Authority meeting in Columbia for you yesterday, and he would be back this afternoon. He didn't say anything about going to Columbia on personal business to handle our insurance or getting his brakes fixed today."

"That doesn't sound like John. I have no idea why he told you that. I was happy to give him a couple days off, but I don't have any meetings scheduled in Columbia this week."

Now she was certain something was wrong. "Sorry to have bothered you, Mr. Lindstrom. I'm just worried about him. If I don't hear from him soon, I'm not sure what I'll do. If he was in an accident, I should've heard from someone by now."

The thought that John might be seeing another woman crossed Pete's mind, but he kept that to himself. "Call me when you hear anything, Mandy, and I'll do the same. And try not to worry. I'm sure he'll turn up with a logical explanation."

"I hope so. Thank you, Mr. Lindstrom."

When Mandy hung up, she was paralyzed with fear. Whatever was going on, John would've called her. Unless he couldn't.

***

Chuck's best friend George Cooper stopped by T.W. Graham's on Tuesday afternoon to talk to Marge Mason before the restaurant got busy for dinner. He spotted his favorite waitress wiping down some tables and called out, "Hey Margie, did you happen to see Chuck on Saturday night? We were supposed to have dinner together, but I must've missed him. Just wanted to make sure he's OK."

Marge put her cloth on the table and said, "Hi George. Have a seat and take a load off. Chuck wasn't here on Saturday. Maybe he had to get an early start on his next trip. Did you call him?"

"That's the thing, Marge. I left a couple messages on his cell yesterday and stopped by his cabin. His cab is still in the yard, but that old pickup of his is not where he parks it in back. I called him again twice today and left messages, but he hasn't called me back. Chuck always gets back to me, especially when I leave him a message. I'm starting to get worried."

"That piece of junk pickup he drives probably broke down, and he's getting it fixed someplace."

"Could be, except he told me when we had dinner here Saturday before last that he'd be back in town by Friday and would see me for dinner here on

Saturday. He said he'd be heading back out of town with another port container yesterday, but his cab is still at the cabin."

Marge thought some more about it and suggested, "Maybe his trip got canceled, and he drove the pickup out of town to bring back something for the cabin."

"Maybe, but he still would've called me. I'm honestly afraid something's happened to him. If he stops in, please let me know. I'll do the same if he calls me. I just hope our boy isn't in any trouble. If I don't hear from him by tomorrow, I'm calling the port."

Chapter 25

August 2018

Early that same Tuesday evening, Emily was sitting at the dining room table with Chuck, John, and Jamison. On one end of the long table that comfortably seated eighteen were several cold cut sandwiches, small bags of chips and cookies, a large bowl of fresh fruit, and bottles of water, iced tea, fruit juice, and soft drinks. There was also a pot of coffee and a variety of condiments.

After a long day, despite their fear of the unknown, everyone was hungry and ate in silence as Jamison began talking. "I trust all of you have found your accommodations satisfactory. We may be here for a few days, depending on when my boss says we can leave. In the meantime, make yourselves comfortable. The TVs have all been disconnected, but there's a DVD player in your rooms and some old movies you can watch. You're also free to help yourselves to any of the books in the library room."

"Why are we here?" persisted John, despite the warning he got earlier from ceiling man.

"Unfortunately, I'm not at liberty to discuss why you were brought here. But you will all remain safe as long as you follow a few simple rules. Breakfast will be available here in the dining room each morning starting at seven a.m. Lunch will be served at one and dinner at seven. Help yourselves to coffee and tea in the kitchen any time between seven a.m. and nine p.m. Frankie is a terrific cook and will be your chef. Everyone must be in their own rooms no later than ten p.m. every night until seven a.m. the next morning, no exceptions."

"What about our clothes?" asked Emily.

"Your carry bags and personal items from the hotel, as well as some extra clothes, will be delivered here late tonight by one of our drivers. My apologies for the delay. You can get them from the foyer in the morning. In the meantime, there's plenty of linens and extra toiletries in your bathrooms.

Most importantly, do not attempt to leave this house under any circumstances. My men are armed and under strict orders to stop you and, if necessary, use force if you try to escape. There are security cameras we're monitoring around the clock, both outside and throughout the house, except in your bedrooms and bathrooms."

He then introduced everyone with their real names. "Emily Baker teaches fifth grade at Mt. Pleasant Elementary and was a scholarship athlete on the Clemson track team." Pointing, he continued. "Chuck Wilson here is a truck driver who hauls containers for the Port of Charleston and lives alone in McClellanville. John Simpson is married and works on the docks at the Port of Charleston."

Jamison paused to study the faces of his guests before adding, "You may use your real names among yourselves, but talking is only permitted downstairs and on the rear porch. No talking to anyone on the upper floors, where you must remain in your own rooms."

When Jamison finished his little briefing, John took a chance and said, "Mr. Jamison, you've gone to a lot of trouble to kidnap the three of us. I just hope you know what you're doing. If this is about getting a ransom for our release, you may be very disappointed by the amount of money my wife could raise."

"Mr. Simpson, please don't trouble yourself about why you're here. You don't have a clue. Just follow my rules and you'll be fine. We don't wish to harm anyone unless you force our hand. You've already been warned by my boss. Now if you'll all excuse me, I have to make some calls."

After Jamison disappeared down the hall and into one of the first-floor bedrooms, Emily lowered her voice and quietly said, "Hi Chuck. Hi John. I can't believe someone went into my apartment and packed some of my clothes. These people are unbelievable. I still can't figure out why the three of us are here. I wonder how many others got that letter and threw it away. I wish I had. I don't think we have any choice except to do what they say, at least until they tell us what they want."

Now on his third sandwich, Chuck said with his mouth half-full, "Nice to finally be able to talk to you guys. I agree with you, Emily, it was really stupid of us to believe that letter. John, thanks for speaking up for all of us. Just don't push them too hard until we find out what's going on. The maniac behind all this is dangerous and has gone to a lot of trouble and expense to get us here. I'm convinced he won't hesitate to hurt us if we cause any problems."

"No worries, Chuck, we'll be fine," said John. "Let's all keep our eyes and ears open. We'll figure out something when we know more, but one thing is certain. They can't keep us here forever. Sooner or later, we'll find out what they're up to."

Chuck changed the subject and asked John, "How long have you worked at the port? Surprised we haven't bumped into each other."

"A little over five years on the dock, Chuck. My wife Mandy works in the accounting office of a marketing company in downtown Charleston. I told her that Pete Lindstrom, my boss at the port, asked me to handle a meeting for him in Columbia yesterday, and I would be back home this afternoon after getting new brakes put on my truck. By now, she's probably already called Pete and knows I lied to her."

Emily said, "I told the principal at my school I had to take my aunt to the hospital for some minor surgery yesterday. After my parents died, she's the only family I have. I'm sure she's already called my principal to ask her if I've been at school this week. I started to call my boyfriend Richard after I read the letter but got cold feet."

Chuck said to her, "Sorry about your parents. Lost mine a few years ago. I told my contact at the port last week that I had to leave town yesterday for a family emergency, but I'd be back home by tomorrow. I live alone, so I doubt anyone is even looking for me."

John said, "We all lied for these clowns, and now we're stuck in the middle of nowhere. Let's not beat ourselves up, what's done is done. I'm just wondering if Jamison really sent that text message he mentioned before we left Daufuskie."

"Not a chance," said Chuck. "These guys are the real liars. They're not gonna risk sending anyone any text about us. Just like we're never seeing any two hundred and fifty grand. It's all bullshit. They wanted to get us here without any problems, and we all fell for their smokescreen. We just don't know what they want yet."

Emily was suddenly exhausted. "It's been a long day. I'm going to head up to my room. Good night, see you both in the morning."

After locking her bedroom door, she sat on the edge of the king-size bed and thought about how worried Richard and Aunt Marie must be by now. She also hoped Jamison would send the text he mentioned to either Aunt Marie or Richard to let them know she was OK. At least so far. She was more afraid than at any time in her life. She still couldn't believe how stupid she'd been to put herself in this nightmare.

She felt grungy from the day's travel and decided to soak in the oversized tub next to the huge glass-enclosed rain shower. By the time she got out and tucked into bed, it was almost dark. As soon as her head hit the pillow, she fell into a restless sleep.

***

Just before midnight, Mark Davis arrived from Hilton Head with the luggage. Jamison met him at the door. "How was the drive, Mark?"

"Fine, no problems. I stayed at the speed limit all the way to make sure I wasn't stopped. Took a little longer than I expected, but better safe than sorry."

"Thanks for taking care of everything on Hilton Head and Daufuskie. I told our friend who owns the cottage that we'd leave everything exactly as we found it."

"I removed all the surveillance equipment myself. After I left, the head of the cleaning team called me when they were finished. They made a final sweep of the cottage and assured me no one will ever know anyone was there. After locking up, the cleaners left the front door key under the mat outside the door as the owner instructed. The three vehicles you borrowed are all sitting in front of the cottage unlocked with the keys under the rear floor mats."

Davis handed Jamison the three license plates from the basket in the cottage. "Wasn't sure what you wanted me to do with these, so I just brought them with me."

"On your way back, stop someplace with no houses around so you won't be seen, and bury them well off the road."

"OK, I plan to shove off early tomorrow morning and head back to Miami."

"You can crash on the third floor in the bedroom on the right at the top of the stairs. Frankie will have breakfast ready by six a.m. for my team, I'll join you then. Our guests aren't allowed downstairs until seven. You need to be gone by then."

Before Mark had a chance to mention something else to Jamison, the security guy watching the monitors came out of one of the first-floor bedrooms for some coffee. He walked over and shook hands with Mark. "Saw you come in on the monitors. How was the drive?"

Mark wasn't about to start a conversation with him. "No problems. Sorry guys, but I'm beat and heading upstairs. See you in the morning."

Chapter 26

May 2018

Two days after Emily identified the second man in the argument she saw at the port on the morning of Jorge's murder, Steve called Dale for an update. His gut told him this was the break that would move his investigation forward.

Steve said, "Just checking in to see if you've made any progress on your end putting a name to the face Emily Baker recognized in one of the photos you sent me. Assume there was no joy when you ran it through facial rec."

"Steve, I was actually going to call you shortly with an update. Sorry it's taken so long, but I think we've finally got something. As you guessed, our photo of the possible shooter Emily identified isn't clear enough for facial rec, but we did just get something interesting from one of our informants inside the cartel."

Dale recounted the story. "My guy was shooting the breeze a few days ago with one of the cartel guys he works with. Cartel guy asks my man if he's ever met the boss. My guy says he doesn't even know who the big boss is and asks cartel guy if he ever met him. Cartel guy says no, but he did meet a man who's very close to the top."

"Did he get a name?"

"Cartel guy says he saw the man a few months ago at some big meeting of the organization's top lieutenants. He told my guy he just got his first name, Teddy. Said he heard through the grapevine that Teddy used to work in New York for the Bruno family."

"Get anything from the DEA in the Big Apple?" asked Steve.

"The only person named Teddy who they thought might be a possible was a guy who used to handle wet work for Happy Bruno, head of the Bruno crime syndicate. Turns out this Teddy was caught on a surveillance camera at La Guardia boarding a flight to Miami about six years ago but hasn't been seen since. His full name is Teddy Francisco, a real hothead thug."

115

"Any more recent photos?"

"New York DEA emailed me a still shot from that airport surveillance video. It's the only photo they have of him. What got my attention was that DEA New York thinks Happy Bruno may have owed the Camino cartel a favor and sent Teddy to Miami to lend his 'heavy lifting' skills to Camino's Miami operation. They can't be sure since he hasn't been spotted anywhere since he showed up on that surveillance video."

"Could be promising, Dale. Any chance this Teddy is the same guy in that more recent photo you sent me that Emily recognized from your Camino surveillance files? I could use some good news right about now."

"Why didn't you say so?" Dale teased. "There's about a six-year age difference between the two photos, but our photo analyst says there's not much doubt Teddy's photo from that old New York airport surveillance video is a match to our more recent surveillance photo I sent you. This guy could definitely be your port murderer."

Steve couldn't contain his excitement. "Hot damn, now you're talkin' my language! All we need to do is find this wise guy and arrest him for the murder of Jorge Rodriguez. Any idea where he is?"

"We've got every informant, snitch, and undercover on the lookout with his photo and a bonus for information on his whereabouts. Just a matter of time before we find him. And if Emily can testify he was the man she saw, and we can put him in your neck of the woods at the time of the murder, we've got a real shot at solving your case and taking Mr. Francisco off the board."

"Anything you need from here?"

"Not right now, Steve. After we find Teddy, make that *when* we find him, we'll need Emily to identify him in person and testify in court about what she saw at the port."

"She's been very cooperative every time I've talked to her. I think she'll help us. I did some digging and checked her out. Parents died in a plane crash a few years ago, and she moved in with her aunt. She was a scholarship athlete on the Clemson track team. Her coach told me she was well-liked by everyone."

"That's good because we're going to need her."

Before ending the call, Steve said, "For now, I don't want to get Emily worried. Let's just keep her identity to ourselves until we see how things play out."

A week later, Steve called Dale again. "We finally got a lead on our search for the port mole."

"I'm all ears, talk to me," said Dale.

"Joe Cartwright, our Wando Welch Terminal Director of Security, you met him at our briefing in Mt. Pleasant last November, told me yesterday he thinks they have a line on a possible suspect. Guy's name is Jerry Reardon, forty-five, been working at the Wando Welch Terminal as a shipping clerk for the past six years."

"What makes you think he's your man?"

"Joe's security team at the Wando terminal has reviewed all the shipping documents for the container that was seized two days before the murder last August. Reardon handled all the paperwork and logged in the container from South America with the hidden stash of drugs we seized. The fax machine log in his office shows a fax sent to an unknown number with a Miami area code. We think he may have sent a warning and faxed the manifest and container number to someone down there."

"Tell me you traced the number."

"We can't prove Reardon sent it, but the phone company's billing records show that the fax was sent to a number registered to…wait for it…Auto Warehouse."

Now it was Dale's turn to get excited and almost shouted into the phone, "That's the link we've been looking for! If your mole is in contact with someone at Auto Warehouse and tipped off the cartel that their container with the drugs was going to be searched, that would explain why Jorge was in the dark and was taken out before anyone found the link. It's no coincidence Teddy Francisco showed up at the port two days later and made Jorge redundant."

Steve agreed, "It all fits. But we still don't have any proof Jerry Reardon is our mole, or if he's working with anyone else at the port."

"What's your next move?"

"We're thinking an old-fashioned sting," answered Steve. "Here's what we need. You get your undercover at Auto Warehouse to send a routine fax to Reardon's attention on the fax machine in his office. The fax will request confirmation of a specific container on a ship scheduled to arrive at the port on a specific date. A real container number on that ship's manifest will be in the fax. If he checks that manifest and faxes back a confirmation to the same Auto Warehouse fax machine, we've got him."

"I'm with you so far, it might actually work."

"To make it happen, we're also going to need you to get a warrant to tap that fax line at Auto Warehouse. If we can trace a faxed confirmation from Reardon's office back to that same fax line, we'll know it had to be Reardon who sent it."

"I like it. Definitely worth a shot if our undercover man can access that same Auto Warehouse fax machine. Hopefully they only have one. Meantime, I'll get with our team and start working on the warrant. I have a judge in mind to see about signing off on it when we have all the paperwork ready. I'll give you a heads up before we meet with him, in case he needs anything from your end."

"I'll let our people know. We're keeping a tight circle on this for the time being, just Chief Hartman and Rob Campbell, the State Ports Authority security head you met at the briefing up here last November, plus Joe Cartwright and our County Prosecutor Jill Carrington."

"Sounds like a plan. Let's touch base again tomorrow."

"Thanks again, Dale. And let me know as soon as something breaks on your Teddy Francisco search."

When Steve hung up, he could feel it. He'd finally turned the corner on the murder investigation he started nine months ago.

Chapter 27

June 2018

In mid-June, five weeks after Emily identified him from Dale's old surveillance photo, Teddy Francisco was spotted talking to Art Winston at a private Miami nightclub that evening. Winston was under 24-hour surveillance by the DEA as soon as he was hired to replace the previous Auto Warehouse owner Paul Franco, who had been found murdered three weeks earlier.

The undercover called Dale and told him he had eyes on a guy who matched Dale's photo of Teddy Francisco. He gave Dale the address and told him Teddy might be at the club for a while at a corner table with three young women in their twenties, definitely not schoolteachers, and two oversized apes on steroids posing as armed bodyguards.

As soon as Dale explained the situation to Miami SWAT, eight elite SWAT team officers were dispatched to the club. To protect the DEA undercover inside the club and avoid compromising the ongoing surveillance operation at Auto Warehouse, the SWAT team deployed outside and waited.

Four members of the team hid between parked cars along both sides of the club entrance. Both ends of the street and sidewalk were blocked by Miami PD patrol officers. Alongside the building and out of sight of the club's covered concave entrance, two more armed SWAT officers took up a position on each side of the entrance.

The final two SWAT team members replaced the parking attendant in Francisco's Lincoln Town Car and were invisible behind the limo's heavily tinted windows.

When Teddy and his men got up from their table to leave, the undercover punched a button on the phone in his pocket to signal the SWAT team leader and followed Teddy and his two men at a discreet distance to the front door. He paused there and quietly said something to the doorman as the three men exited the club.

As soon as the Town Car arrived at the entrance and Teddy started toward it, the SWAT team surrounded all three men and yelled at them with weapons drawn to get their faces on the sidewalk. At the same time, the DEA undercover remained just inside the club's entrance door to keep anyone else from trying to leave.

Before one of the bodyguards could reach the weapon inside his jacket, he was knocked unconscious for his trouble with the butt of a SWAT team shotgun. All three men were cuffed and loaded into the back of the black Miami SWAT van that was waiting down the street. The entire operation was over in less than ten minutes.

Teddy Francisco was taken into custody and charged with the August 2017 murder of Jorge Rodriguez at the Port of Charleston, as well as federal drug charges, including the transportation of illegal drugs across state lines. Teddy lawyered up with the Camino cartel's high-profile Miami attorney, Louis Franklin, well-known in legal circles as the defense attorney for the rich and famous of the criminal underworld.

At his bail hearing, given his suspected ties to organized crime in New York and Miami, plus the high probability of fleeing the country or going underground under the protection of the Camino cartel, bail was denied. To await trial, given his suspected high-ranking status in the Camino pecking order, Teddy was transferred to Coleman, a high-security federal penitentiary in Sumterville, Florida.

The DEA and FBI agreed to delay Teddy's trial on federal drug charges until after his murder trial in Charleston County. Teddy's two goons were detained for carrying a firearm without a license or concealed carry permit, pending further investigation.

Steve had never considered the arrest of Teddy Francisco would put the prosecution's star witness in jeopardy, especially since Emily's identity had been kept a carefully guarded secret from the public and the press.

By the time he realized his mistake, it was too late.

Chapter 28

August 2018

When Marie hadn't heard from Emily by Tuesday evening, nearly two days after her niece went missing, she called Hank Reed back on Wednesday morning.

"Detective Reed, this is Marie Parker. Emily still hasn't called, and I'm frightened. What should I do?"

"Miss Parker, we've checked all the local hospitals, and no one named Emily Baker has been admitted. None of the other teachers at her school have any idea where she might be. Yesterday afternoon, I went to her apartment complex and talked to some of her neighbors, but no one has seen her this week. We've decided to open an official missing persons investigation."

Marie started crying and Reed said, "Miss Parker, I know this is stressful for you, but try to stay positive. I'd like to come and see you this morning if you would be available. We need a recent photo of Emily and as much as you can tell me about her whereabouts for the past few days, including the last conversation you had with her."

"Of course, Detective. I'll be here all day. When can you come?"

"You told me yesterday you live on Daniel Island; I just need your address. I can be there at ten a.m. if that works for you."

"Thank you, I'll be here and will have a photo of Emily for you." After giving Reed her address, Marie went to get her favorite photo of Emily from the mantel in the living room.

Reed knocked on the door of Marie's townhome just after ten. Her eyes were red from crying when she opened the door and invited him into the living room. "Thank you for coming, Detective Reed."

"Hank will be fine, Miss Parker. That's a pretty photo of your niece," he said when he noticed what must have been Emily's picture on the coffee table.

"Everyone says she looks like a runner."

"Well, they're right. I talked to her assistant coach at Clemson, and he told me Emily was a terrific athlete and a star on the track team."

Reed then explained to her what would happen next. "Our first step will be to circulate Emily's photo and profile to all our officers. We'll also send out a missing persons alert to every police department and law enforcement agency in South Carolina, including the Highway Patrol and the FBI, in case she may have been taken against her will."

Marie sobbed, "Oh no, please tell me she wasn't kidnapped. I just can't bear to lose her."

He didn't want to frighten her, but he knew there was a very real possibility that Emily had been abducted. "We have no idea at this point, Miss Parker. We just want to cover all our bases so we can find her as soon as possible."

Reed quickly changed the subject and asked, "Tell me about the last conversation you had with her in as much detail as you can remember."

Marie composed herself and said, "We had an early dinner Sunday afternoon, and she seemed fine. She talked about the new school year starting on Monday. We also talked about how her training was going for the Charleston Marathon this January. It's her first marathon. She mentioned to me that she and her boyfriend, Richard, had a nice dinner on Saturday evening at a new restaurant. They've known each other since high school and reconnected after Emily graduated from Clemson. He's a nice young man, and he and Emily are very close. It wouldn't surprise me if they got engaged soon. You have to find her."

"Have you talked to Richard this week?"

"I called him Monday evening to see if he'd talked to her since the weekend. He told me Emily said she was not feeling well during their dinner on Saturday and went straight home as soon as they finished eating. He called her late Sunday morning to see how she was feeling."

"What did she tell him?"

"She said she was feeling a little better after a good night's sleep, probably just a stomach bug or something she ate, and she was just going to rest in bed on Sunday. In hindsight, Richard told me she seemed a little out of sorts at dinner, like something was bothering her, but he couldn't put his finger on it. He thought she might have just been nervous about the new school year starting on Monday. Now that she's missing, he's certain something else was going on. He's very worried about her."

"What did he think might be going on?"

"Richard told me he had no idea, just that she wasn't herself. I called him again yesterday, and he told me he still hadn't heard from her and had left several voice messages. Maybe you should talk to him."

"Yes, I was planning to. Can you give me his cell number?"

Reed got the number and thanked her for the photo. He told Marie he would let her know as soon as he had any news. After calling Richard from his car and not learning anything new beyond what Marie had already told him, he headed back to his office to get the missing persons alert underway. He also ran a quick background check on Richard, but there were no red flags.

***

After a sleepless Tuesday night and still no call from John, by Wednesday morning Mandy Simpson was gripped with fear in the pit of her stomach. They needed her at work to finish preparing for the annual audit, but she had to do something!

She didn't think the police would do anything, at least not right away. Especially since John had made up a story about why he had to be in Columbia in the first place. Now she doubted he even went to Columbia, but why lie about it and still not be home by now, or at least call? She'd known John since grade school, and this just wasn't like him.

As she was sitting at the kitchen table, drinking her third cup of coffee and trying to decide if she should even go to work with John missing, she remembered something. Down the hall from her office in the old cigar building, she'd noticed the name stenciled on the door to another office.

It read *Jones Investigations*.

She quickly showered, dressed, and headed for her office building on East Bay Street. When she reached the office door at nine a.m. she knocked before opening it. An attractive receptionist, with auburn hair and wearing a bright blue blouse that matched her eyes, looked up from a file and smiled. "Welcome to *Jones Investigations*, I'm Molly Jones. How can I help you?"

Mandy noticed her name on an old-fashioned combo business card holder and name plate sitting in the front of her plain wooden desk. Mandy said, "I'm not sure. Are you a private investigator?"

"No, no," Molly laughed. "That would be my husband, Billy."

"My name is Mandy Simpson, and I was wondering if I could talk to Mr. Jones about my husband, John. He was supposed to be home from a business trip by yesterday afternoon, but I haven't heard from him."

Molly said, "Mrs. Simpson, if you'll take a seat over there, I'll see if Billy can see you. He has to leave for a meeting out of the office this morning. I'll find out if he has a few minutes now to talk to you before he goes."

Molly got up and knocked on one of the two doors behind her desk and went in. She returned with Billy, who was wearing a blue sport coat, tan slacks, and a white shirt with an open collar. Locals call the outfit a Charleston tux.

"Hello Mrs. Simpson, my name is Billy Jones. Please call me Billy. How can I help you?"

***

George Cooper called Marge Mason at home on Wednesday morning to see if she or anyone at the restaurant had heard any news about Chuck. Marge told him one of her customers happened to notice him last Friday morning fishing at his favorite spot on the creek. Nobody else she talked to had seen him since then.

George found the business card Chuck had given him last year with the phone number of Greg Stevens, his transport contact at the port in case of an emergency. George felt that Chuck being missing definitely qualified.

"Mr. Stevens, my name is George Cooper. I'm a friend of Chuck Wilson, one of your container drivers. I haven't heard from him since I tried calling him on Monday, and I've also left several messages on his voice mail. Chuck and I go way back and have been close friends forever. We both grew up in McClellanville. It's not like him not to return my calls. I checked around the neighborhood and nobody's seen or heard from him since last Friday. I'm getting pretty worried about him. His sleeper cab is still at his cabin. Do you happen to know where he is?"

"Hi George, Chuck's last trip for us was Monday before last to Birmingham. After he got back, I forget which day it was, he called me and said he had a family emergency and would be out of town early this week. He said he expected to be back home before the end of the week."

"Thanks, Mr. Stevens, Chuck never mentioned that to me. He always returns my calls, even when he's on the road. We were supposed to have dinner last Saturday, but he never showed. I didn't even know he had any family, other than his friends. He's an only child and his parents died a few years ago. He was married once, but it only lasted a few months before his wife divorced him. Guess I'll just have to wait 'til he gets back."

"Sorry I couldn't be more helpful, George. Give me your number. If I hear from him, I'll give you a call. Chuck told me he'd be picking up his scheduled container shipment next Monday, so I'm sure he's planning to get back home by this weekend latest."

George thanked Stevens again and hung up. He was still convinced Chuck was in trouble.

Chapter 29

August 2018

On Wednesday morning, two days after the nightmare began with her drive to Hilton Head, Emily was awake by five a.m. During the school year, she would now be putting on her running clothes, heading downstairs for a banana topped with peanut butter, and be out the door before five-thirty. Now she was being held captive and forced to stay in her bedroom until seven.

After brushing her teeth and taking a quick shower, she pulled on the only clothes she'd been wearing since yesterday morning and tied her damp hair into a ponytail. When she opened the remote-controlled blackout blinds, the view was spectacular as the brightening sky signaled the imminent appearance of the sun at the far edge of a calm ocean. She stood at the window until the bright orange ball broke the plane of the horizon.

Before she was allowed to leave her room at seven, she thought back to everything that happened since she got the mysterious letter. She tried to think of a rational explanation for why she was targeted, but still couldn't come up with anything that made sense. The only thing she could think of that was out of the ordinary was talking to that Mt. Pleasant detective back in May.

She tried to recall her conversations with him. What was his name? Harris, that was it. Detective Harris. She remembered first talking to him last December, right after she was stopped at the port entrance by a security guard on one of her early morning runs. Harris had asked her if she'd seen anything unusual on one of her morning runs near the port entrance last August.

She'd told him what she'd seen and didn't hear from him again until May when she had two meetings with him in her apartment, a couple weeks apart.

She replayed those two meetings in her mind. Harris had come to her apartment and showed her photos both times. He'd asked her if any of the photos looked like one of the men she'd seen last August having an argument near the port entrance. She'd identified one of the men from the first group of

126

photos he showed her at their first meeting, and the other man from a photo she recognized in their second meeting.

He never told her what it was about and never called her back. She thought about it some more but couldn't see how any of that could have anything to do with being lured to Daufuskie Island with two strangers and ending up here.

She looked at the clock on the nightstand. Six-thirty a.m. She still had to wait another thirty minutes before she could leave the room for breakfast. To kill some time, she replayed the conversation she had with Chuck and John last evening. Out of the blue, a thought popped into her head. She recalled Jamison mentioning Chuck drives containers from the port and John works there. Just a coincidence? Or could the port and that incident she saw somehow be the connection they've been missing?

She needed to find out if either of them had ever talked to Detective Harris.

At one end of the dining room table, when all three of them were alone drinking coffee after finishing their breakfast of bacon and eggs, compliments of Frankie, Emily quietly said, "Keep your voices low. I need to ask you both about something important, and I don't want them to hear us. Did either of you ever meet or talk to a Mt. Pleasant Detective Harris last year?"

They both thought about it, and John answered first in almost a whisper. "I can't remember his name, might have been Harris, but a Mt. Pleasant detective did ask me if I'd seen anything unusual on an early morning last August as I was driving into the port for my six a.m. shift. I forget what date in August he asked me about, but I told him I didn't see anything out of the ordinary that day."

"When did he call you?" asked Emily.

"I think it was sometime last November."

"How about you, Chuck?"

"Now that John mentions it, I also remember talking to a detective last November. Could've been a Detective Harris, I'm not sure. Anyway, he asked me the same question he asked John. Did I see anything unusual around the entrance as I leaving the port with a container one morning last August? The day he asked me about was a Monday, but I don't remember the date. I told him I didn't notice anything unusual."

It was Emily's turn. "The reason I asked if you guys talked to a Detective Harris is because I talked to him last December and met with him a couple times in May."

"You're kidding," said John. "We're both in and out of the port all the time, but you're a schoolteacher. What could you possibly have to do with the port?"

"My apartment is on Whipple Road and sometimes I run to the port entrance and back on my morning runs. It's about a five-mile loop."

"What did Harris want?" whispered Chuck.

"He told me he needed some help with an investigation and asked me the exact same question he asked both of you last November. Did I see anything unusual at the port entrance last August during one of my early morning runs?"

"Did you see anything the morning he asked you about?"

"Actually, I did," she said, her voice now barely audible. "When I first talked to Harris last December, after I'd given my cell number to a security guard who stopped me at the port entrance on one of my runs, I told him I saw two men arguing several yards from the main entrance gates, down along the security fence. I had just rounded in front of the main entrance gates when I saw them that morning."

"Did he ask you if you could identify the two men you saw?" asked John.

"On his first visit to my apartment in early May, he showed me six photos and asked if I recognized either of the men I saw. I pointed to a photo of one of them who was there. Harris came back a couple weeks later and showed me six more photos. One of them matched the face of the other man I saw that morning."

Chuck asked, "Did he tell you what he was working on or why he wanted to know who you saw?"

"No, he just thanked me and said he was tying up some loose ends, nothing for me to worry about. He made it all seem like it was no big deal. I haven't talked to him since May and forgot all about it."

John said, "Emily, this is way too much of a coincidence. Whatever Harris was working on, that incident at the port last August has to be the link that connects the three of us and why we were targeted. I think someone may be worried one of us, or all three of us, saw something we shouldn't have seen that morning. Those guys you identified are the key. Did Harris happen to tell you tell who they were?"

"He didn't share anything with me. Now I wish I'd pressed him harder to at least tell me something about what he was working on."

John had another thought and asked, "Do either of you remember seeing or reading anything about a dead body found outside the port last summer? I think I saw something in the paper about it last August, but there wasn't much information in the article."

"I never saw anything about any dead body at the port last year," said Emily.

"Me neither," said Chuck. "I'm on the road so much, I don't get the local paper and don't catch the news on TV very often. But nobody at the port ever said anything to me about it."

Emily looked around to make sure they were still alone. "If what I saw did have something to do with a suspicious death, and these people holding us had anything to do with it, we could all be in trouble. At some point, Jamison or his mystery boss might ask each of us the same question Harris asked us."

John stared at Emily and warned, "If they do, don't ever tell them what you told Harris, no matter what. Got it?" Emily nodded in agreement.

When they later trudged upstairs to their bedrooms on the second floor before their ten p.m. curfew at the end of another boring day, they still hadn't been asked any questions about the incident. So far.

***

Early that same morning, just after six a.m., Jamison met with his security team and checked the monitors set up in one of the two downstairs bedrooms to make sure all the surveillance cameras were working. Satisfied everything was in order, he sent a short text to his boss and went into the other downstairs bedroom where he had set up his office.

Just as he sat down, his phone vibrated with another text from an unknown number.

Are you alone?

Jamison typed a short reply. *Yes. Who is this?*

Text me the number of a safe burner and good time to talk in private. I'll call you.

Jamison texted back the number of one of his unused burner phones and the time he could take the call, then deleted the incoming texts and his replies from his regular cell phone.

At ten a.m., he checked on his guests. Emily and John were in the library reading. Chuck was rocking on the back verandah facing a great ocean view he didn't even see with his eyes closed for a morning nap before lunch.

Thirty minutes later, Jamison left in one of the SUVs and switched on his burner phone. He drove south on Highway 12 to a quaint restaurant in the small town of Duck. He went inside, sat in a corner booth, and ordered coffee. His watch read ten forty-five a.m.

Jamison was ready and waiting for his 11 a.m. callback.

Chapter 30

August 2018

At eight forty-five a.m. that same morning, Steve headed downtown to catch up with Billy Jones, his army basic training buddy, for a late breakfast to see how things were going with *Jones Investigations*. He also wanted to run a question by Billy about his port investigation. Steve, Billy, and their wives had become good friends since Billy retired from the army and moved to Charleston almost two years ago.

Billy was drinking coffee and waved when Steve walked in. An attractive waitress wearing a red and white checkerboard apron that matched the artwork on the Checkers Restaurant sign above the front door, followed Steve with a pot of coffee.

The two friends shook hands and Billy said, "Good to see you, Steve. How are Janet and the girls?"

Steve had met Janet in Hawaii during a five-day R&R leave after his first Iraq deployment. He was sharing a hotel room with an army buddy and noticed a pretty girl sitting alone at the hotel pool when he went for a dip one afternoon. When he sat down next to her, she looked up from her book and smiled. They started chatting and quickly discovered they were both from Charleston. Janet worked at a bank in Charleston and was in Hawaii for a banking conference. They made a date for dinner that evening and saw each other every day for the rest of his leave.

"All good, Billy. Jan and I celebrated our eighteenth anniversary last month. We were married shortly after I left the army. Best decision of my life. Glen was going to be my best man." The mention of his brother's name suddenly interrupted Steve's train of thought like it always did, and he looked away for a moment.

Billy guessed what his friend was feeling and said, "Sorry I never got a chance to meet him, but from the stories you've told me, Glen was a very special guy."

Steve looked back at his friend and refocused. "Thanks Billy, he was. Sorry, where was I? The girls are both doing great. Jeanie is a senior this year, and we're starting to check out colleges. They both get their smarts from their mother. Mags is a freshman and going to try out for the high school soccer team this year. She's got some skills. They've both grown up way too fast, and I have no idea where the time has gone. Your boys still doing well at Clemson?"

"Yes, and they love it. And Molly still enjoys helping me out in the office. Speaking of which, I had an interesting missing person's case walk through the door this morning just before I got here. Woman said her husband was supposed to be back yesterday from a short business trip to Columbia on Monday to attend a meeting as a favor for his boss at the port. He was due back home yesterday afternoon, but he's still not there and hasn't returned her phone calls."

"You talked to his boss?"

"Not yet, but she called him yesterday afternoon. Here's where it gets a little weird. His boss at the port told her that last week her husband asked him for Monday and Tuesday off this week. He told his boss he had to take care of some personal insurance business in Columbia on Monday, and he had an appointment yesterday to get some work done on his car."

"Sounds to me like there might be another woman in the picture."

"She insists there's no one else. They've known each other since grade school and been happily married for over five years. Anyway, I told her I'd look into it. What about you? What's Mt. Pleasant's ace detective been up to?"

"One of the cases I'm working on is a murder investigation that started last August, if you can believe it. This one's been a real rollercoaster ride. I'll tell you all about it if I ever figure it out."

"Making any progress?"

"We think we've got the bad guy in custody. Trial is scheduled next month. So far, this case has had more twists and turns than an Agatha Christie mystery. Since I became a homicide detective, this is without a doubt the most complicated murder investigation I've ever handled. And we won't cross the finish line until the man we arrested is convicted."

"Sounds interesting. Anything I can help with?"

"There actually is something I wanted to run by you. Without getting into too many details, and I shouldn't even be sharing this with you, the surveillance tapes from an incident at the port that have a direct bearing on the case were stolen from the port security office. Fortunately, all the port video footage is automatically backed up, and I've reviewed copies of the footage."

"So, what's the problem?"

"What I don't understand is why someone who works at the port with access to the security office would steal tapes they must know are backed up on the port's off-site digital storage system."

"Only one reason, Steve. Whoever stole those tapes wanted to see what was on them before the police did. I'm assuming the footage shows your suspect, and possibly a witness. Seeing the footage first would give them some time to cover their tracks."

"That makes sense. The Miami DEA agent I'm working with had the same thought about the witness angle. I just wanted to make sure we weren't missing something."

"Did you find out who stole the tapes?"

All Steve was comfortable answering was, "Working on it."

Billy said, "Well, I've got to get back to the office. I've got a client lunch meeting, and I want to follow-up on my missing husband case this afternoon. I need to call the man's boss at the port to see what else I can learn."

"Good luck with the new case. I know some security people at the port if that would help. Just let me know. Sounds to me like *Jones Investigations* is doing well. I know you told me you were a little nervous about taking the leap to start your own company, but I had a hunch you'd make a great private investigator."

"Thanks, Steve, so far, so good. Let's get together for dinner with the wives, sooner than later."

Steve picked up the check before Billy could get to it and headed back to police headquarters.

When he got there, he stuck his head into Hartman's office. "Got a sec, Chief?"

"Sure, what's up?"

"Just wanted to let you know I talked to Dale Hawkins late yesterday, and he still doesn't have the warrant we need to tap the fax line at Auto Warehouse.

Says he needs to dig up some more evidence for the judge. His undercover at the warehouse is working on it, but so far nothing. Joe Cartwright has twenty-four-hour surveillance on Reardon, but the guy's been acting like a choir boy ever since we tracked the fax log in his office and put eyes on him."

"You think he's on to us?" Hartman asked.

"I don't see how. Joe and his guys are being super careful not to spook him. Keep you posted when something breaks. Jill Carrington would love to have another trial witness to tie Teddy Francisco to the Camino organization and the port."

"Thanks Steve, appreciate the update. If Reardon's your guy, he'll make a mistake. Just a matter of time."

As he was leaving the Chief's office, Steve bumped into Hank Reed, who was rushing down the hall like his pants were on fire. "Whatcha workin' on, Hank? Did I miss the fire alarm?"

Hank stopped and said quickly, "Just got back from an interview on Daniel Island, and I need to get a statewide missing persons alert underway ASAP."

"I won't keep you. Who is it?"

Before Hank started hustling to his office again, he said, "Young local schoolteacher named Emily Baker."

Chapter 31

August 2018

Steve stopped in his tracks to process what he'd just heard before hurrying down the hall to catch up with Hank. His port murder investigation and upcoming murder trial was just turned on its head. His first thought was that Emily had been kidnapped. And if he was right, he had a good idea who was behind it and why.

He also realized too late that he should've kept closer tabs on Emily, especially with the Francisco trial about to start. He hadn't even told Emily yet that she needed to be a witness at the trial so she wouldn't worry about it. He was now afraid it was too late, and the cartel had taken her.

Something Billy mentioned to him earlier that morning over coffee was still stuck in Steve's head. Billy and Dale both suggested whoever saw the stolen the port surveillance videos wanted to see if there were any witnesses on the tapes. Emily was missing, and he had no doubt Billy and Dale were right. The cartel needed to keep any potential witnesses from testifying by hiding them away, maybe permanently.

He made a mental note to review the security tapes again. He also needed to follow-up with the container driver and dock worker who were both in their vehicles at the port entrance last August at the same time Emily saw the two men arguing along the security fence. When he interviewed them last November, neither man recalled seeing anything unusual that morning. He wondered if either of them might have noticed Emily.

Steve followed Hank into his office and started talking to his back before Hank had a chance to sit down. "Hank, Emily Baker is a key witness in the upcoming trial of my port murder suspect. If she's missing, it's almost certain her disappearance is related to my case. Do you have a photo of her?"

Hank handed Steve the photo of Emily that Marie gave him. "Slow down, Steve, you've lost me. What's going on?"

Steve looked at the photo and blurted, "That's her. Back in May, Emily Baker identified both the victim and the shooter in the port murder I've been investigating since last August. Later that same month, the Miami DEA arrested a man named Teddy Francisco for the murder based on Emily's eyewitness ID from surveillance photos I showed her. The man who was arrested has been linked to the Camino drug cartel, and his trial is scheduled to start soon here in Charleston."

Hank interrupted, "Emily Baker is a schoolteacher. How in the hell did she get mixed up in your port murder investigation?"

Steve shut the door to Hank's office. "Hank, there's a lot of moving parts to this case, most of which have been kept confidential to make sure the media doesn't get wind of what's going on. I've been working with a Miami DEA agent since my investigation started, and we're now trying to gather as much evidence against Francisco as we can. Emily Baker is our only witness who can put Francisco and Jorge Rodriguez, the murder victim, together only minutes before the murder."

Hank couldn't hide his surprise. "What? Are you saying Emily Baker is involved in all this? Who besides you are in the loop?"

Steve didn't want to start explaining any more details until he talked to the Chief. He quietly said, "Hank, let's do this. Right now, your missing persons alert takes priority. If I'm right, Emily Baker may be in serious danger. You need to get the alert going, and I need to update the Chief. I'll see how soon the three of us can meet. How much time do you need?"

"Give me about thirty minutes or so to get the alert going. I'll hang here until I hear from you."

"Deal, thanks Hank. Just keep what I just told you to yourself until we meet with the Chief."

Steve left Hank's office and made a beeline to see the Chief. He barged into his office and shut the door behind him. "Chief, sorry to interrupt. I just found out from Hank that Emily Baker has gone missing. I think the cartel has grabbed her."

"Take a seat and tell me what's happening."

"Hank is getting a statewide alert out on Emily right now. He'll be ready to meet with both of us in thirty minutes to brief us on the details. I just found out. All I know is she's missing. I told Hank she's a key witness in our port investigation but didn't discuss any details. I thought we should do that together."

Hartman picked up his phone and buzzed his secretary. "Judy, something's come up. I need you to reschedule my meeting with Hal. And hold all my calls. Thank you."

As soon as he hung up, Steve said, "Chief, we need to put a full-court press on this. Before we meet with Hank, I'd like to let Dale, Rob and Joe know what's going on before any news gets out. The media are going to be all over this. Right now, only our inner circle knows how Emily is linked to our port murder investigation, and we need to keep it that way. If the cartel gets wind that Emily is the star witness in Teddy Francisco's trial, assuming they don't already know, we may never find her."

"You're right, if that gets out, she'll be in even more danger. And if they have her, time is not on our side. Make those calls and bring Hank back here with you when he's ready. We need to find out when she went missing, who Hank has talked to, and everything else he knows about what's going on."

Steve's first call was to Dale. He left an urgent message, and Dale called back five minutes later.

"Just got your message, Steve. Sounds important, what's up?"

"We've had a major development here. Emily Baker has gone missing."

"Missing? As in disappeared? When did this happen?"

"I don't have all the details yet. Hank Reed, one of our detectives, found out yesterday and is putting out a statewide missing person's alert to all South Carolina law enforcement agencies. Chief Hartman and I will be meeting with Hank shortly to get updated. I'll get back to you when I know more, just wanted to give you a heads up right away."

"Sorry to hear that, keep me in the loop. By the way, nothing new on our end. We'll pitch the judge again on the urgency of identifying your suspected port mole, especially if the mole is implicated in the disappearance of a key witness in Teddy's murder trial."

"Good idea. The main thing is to make sure it doesn't leak out, especially down there. And let's keep Emily's name out of it for now. If the cartel learns she's an eyewitness in Teddy's trial, she'll be toast, if she isn't already."

"You really think the cartel has her?"

"It's a damned strong possibility. She's on those surveillance tapes that were stolen. Somebody in the cartel may have decided it was time to grab her and find out if she saw anything that morning. I'll know more when we talk to Hank."

Steve made similar calls to Joe Cartwright at the port and Rob Campbell in his State Ports Authority office in Columbia. He promised both men he would get back to them as soon as he had more information. He also stressed the absolute need to keep a tight lid on Emily's involvement in his murder investigation. "The cartel can't find out about Emily's positive ID of Francisco. Her life may depend on it."

After finishing the calls, Steve headed for Hank's office. He was on the phone, and Steve waited in the doorway. When he hung up, Hank handed Steve a copy of the missing persons sheet with Emily's photo and profile. Hank said, "That was the Charleston County Sheriff's office calling to confirm they got the alert on Emily and will make sure it gets distributed to their people immediately."

"Very good. You ready to meet with the Chief?"

"Let's do it."

In Hartman's office, Hank updated them on everything that happened since Marie Parker came in yesterday to report her niece missing. "What convinced me to open a missing persons investigation was talking to Miss Parker and also Mary McCarthy, her school principal. They both insisted it was completely out of character for Emily to just go off the grid without at least telling someone where she was. And nobody's heard from her since Sunday when her aunt last talked to her."

Steve said, "Hank, you mentioned her boyfriend Richard Barnett told you she seemed a little off when they had dinner together last Saturday. Any chance he's involved?"

"Very unlikely. He's a successful engineer with a major downtown Charleston construction firm, and he's known Emily since they were both on the Mt. Pleasant High School track team. Marie Parker told me she expects them to get engaged soon. When I met with him, he came across as a straight arrow. I'll run a deeper background check on him, but I don't think Barnett has anything to do with it."

"Is her car at her apartment?"

"I had a patrol officer check the parking lots in her entire apartment complex, and also the lot at her school. Her car's not at either place. I've included a BOLO on the car and the plate number with the missing person's alert."

Hartman said, "We need to go through her apartment with a fine-tooth comb. There must be something that will give us a clue to work with. I'd rather not get the apartment manager involved to let us in if we don't have do. Also be a good idea to see her school principal and find out exactly what Emily was doing there last Thursday, and anything she said. Hank, can you get a spare key to her apartment from Miss Parker?"

"Already got one and was planning to look around Emily's apartment this afternoon. I'll also set an appointment to meet with Mary McCarthy as soon as possible at Emily's school."

Steve said, "Mind if I join you at Emily's apartment? Can't hurt to have two sets of eyes to look around."

"No problem, that's probably a good place to start until we get something from the alert."

Steve filled Hank in on the highlights of his ongoing investigation of the port murder and how Emily got involved. He left out anything about the search for a mole inside the port. The fewer people who knew about that, the better. If it got out, the entire sting operation could be blown.

When he finished briefing Hank, Steve told him, "Give me fifteen minutes. I need a quick chat alone with the Chief."

"No problem, swing by my office when you're ready to go."

After Hank left, Steve said, "Chief, I didn't think Hank needed to know about the port mole investigation. I've talked to Dale and filled in Joe and Rob on Emily's disappearance. Everything that's happened, starting with the port murder last August to Emily going missing, is somehow tied to the Camino cartel. I can feel it."

"It's definitely starting to look like a real possibility."

"It's my own damn fault Emily is missing. I can't believe I didn't see it. I needed to keep an eye on her after she identified the port shooter back in May, but I didn't. I should've realized she'd eventually be on the cartel's radar after those tapes were stolen. I'm just not sure why they waited so long to take her."

"Don't beat yourself up, Steve. We don't know for sure the cartel even took her. And none of us figured she was in any danger. Let's just concentrate on finding her. Use whatever resources you need. This entire department is at your disposal."

Steve nodded and said, "I know somebody who might give us a hand."

Chapter 32

August 2018

On their way to Emily's apartment, Hank filled Steve in on his interviews with Marie Parker, Richard Barnett, and Mary McCarthy. "After talking to Richard, he told me he was pretty certain something was bothering Emily. He said they'd been planning to make a night of it after their dinner on Saturday, but Emily told him she wasn't feeling well and went right home. Given she's now missing, it's pretty clear something was going on that she couldn't talk about, even with Richard."

Steve asked, "What's your take on Marie Parker's relationship with Emily?"

"All through high school and whenever she was home from Clemson, Emily lived with her. Miss Parker told me they've been extremely close since her parents' plane crash. She insisted Emily would never lie to her unless she was in serious trouble. Richard also confirmed that Emily and her aunt were very close."

"What about her meeting last Thursday with the school principal? Did McCarthy sense Emily was upset or act like anything was wrong?"

"She told me everything seemed normal. Emily made an appointment last Wednesday to see her on Thursday to review some ideas she had for her new fifth grade class. What was interesting was they never really talked about that. Emily told her she just needed to make some copies of her old lesson plans. McCarthy thought the real reason Emily went to see her was to ask for a substitute teacher for the first two days of school this week so she could take her aunt to the hospital on Monday for some minor surgery, which we now know was not true."

"Hank, it sounds to me like something or someone spooked her, and she had no choice but to make up a lie about what was really going on."

When they arrived at her apartment, Steve said, "I'll look around upstairs, you take this floor. I want to check her closet and dresser to see if it looks like any clothes might be missing, or any basic toiletries are not in her bathroom. Maybe she had to leave town for a couple days for something personal and didn't want anyone to know."

Hank was skeptical. "Maybe, but it's now Wednesday afternoon, and she hasn't called anyone yet. We've been monitoring her phone number since yesterday. According to her phone records, her last call was to her aunt on Sunday. As of this morning, we can't even get a signal to locate her cell. If the cartel did grab her, it's likely they removed the SIM card and tossed the phone."

Steve checked her closet, but it was impossible to know if any clothes were removed. Same with her dresser. A box in the back of the closet just had some old school materials and lesson plans in it. Everything looked normal in her bedroom. However, her toothbrush, toothpaste, and a few other basic toiletries were nowhere to be found in the bathroom.

He went down to the first floor to see if Hank had turned up anything. "Nothing looks out of place down here. Nothing out of the ordinary, dishwasher is empty, fridge has usual stuff you'd expect, couple of frozen dinners in the freezer, no red flags."

"You see any old mail lying around from last week, junk flyers, anything?"

"Trash can is empty, maybe she emptied it on Sunday. Probably should check her mailbox anyway," said Hank.

"Can't hurt, these apartments usually have mailboxes for each unit in the office lobby or sometimes outside each building. We may need a search warrant to access her box. I'll check with the office to see if they'd be willing to open it for us."

Steve headed for the apartment rental office and was met by a middle-aged woman dressed in casual dark slacks and a white blouse. Office Manager Janice Peterson smiled and said, "Welcome to Anchor Apartments. Are you looking for a rental unit?"

He showed her his creds and explained the situation. "Miss Peterson, one of your tenants, Emily Baker, who lives in apartment number seven in Building C, has gone missing. A statewide missing person's alert went out this morning. She hasn't been seen since Saturday evening. I'm here with another Mt. Pleasant detective to look around her apartment. Her aunt gave us a spare key."

"Oh my goodness, that's terrible. Is there anything I can do to help?"

"Actually, there is. We'd like to check her mailbox. We can get a warrant, but time is of the essence. If you could open her mailbox for us, we just want to look through any mail she may not have picked up. We're happy to do that in your presence, and you can return any mail back into the box and lock it."

She hesitated, "I really shouldn't leave the office, and I don't think I have the authority to let you look through someone's mail."

"Miss Peterson, I understand your reluctance, but we need to find this young woman, and this could be helpful. Is there any chance you can make an exception given the circumstances? I can promise you won't get into any trouble. We don't want to take any of her mail, just look through it. Five minutes at the most and we'll be out of your hair."

"Well, if you promise just to look through it and put it back, I guess I can make an exception. I see Emily once in a while when I come in early to catch up on paperwork. She's a runner, you know, and she's a model tenant."

"Yes ma'am, we just need to find her. Thank you."

As they were walking to the outdoor mailboxes for Building C, Steve asked, "When was the last time you saw Emily?"

Peterson thought for a moment. "I came in early a couple Saturdays ago and passed her running along Whipple Road. It was very early in the morning, around six a.m."

"Did anything strike you as unusual or out of the ordinary that morning?"

"No, nothing. Her ponytail was swaying back and forth, and she was running fast, like she always does."

When they got to the mailboxes, Peterson opened the box with her master key. There were three pieces of mail. Before Steve touched the mail, he gloved up and took it out of the box. The first two envelopes were routine bills. The third piece was a standard #10 business envelope hand-addressed to Emily Baker.

On the upper left corner was printed the name and address of the Mt. Pleasant Elementary School. It was postmarked last Thursday from Mt. Pleasant. The other two pieces of mail were postmarked on Monday, the day Emily apparently went missing.

Steve put the envelope in an evidence bag from his pocket and said, "Miss Peterson, I'm afraid I'm going to need to see what's inside this one. It's from Emily's school and might be important. I'd like to take it with me to dust the envelope and its contents for prints. If it's nothing, I'll return it to you, and you can put it back in her mailbox."

"Detective, I'm really not comfortable with that. Opening someone's mail without their permission is a crime, and I'd prefer if you had a search warrant before you open it."

"OK, Miss Peterson, I understand your concern. Let's go back to your office. I need to make a couple of phone calls."

On the way to Peterson's office, Steve called Hank and told him to meet him at the rental office. He then called Mary McCarthy at the school.

"Mrs. McCarthy, this is Mt. Pleasant Detective Steve Harris. I'm working with Detective Reed, who you spoke to yesterday. Emily Baker is still missing, and we've issued a statewide alert. I'm at Emily's apartment building and the manager has allowed us to check the mail in Emily's box. There was one of your school envelopes hand-addressed to her. It was probably mailed last Thursday or Friday. She may not have checked her mail over the weekend."

"How can I help you, Detective Harris?" asked McCarthy.

"Were there any routine mailings last week from the school to your teachers or staff?"

"No, all our teacher and staff correspondence were already mailed before last week since school started this Monday."

"What exactly did you and Emily discuss last Thursday?"

"As I told Detective Reed, when Emily got here, she stopped in my office to tell me she had to copy some lesson plans before we met. She had called on Wednesday and asked if she could see me on Thursday, to discuss some ideas she had for the new school year. She went back to her office and returned to meet with me about thirty minutes later."

"Besides asking you for a substitute for Monday and Tuesday, did she talk about anything else?"

"Not really, she just said she had to make copies of some lesson plans that she had in her shoulder bag. After our meeting, she told me she had to mail something on her way home and asked if there was anything she could mail for me. I did have a letter I was going to mail myself and gave it to her. She said she'd mail it for me and left."

"Mrs. McCarthy, you've been very helpful. We'll keep you posted as soon as we know anything."

Before he finished the call with McCarthy, Hank walked into the rental office. Steve waved him over and held up the evidence bag. When he hung up with McCarthy, he said, "Miss Peterson is the rental manager for the apartments and was kind enough to allow us to look into Emily's mailbox. This envelope from her school is addressed by hand to her. We're going to need to dust both the envelope and whatever's inside it for prints."

"What's in the envelope?" asked Hank.

"We haven't opened it yet. Miss Peterson wants us to get a warrant before we do that. Call the Chief and get a warrant going. If a judge is available, see how fast he can get it for us."

Steve then asked Peterson, "Do you have a safe on the premises where you can secure the envelope until we get the warrant?"

"We have one in a locked cabinet in our conference room to hold rental checks and applications that are in process. I can put your evidence bag in there."

"Miss Peterson. I may call you after hours, depending on when we can get the warrant. Would that work for you?"

Peterson gave Steve her cell number and told him she lived close by and to call her when he had the warrant. She apologized for causing any trouble. Steve thanked her and told her not to worry about it.

On their way back to police headquarters, Steve said to Hank, "I think whatever's in that envelope is something important. I have a hunch Emily may have mailed it to herself after she left her meeting with Mary McCarthy last Thursday."

"That's some hunch, Steve. If you're right, what's in that envelope could tell us a lot. We'll need prints from Emily's apartment in case we need to match them against whatever's in the envelope. We can also compare the handwriting on the envelope with Emily's. Maybe there's something with her handwriting in her apartment, or we could get something she's written from the school."

"Hank, see what you can learn and have one of our forensic guys get some prints from the apartment as soon as possible. If the contents of that envelope are important, we need to make sure she sent it."

Chapter 33

August 2018

At one p.m. on Wednesday, Frankie had sandwiches, fresh fruit, chips, and a plate of cookies just out of the oven on the dining room table for lunch. The chef was a short, round man in his forties with a double chin, compliments of a sweet tooth and a fetish for his own homemade desserts. Emily wasn't hungry and settled for some of the fruit and a glass of lemonade. John went for one of the sandwiches. Chuck already had two on his plate with two of the cookies.

Making small talk, Emily said, "Wonder where Mr. Jamison went. He left the house around ten this morning and hasn't gotten back yet."

"No clue," said John. "I'm more concerned about his redneck security goons and their guns. I saw one guy on the front porch and one behind the house this morning. The other one must be watching the monitors in one of the bedrooms. I'm sure someone is keeping tabs on every move we make. We should probably keep our voices down at all times in case they're listening."

Chuck was getting antsy and asked, "How long do you think they can keep us here? We don't even know why we're here. What are they waiting for?"

Before Emily and John had a chance to reply, Jamison came through the front door and headed straight for one of the downstairs bedrooms without even looking at them.

Emily was watching him closely before he disappeared down the hall. After she heard a door close, she said, "That was strange. He looked like he just saw a ghost."

***

Earlier that morning, Jamison was sitting alone inside the Duck Diner, sipping coffee in a back booth with a perfect view of the front door. The breakfast crowd was long gone, and there were only a handful of customers sitting around a couple of four-tops past the booths. At exactly eleven a.m., his burner phone rang.

"Hello, who's this and what do you want?"

The artificially muffled voice on the other end asked, "Jamison, are you alone?"

"Yes, who are you?"

"I'm a friend with some news about your mother and father. I know you're going to be skeptical, but your parents are both alive and your father wants to talk to you."

"Bullshit! Put him on the phone," Jamison demanded.

"I'm not with him, but I am in contact. Before he talks to you, he needs to be sure you can be trusted."

"What do you mean 'trusted'? My father disappeared two years ago, and no one, including me, has heard from him or my mother since their boat disappeared on a sailing trip. I'm asking you one more time before I hang up, who are you and what do you want?"

"I know for a fact your boss was responsible for sinking their boat and attempting to murder them. He thinks he succeeded, but your parents were able to barely escape in a small emergency raft just before the boat went down several miles east of the Keys."

Jamison was getting angrier. "How do you know all this? If my parents were alive, they would've called me a long time ago. Give me one reason I should believe you."

"Your father knew you wouldn't believe me, so he told me to tell you he's sorry he missed your high school graduation. He was stranded in New York because his flight to Miami was canceled, and he couldn't get home until the next day."

Jamison went silent. Was it really possible they were alive? He remembered how disappointed he was when his father missed the graduation and his mother had to explain why he couldn't be there.

The voice said, "Are you still with me, Jamison?"

"Y-Yes, I'm still here," he stuttered, still trying to process what he'd just heard.

The voice continued, "They were both up top on their way to the Bahamas under full sail when the engine exploded, and they were both thrown into the water. Before the boat sank, the small raft on the bow came loose, and they

146

managed to reach it. The engine wasn't even running, and your father knew there was no reason it should've exploded unless it was sabotaged. He and your mother have been hiding in the Caribbean since they found out who was behind it."

"How could my father possibly know who it was if the evidence sank with the boat."

"Because he told me."

"He told YOU? Prove it. Tell me who you are."

"I also work for your boss and know everything that's going on. I've been involved from the start when you had those letters delivered to the three innocent people you're now holding on the Outer Banks. I know who they are, how they got there, and I know why."

"Are you threatening me? How could you possibly know all that?"

"I'm trying to help us both, but you need to trust me. Your parents didn't deserve what happened to them, and neither do your guests. I want to bring down the man responsible, but I can't do that without you."

Jamison gritted his teeth and fought to control his voice, "Why are you telling me all this? If my father is alive, I need to talk to him. Tell me how to reach him."

"Jamison, I need to go. I can't stay on this phone, but I'll call you again at the same number and same time this Friday. Answer your burner on the third ring. If you don't answer, I'll call you again on Saturday at the same time. And don't mention this call to anyone for both our sakes."

"Tell me who you are," demanded Jamison one final time.

The electronically altered voice answered, "Mark Davis."

Chapter 34

August 2018

Shortly after six p.m. on Wednesday evening, the Chief came to Steve's office and handed him the signed warrant. Hartman said, "Caught Judge Collins in his office just before he left for the day. I showed him our warrant request for the envelope and its contents and explained that the scope of the warrant is limited to allowing us to inspect it after it was retrieved from a private mailbox by the office manager of a local apartment complex."

"Did he agree to the warrant?"

"When I told him the mailbox was used by Emily Baker, the local schoolteacher who's missing, and the envelope may contain important information related to her disappearance, he quickly signed it."

"This is important, Chief, I can feel it. I'll call Janice Peterson right now and see how soon she can meet me at her office to open the envelope. It's in an evidence bag locked in her office safe. She told me she'd meet me there as soon as we got the warrant. Peterson said she could be at the rental office in thirty minutes."

Steve got there shortly after Peterson arrived and showed her the warrant. She'd already retrieved the sealed evidence bag from the safe and handed it to him.

With gloved hands, Steve carefully slit open the envelope without damaging the flap so forensics could retrieve any DNA from whoever may have licked the seal. There were three pages in the envelope, including a short hand-written signed note and a two-page typed letter.

He read the note first. It was dated Thursday, August 30, 2018.

I received the original of this letter last weekend in my mailbox. There was no return address or postmark. If something happens to me, it will explain where I've gone and why. I have no idea who delivered this letter, but I have decided I need to find out on my own. Please tell my Aunt Marie and boyfriend Richard Barnett that I love them both very much. Emily Baker.

Steve put the note aside and began reading the two-page letter. Halfway through, he sat down slowly on a nearby chair and kept reading, his eyes never moving from the paper.

When he finished it, he read it again, then made a call. "Chief, I just read a note from Emily and a two-page letter that was with it in the envelope. You need to see these right away. I'll be back in twenty minutes. If Hank's still there, ask him to meet us in your office."

Before explaining what was in the letter, Steve said to Peterson, "I need take this letter and the envelope with me. I'll return both when we're finished with them."

Before she had a chance to object, Steve was out the door and running to his car. He raced back to police headquarters, where Hank and the Chief were waiting for him in the Chief's office. He stuck his head in and said, "I need to make copies, be right back."

Returning the original of the note, letter, and envelope back into the evidence bag, Steve hurried back to Hartman's office with the copies and closed the door. He handed them the copies and remained standing. He rushed his words like he was racing against a bomb timer about to hit zero. "This explains why Emily is missing and where's she's been since Monday."

After reading the letter, Hartman spoke first, "Son of a bitch! This is unbelievable. How did it end up in her mailbox?"

Steve had already figured it out. "She knew she was in trouble and somehow figured out a way to mail a copy to herself, hoping someone would find it and come looking for her if she got into trouble. We need to dust the originals in my office for prints to see if any match Emily's. But there's not much doubt it was Emily who wrote the note and mailed it with the letter to herself. Hank, did you get a sample of her handwriting from McCarthy."

"Got it right here. I'm no handwriting expert, but it definitely looks like a match."

The Chief said, "Smart girl. Her life was threatened if she didn't follow the instructions in the letter. Took some guts to copy it and send it to herself without letting anybody see her do it."

Steve was already getting antsy. "Whoever sent her this letter is smart, wealthy, and dangerous, with unlimited manpower and resources. This whole scheme took an enormous amount of planning, money, and a team of professionals to pull it off."

He took a breath to calm himself. "We now know she was lured to Daufuskie Island, but I doubt she's still there. I'm driving to Hilton Head as soon as we're wrapped up here to see if I can pick up her trail. I've got a go-bag in my office. Chief, can you have Judy get me a reservation at the Heritage for tonight?"

"No problem, I'll have her text you the confirmation and let you know as soon as we confirm Emily's handwriting and any prints on the letter and envelope."

Steve reviewed his next move. "When I check in, I'll see what I can get on her reservation, when she checked in and checked out, and if they can tell me who made the reservation. In the morning, I'll take the ferry over to Daufuskie and find out who owns Blaine Cottage, maybe get inside. The ferry captain may have also noticed her, hopefully he's working tomorrow. I'll also take along a few of Hank's missing persons alerts with Emily's photo. The letter says a car would be waiting for her at the dock, maybe somebody remembers seeing her."

Hartman said, "I'll call the Hilton Head Police Department to let them know you're coming. I know Chief Calhoun, and he'll help out with anything you need. I'll give him your cell."

"Thanks Chief. Hank, see what you can find out at the Bank of Charleston in the morning. There must be a safety deposit box in Emily's name. She had to meet with someone to get access to the box. Also see if you can find out who opened it for her."

"Will do," said Hank.

Steve added, "We also need to run down a description of her car. DMV should have it if it's in the system in her name, or her aunt should be able to tell us. Chances are her car is still in one of the airport long-term parking lots. We need to find it. And someone needs to check with Avis about her rental and text me the details. Find out who made the reservation. The rental car may still be in the Heritage parking lot."

They all read the letter one more time to make sure they didn't miss anything. When they finished, Steve said, "It's clear someone got into her apartment without her knowing it. Hank, send a tech team over there first thing tomorrow to dust the entire apartment for prints, check for fibers, and anything else they can find. Somebody put that safety deposit box key in her bedroom. Also check for bugs and cameras in case they left any behind."

Before Steve got up to leave for Hilton Head, he said, "These people are pros, and I doubt we'll find anything useful. They've probably already removed their surveillance cameras, but maybe we'll get lucky, and they missed one. Let's plan to meet back here on Friday morning at eight a.m. That work for you, Chief?"

Hartman nodded and said, "See you both on Friday morning. She's been missing since Monday, and the clock is ticking. We'll call you with any new developments here. You and Hank need anything else, just holler. Let's find her!"

As soon as the meeting broke up, Steve hurried to his office to call Janet and tell her what was going on. She asked, "Is this about the missing girl I saw on the news?"

"Yes, and we just got a lead I need to check out right away. I'll be back sometime tomorrow night. I'm about to head to Hilton Head now and will be staying at the Heritage Hotel. I'll call you when I get in. Love you."

"Love you too, hon. Be careful."

Steve grabbed his go-bag and headed for his car. He had several more calls he needed to make as soon as he got on the road.

His first one would be to Billy Jones.

Chapter 35

By Thursday, boredom had officially set in on the Outer Banks. Nothing was happening. Emily had figured out the routines of her captors, who kept to themselves. During the day, the three armed men rotated every two hours from the front of the house, then to the rear, and finally to one of the bedrooms on the first floor, where she guessed the surveillance monitors were located.

She noticed Jamison spent most of his time in the other downstairs bedroom, which she assumed doubled as his office. She figured the three bedrooms on the top floor were being used by the security guards and the chef. She guessed at night the three guards probably rotated in shifts, two on duty while the third guard slept. If she was right, only one guard would be patrolling outside after dark.

By the time she got downstairs shortly after seven a.m., Chuck and John were already there. They all had coffee together in the dining room while Frankie prepared breakfast in the kitchen. Emily assumed Jamison and the guards ate every morning before they were allowed out of their rooms.to come down.

The armed guards never spoke to their captives. In her mind, she gave each one a name.

Sarge was by far the biggest of the three. The tall black man was at least six-feet-six, and his face was set in a permanent scowl. He wore tight-fitting T-shirts with sleeves that might rip at any moment against his bulging biceps. His shaved head was as shiny as a cue ball.

Shorty was a good foot shorter than Sarge, with a barrel chest and a face that looked like it had just gone ten rounds. He had an XL crooked nose, no doubt broken more than once, menacing small eyes set too close together, cauliflower ears, and a droopy Yosemite Sam mustache. Definitely a face made for radio only.

Tonto was a Native American with long black hair tied in a ponytail. His pockmarked face featured a two-inch scar over his left eye and reminded her of a bad tree stump carving by a drunken chainsaw artist. Looped on his belt was a large hunting knife in a worn leather sheath with a strap snapped around the handle.

After breakfast, Emily and John sat on rocking chairs on the back porch. Shorty was sitting in a chair on the manicured lawn that led to the sand dunes along the ocean. His chair faced the house, and he was watching both of them carefully.

Emily said, "What do you suppose that guard is thinking right now?"

"He doesn't strike me as a thinker. I think he's as bored as we are."

"Any ideas how we can get out of here? Sitting around all day is driving me crazy."

"They're watching our every move, they're heavily armed, and I think they'd like nothing better than to see one of us make a run for it. Other than that, we could try to bribe them with that thousand dollars we still have from the safety deposit box. What in the hell did they give us that for?"

Emily laughed and said, "Very funny. I think that money was just another carrot to get us here. Maybe you should leave Frankie a generous tip with some of yours after lunch."

"Now who's the comedian? I wish I could figure out their end game. Jamison is clearly running the show here, but someone else is pulling his strings. The guards are just following orders. I'd love to know where Jamison went yesterday morning. Since he got back yesterday after lunch, he hasn't said a word to us. Something has changed."

They chatted some more before heading into the library room, where Chuck was stretched out on the sofa with his eyes closed, waiting for lunch to be served.

***

On the way to Hilton Head, Steve called Billy's cell and got him at home. "A lot has happened since we had coffee this morning. Got a minute to talk?"

"Sure, Molly and I just finished dinner. I'm reviewing my notes on that missing person's case I mentioned this morning. What's up?"

"When I told you about those port surveillance tapes that were stolen, you told me one of the reasons might have been that someone wanted to see if there were any witnesses on the tapes. I now think you were right, Billy. I found out when I got back to my office this morning that my star witness has gone missing. I think she was taken by the same people responsible for the port murder I've been investigating."

"Sorry to hear that. How can I help?"

"You've handled a lot of missing persons cases, and I was wondering if you could give me a hand as a paid consultant. I haven't talked to the Chief about it yet, but I think he'll approve it when I tell him about you and your career as an Army CID Special Agent with a lot of missing persons experience."

"Be happy to, Steve. I've got a pretty full plate, but I'll help however I can. When do you want to meet?"

"I'm on my way to Hilton Head right now to check out a lead, back tomorrow night. I have a meeting with the Chief at eight a.m. Friday. I'll ask him then. How about lunch in your office Friday around noon?"

"I'll make it work. See you then. Be safe."

Steve then called Dale to fill him in on Emily. When he finished, Dale said, "Let me know if there's anything I can do on my end, Steve. We still need her to testify at Teddy's trial."

"Where are you with the wiretap warrant?"

"Better news there. The judge just signed our warrant this afternoon to tap the only Auto Warehouse fax line. We'll be set up shortly to start monitoring it round the clock starting on Monday. If the mole turns out to be Reardon, maybe we can get him to turn on Teddy."

"Fat chance of that, but good news. I'm about to call Rob Campbell and Joe Cartwright to update them on Emily. I'll tell Joe you'll be in touch with him to coordinate the sting. If Reardon takes the bait, we'll have him arrested. I'll be back in Mt. Pleasant by tomorrow evening, call me day or night if you need me."

When Steve checked into the Heritage on Wednesday evening a little after ten p.m., he was beat. He dropped his bag in his room and returned to the lobby to see the manager on duty. He hoped no one had checked into Emily's room yet so he could take a look around.

He showed his credentials and the missing persons alert with Emily's photo to Robert Sherwood, the night manager, and asked him to confirm an Emily Baker checked in on Monday afternoon. Sherwood looked up the name in the computer, but told Steve the only woman who checked in as a single on Monday afternoon was a Kathy Ritter, Room 120.

Steve asked, "Any chance you can let me see that room?"

Sherwood said, "Let me check to see if her room is still vacant."

It was empty, and Steve and Sherwood went to Room 120 for a look around. The room was already cleaned after someone had checked her out on Tuesday afternoon. There was no trace Emily had been there. Back at the reservation desk, Steve was told her reservation was made by credit card, no doubt the number of Emily's fake card. No email address or phone number were on the reservation.

Sherwood said the reservation agent on the front desk who checked in Kathy Ritter on Monday afternoon would be on duty in the morning.

Thursday morning, after an early breakfast in the hotel dining room, Steve called Hank to let him know Emily's fake credit card was in the name of Kathy Ritter, then met with the woman who was on the reservation desk on Monday. She recognized Emily from her photo and confirmed she had used a credit card in the name of Kathy Ritter, the same name on the reservation. She said there was nothing out of the ordinary.

Dead end.

Before Steve left the hotel for the ferry, he got a call from Hank. "I've got the details from Avis on the car Emily rented on Monday afternoon. Dark blue 2018 Toyota Camry. Here's the plate."

Steve jotted it down and said, "Thanks Hank, I'll see if it's still here. Any luck finding her personal car in the airport parking lot?"

"Not yet, but I've got what we need from DMV. Three of our patrol guys are walking the parking lots looking for it. I'll let you know when they find it."

Steve had better luck with the ferry captain on his ten a.m. trip over to Daufuskie. The captain recognized Emily's photo on the missing person alert Steve showed him. He told Steve she seemed to be traveling by herself and was met by an SUV at the arrival dock on Daufuskie.

"Did you happen to notice anything about the SUV, color, make or model, anything?"

"Not really, I think it was gray or silver, but I wasn't paying much attention. There were some other people who were also met with rides at the dock. It's not that unusual since there are a few private vehicles on the island. The local residents use them to get around instead of golf carts. When they have visitors arriving by ferry, they pick them up in their cars."

Another dead end. They were piling up.

Steve got the name of the rental agent for Blaine Cottage at the Daufuskie Real Estate Agency. He said they manage most of the rentals for that cottage, but sometimes the owner, James Hartley, books rentals himself, mostly for friends. Since Hartley lived on Daufuskie, Steve talked to him in person.

Hartley confirmed he had booked a one-week private rental for Blaine Cottage recently. That reservation ended on Tuesday. He said the rental was paid in cash and gave Steve the name and a description of the person who paid for the reservation. Steve guessed that would also lead nowhere.

The owner agreed to show Steve around the cottage, which was clean as a whistle. It was isolated on the back side of the island with no other residences nearby. The chances of anyone seeing something going on at the cottage were close to zero.

Steve knew Emily was taken from Daufuskie, then likely driven or flown away from Hilton Head. He would need more manpower to find out how.

When he got back to the Harbor Town Marina, he returned to the Heritage to look for Emily's rental car. He found it empty in the hotel parking lot. The doors were locked.

His next stop was the Hilton Head Police Department to meet with Police Chief Bobby Calhoun to fill him in on what little he'd found so far. Calhoun agreed to have some of his officers check all the marinas on Hilton Head where a boat might have brought Emily from Daufuskie. He would also get Steve a list from the Hilton Head Airport of all the private flights arriving and leaving that week.

Calhoun added, "Of course, if they left Hilton Head by car, we'd have no way of knowing where they were headed."

"Thanks Chief, here's some extra missing person flyers and my card. Call me day or night if you turn anything up."

Late Thursday afternoon, Steve started the drive back to Mt. Pleasant. Emily's trail was already cold, and he needed a new lead. On the way home, Hartman called to let him know the only prints on the letter were Emily's, and the handwriting sample Hank got from her school was also a perfect match. Steve told him he'd report on his trip in the morning.

He hoped his lunch with Billy tomorrow would give him some fresh ideas.

Chapter 36

August 2018

Janet had dinner ready when Steve got home from Hilton Head early Thursday evening. He dropped his overnight bag in the hallway and was greeted with a kiss and a cold beer.

"How'd it go?" she asked.

"First, I'll have another one of those," he said before kissing his wife again.

She smiled and said, "Let's sit down, I've got your favorite dinner ready. You can tell me all about it."

She dished out the shrimp and grits, made from an old family recipe, and he gave her the Cliff Notes version of his trip. "Emily was definitely there. I confirmed she was registered at the Heritage Hotel on Monday and found her Avis rental car in the hotel parking lot."

Steve took another helping and said with his mouth full, "These are awesome, as usual. Thanks hon, I haven't eaten since breakfast."

After a swig of beer, he finished his recap of the trip. "I talked to the ferry boat captain who remembered seeing her on his ten a.m. Tuesday morning trip to Daufuskie when she got off the ferry and was picked up by a driver in an SUV. He doesn't remember seeing her on any of his return trips back to Hilton Head as of this morning. From there, I have no idea where she went."

"You think she might still be someplace on Daufuskie?"

"I doubt it. I'm guessing she left from a private dock on Daufuskie and was taken back to Hilton Head by private boat. I found the owner of Blaine Cottage, and he confirmed a rental this past week, but the renters paid in cash and left on Tuesday afternoon. I think Emily was there, but I can't prove it. The cottage had already been cleaned and sanitized before I got in to look around."

"So now what?"

"The Hilton Head Police Chief is going to have his men check all the marinas with Emily's photo to see if anyone saw her on Tuesday or

158

Wednesday. They're also getting a list of all private flights in and out of the Hilton Head Airport both days. She could be anywhere."

"Well, maybe you'll get lucky, and someone saw her."

"I'm meeting with Hank and the Chief tomorrow morning at eight. I'm also having lunch with Billy at noon in his office. I want to pick his brains for any ideas he might have. He handled a lot of missing persons cases in the army, and he's probably forgotten more than I know about finding someone."

***

After an early night that went a little longer than planned when Janet climbed into bed with him, Steve was out the door on Friday morning by seven a.m. The drive from their house on Pitt Street in the historic Old Village of Mt. Pleasant to the police headquarters building on Ann Edwards Lane took less than ten minutes. He wanted to review his notes before the meeting.

The Chief and Hank were sitting around the conference table in Hartman's office at eight, waiting for him to finish a phone call and get the meeting started. When he hung up, he asked, "How'd it go yesterday, Steve?"

Steve reviewed his day, starting with Emily checking into the Heritage Hotel on Monday afternoon and getting off the ten a.m. ferry to Daufuskie on Tuesday. He covered his meeting with the owner of Blaine Cottage and his inspection of the cottage. He finished his recap with his meeting with Chief Calhoun.

Hank asked. "Did you locate her rental car?"

"Sorry, forgot to mention that. It was in the hotel parking lot, nothing suspicious. She apparently drove to the hotel from the Charleston Airport in an Avis rental to the Heritage and parked it there, just like the letter told her to."

Steve asked Hank, "What did you find out at the Bank of Charleston?"

"She was definitely there on Monday morning to access her safety deposit box. One of the bank managers, a Mr. Ellis Gordon, told me he personally went with her to the box. He said she left the bank right after she accessed it."

"Did he know who applied for the box?"

"He directed me to Mrs. Joan Haskins, the person who oversees the safety deposit box applications and access cards. She told me the box application was handled for Emily by someone claiming to be her mother, who paid for the first month's box rental fee in cash. Haskins gave me a vague description of

159

the woman who filled out the application, but we know Emily's real mother died in a plane crash several years ago."

Steve said, "These people are too smart to drop breadcrumbs. Whoever applied for that box is long gone. Any luck finding her personal car in the airport parking lot?"

"Yes, we found it in a middle row in one of the long-term parking lots, just where the letter told her to leave it. And the license plate had been removed."

Hartman asked, "What about her apartment, Hank? Did the tech team come up with anything besides Emily's prints?"

"The only prints they found were Emily's and another set that turned out to be Richard's after he agreed to allow us to print him. They searched for hair and fibers and are analyzing what they collected, but whoever was in her apartment was probably wearing gloves and booties. No surveillance cameras found inside or out."

"They must've removed them on Monday or Tuesday after Emily left her apartment," said Steve.

Hartman added, "We know she followed the instructions in the letter and most likely left Daufuskie Island sometime on Tuesday. She didn't return to her hotel, and someone checked out for her. Let's keep digging and hope Chief Calhoun comes up with a lead on any sightings of her after she left Daufuskie."

Steve looked at Hank and said, "I need another few minutes to update the Chief on my port murder investigation. Let me know if you get anything from the missing person's alert."

After Hank left, Steve closed the door and discussed his idea to add Billy Jones to the investigation as a temporary paid consultant. He went over Billy's background as an Army Special Agent and why he thought Billy would be a strong asset to the team.

"Steve, I trust your gut on this. Find out what Billy would charge to help us and get back to me. I'm going to have to squeeze something out of the budget and see if I can make it work. If he's too expensive, it's not happening."

"Appreciate that. I'm meeting him for lunch today in his office downtown. I'll call you as soon as we finish. I've known him since we were in basic training together, and I would trust him with my life. He's smart and a relentless investigator. We need to find Emily, and I know Billy can help us."

160

"I don't doubt your instincts. If we can afford him, I'd like to meet him as soon as he's available. We have a lot of balls in the air right now, and we need some results fast."

***

Steve knocked and opened the outer door to *Jones Investigations*. Molly looked up from her desk with her trademark smile. "Hi Steve, he's in his office waiting for you. I got some sandwiches and chips for you guys, what can I get you to drink?"

"Thanks Molly, just water for me. Billy said you're enjoying the job. He's lucky to have you."

Molly grinned and said, "Flattery will get you everywhere, Mr. Detective Harris."

Steve sat down with Billy at a small table in his office. "I talked to the Chief this morning about bringing you on as a paid consultant. After some arm twisting, he finally agreed, depending on your fee and the Chief's budget."

Billy said, "Let's do this. I owe you for helping us get settled here in Charleston, and I'd like to return the favor. You tell me what the Chief can afford, and that will be my fee. I'd like nothing better than to help you find Emily Baker, and I'd like to think I can help. How does that sound?"

"You don't owe me anything, but I could really use your help on this case. It's a lot more complicated than you can imagine and leads all the way to the Camino drug cartel in Miami."

Steve opened a thick file and spent the next hour summarizing everything, from the day he was called to the murder scene at the Port of Charleston a year ago, to the arrest of Teddy Francisco, and finally a review of his trip to Hilton Head yesterday.

Billy made notes and didn't speak until Steve was finished before he said, "I have some questions and a couple thoughts."

Chapter 37

August 2018

Since his phone call with Mark Davis on Wednesday morning, Jamison was struggling to wrap his mind around what Mark had said. He kept replaying the conversation in his head, but it still made no sense. Mark had been working for the boss a lot longer than him and handled numerous covert, and often illegal, surveillance operations over the years. In fact, it was Mark who came up with the surveillance scheme to make sure their three guests complied with the letter.

Bottom line, Mark Davis was a loyal and trusted member of the boss's inner circle, and Jamison had questions. *What could Mark possibly be up to? How long had he known about my father? Was he even telling me the truth?* He needed some answers.

After his daily six a.m. meeting with the security team on Friday, Jamison grabbed some coffee from the kitchen while the men ate breakfast before the guests came downstairs. The house was quiet as he walked to the back porch to watch the sunrise over a calm ocean. Before he left for the Duck Diner and his eleven a.m. call with Mark, he needed to call the boss with his daily eight a.m. status report. He had no idea how long his guests would be staying or what the boss was planning next.

Jamison was frustrated. His boss should've been here by now. That was the original plan. Something was going on, and he was getting more uncomfortable by the day being in the dark.

Back in his office, he made the call at precisely eight a.m. "Boss, everything is quiet here, no problems. When should we expect to see you?"

"There's been a development I need to deal with here in Miami. When I get it sorted out, I'll let you know. I should be up there sometime next week. Meantime, just make sure the guests stay put. It's important I talk to all three of them when I get there."

"Yes sir, understood."

The boss clicked off. He said next week. Next week! The house was rented for a month so that was no issue. But Jamison sensed something was definitely up, and it had to be serious. He wondered if the police could possibly be on to them. He convinced himself there was no way anyone could know where they were. He would ask Mark Davis what he knew.

At exactly eleven a.m., he answered his burner on the third ring. The muffled voice said, "Are you alone in a safe location?"

"Yes, is that you, Mark?"

"Hang on, I'm going to call you back on a different phone in two minutes. Answer on the third ring. No names."

When he called back, Jamison recognized his voice and asked, "What was that all about?"

"Just some extra precautions. I switched to a different secure phone that doesn't require a voice modulator. I know you have more questions, and I'll try to answer them. First, what's happening on your end?"

"I talked to the boss this morning. He told me he wouldn't be up here for a few more days, sometime next week. He told me he had to deal with a situation in Miami first and ordered me to make sure our three guests stay right here until he arrives. I think there's a problem. What's going on?"

Mark paused to give Jamison a moment to calm down before he asked a question of his own. "Can you promise me everything I'm about to tell you will go no further? I trust you, but if you share any of this with anyone, both our lives could be in jeopardy."

"Yes, of course. Who would I tell anyway, the three guard dogs I'm rooming with?"

Mark smiled and said, "There's a problem with the hit on Jorge Rodriguez at the Port of Charleston last year, and the cops have already arrested Teddy Francisco. Somehow, they figured out he was the shooter. The boss thinks there may be a snitch in the organization and has me recording everyone's cell phones."

"OK, thanks for the heads up. At least that explains why he's delayed coming up here. Did you really mean it when you told me you want to take him down? I'm lost, help me out here."

"For now, I'm keeping my head down and doing my job. But after I talked to your father and found out what happened to your parents, I started working on a plan. I'm just not ready to share it with you yet."

"When did you first speak to my father?"

"Last week. I was going to tell you right away, but we were both in the middle of final planning to snatch your guests, and I couldn't risk the boss finding out what I knew. He has no idea your parents survived the explosion."

Jamison kept chasing answers. "How did you find out?"

"Jake Thomas is your father's closest friend in the cartel ever since the organization acquired a majority ownership in Walters International. He was contacted by your father shortly after they were rescued drifting in a raft by a fishing boat off the Bahamas. He told your father that the boss was behind the explosion. Your father told Jake he had a rainy-day numbered account in the Caymans and would remain in seclusion in the Caribbean. He never told him which island."

"Who's this Jake Thomas?"

"Jake is a financial wizard who was initially hired by the boss's father over twenty years ago, on the recommendation of a trusted cartel contact at a large Miami bank. When the boss was put in charge of the Miami cartel operation, he was so impressed by Jake's financial chops that he brought him into his inner circle to handle the cartel's complex financial transactions. What the boss never figured out was that Jake was never the loyal friend he thought he was. Jake was only ever in it for the money and never trusted the boss to have his back if the shit ever hit the fan."

Jamison was still trying to process what Mark was telling him and fired another question. "Why didn't Dad ever try to contact me after he was safe?"

"Your father made Jake promise not to tell you. He was afraid the boss would find out he and your mother were still alive, and he'd come after you. He told Jake he didn't want to put you at any risk."

"I would never have agreed to work for the boss if I had known. Why did Jake wait so long to tell you all this?"

Mark told him what he knew. "Jake said the boss told him recently that he suspected he had a traitor in the organization close to the top and decided to give me a heads up. Jake's been in regular contact with your father since he and your mother have been hiding in the Caribbean. Two weeks ago, your father told him it was time to talk to you, and Jake contacted me to set it up."

"When can I talk to my father?"

"When I spoke to him, he asked me to set up a secure link so he could talk to you. As soon as he gives me a date and time, I'll let you know the protocols I'm setting up for you to call him. The boss is on high alert and paranoid right now. We both need to be very careful not to put your parents, or us, in his crosshairs."

"Why didn't you tell me all this when you were at the house with me on Tuesday night after dropping off those bags you brought from Hilton Head?"

"I didn't think it was safe. I was going to say something to you that night, but you may remember one of the security guys saw me at the front door talking to you and wanted to shoot the shit. I don't trust those three goons, and I couldn't risk being overheard or recorded. The surveillance stuff we set up in the house is pretty sophisticated."

Jamison was still struggling to wrap his head around what Mark was telling him. "I still can't believe my parents are alive. The boss told me he was sorry they died when he came to our Miami house shortly after they disappeared. I asked him how he knew that, and he said it was obvious since I hadn't heard from them. You took a big risk telling me all this, thanks for trusting me."

"Bottom line, the boss is under pressure, and I think it's time for both of us to get out of Dodge. You've been a straight-shooter and deserve to be with your parents. That's not gonna happen until the boss is stopped. If we work together, we just might come out of this on the other side. Meantime, keep doing what you're doing. I'll be in touch."

Jamison turned off the burner. It was a lot to process, but one thing was certain. He would need to be very careful in the days ahead.

Chapter 38

At nine a.m. on the last Friday in August, veteran Charleston County Prosecutor Jill Carrington and well-known crime family defense attorney Louis Franklin were sitting in Judge Harvey Templeton's Charleston County Courthouse chambers in downtown Charleston.

The purpose of the meeting was to discuss a request by the prosecution to delay the start of the Teddy Francisco's trial for the August 2017 murder of Jorge Rodriguez. The trial was scheduled to begin on Monday, September 17, just over two weeks away.

Since his arrest three months ago, Teddy was being held without bail for murder, as well as additional federal charges, including the illegal distribution and sale of drugs across state lines. The DEA and FBI agreed to allow him to stand trial in Charleston County for the murder before trying him on the federal drug charges in the Southern District of Miami.

The meeting was off the record. Templeton was dressed casually behind his ornate antique mahogany desk. Carrington and Franklin sat in matching upholstered leather chairs in front of him.

Jill Carrington was a hard-nosed prosecutor in her mid-fifties. She was well-known by local Charleston County residents for her steel-gray eyes, sharp jawline, and sharper tongue. She had been re-elected twice for her take-no-prisoners hard line on prosecuting criminals.

Louis Franklin was in his late forties. He was born in New York and raised by a single parent in a hard-scrabble Brooklyn neighborhood. After finishing near the top of his class at NYU on an academic scholarship, he got his law degree from Columbia Law School, finishing first in his class.

Franklin accepted a lucrative job offer from a prominent law firm in New York City that specialized in defending organized crime defendants. He gained national notoriety, along with a seven-figure bonus, for successfully getting a not-guilty verdict for a high-ranking member of the Bruno crime family.

Given the high-profile nature of the trial, the long-serving judge, well-known for his no-nonsense demeanor on the bench, requested an informal meeting with both attorneys before any official pre-trial motions were filed.

"Thank you both for coming in and agreeing to meet with me in chambers," Templeton began. "Since Mr. Franklin requested a speedy trial, I wanted the three of us to informally discuss Miss Carrington's request for a delay ahead of the trial. At the moment, I'm reluctant to grant the prosecution's request, but I want to hear from both parties before we move forward."

Looking directly at Carrington, Templeton said, "Miss Carrington, you've already agreed to the fast-track trial schedule. Please explain why you need a delay."

Softening her usual courtroom attack mode, Carrington explained her request. "Thank you, your honor. It has come to my attention this week that my investigator has been unable to contact one of our key witnesses. While our case is still very strong, the prosecution believes all of our witnesses are essential to insuring a fair verdict beyond any reasonable doubt."

"Is your witness on the prosecution witness list?"

"Not yet, Judge. We wanted to make sure each of our witnesses would be available for trial before submitting their names to the defense. We have not disclosed the identity of this witness yet for the very reason we were forced to request this delay. Given the defendant's questionable background, we're concerned we might risk ending up in the exact situation we're in today."

Franklin exploded, "Judge, that is an outrageous accusation! My client is innocent of this bogus murder charge, and to suggest some kind of conspiracy to eliminate a witness is completely unfounded, ridiculous and offensive on its face. The prosecution is grabbing at straws at the last minute because they know they have a weak case. My client is innocent, and we look forward to proving it without any further delay of the trial date agreed to by the prosecution."

Before Franklin could continue, Templeton interrupted him. "Hold on, Mr. Franklin, you'll get your turn. Miss Carrington, do you have anything else to add?"

Carrington continued to keep her normally confrontational demeanor in check and calmly replied, "Judge, we have every resource at our disposal looking for this witness. We just need a little more time so we can confirm the availability of the witness for trial."

"Mr. Franklin, you may now state the defense's position on delaying the trial to allow the prosecution more time to locate a witness."

Franklin's expected rant did not disappoint. "Judge, the prosecution has had ample time to prepare their case against my client and find their witnesses. This case is totally circumstantial and a waste of everyone's time and expense. Now, at the last minute, the prosecution wants a delay? The defense strongly objects and reiterates our demand for a speedy trial on the start date that was agreed to.by the prosecution."

"Miss Carrington?"

Carrington took the kid gloves off and shot back, "Judge, I understand Mr. Franklin's passionate and over-the-top objection, but the people also have a right to a fair trial, and that includes the testimony of every relevant prosecution witness."

"How much time are you requesting, Miss Carrington?" the judge asked.

"Your honor, the prosecution respectfully requests a one-month delay. If we're unable to locate our witness by then, we'll be prepared to start the trial on the new date regardless. Thirty more days is not going change the outcome of the trial one way or the other."

The judge looked at his trial calendar and said, "I'm going to allow the prosecution a one-week delay in the interest of fairness to all parties. Mr. Franklin, your objection is noted. If you want to file a motion for the record, you may do so, but it won't change my ruling."

"Thank you, your honor," said Carrington.

Franklin was furious. "Judge, I disagree in the strongest possible terms, but apparently my client has no choice but to abide by your decision. I absolutely want my objection noted in the record."

***

After the meeting, Franklin called a private number in Miami. The boss asked, "What is it, Mr. Franklin?"

"Looks like you were right. I just left a meeting with Teddy's trial judge and Charleston County Prosecutor Jill Carrington. She tried to get a thirty-day delay because of a missing witness they haven't been able to locate."

"Did you find out the name of the witness?"

"No, the prosecutor won't disclose it yet, but there's now not much doubt it's one of the three people you're holding."

"What did the judge say?"

"He only gave her a one-week delay. The trial is now scheduled to start in Charleston on Monday, September 24."

Never one for small talk, the boss said, "Keep me updated," and abruptly hung up. The clock was still ticking.

Chapter 39

Friday, August 31, 2018

At five p.m. on that same Friday, Steve was back in the Chief Hartman's office sitting at his conference table, this time to introduce Billy and discuss some of his ideas to accelerate the search for Emily.

Hartman said, "Welcome, Mr. Jones. Steve's told me all about your extensive missing persons experience, and we appreciate your input. We're not in the habit of hiring outside consultants, but in this case, I agree with Steve's recommendation to bring you on board to assist us. Thank you, and I look forward to working with you."

"Please call me Billy, Chief. My mother once told me that's what my dad first called me when I was born, and everybody's called me Billy ever since. I know Steve already filled you in on my military background before I started *Jones Investigations* here in Charleston a couple years ago. I'm happy to dig in and help any way I can. Steve briefed me on the situation in my office earlier today."

"Thanks Billy. Steve, why don't you briefly run down where things stand before we get Billy's thoughts."

Steve began with an update on the port murder investigation and why he was convinced the Camino cartel was responsible for Emily's disappearance. "We know there's a mole at the port who stole the surveillance tapes from the morning Jorge Rodriguez was murdered by Teddy Francisco. The Miami DEA and our port security team are ready to initiate a joint sting operation to flush out the mole. We're launching it on Monday morning.

There's no question in my mind the stolen tapes ended up with the cartel. If our sting works, we'll have proof that the person who stole the tapes is working with Camino. We're prepared to offer him a deal in exchange for information about the cartel's network and who got the tapes."

Steve looked at Hartman and said, "We know Emily is on those tapes. Billy convinced me there's a strong possibility that the cartel wanted to see if they included any potential witnesses who could identify Francisco as the man seen with Rodriguez just before the murder. I think they've taken Emily to find out if she saw anything and make sure she's not available to testify in Teddy's trial."

He then reviewed the highlights of his trip to Hilton Head. "We now know Emily was following the instructions in the anonymous letter she received. She was at the Bank of Charleston and accessed a safety deposit box, rented a car from Avis, and checked into the Heritage Hotel on Monday. She took the ferry to Daufuskie Island Tuesday and was then driven to Blaine Cottage."

Hartman added, "From there, we don't know where they took her. What we do know is that somebody has spent a lot of time and money to kidnap her. If they were so afraid of what she may have seen, why go through this whole charade? We're missing something."

Billy stopped scribbling on his notepad and said, "This might be a good place for me to jump in, if that's OK with you guys."

"Absolutely," said Steve. "Unless the Hilton Head Police Department comes up with anyone who saw her at one of the marinas where she may have been taken by boat from Daufuskie, or saw her at the Hilton Head Airport, I'm not sure where we go from here. So far, our statewide missing persons alert has turned up zip except a bunch of false leads."

Billy looked at his notes from his earlier meeting with Steve. "I think several of the people who saw her on Monday and Tuesday need to be reinterviewed, starting at the Bank of Charleston, specifically Ellis Gordon and Joan Haskins. Somebody at the bank is involved in this up to their eyeballs. You don't normally open a safety deposit box for someone else.

And someone got the key to her box and planted it in her bedroom. The story Haskins told you about how her mother took care of getting the box in Emily's name is either lax on her part or false. We need to get background checks on both Gordon and Haskins.

Somebody also needs to run down the credit card that she used for the Avis rental and her room at the Heritage. Also, anything on whoever made her rental car reservation, room reservation, and checked her out of the hotel."

Billy finished reviewing his notes. "Just a couple more thoughts. The owner of Blaine Cottage needs to be looked at carefully, including a full background check. It's pretty convenient that he took a private rental reservation for the exact location that Emily was directed to, in the exact time frame, and was paid in cash. We need to run down who made that reservation. Someone from the cartel obviously paid the owner directly."

Steve said, "It's also strange that the cottage was cleaned and sanitized so quickly in the middle of the week, especially since it was still not rented when I went there yesterday. What was the rush? A forensic team needs to scour that cottage for anything that the cleaning people might have missed. A search warrant shouldn't be a problem if the owner objects."

"Good point, Steve," said Billy. "Then there's the vehicle that picked up Emily at the ferry dock on Daufuskie and drove her to the cottage. We need to get a list of the owners of every private vehicle on Daufuskie. Who picked her up? Anyone notice the driver or the vehicle?"

Billy added some final thoughts. "Since Emily apparently copied the letter at her school and mailed it to herself, it might be worth interviewing her principal again to see if there's anything else she can add from her conversation with Emily. I'd also like to interview Emily's boyfriend and her aunt to see if there's anything else they might remember, given they were the last people to talk to her before she went missing on Monday."

Steve was making a list and asked Billy, "What about going public and doing a press conference with the local media to get her photo out to the general public? If she's still in South Carolina, maybe someone has seen her. We just can't get into any details about our suspected link between her kidnapping and the Camino cartel or the port murder investigation. A press conference appealing for any information on her whereabouts would be expected by the cartel. If we stay silent, they might suspect we're on to them."

"Works for me," agreed Billy. "A press conference makes sense as long as you don't disclose any specifics about your investigation. Chief, I think you should handle it. The media already knows Steve's leading the port murder investigation. The more separation between the two lines of inquiry, the better."

Hartman, who had been mostly just listening, spoke up. "Good stuff, Billy. I'll set up a press conference. Now I know why Steve pressed me so hard to get you involved. Steve, what kind of manpower would you need to follow-up on Billy's suggestions?"

172

"Right now, if I can keep Hank on the Emily search full-time and add one more of our senior detectives, I think we can quickly jump on most of the list. We need to find a lead on Emily's whereabouts, and we need it fast."

Billy said to Steve, "I also think you should follow-up with Chief Calhoun as soon as possible for an update. I'm especially interested in the list of private planes that landed and departed this past Tuesday. If we can find any suspicious flights or planes that may have flown Emily off Hilton Head, we could get back on her trail."

The Chief wrapped up the meeting. "I'll get Hank in here to meet with us at eight a.m. in the morning, and I'll ask Robby Girard to join the team for a few days. Robby's a smart investigator and could handle some of the follow-ups. Billy, if you're available, you're invited to join us. Hate to ruin everybody's weekend, but we can't wait until Monday to get some of this moving. If Emily's still alive, she's counting on someone to find her."

***

Steve met with Billy in his office for another thirty minutes before they left the building together. Billy asked, "Did you ever re-interview those other two potential witnesses from the stolen port surveillance footage?"

"Actually, I got around to calling both of them this past Monday afternoon but didn't reach either of them on their cellphones. I left them both a message to call me back soon as possible. With everything else going this week, I've put it on the back burner. Since I still haven't heard back from either of them, I'll try to reach them again next week."

As they were about to head to their own cars, Steve asked, "Just out of curiosity, if you're at liberty to tell me, what's the name of your missing person?"

Billy answered, "John Simpson."

Chapter 40

Friday, August 31, 2018

It took Steve a moment for the name to register. John Simpson was one of the two men he was trying to reach to follow-up about anything they might have seen at the port entrance around the same time Emily saw two men arguing along the fence.

Before Billy reached his car, Steve ran over to him and said, "Billy, wait. I think John Simpson is involved in my murder investigation, and he could be with Emily."

That stopped Billy in his tracks. "That makes no sense, Steve. Are you telling me you think my client's husband may have also been kidnapped by the cartel?"

"That's exactly what I'm saying. I interviewed John Simpson last year. He was one of the two men I mentioned who was at the port entrance exactly the same time Emily was running past the gates last August. I've been waiting for him to return my message."

Steve thought about it some more and added, "It can't be a coincidence. John is also on the stolen surveillance tapes. If we're right and the cartel was looking for potential witnesses on those tapes, whoever took Emily may also have John. I can't believe I never made the connection to your missing persons case until you just said his name."

"Steve, if that's what happened, Emily's disappearance and possible kidnapping by the Camino cartel just turned the missing persons investigation into is a whole new ballgame."

"I need to head back into the office before the Chief leaves. If you need to get home to that pretty wife of yours, I'll see you here in the morning. The Chief and I may be here for a while."

"Forget it," said Billy. "If the cartel is holding both John and Emily, you're going to need all hands on deck. I'm going back in with you."

"You can't be serious," said Hartman after Steve told him what they'd just discovered, "You think Billy is working on a missing person's case of someone you interviewed last year as part of your port investigation? What the hell's going on?"

Steve said, "Chief, that's not all. I'm now worried there might be a third person."

"Tell me you're kidding."

"Sorry Chief, but I also tried to reach a man named Chuck Wilson earlier this week. He was the container driver who was leaving the port at that same time John Simpson was heading in for his early shift. I left messages on both Wilson's and Simpson's phones Monday afternoon, but they haven't called me back. Wilson's truck was also on the stolen port videos."

"Steve, we've got to get on top of this. Why do you think the cartel has also taken both of them?"

"When I mentioned to you guys this afternoon that I wanted to reinterview a couple guys who were also on the tapes, it wasn't that urgent. Emily has already identified both our dead guy and the shooter. Wilson and Simpson told me last year they didn't see anything that morning. I just wanted to talk to them again to make sure. If all three of them are together, I think the cartel got nervous about Francisco's murder trial and decided to cover their ass and take all three of them off the grid."

"Look, we still don't even know for sure if Simpson and Wilson are with Emily. And until we find out more, I sure as hell don't want to involve the media," warned Hartman.

"I need to call Joe Cartwright at the port and find out who handles Wilson's container schedule," said Steve. "We also need to get warrants to search both Simpson's and Wilson's homes ASAP to see if we can find anything that might give us a clue if they got that letter."

Billy said, "I'm sure John's wife will let me search their home. She's desperate and will do anything that might help us find her husband."

"OK," said Hartman. "Billy, give her a call and see if she can meet you now. I'll get a couple of patrol guys to join you there. We'll need her address. Steve, fill Joe in and see what you can find out about this Chuck Wilson. And get me his address for a search warrant."

Billy called Mandy Simpson and explained what he needed. He told her he'd see her in thirty minutes with two police officers.

Joe Cartwright answered his phone immediately. "Steve, what's up? We're ready to initiate the sting with Dale and the Miami DEA on Monday. The tap on the fax line is all set up."

"Joe, something else has come up, and I need to find one of your port container drivers right away. Can you get me the name of your container transport contact for Chuck Wilson? He's an independent trucker and a regular container driver. I interviewed him last year in connection with my murder investigation, and I need to talk to him again as soon as possible."

"Give me a few minutes, I'll call you back."

Fifteen minutes later, Joe was back on the phone. "This is going to sound a little strange. I just talked to Greg Stevens, our transport manager who handles Chuck Wilson's container schedule. He told me one of Chuck's friends, who also lives in McClellanville, called Greg twice this week asking about Chuck. He told Greg this afternoon that no one has seen or heard from Chuck since last weekend. His friend's name is George Cooper."

Joe gave Steve the cell numbers for Cooper and Stevens, and the address of Chuck's cabin in McClellanville. "Thanks Joe, anything else?"

"Cooper told Greg that Chuck's sleeper cab has been parked next to his cabin all week, and his old pickup truck is gone. He said it wasn't like Chuck to ignore his calls, and he's convinced something's happened to him. What's going on, Steve?"

"Not sure yet, Joe. I'm following up a couple leads right now. I'll talk to you before Monday morning about the sting operation and touch base with Dale. We need to smoke Reardon out and find out fast what he knows. We're running out of time."

When Steve hung up with Cartwright, Hartman asked, "What did he say?"

"Believe it or not, sounds like Chuck Wilson may also be missing. I'm going to try Wilson again on his cell. If he doesn't answer, I'm going to call one of his neighbors in McClellanville to see what he knows. George Cooper has been calling Greg Stevens at the port all week about Chuck. He told Stevens no one around town has seen or heard from Wilson since last weekend."

An hour later, Steve had the search warrant in his pocket and left Mt. Pleasant for the forty-five-minute drive on Hwy 17 North to Chuck's cabin in McClellanville. George Cooper told Steve he'd meet him there before dark.

***

All was quiet on the Outer Banks when they sat around the end dining room table for dinner on Friday evening. Frankie brought out some fresh sea bass, a bowl of wild rice, asparagus, and a basket of rolls. The guards had already eaten in the kitchen in their usual shifts. Sarge was on the front porch and Tonto was out back. Shorty was manning the downstairs bedroom monitors.

Jamison came from the other downstairs bedroom and sat with them. "Mind if I join you for dinner?" He waved Frankie over from the kitchen. "Please bring me a plate. I'll have what they're having."

Since they arrived on Tuesday, Jamison rarely ate with them. He said, "I hope you're all comfortable with the accommodations. There's been a delay in the proceedings, and it looks like you'll be here for a few more days. Thank you again for cooperating, I'm sure this has been inconvenient for all of you."

John snapped, "Inconvenient doesn't begin to cover it. When are you going to tell us what we're doing here? By now, a lot of people are bound to be looking for us. Just tell us what you want and let us go."

Jamison calmly replied, "Mr. Simpson, I'm not at liberty to discuss any of that. We've already been over it, and you already know it's not up to me. The man I work for is calling the shots." He chuckled and added, "Sorry, bad choice of words."

Frankie brought Jamison a plate and everyone helped themselves. Jamison said, "As I've also already told all of you, as long as you follow my instructions and don't try anything stupid while you're here, you'll all be safe. Since we're going to be here longer than I anticipated, if there's anything Frankie can add to the menu, he'll do his best to accommodate your requests."

Before starting to eat, Jamison added, "Since we didn't bring you enough clothes for this long a visit, I've opened the utility room on the first floor. Help yourselves to the washer and dryer. In the meantime, relax and enjoy your dinner. Looks like another beautiful evening on the Outer Banks."

John looked over at Emily and Chuck and rolled his eyes.

177

Chapter 41

Friday, August 31–Saturday, September 1, 2018

On the way to Chuck's cabin Friday evening, Steve began mentally reshuffling his priorities. He recorded a list on his cell.

- Confirm John and Chuck missing.
- Call Chief Calhoun for update on Hilton Head marina searches.
- Review Hilton Head Airport flight logs.
- Discuss Monday press conference with Chief.
- Call Dale to review sting operation.

He knew the fastest way to find Emily, and maybe John and Chuck, was to find someone with inside information about the cartel and Emily's kidnapping. He hoped the port sting operation on Monday would flush out Jerry Reardon.

When he arrived at Chuck's cabin, he pulled next to an old Ford F-150 parked next to a large sleeper cab in the front yard with *Chucktown Special* painted on the door. George Cooper was sitting on the porch, wearing an old pair of shorts, white T-Shirt, sandals, and a stained baseball cap. He looked to be close to sixty, with a thin frame and spindly legs. He stood up and slowly limped over to greet Steve.

They shook hands and George said, "You must be Detective Harris. George Cooper, thanks for driving out here in person. I'm a good friend of Chuck, and I've been worried sick about him all week."

"Nice to meet you, George. I appreciate you meeting me. I talked to Greg Stevens at the port this afternoon, and he told me about your concern for Chuck's whereabouts. I'm investigating another case, and I'm trying to figure out if there's any connection with Chuck being missing."

Before he could continue, George said, "You mean that port investigation you were working on last year." It was a statement, not a question.

"What makes you say that?"

"Chuck told me a Mt. Pleasant detective interviewed him, I think it was around last November, about some investigation he was handling. He never told Chuck exactly what it was about, but I'm guessing it might have something to do with why he's missing. Chuck and I talk about everything. He's probably the closest friend I got. Were you the detective who talked to him last year?"

Steve smiled and said, "You sure you're not a detective yourself? Tell me again why you think Chuck is missing." George told him.

"George, I have a warrant to look around the inside of the cabin to see if there's anything that will tell us where Chuck might be. When I called, you mentioned you had a spare key to the cabin from Chuck. You can join me inside if you want, just don't touch anything. Some techs will be back here tomorrow to search for prints and anything else that might tell us if a stranger has been in the cabin. Mind if I borrow your spare key? I'll make a copy and get it back to you."

They both gloved up and covered their shoes. George opened the front door and handed Steve the key. There was no sign of the letter or any surveillance equipment. Steve was not surprised. He already figured if Chuck got that letter and followed the instructions, he would've taken the letter with him to Hilton Head. He did notice Chuck's laptop in the kitchen and put it in an evidence bag. He couldn't tell if any of Chuck's clothes were missing, but his wardrobe was pretty sparse.

"George, can you describe what Chuck might be driving?"

"He's got an old beater Chevy pickup he mostly uses to drive around town. Chuck spends most of his time on the road driving his *Chucktown Special* parked out front." Steve wrote down the description of the pickup, told George he needed to make a call, and stepped outside to call Hartman.

"Chief, I thought of something driving out here. I just got a description of Chuck's pickup truck from Mr. Cooper. Since it's going to be dark soon, can you get a couple of patrolmen to check the airport parking lots for it first thing in the morning? If his pickup is there, especially if the license plate is missing, we can be pretty certain he followed the instructions in the same letter Emily

179

got. I'm also going to call Billy and get a description of John's vehicle to you so the patrol guys can look for both."

"Good idea, Steve. Anything helpful out there?"

"I'm bringing back his laptop. Techs can check it in the morning, it's not password protected. Looks like some of his clothes might be missing, but hard to tell. He's definitely no clothes horse. I'm heading back in a few minutes. I'll see you for our meeting at eight tomorrow morning."

"See you then, get some sleep."

***

Hank and Robby Girard joined Steve, Billy, and the Chief around his conference table on Saturday morning. Hartman put down his coffee cup and said, "Thanks everyone for coming in early on a Saturday morning. Steve told me he's already filled you in on the basics. There are four patrol officers searching the airport parking lots as we speak for Simpson's and Wilson's personal vehicles. I'm expecting to hear from them shortly."

Steve recapped his search of Chuck's cabin and conversation with George Cooper. "Chuck has definitely not been around McClellanville this past week. Josh is looking through his laptop in the lab. I told him to interrupt us if he finds anything. I searched the cabin and didn't see anything that looked out of place. Stu and Frank are headed out to the cabin this morning to dust for prints and collect any forensics, then head to Simpson's house to do the same."

Billy said, "The only interesting thing I found at John's house was a heavy white envelope addressed to him in the bottom of his toolbox in the garage. The envelope was empty but probably contained the letter. It's being dusted for prints, but I'm not holding my breath. What caught my eye was the outside of the envelope. It was stamped **Personal and Confidential** at the top. Along the bottom, under John's name, it said **Urgent for Your Eyes Only**."

"Did his wife recognize it?" asked the Chief.

"She never saw it before and had no idea why John would've hidden it in his toolbox. My guess is John didn't want her to know anything about the letter, if that's what was in the envelope. One thing that's strange is some kind of logo on the back flap with the script letters *WSB* inside a horizontal box. No idea what it means."

Hartman's phone rang. "Hang on, Tommy, I'm putting you on speaker." He punched the speaker button and said, "OK, go ahead."

Mt. Pleasant patrol officer Tommy Carter said, "Chief, we found the old Chevy pickup matching the description you gave us. The license plate is missing. We'll open the truck and get the VIN number, but I wanted to let you know right away. Still looking for Simpson's white Explorer. Hang on a minute, Chief."

After a long pause with muffled voices in the background, Tommy said, "Just found the Explorer, Chief. No license plate."

"Nice work. Text me those VIN numbers when you get them and leave the vehicles right where they are."

Steve gave a thumbs up and said, "Looks like we're now searching for three people who are probably together. Assuming they all left Daufuskie at the same time by boat, I need to call Chief Calhoun and tell him to recheck every marina on Hilton Head for any boat that dropped off at least five or six people on Tuesday afternoon. He already has Emily's photo. Robby, call the DMV and have them email us Chuck's license photo. Billy, see if Mandy can email us a photo of John. I'll email both photos to Calhoun."

"Did you get those airport logs from Calhoun yet?" asked Billy.

Steve handed him a file folder. "He emailed them to me last night, and I printed them this morning. Can you review these and see if anything jumps out? If we're right about the time frame, and they left Daufuskie on Tuesday afternoon, start with the private flights leaving Hilton Head on Tuesday. If this Jamison guy mentioned in the letter is with them, along with two or three armed guards, the plane would have to be big enough for at least six or seven passengers."

"I'm on it. Is there a spare office I can use?"

"Use the office next to Steve's," said Hartman. "Robby, give Billy a hand going over those logs. Before everyone leaves, let's discuss our strategy for the press conference now that we're dealing with three missing people who may have been taken by the same group."

Hank said, "If the Camino cartel is hiding all three of them, we can't get that out to the media yet. If they're still safe and the kidnappers find out what we know, it might force their hand and put them in worse danger."

"Hank's right," said Billy. "We don't want what we know getting out to the public. There's a statewide alert on Emily, so a press conference talking about her disappearance would be normal. We just can't mention anything about John and Chuck. The main objective is to get Emily's picture out to the public and a phone number for any information."

Hartman said, "Agreed. I'll have Judy contact all the media around the state and set up a tip hotline for anyone who may have seen Emily. We'll schedule the press conference for two p.m. on Monday to allow time for coverage in the local evening newscasts. Hank, please alert Marie Parker and Richard Barnett. If Miss Parker wants to join me at the press conference to appeal for any information on Emily, she's welcome to come."

Hank said, "I've been talking to Marie Parker every day to keep her up to date on our search. As Emily's closest family member, I think she'd welcome an opportunity to make an appeal to the public for any information that would help us find her niece."

"Good," said Hartman. "And just so we're all on the same page, Steve and Billy should be nowhere near the press conference. Hank, you can join me at the podium since you started the Emily investigation and are familiar with the details. Steve, talk to that rental agent at Emily's apartment and make sure she doesn't discuss anything about that letter with anyone. Keep me in the loop on everything."

Before the meeting ended, everybody had their marching orders to hit the ground running on Monday morning. Steve would call the owner of Blaine Cottage with some additional questions and follow-up with Chief Calhoun. Billy said he'd re-interview Ellis Gordon and Joan Haskins at the Bank of Charleston. Robby was tasked to run down the credit card used by Emily under the name Kathy Ritter for her Avis rental and hotel reservation. Hank and the Chief had a press conference to prep.

Emily, Chuck, and John had already started a quiet weekend on the Outer Banks.

Chapter 42

Saturday, September 1, 2018

Steve was fired up when he called Dale to update him on everything that was happening, including why he thought the Camino cartel was responsible for kidnapping two more people linked to Emily.

When he finished, he said, "I'd like to see if our sting operation is successful and follow-up on a few other leads before we call in the FBI. Once the cartel gets wind of what we suspect, I'm afraid it might put all three of our missing people in more jeopardy."

Dale said, "If you don't get any traction soon, I don't think you'll have any choice. If the cartel is holding all three of them, they may just eliminate them if they find out one of them is scheduled to be a witness in Teddy Francisco's murder trial."

"What's your take?" asked Steve.

"If I had to bet, assuming they're still alive, I'd guess they're being held as hostages in case the cartel wants some leverage to try to cut a plea deal if the prosecution's case looks like a slam dunk. That would keep them alive, at least until the trial is over. Since Emily happens to be the only prosecution eyewitness, if she doesn't show for the trial, Teddy could definitely walk on the murder charge. Keeping all three potential witnesses away from the trial is just being prudent from the cartel's point of view."

"Makes sense, Dale. We just need to find them before the trial starts. If the cartel finds out Emily is the one who identified Francisco, game over."

Steve brought Dale up to speed on the trial. "Jill Carrington is still withholding Emily's name from the defense. She won't add her to the witness list at all if she's still missing when Jill is compelled to disclose her final witness list to the defense."

"That's scheduled in a few days, right?"

"Jill called me yesterday and said the judge granted her a one-week delay. If we don't find Emily soon and she's not around to testify, her case against Teddy basically goes on life-support. And we're running out of time."

"Steve, if those airport logs Billy's checking turn up anything suspicious, I have a good friend I trust in the FBI who might be able to help. If I was kidnapping three people at the same time on an island, the easiest and safest way to get them to a secure location would be to fly them off Hilton Head in a private plane. Eliminates the risk of being stopped on the highway, and they could land anywhere."

"That's exactly what Billy thinks. He's still reviewing the logs of all planes leaving Hilton Head last Tuesday and Wednesday and running down the tail numbers to find out who owns each one. He's also getting information on any flight plans that were filed. I'll let you know what he turns up and if we need any help."

***

An hour later, Billy went into Steve's office and said, "Think we may have something. The controller on duty told me the pilot of one of the planes that left Hilton Head Airport on Tuesday afternoon turned off the plane's transponder shortly after takeoff."

"Why would he do that?" Steve asked.

"With the transponder off, the plane couldn't be tracked."

"How did you figure out which plane it was?"

"Robby and I already had a list of all the flights that left Hilton Head on Tuesday and Wednesday. The plane that turned off its transponder was a privately-owned King Air. The pilot also didn't file a flight plan. Most private flights do, but it's not an FAA requirement."

"Were you able to track the tail number to the owner of that plane?"

"It's complicated, Steve. The plane is owned by an offshore shell company. I have a guy who traced that company to a mostly invisible corporate entity based in South America with suspected ties to the Camino cartel in Mexico. We're still trying to piece it together, but so far, all the dots connect."

"Text me the tail number. Dale told me he has an FBI buddy he trusts who can help us. He understands it could cost Emily her life if the cartel even gets a whiff we're on their trail. Let's say you're right and that plane is the one that flew everyone from Hilton Head. That still doesn't tell us where they landed."

Billy explained, "Without a flight plan, the pilot must fly by VFR, Visual Flight Rules, which require the pilot to stay below eighteen thousand feet. If I needed a place to drop off several passengers without being noticed, I'd want to land sooner rather than later at a relatively small and isolated municipal airport or private air strip with no radar control tower. Most small airports don't have one. And the King Air also doesn't need a long runway."

"Any ideas?"

"It's a longshot, but I've already asked Robby to start making a list of small airports with runways around five thousand feet long. He's starting with the coastal areas of South Carolina, North Carolina, and Georgia. It could be a long list, but something might jump out as a likely landing spot. We gotta start someplace."

"OK," agreed Steve. "I don't have a better idea, but we're still looking for a needle in a haystack. I'll find out if Dale's FBI contact can help us get that list faster from the FAA."

Before he had a chance to call Dale and also update Hartman on the possible flight they were looking for, Steve got a call from Chief Calhoun on Hilton Head.

"Steve, we may have something from our marina search. A retired veteran fishes almost every day off the dock at the Skull Creek Marina. He told us he saw a large yacht briefly tie up at the marina on Tuesday afternoon and several passengers get off. He said a young woman with a long blond ponytail could have been the woman in the missing persons flyer we showed him."

"Did he recognize anyone matching the other two photos of Wilson and Simpson?"

"He told us he also saw a big man that could have been Wilson but didn't get a real good look at any of them. He said they all basically just walked along the dock and got into a couple of SUVs that were waiting for them. He gave me his cell number if you want to call him. Unfortunately, there are no CCTV cameras at the Marina."

"That's gotta be them. It fits with our theory that all three of them were flown off Hilton Head together on Tuesday afternoon. Do me a favor and have a couple of your guys go back to that marina with the photos and see if they can find anyone else who may have seen that boat and the people who got off. Same thing at the airport."

"Will do, I'll call you when I have something."

Steve unconsciously looked at his watch. Tick-tock.

Chapter 43

Monday, September 3, 2018

After a quiet Sunday at home with Janet and some much-needed downtime, Steve had a lot of balls in the air when he got to the office early Monday morning. He was hoping to find any lead this week that would get him closer to finding out where Emily, Chuck, and John were being held. He still believed they were alive, although he also realized that might just be a hope and a prayer.

His first call was a little after eight a.m. to Dale for a final run through before the port sting operation was launched. "Morning Dale. Know you're busy, just wanted to review the plan with you one more time."

Dale said, "Joe Cartwright and his security team at the port are all set, including two of your undercover detectives somewhere in the building waiting for a call from Joe if we get a hit."

"What time are you going to send the fax to the port this morning? How exactly do you see it playing out?"

"The basic plan hasn't changed. At ten a.m. this morning, our undercover is going to try to send a routine-looking fax from the Auto Warehouse fax machine that we identified from the fax log in Reardon's office."

"What happens if your inside man can't access the fax machine without being seen?"

"If he can't send a fax from that machine undetected at ten a.m., he'll send a group text to alert me and Joe. My guy will then try again at eleven a.m. and every hour on the hour after that if necessary until he's alone to send the fax. I'll have my guy add your cell to the group text."

"What happens when he sends the fax?"

"It will be faxed to Reardon's attention and request a routine confirmation of a specific container on a ship scheduled to arrive at the port on Wednesday. If our wiretap picks up a return fax from Reardon's office back to the same

Auto Warehouse fax machine that sent the original fax to his office, game over. Your detectives there will arrest him and keep him in custody. No doubt he'll lawyer up. Joe told me you have a judge standing by ready to sign a search warrant for his office, including his phones, computer, and anything else they can find."

"Dale, we're good on this end. We've got a judge on call, and we'll be all over his office like flies on roadkill."

Steve rang off and called Chief Calhoun to ask him about any more news on his marina search.

Calhoun said, "We found another person who might have seen your missing people last Tuesday afternoon at the Skull Creek Marina. One of the women who works at the bait shop near the dock was outside taking a smoke break."

"What did she see?"

"She told us she saw a large yacht tie up at the end of the dock and recalled seeing six or seven people get off. She also remembered a young woman with a blond ponytail that looked like Emily in the photo we showed her."

"Did she happen to see the name of the yacht?"

"Unfortunately, she didn't. The boat's size is what initially caught her attention, but the bow was facing her, and she didn't see the stern where the name would be easily seen. She wasn't paying a lot of attention and went back into the store before it left."

"At least that confirms what the other witness saw. Did she say what the woman was wearing?"

"She remembered the young woman wore a white blouse and maybe jeans, same description we got from the fishing guy."

After hanging up, Steve decided to call James Hartley, the owner of Blaine Cottage. As expected, Hartley had nothing new to add to what he'd already told Steve last Thursday. When Steve asked him why the cleaning team was there so quickly, Hartley said he always books his cleaning team in advance to clean the rental as soon as it's vacated.

Billy was next on Steve's call list. He was on his way downtown to interview Ellis Gordon and Joan Haskins again. Steve said, "I talked to Dale last night. He'll have that list of small airports emailed to me shortly. Did you run background checks on Gordon and Haskins?"

"I asked Robby to take care of that this morning, along with a background check on Hartley. He's also running down the credit card number Emily used for her Avis rental and Heritage Hotel reservation, but no luck so far. It's obviously a fake and won't lead us anywhere."

Steve said, "I just talked to Hartley, nothing worthwhile there, unless his background check shows any red flags. Let me know what you learn from your bank interviews. I'm waiting on the forensics report for Chuck's cabin and John's house, but these people are smart. I doubt our techs will come up with anything."

"What about Chuck's computer?"

"Nothing helpful on his laptop, just mostly his driving schedule. We're still spinning our wheels."

"Something will break our way, Steve. We just need to stay with it."

"You're right, but we're running out of time. By the way, the Chief is all set for his two p.m. press conference today with Hank. Emily's aunt agreed to join them."

Before Billy rang off, he said, "I'll see you in your office when I'm finished the bank interviews. I have to stop by my own office when I'm finished to drop something off to Molly before I head your way."

***

On the Outer Banks, Jamison got a text on Monday morning from Mark. *Will call Wednesday morning, usual time. Important. Confirm if OK.* Jamison confirmed.

Emily started the new week just like she started every day since she was taken captive. Everyone in the house went through the same boring routines, including the armed security guards. Frankie had added steak to the menu, and the meals were about the only thing she looked forward to between reading, exercising, sleeping, and worrying about what would happen to her.

She missed her daily running regimen more than she could imagine. Instead, she was forced to settle for a hard forty-five-minute aerobic exercise routine, once in her room before breakfast, and again on the back porch in the afternoon.

What none of them realized was that it was the calm before the storm. A strong tropical wave had come off the west coast of Africa and was beginning a slow two-week trek across the Atlantic. The tropical system would eventually become a Category 4 hurricane heading in the direction of the Outer Banks.

Hurricane Florence was getting ready to make a house call.

Part Three
End Game

Chapter 44

At ten a.m. on Monday, Steve was on the group text with Dale and Joe Cartwright, all waiting for a text from Dale's undercover at Auto Warehouse.

Five minutes later, a message came through. *No go, trying again eleven a.m.* Someone else must have been around the fax machine, and the undercover would try again in an hour.

At eleven a.m., they all received the message they were waiting for. The two-word text read *Fax sent.* Dale sent a reply. *Message received, standing by.*

Dale then called Steve. "Since our undercover will be nowhere near that fax machine, our team coordinating the wiretap will call me if there's a return fax to the same machine. If the fax number of the sender is from the fax machine in Reardon's office, he's toast."

Two hours later, Joe Cartwright called Steve from the port. "Reardon just sent a text to an unknown number with a Miami area code, no doubt a burner."

"What did it say?"

"Reardon's total message was only a series of eight numbers and a letter, and the numbers don't match the container numbers in the fax Dale's guy sent him. The container number in the fax from Auto Warehouse to Reardon's office was 43654297. The numbers plus a letter that Reardon texted to the unknown number were N68134523. Definitely some kind of code."

"Shit, somehow Reardon knows or suspects something's up. I'll call Dale and let him know."

When Steve relayed Reardon's cryptic text, message, Dale said, "Send me the two sets of numbers. I'll get the FBI Cryptanalysis Unit to see if they can figure it out."

Steve was quickly running out of patience. "What the hell is he up to? Either someone inside tipped him off, or he's not taking any chances and just being cautious. Those numbers Reardon texted had to be to someone in the cartel. We could just bring Reardon in for questioning, but we still need more proof he's the mole. And texting eight numbers is hardly a crime. If the FBI figures it out, we might want to try it again and see if he uses the same code."

"Sorry, Steve. I really thought the sting would work."

"Me too. But Reardon is up to something. We'll still keep him under tight surveillance at the port. Anyway, good work on your end, it was worth a shot."

Dale said, "If we get any info from our undercover that Auto Warehouse is tracking any container ships scheduled to arrive at the Port of Charleston, we're getting a search warrant to tear Auto Warehouse apart. It was no accident that Teddy met Art Winston at that private club in Miami last May. We know Winston and some of his Auto Warehouse people are up to their necks in Camino's distribution network, we just have to prove it."

"What's the security at the warehouse look like?"

"It's tighter than a drum. Our guy can't get close to any files, too many armed security guards all over the warehouse twenty-four seven. About all he can do without giving himself away is just keep his eyes and ears open for anything suspicious."

Agitated and frustrated, Steve said, "Somehow, we've got to find Emily before Teddy's trial starts. We're pretty certain they flew her off Hilton Head with Wilson and Simpson on Tuesday afternoon, but we have no clue where they landed. I'll be in touch."

When he calmed down, Steve called Cartwright back. "We need to beef up the surveillance on Reardon. I don't want him to even take a piss without us knowing where and how long it took. I'd love to just arrest his ass right now and put some pressure on him, but he'd just lawyer up. And we've got nothing to hold him."

Cartwright said, "When he didn't take the bait, I told your two detectives they could take off. This guy may be smart, but he'll eventually screw up."

The week was off to a bad start, and the clock was still ticking.

***

Billy was in the back of the police headquarters conference room on Monday afternoon to watch the two p.m. press conference about Emily's disappearance. Standing on either side of Chief Hartman were Hank Reed and Marie Parker.

Hartman held up the missing persons alert with Emily's picture and profile. "Thank you all for coming. We have copies of this alert in the back for all of you. We're appealing to the public for any information on the whereabouts of Emily Baker, a Mt. Pleasant school teacher, who went missing last Monday. With me here at the podium are Mt. Pleasant Detective Hank Reed and Marie Parker, Miss Baker's aunt."

The Chief paused to look directly into the TV cameras and added, "We've set up a tip hotline at the number on the screen. If anyone has any information that might help us find Miss Baker, please call the hotline. Thank you."

After Hank and Marie added a few words, including a heartfelt appeal from Marie, Hartman said, "I'll take a few questions."

"Chief, who reported Miss Baker missing?"

Hartman looked over at Marie and answered, "Miss Parker here alerted the Mt. Pleasant Police Department last Tuesday after several calls to her niece went unanswered. Detective Reed visited her school and Miss Baker's residence, but no one has seen her since last Sunday. Her car was not at her apartment or the school."

"Do you suspect there was any foul play involved?"

"At this time, we're not able to confirm any details of her disappearance. We're pursuing a number of leads and will continue to follow-up any credible information we receive."

After a few more questions, the press conference ended. Nothing was mentioned about the possibility Emily was kidnapped and being held with Chuck Wilson and John Simpson. And no mention of any link to last year's port murder and the Camino cartel.

When it was over, Billy headed for Steve's office. "How'd it go?" Steve asked.

"About as you'd expect. The Chief didn't provide any details despite the local media pressing him for more information."

Steve waved a file folder. "Dale just emailed me this list of small airports with no radar control towers in North and South Carolina and Georgia. He suggested we initially shorten the list to those airports within a mile or so of the coastline. His thinking is that it would probably be safer to fly over the ocean to a small airport near the coast to minimize being seen, especially if they were flying VFR with their transponder off."

"Makes sense. I'll sift through them to see what airports fit those criteria."

"How'd your bank interviews go?"

Billy said, "Joan Haskins has worked at the bank for ten years and is well-liked by everyone there. She worked her way up from teller to administrative assistant after getting an Associate Accounting Degree online. She's been in charge of the safety deposit boxes for the past two years. She was very friendly, answered all my questions, and didn't appear nervous or hiding anything."

"What about Emily's security box application?"

"She didn't think anything was out of the ordinary. The woman who applied for the box had also requested access for Emily, who she said was her daughter. The woman's ID looked fine. Haskins also mentioned that Ellis Gordon approved the application, which she showed me."

"You think she's involved?"

"I didn't pick up any red flags, at least on the surface. I just don't see her mixed up in this."

"What about Ellis Gordon?" asked Steve.

"Mr. Gordon is another story. According to a senior manager I talked to, he was hired a few months ago with a strong recommendation from, no surprise, a bank in Miami. He told me Gordon runs the bank's personal investment department. Haskins mentioned that Gordon keeps to himself and doesn't socialize with any of the bank's employees, at least as far as she knows."

"Did you talk to Gordon?"

"I did, and he was friendly enough but seemed a bit nervous. He wanted to know what I was looking for. When I told him I was investigating some missing items from a safety deposit box for one of my clients, his eyes shifted away from me for just a second. I got the feeling I'd struck a nerve. The kicker was that he didn't ask me for the name of my client. Before we could discuss it any further, he apologized and said he was late for a client meeting outside the bank. He told me he'd be available to meet with me tomorrow."

"You think he might be the cartel's inside man at the bank?"

"Somebody helped set up those three safety deposit boxes and put in the phony documents. My money's on Gordon."

"Billy, see if Robby has those background checks yet for Haskins, Gordon, and James Hartley, the Blaine Cottage owner. And let's dig deeper into Ellis Gordon. Let me know what you find. I'm going to set up an appointment with Gordon myself, tomorrow."

Steve next called Jill Carrington and left a message to call him back for an update on Teddy's case. He had to find out how much time he had left to find Emily before Jill had to submit her witness list to Teddy's defense team.

Chapter 45

Tuesday, September 4, 2018

After a week in captivity, they still had no idea what the man behind the curtain was waiting for, but they were determined to stay positive.

Their second Tuesday on the Outer Banks was sunny with a high forecasted in the low 80s later in the day. As the three of them sat around their usual end of the dining room table, Emily said, "I'm going to ask Jamison if he would let us to watch thirty minutes of news on the TV in the living room. What do you guys think?"

"Can't hurt," said John. "We've been here for a week and have no clue what's going on in the outside world. But I seriously doubt we've made the national news."

Chuck weighed in and said, "Give it a shot, Emily. Jamison wants us to feel like we're just on vacation, let's see if he means it. What's the harm?"

Before they left the table, Jamison walked by and headed for the front door. Emily stood up and put on the biggest smile she could muster. "Mr. Jamison, excuse me, I'd like to ask you a favor. You told us to let you know if we need anything."

Jamison stopped and turned toward her. "Miss Baker, as I told you, if you have any menu requests, please ask Frankie. He's in charge of the food service."

She responded quickly before he got out the door. "It doesn't have anything do with our meal plan. We were wondering if you would consider allowing us to watch thirty minutes of the news on TV before dinner. We could watch it in the living room, and you could join us or have one of your security team sit with us. Just thirty minutes a day. We haven't given you any trouble since we've been here and would be very grateful."

"I'll think about it," Jamison said tersely and left the house.

"Well, at least he didn't say no," Emily said as they all headed for the back porch. Chuck waved at Sarge, who had backyard guard duty. Sarge didn't wave back.

***

That same morning back in Mt. Pleasant, Steve, Billy, Hank, and Robby were meeting in Chief Hartman's office to organize their next moves in the search. Hartman said, "Steve, let's start with an update on where things stand."

"I talked to Jill Carrington this morning. Teddy Francisco's trial is scheduled to start on Monday, September 24. Jill needs to have her witnesses prepped and ready to go before then. Her final witness list has to be submitted to the defense ahead of the trial, which give us less than three weeks to find Emily."

"What other evidence does she have besides Emily's eyewitness testimony?" asked Hartman.

"Airport surveillance footage shows Teddy arriving at the Charleston airport last year on Friday, August 4th. That puts him in the Charleston area three days before the murder. He was picked up on camera again in the airport on Monday afternoon, August 7th, the day of the murder."

"Carrington have anything else?" asked Billy.

"There's a possible match to Teddy's prints with the partial taken from one of the shell casings that was recovered under Jorge Rodriguez's body. Although the defense will argue it's not conclusive, Carrington feels it's a solid building block for the prosecution's case. There's also a lot of circumstantial evidence linking both Teddy and Jorge to the Camino cartel, including the seizure of the drugs from that container ship at the port on the weekend before the murder. The problem is, without putting Teddy at the port on the morning of the murder, he could still walk on the murder charge."

Hank said, "What about the letter that lured Emily, Chuck, and John to Daufuskie Island? Didn't you tell us the ferry boat captain identified Emily on his ten a.m. trip from the Harbor Town Marina to Daufuskie? And we know she was at the Bank of Charleston the day before. You also confirmed she checked into the Heritage Hotel under an assumed name. All of which seems to prove the authenticity of the letter."

"She told me she would certainly enter the letter into evidence, but there's no hard proof linking Emily's disappearance and the letter to Teddy or the cartel. There's some other evidence, but nothing definitive. We have the surveillance footage of Emily at the port that morning, but no footage clearly showing Teddy's face. Without Emily's identification of the two men on the video, there's no smoking gun. Carrington needs her testimony."

Billy looked at Steve and asked, "Will you be testifying about Emily's positive ID of the two men from the photos you showed her?"

"Those two photos Emily identified will be put into evidence, but my testimony will no doubt be attacked as heresy without Emily's direct testimony. Bottom line, we would still have an outside shot to convict Teddy for the murder without getting Emily on the stand, but it's a longshot, especially going up against his hotshot defense attorney, Louis Franklin."

"Where are we on the missing person's search?" asked Hartman.

"We have two tracks we're running on. We're virtually certain our three kidnap victims were flown off Hilton Head, and we're identifying likely small airports along the coast, starting in the Carolinas and Georgia. Once we get a target list, our plan is to narrow it down with some aerial reconnaissance of the airports on our list that look like good possibilities. We'll also use Google Maps to identify the most isolated airports. We're shooting in the dark, but maybe we get lucky."

"And the other track?"

"We're looking for a link with someone Emily came in contact with in the two days before she fell off the radar at Daufuskie. The best candidate right now is Ellis Gordon, a manager at the Bank of Charleston. We're going to dig deeper into his background and put some pressure on him about the safety deposit boxes. Someone at the bank had to access them to put in those bogus credentials before our missing people emptied them on Monday."

Billy mentioned a third option. "If the FBI can figure out the code that Reardon used in that text he sent to an unknown number, we could send another fax to him from Auto Warehouse and see if he responds with another coded text."

"If the FBI can crack his code that may be worth a shot," Steve said without much enthusiasm.

Hartman gave the group some final marching orders. "Hank will coordinate any tips we get from the hotline and his statewide missing persons alert on Emily. Robby, keep digging into Gordon's background and Emily's bogus credit card. As you all know, the forensic tech guys came up empty at all three residences. No surprise there. Steve, if you need more manpower, just holler."

Steve ended the meeting. "OK everybody, let's get back to it. We're running out of time."

***

The strong tropical wave of heavy showers and thunderstorms that had moved off the west coast of Africa was now organized into a tropical depression near the Cape Verde Islands. Strong thunderstorms were wrapping around a closed low-pressure center and generating high winds and heavy rain squalls. The weather system's labor pains were intensifying as a new tropical storm was being born. Fueled by the warm tropical waters of the Atlantic as its primary energy source, the storm was forecast to continue strengthening into a major hurricane during its thirty-five-hundred-mile journey across the Atlantic to the east coast of the United States.

Chapter 46

Before Jamison left the house on Wednesday for his eleven a.m. call from Mark, he found Emily reading in the library. "Miss Baker, I've decided to turn on the TV in the living room at six p.m. so you and your friends can watch a half hour of news. One of my men will join you. The TV will be disconnected again at six-thirty."

Emily looked up at him with a genuine smile. "Thank you. We still don't know what you want from us, but if you have any questions, we'll be happy to answer them if it will get us home faster."

"Miss Baker, I appreciate the offer, but as I've said, my boss is in charge of the agenda, not me. You'll be informed when the time comes, not before. If you continue to cooperate with my instructions, access to the TV at six p.m. for thirty minutes will also continue, unless and until something changes. Have a nice day."

Earlier that morning, after his usual six a.m. meeting with his security team, Jamison called the boss with his daily update. "Everything normal, sir, no problems. Anything I need to know from your end?"

"Thank you, Mr. Jamison. There's an ongoing situation here that still requires my full attention. For now, sit tight and keep our guests comfortable. You have your orders if there's any trouble."

"Yes sir, understood," said Jamison before the boss, as usual, abruptly ended the call. Jamison was getting more and more anxious to know what was going on in Miami. He was sure that something was definitely off. He hoped his call with Mark would shed some light on things.

At the Duck Diner, he took his usual spot in a back booth and waited. On the third ring at precisely eleven a.m., he answered his burner. Before Mark even had a chance to tell him why he called, Jamison wanted some answers. "Mark, I need to know what's going on with the boss. He keeps telling me he's been dealing with a situation there, and we're still in a holding pattern at this end. I'm in the dark. What's going on?"

"All I know is that he's concerned about Teddy's trial, which was postponed for one week since the prosecution hasn't been able to locate one of their witnesses. The new trial date is September 24. He's convinced the missing witness is one of your three houseguests. As long as they're squirreled away, he doesn't think there'll be a problem."

"Why hasn't he flown up here yet?"

"He's got bigger issues to deal with at the moment. His inside guy at the Port of Charleston texted one of cartel's lieutenants at Auto Warehouse with a mayday message. Seems someone at the warehouse sent a fax to the cartel's mole at the port asking for confirmation of a container shipment this week. But his warehouse people told him they didn't send any fax to the port. He's now concerned the port security people may be on to his inside man. For the time being, he's decided not to use the Port of Charleston for any more shipments from South America."

"What does that have to do with Teddy's trial?"

"If the police arrest his guy in the port security office, he's worried they'll squeeze him for information, especially if he puts Teddy at the port on the day of the murder. If his port guy gets another bogus fax, he's been ordered to disappear."

"Sounds like Auto Warehouse is compromised," said Jamison.

"Now you understand what the boss is dealing with. His distribution pipeline is being disrupted, and Teddy's trial is on the back burner for the time being. As long as any potential witnesses who were seen on the port surveillance tapes aren't available to testify, he's OK to just keep them there on ice with you until he figures out what's going on."

"You think the cops have any idea we're here?"

"Not yet, but they're working on it. The boss asked me to monitor the press coverage of the police investigation into Emily Baker's disappearance. There was a press conference at the local police headquarters in Mt. Pleasant on Monday afternoon, but the news coverage didn't include anything about Wilson or Simpson. If the police know something, they're keeping a very tight lid on it. Except for one thing."

"What's that?" asked Jamison.

"Ellis Gordon said he's been interviewed twice, once by a private investigator and once by a local detective. They both asked Gordon about items missing from a safety deposit box, and he's getting nervous."

Jamison's heart rate accelerated. "How could they possibly know about that?"

"That's what has the boss worried. Trouble is, there's nothing coming out of the Mt. Pleasant Police Department. Whoever is working on Emily's investigation, besides a Detective Hank Reed, who was at the press conference with his police chief, they're not making anything public."

Jamison took a nervous sip of coffee. "This is not good, Mark, we're sitting ducks up here."

"Just stay calm and locked down. And don't panic. I'm working on a plan to get us both out of this mess."

"Have you talked to my father since last Friday?"

"Yes, I've been in contact with him. He and your mother are both fine. He knows you and I have talked, and he said to tell you to hang in there."

"When can I talk to him?"

"Very soon. The plan I'm working on is risky. I need to go over the details with you in person, not over the phone. I have an early flight to Raleigh in the morning and a rental car reserved. I should be on the Outer Banks by tomorrow afternoon. I have a reservation at the Duck Inn for tomorrow night. The boss doesn't know I'm coming. Can you meet me there tomorrow around six p.m.?"

Jamison thought about it and said, "Let's make it seven. Our guests will be eating dinner then, and I'll just tell my guys I'm heading down to Duck for a bite to eat. They know I've eaten there before and won't be suspicious."

"See you at seven p.m. tomorrow," said Mark.

"Text my burner when you arrive at the motel. What name are you using for your room reservation?"

"Davis Walters."

***

Wednesday afternoon, Dale called Steve. "The FBI Cryptanalysis team thinks they've cracked Reardon's code."

"Tell me."

"The number of the container we faxed to Reardon from the warehouse was 43654297. His text numbers were N68134523. He changed each number to one number less and then reversed the order of the numbers. We suspect the letter N was a warning to whoever he texted, even though he couldn't have known whether the fax came from the cartel or someone else. We think he was alerting the cartel that someone may be on to him."

Steve said, "If we try sending another text to him from the warehouse, he might just bolt. For now, we'll just continue keeping a tight watch on him."

"One other thing, Steve. We tracked the burner number he texted to a phone bought in Miami from a small drug store. The manager told us he sells lots of them, and over half are paid for in cash. No doubt that burner is long gone."

Steve told him, "By the way, we're narrowing down that list of small airports you sent us. Not sure if that will get us anywhere, but we're turning over every rock we can think of. If they're still alive, our hope is they're safe and just being kept hidden until after Teddy's trial."

"Assume they're alive. Just hang in there, Steve. We're still working on a search warrant for Auto Warehouse. Even though our sting operation was a bust, we're hoping it will help convince a judge that the cartel is using the warehouse to direct international drug shipments into the country."

Steve was still running into brick walls, and the walls were still winning.

Chapter 47

Steve got to the office on Thursday before seven a.m. Sleep was a luxury he couldn't afford these days. He began reviewing the airport list again when he got a call from Billy. "Hey boss man, you're in a little early, aren't you? I just talked to Molly, and she said you left the house at six-thirty this morning. What's the plan for the day?"

"I'm just going over these airport lists. When the Bank of Charleston opens, I'm going to make an appointment to see Ellis Gordon again. And I need to call Dale this morning to find out when he expects to get his search warrant for Auto Warehouse. I'm also thinking about seeing Jerry Reardon at the port for a friendly chat. We can't keep waiting around. We need to make something happen and shake things up before we run out of time."

"How can I help?" asked Billy.

"Hang tight for the moment. I'll call you when I have something."

Steve called the Bank of Charleston shortly after nine a.m. A pleasant receptionist said, "Good morning, how may I assist you?"

"Ellis Gordon, please."

"I'm sorry, sir. Mr. Gordon no longer works for the bank. Is there someone else who can help you?"

"Why did he leave?"

"I don't know, sir, you'll have to talk to one of the other bank managers about that."

Steve was no closer to finding Emily than when he learned she was missing. Dale was still waiting for his search warrant, and it was Jerry Reardon's day off. The search for Emily was at a standstill. After cleaning up some paperwork from another case, he decided to head home for an early dinner with Janet and start fresh in the morning.

***

On Thursday evening at the beach house, the cable to the TV in the living room was disconnected at six-thirty after Jamison watched the six p.m. newscast with them. As expected, there was nothing about any of them being missing. With several thousand people reported missing in the US alone each year, Jamison knew very few cases ever made the network news, unless the missing person or their family had some kind of celebrity status or went viral on the internet. A missing schoolteacher, truck driver, and dock worker hardly qualified, unless the media discovered all three of them were kidnapped together by a Miami drug cartel.

A few clouds began drifting over the house from the ocean when Jamison headed out the door soon after the newscast for the short drive to the Duck Inn. He'd gotten a text on his burner a little past six p.m. telling him Mark had arrived at the motel and would see him at seven.

The Duck Inn was a small but popular two-story motel used mostly by tourists and visitors to the Outer Banks all year round. When Jamison entered the lobby, he was greeted by a friendly receptionist behind a dark brown reservation counter. A large reproduction print of sand dunes sprinkled with wild sea oats hung on the wall behind her.

"Welcome to the Duck Inn. How may I help you, sir?"

"Would you mind calling Mr. Walters to let him know Jamison is here to see him?"

"Certainly, sir, I'll be happy to." After calling his room, she said, "Mr. Walters is expecting you in Room 214. The elevator and stairs are on your right."

Jamison took the stairs and knocked on Mark's door. They shook hands and Jamison stepped inside. Mark said, "Good to see you, Jamison. Assume everything at the house is normal? I ordered some coffee from room service, help yourself."

"Thanks for coming, Mark. The house is quiet, and the guests have been cooperative since we all arrived, although the boredom has become tedious for all of us. After our last conversation, I'm anxious to catch up and find out more about what's going on. By the way, clever fake name."

"Sorry for all the cloak and dagger. Things are happening in Miami, and I'm getting mixed signals. The boss is pissed off and has become paranoid

207

someone in his organization is working with the cops. I didn't want to take any chance of him finding out about the plan I've put together."

"You told me his distribution network has been compromised," said Jamison.

"It's worse than that. Besides the security issue at the port I told you about, the boss is convinced one of his people must have tipped off the police about the safety deposit boxes. I told him our surveillance cameras in their hotel rooms on Hilton Head confirmed all three letters were torn up and flushed away. I even emailed him copies of the videos. The boss also decided Ellis Gordon has now become a liability. Yesterday he ordered Gordon to get out of Charleston."

"Does he think you or me are working with the police?"

"Right now, he's suspicious of the entire team, including us, at least until he figures out how the cops found out about the safety deposit boxes."

"What's this plan you mentioned?"

Mark pulled out a satellite phone from his briefcase. "Before we get to that, there's another reason I came up here to meet with you. I've set up an encrypted link to call your father on this satellite phone. You ready to talk to him?"

"Now?"

"Yes, right now. I told him yesterday I was coming up here to meet with you and would be calling him tonight around seven-thirty to talk to you."

Jamison's thoughts were suddenly jumbled. "Give me a minute. It's been over two years. I need to think about what I want to say to him. How much time do we have to talk?"

"The link I've set up on this phone is secure. Just tell him you've missed him and your mom. He just wants to hear your voice and make sure you're doing OK."

Mark put the call through and handed the phone to Jamison. When a man's voice answered, questions started tumbling out from Jamison, "Dad, is that you? Are you alright? How's Mom? Where are you? What happened to the boat?"

Before Jamison could continue, Harrison Walters interrupted him. "Slow down, son. I can't tell you how good it is to hear your voice. Your mother and I are fine. Mark told me he explained how we survived the explosion on the boat. We were just lucky we weren't far from the Bahamas and managed to hitch a ride with a fishing boat to the coastline. We now have proof my boss, and now also yours, was behind it, thanks to my good friend, Jake Thomas. He assured me Mark could be trusted."

Jamison became emotional and started tearing up. "Dad, we've got to get you and Mom back home. I need to see you. I'm so sorry about what happened. I had no idea my boss was behind it. I didn't realize who he was until it was too late. He told me he was the majority owner of Walters International. I didn't know he was also head of the Camino drug cartel when he hired me. And you can't just walk away from these people once you start working for them. But you already know that."

Wishing he could take back those last words, Jamison wiped his eyes and quickly said, "Sorry Dad, I didn't mean that."

"It's OK, Jamie. You're right. I've made a lot of mistakes in my life, but the biggest was agreeing to join his organization. I knew it was wrong, but I was too weak to resist the temptation of all the money he was offering me. I've regretted that decision ever since, but like you said, once you're in, you're in. When Jake told me you were working for the cartel, I was angry and heartbroken. Not with you, with the boss. And myself."

"Don't blame yourself, Dad. It was my decision. But why did he try to get rid of you?"

"A couple months before your mother and I took that sailing trip, there was a problem with a shipment from Mexico City to Miami, and the shipment was lost. The boss blamed me, even though I had no idea what happened. Turned out some guy named Manny Rodriguez, who I'd never met but was on my payroll, fouled up some paperwork, and the shipment disappeared. The boss chewed me out and threatened to clean house if I didn't get rid of this guy. So, I fired Manny and thought that was the end of it. Until the boss had my boat blown up."

"We're going to figure something out to get you home. Mark told me he has a plan."

"Mark shared it with me, and it just might work. But it's very risky. I would never forgive myself if something happened to you."

"Please don't worry, Dad, I'll be fine, and I trust Mark. Is Mom there? Can I talk to her?"

Charlotte Walters took the phone from her husband and said, "Jamie, are you OK? I've missed you more than you'll ever know. Your father and I have been talking to Mark, and he says he has a way for us to finally get back home. We're tired of hiding and looking over our shoulders every day. We miss you, but we don't want to put you in danger."

"Mom, I promise I'll do whatever it takes to get you back home safe."

When Jamison choked up, his mother said, "Jamie, I know you will. Just be careful. The man you're working for tried to kill us, and he won't hesitate to try it again if he finds out we're still alive. You were always the smartest person in the room, just don't take any unnecessary chances. We love you."

Mark took the phone. "Mrs. Walters, please put Mr. Walters back on the line, thank you."

Harrison Walters got back on, and Mark finished the call. "Sir, I'll be in touch when we're ready to make our move. Meantime, sit tight and stay safe."

Jamison was emotionally drained and buried his face in his hands. His parents were alive but still in danger. When he collected himself, he said to Mark, "Tell me about your plan."

Chapter 48

Friday, September 7, 2018

Steve left his house early again on Friday morning to meet Billy for breakfast at his favorite local diner on Coleman Blvd., which was right on the way to police headquarters from his house in the Old Village.

Sleep had become increasingly elusive as he struggled to come up with his next move. He was tired and frustrated with more dead ends. Billy had also been burning the candle at both ends all week to juggle his own cases and help with the search to find Emily, Chuck, and his client Mandy Simpson's husband John.

When Billy walked into the diner, Steve was already on his second cup of coffee and waved him over. "You look like shit," he said as Billy sat across from him in one of the diner's tiny booths. Other than a few early birds stopping in for their morning coffee fix to go, the diner was nearly empty.

Billy greeted Steve with tired eyes and a smile. "You don't look so hot yourself. Reminds me of our army basic training days when we'd be leaving the mess hall about now for another day of fun and games. By the way, I talked to John's wife Mandy yesterday afternoon and told her to hang in there. I didn't share with her that John is likely with Emily, the missing schoolteacher seen on the news, and Chuck Wilson, a man Mandy would never have even heard of."

Steve said, "Hank told me he talks to Emily's aunt every day, and I called Chuck's friend George Cooper yesterday. I just wish we had some better news for these people. They're all scared and dreading the worst."

After the waitress refilled their cups, Steve glanced out the window, gathering his thoughts. He turned back to Billy and said, "I tried to set up an appointment with Ellis Gordon at the Bank of Charleston yesterday afternoon and was told Mr. Gordon has left the bank."

"You mean left as in quit?"

"The receptionist wouldn't say, but I'm assuming it was his decision, probably on orders from Camino. I'll try to get a forwarding address from the bank's senior manager, but I doubt Gordon left a real one. The FBI now has a BOLO out to question him about Emily's disappearance, but my guess is he's long gone with fake creds from the cartel. I should've brought him in earlier. We can't seem to catch a break."

"Not your fault, Steve. I'm not sure Gordon even knows where Emily and the others were taken. I think only a few people are in the loop with all the details, including where they're being held."

Steve said, "I'm going to the port this morning to meet with Joe and have a chat with our friend Mr. Reardon. He's up to his neck with the cartel, I can smell it. I'm going to rattle his cage and see if I can pressure him into saying or doing something stupid. I want him to know we're on to him and see what he does."

"Can't hurt. Want me to come with?" asked Billy.

"No, you've got enough on your plate. Right now, I'm just grabbing at straws, no sense wasting both our time. We pretty much know what happened, thanks to the letter Emily cleverly left for us to find. We know our three missing people were likely flown off of Hilton Head on Tuesday. We're also pretty sure they were taken out of circulation so none of them could testify at Teddy's upcoming murder trial. We just have no idea where the hell they are."

"Look partner, we've come a long way in the past week. We just need to stay with it. Let me know how you do with Reardon."

"What about that airport list, any progress?"

Billy said, "I went over the list again last night and narrowed it down to five isolated airports along the coast, all private with no control towers. I'm going to talk to a buddy of mine to see if we can borrow a helicopter and fly over each one. If the areas around any of those airports look like good places to hide people, we might want to consider having the Chief call the local cops near each airport. Maybe they'd agree to patrol a mile or two radius around their local airport for anything suspicious or out of place."

"Good idea. It's another long shot, but let's keep pushing until the clock runs out."

Billy headed downtown when they left the diner, and Steve drove to his office. He swiped his key card and entered the lobby of the Mt. Pleasant Police

Department. He was greeted by Tiny, a six-foot, seven-inch overnight security guard who was ready to go off shift.

Francis 'Tiny' Tilden had been a second-team All-American defensive tackle in his playing days at the University of South Carolina. Graduation was now twelve years in his rearview mirror, but he still looked like he could manhandle the usual offensive line double-team he got to slow down his powerful bull rush toward the opposing quarterback.

Tiny said, "Hi Steve. If they're paying you overtime, you should have enough by now to buy a beach house on Isle of Palms."

"Morning Tiny, I've definitely had a few irons in the fire lately. Is the Chief here?"

"Haven't seen him yet. Robby got here around seven, and Hank came in about fifteen minutes ago. Y'all workin' that missing schoolteacher case?"

Steve laughed and said, "Tiny, you don't miss much. When you're ready for the detective's exam, let me know. I'll put in a good word for you with the Chief."

When Steve got to his office, he called Joe Cartwright on his direct line at the port security office. He picked up right away. "Cartwright here."

"Joe, it's Steve. Whatever happened to nine to five? Glad I caught you."

"In your dreams, buddy. What's up?"

"I'm worried Jerry Reardon may be on to us. I'd like to meet him in his office and ask him a few questions. What would be a good time for you?"

"Jerry called in on his day off yesterday and said he wasn't feeling well and wouldn't be in today. You could be right, and he got spooked. How about we pay him a visit at his home this morning? He lives by himself in the Madison Apartments complex in North Charleston. I can meet you there in an hour. Here's the address."

Steve scribbled it down in his notebook. "I'll meet you there at nine. What's he drive?"

"A white Chevy Tahoe. See you there."

When they met at Reardon's apartment, the doorbell and several knocks brought no one to the door. Steve said, "You hang here while I check the parking lot for his Tahoe."

Fifteen minutes later, Steve returned. "No Tahoe in the parking lot, looks like the asshole may have already done a runner."

At ten a.m. on Friday, Jamison found Emily and John reading in the library room. Chuck was in his favorite lounge chair on the back porch, killing time before lunch was served at one. Chuck was never a big reader. Of the three of them, he had the most trouble dealing with the boredom.

Emily was momentarily startled when Jamison said, "Miss Baker, please come with me to my office for a few minutes."

She'd never been in the converted downstairs bedroom that had become Jamison's office. She looked over at John for some reassurance that it was OK to meet privately with Jamison. John gave her an affirmative nod, and she reluctantly got up from her chair and followed him.

Jamison unlocked the door and said in an even voice, "Please come in and take a seat."

He flicked on the light switch. Two free-standing lamps in opposite corners came on and lit the room in soft light. Jamison sat down behind a mahogany desk in the far corner with his back to the wall facing the door. On top of the desk were two computer monitors, a desk lamp, a satellite phone, and a yellow notepad. A leather briefcase was next to the desk. There was also a large TV screen mounted on the wall facing the desk.

"Miss Baker, before we start, would you like something to drink, perhaps some coffee or tea?"

"No thanks, I'm fine," she said nervously. None of them had spoken privately to Jamison since they'd arrived on Tuesday. Emily now wondered if he was finally going to ask her about the men she saw arguing at the port last year. She decided to let him lead the conversation.

"Miss Baker, I'm about to explain what the three of you are doing here. Some information has recently come to my attention that has prompted me to take all of you into my confidence. I don't expect you to suddenly become my friend, but hear me out. What I'm about to tell you could get us both killed if it leaves this room. Do you understand?"

Emily was too shocked and frightened to say anything and just shook her head up and down.

Before he continued, she managed to say, "May I have a bottle of water, please?"

Jamison tapped an intercom button on the side of the desk. A voice came back from the kitchen over a speaker recessed in the wall. "Yes sir."

"Frankie, please bring two bottles of water to my office."

"Right away, sir."

After he put the water bottles on the desk and left the office, Emily took one and quickly drank half of it. When she put the bottle back on the desk, her hand was shaking.

Jamison said, "Miss Baker, I'm sorry this conversation is making you nervous, but it can't be helped. Just listen carefully. I'm going to tell you how you and your friends might get out of here in one piece. After we finish, I'll also have the same talk separately with Mr. Simpson and Mr. Wilson. Until I do, do not discuss with them what I'm about to tell you."

He took a drink of water and added, "A friendly word of warning. If any of my men overhears the three of you discussing what I'm going to share with each of you, none of us will leave this house alive. Do you understand?"

"Yes."

***

At eleven a.m. that same Friday, Marie Parker, Mandy Simpson, and George Cooper each got a short text on their cell phones from an unknown number that belonged to Mark Davis. Marie was reading a book in her living room when her cell phone pinged with the text message.

After she read it, she leaned back in her chair and closed her eyes. Her heart started racing and her hands began to tremble. Her phone slipped out of her hand and dropped to the floor.

The text said *Emily is safe. More later.*

215

Chapter 49

The Caribbean Island of Anguilla is the most northerly of the Leeward Islands in the Lesser Antilles, situated twelve miles north of Saint Martin and sixty miles northwest of Saint Kitts.

For the past three months, it had also been the latest home base of Harrison and Charlotte Walters. Their modest rental was tucked away in a remote section of the island, inhabited mostly by locals who worked in the island's hospitality industry.

At nine a.m. on Friday, Mark called Walters on his secure encrypted phone link.

"Mr. Walters, Mark here. Hope all is well on your end. Jamison and I have reviewed the final details of the plan I discussed with you, and we're ready to put things in motion. Your friend Jake Thomas is also up to speed and on board."

"Hi Mark, we're fine. Charlotte and I have gone over everything again, and we're both ready to move forward. What's the next step?"

"This afternoon, Jamison is going to share the basic outline of the plan with Emily Baker and the other two captives on the Outer Banks. You should be proud of your son, Mr. Walters. He's willing to take whatever risks are necessary to help get you and your wife back to the United States in one piece."

"Keep him safe, Mark. The cartel won't hesitate to take you both out if they get wind of what you're planning to do. Once you start, there will be no turning back. Are you sure it will work?"

"I'm betting my life on it. And I have no doubt Jamison will hold his nerve and see it through. As you already know, your son is a very smart guy, and I'm absolutely confident we can pull this off. For now, stay put and keep your head down."

"No worries. Charlotte and I have learned how to blend in with the locals on these islands for the past two years. We're not about to do anything to draw attention to ourselves now. Please keep us informed."

"Yes sir, I will."

Time for step one. At eleven a.m., Mark sent his short text to Marie, Mandy, and George.

***

As they were walking away from Reardon's apartment empty-handed late Friday morning, Steve called Cartwright at the port for the plate number for Reardon's Tahoe. When he had the number ten minutes later, Steve called Robby to put out an immediate BOLO on Reardon as a person of interest in the disappearance of Emily Baker. He also told him to call the Charleston airport's security office to check if Reardon was listed on any outgoing flight manifests as of yesterday.

Steve then called Hartman to request twenty-four seven surveillance on Reardon's apartment as soon as possible. When he arrived back at police headquarters just before noon, he stopped by Hartman's office to give him a full update.

"Chief, looks like Jerry Reardon has done a runner. I had Robby put out a BOLO on him, but we're probably too late if he decided to leave town yesterday. First Ellis Gordon and now Reardon. Looks like both of them decided to make a dash for the exits, or were told to, no doubt with the cartel's help. Whoever is running the show on their end is definitely getting antsy."

"What's our next step?"

Before Steve could answer, Hank Reed barged into Hartman's office without knocking. "I just got a call from Marie Parker. A few minutes ago, she got a short text about Emily from a blocked number. All it said was *Emily is safe. More later.* She's frightened and asked me what she should do."

Steve let the news sink in for few beats. "Hank, tell her we need to borrow her phone and take her a new pre-paid cell she can use until our tech guys can check hers out. Marie's number was never released to the media, and it seems unlikely one of Marie's friends, or even Richard, would intentionally give her any false hope. Whoever sent her that text may have some information about Emily's whereabouts."

Hartman said, "Could still be a hoax."

Steve was running through the possibilities in his mind, trying to make sense of what was going on. He finally said, "It could be nothing, but to what end? Whoever sent that text had to know Marie would call us. Maybe the message was actually meant for us."

Steve's cell suddenly vibrated with another call, and he said, "Excuse me a minute, it's Billy."

Billy said, "Steve, I just got a call from Mandy."

"Did she get a text saying *John is safe. More later*?"

Billy was confused and asked, "How in the hell did you know that?"

Steve explained, "Because Marie Parker just got the same text about Emily. Let me call you back. I need to call George Cooper and see if he got the same text about Chuck."

Steve got Cooper on his cell and said, "George, this is Detective Harris. Did you happen to just get a text about Chuck?"

"Yes, I was just about to call you. All it said was *Chuck is safe. More later*. How'd you know I got a text? What's going on, Detective?"

"We don't know yet, we're trying to figure that out. Sit tight and call me if you get any more texts about Chuck. I'll call you back when we know more."

Hank had already left Hartman's office and was heading to Marie Parker's house when Steve finished his call with George. He said to Hartman, "Something's going down, Chief. I think someone inside the cartel is reaching out to us. I'm not sure why, but if it's one of the kidnappers who sent those texts, we may be in business. I'm guessing they got the cell numbers for Marie, Mandy, and George Cooper from each of them."

Hartman said, "Maybe the three of them were forced to give the numbers to one of the kidnappers. That would mean they're still alive. But until someone contacts us, there's not much we can do right now one way or the other. If they want us to know they're in control, message received."

"This could be the break we've been hoping for, Chief. There was no reason to send those texts unless the kidnappers want something from us. Let's keep this to ourselves until we find out what's going on."

***

By Friday evening, Hurricane Florence had already reached major hurricane status earlier in the week before strong wind shear briefly weakened her back to tropical storm strength. Now in more favorable conditions, the storm was re-intensifying again and still heading for the United States coastline.

Chapter 50

Saturday, September 8, 2018

After his meeting with Jamison and their call to his parents, Mark drove from the Outer Banks on Friday morning to Raleigh and boarded a private plane to Miami. During the flight, he went over the plan in his head that he had discussed with Jamison. He was ready to set the wheels in motion the next day.

At seven a.m. on Saturday, Mark made the short drive from his Miami condo to his secluded private office. He punched a series of numbers into a keypad next to a heavy steel door and entered a secure and windowless room that housed an extensive array of high-tech encrypted communications equipment.

The temperature-controlled room was dominated by an oversized desk covered with electronic gear, six computer monitors, an oddly shaped desk phone connected to a black box, and an encrypted satellite phone. Shortly after he was hired by the boss over seven years ago, Mark personally installed the entire wiring system for the office to eliminate any digital footprint.

A fully equipped kitchen was situated in one back corner of the room, and an enclosed bathroom with a shower and linen closet was built into the opposite corner. The sparsely furnished space also included a sofa bed with a side table and lamp, coffee table, a four-drawer vertical dresser, and a small dining table with two chairs, just off the kitchen. The entire office was triple soundproofed, including the reinforced dark gray walls, ceiling, and floor.

Mark made some coffee, sat down at the desk, and powered up his sophisticated electronics system, along with the untraceable phone setup he had also designed himself. He called Jamison's burner.

Jamison asked in quiet voice, "Is everything still on track?"

"Are you alone?"

"I'm sitting on the back porch and out of earshot of our security man posted in the backyard. Everything is normal. I've now talked to all three of our guests separately and outlined what's about to go down."

"How did they react?" asked Mark.

"About as expected. Emily was especially nervous. I'm sure they're all skeptical, especially of me. But given the position they're in, they don't have much choice except to let things play out."

"OK, good. Just keep a close eye on them. We can't risk any of the security guys getting suspicious. I'm about to start the clock. Call the boss with your daily update as usual and let me know if he's made any plans yet to fly there to question your guests in person."

"Will do. Good luck with your call to Mt. Pleasant."

***

Mark called the Mt. Pleasant Police Department at eight a.m. and was connected to the duty officer, Sergeant Lynn Demarco.

"Mt. Pleasant Police Department, how may I help you?"

"I have some information about the missing schoolteacher and would like to leave a message for the detective leading the investigation," said Mark in his best impersonation of a helpful citizen.

"May I have your name, sir?"

"I need to talk directly to the detective in charge as soon as possible. Please tell him that Mr. Marks called and knows where Emily Baker is being held. Give him the message and tell him it's urgent that he call me at this number in the next hour."

Mark gave her an encrypted cell number and hung up to wait for a callback.

Demarco immediately called Steve's cell phone and got him at home, just as he was sitting down with Janet for breakfast. She said, "Detective Harris, this is Sergeant Demarco, the duty officer this morning. Sorry to bother you on a Saturday morning, but we just got a call at the station from a Mr. Marks. He said he has information about Emily Baker and insisted the lead detective call him back in the next hour."

This is it, Steve thought to himself. "Thanks Sergeant, no problem. What exactly did he say?"

Demarco relayed the message and gave Steve the phone number.

She added, "Before I could get any more information, he hung up. The man didn't sound like a crackpot, so I thought you should know right away in case the caller was on the level."

"You did the right thing, Sergeant. I'll take it from here."

Steve called Hartman and reviewed the message. "Chief, this is the break we've been waiting for, I can feel it. I'd like to record my call back to this guy and have you listen in. Any chance you can meet me in your office in the next half hour or so? I need to call him back by nine."

Hartman said, "I'll be there in twenty minutes. We can record the call from my office."

Steve disconnected and said to Janet, "I need to hurry into to the office right away. Some guy called in and said he has information about Emily. I need to call him back from the office by nine."

"What did he say?"

"He told the duty officer he knew where Emily was and said I needed to call him back in one hour. Hartman is meeting me there so we can record it. Might be nothing, but I think someone from inside the Camino cartel is reaching out to us."

"Hon, you get dressed and I'll box up your breakfast and fill your coffee mug."

"We've been chasing shadows for so long, I just hope this guy is real. I'll call you when I find out what's going on."

Fifteen minutes later, Steve was on his short commute to police headquarters. He got to the Chief's office at eight forty-five, a few minutes after Hartman arrived, and shut the door behind him.

"Morning Steve, the equipment is all set to record. You can make the call on my desk phone."

"The area code is 850, which is Tallahassee. Doesn't tell us much since he could be calling us from anywhere. We know these guys are using high-tech communications gear, no doubt encrypted, so we're not going to trace it."

"How do you want to handle the call?" asked Hartman.

"I'm basically going to let him talk and tell us what he wants. If he starts making any demands, I'll ask him for proof of life. Let's play it by ear, so feel free to jump in with any questions. Main thing is not to spook him. We need to keep him talking and get as much information as we can."

"We're ready to record, let's do it."

Chapter 51

Saturday, September 8, 2018

At eight fifty-eight a.m., two minutes before the one-hour deadline set by the mystery man calling himself Mr. Marks, Steve punched in the number on the Chief's desk phone, which was already in speaker mode.

Mark Davis looked at the caller ID on his encrypted four-line phone and smiled. He picked up the receiver on the third ring.

"Who am I speaking to?" asked Mark.

"This is Mt. Pleasant Detective Steve Harris and Chief of Police Jon Hartman. Who are we speaking to?"

"For the time being, you can call me Mr. Marks. And don't bother trying to trace this call. I'm sure you've already guessed that would be a waste of time."

"Mr. Marks, your message said you had some information about Emily Baker. We're all ears."

"Not so fast, Detective Harris. Before we go any further, I'm sure you'd like to have some proof that I'm not some crazy with a bogus tip."

"That would certainly be helpful, what do you have in mind?" asked Steve.

"Give me your cell number and I'll text you a photo that I think will be of interest to you."

A few seconds after Steve gave him his cell number, a photo popped up. It was a group picture of Emily, Chuck, and John. Steve showed it to the Chief and gave him a thumbs up.

"You have our attention," said Steve. "How do we know when that photo was taken?"

"The photo was taken yesterday, and depending on how this phone call goes, I'll let you talk to Miss Baker yourself. Does that work for you?"

"This is Chief Hartman. What do you want, Mr. Marks?"

"Before I get to that, let me tell you what I can do for you. I was hired by the boss of the Camino cartel's Miami organization several years ago to handle, shall we say, various electronic surveillance activities. I know that a year ago Jorge Rodriguez, a low-level cartel operative, was murdered in front of your Port of Charleston. And last May, Teddy Francisco, a senior member of the Camino cartel, was arrested in Miami and charged with the murder."

"You were about to tell us what you could do for us," interrupted Steve.

"Patience, Detective. What I also know is that surveillance tapes from the morning of the murder were stolen from the port's security office by a cartel inside man. That same man tipped off the cartel about a large shipment of cocaine from South America. As you know, that same shipment was seized at your port a few days before the murder."

After a short pause, waiting for a reaction, Mark asked, "How am I doing so far?"

Steve looked at the Chief and said, "Keep going, Mr. Marks."

"Gentlemen, we both know that Mr. Francisco's trial is scheduled to start soon, despite the one-week delay your prosecutor was able to get based on her assertion that she needed more time to locate a missing witness. After reviewing the stolen surveillance tapes, my boss suspects that witness is one of our three guests who were seen on the tapes around the main entrance to the port just before the murder went down. He thinks one or all three of them may have seen the killer and Mr. Rodriguez together."

Steve took a chance. "Mr. Marks, so far, you've told us nothing new. We already know our three missing persons were lured to Daufuskie Island on Monday, August 27, and were flown off Hilton Head Island the following day. What we don't know yet is where the plane landed and where you're holding them, but we're getting close. How are *we* doing so far?"

"Very impressive, Detective Harris. So let me make one thing clear. I'm not talking to you as a representative of the cartel to negotiate the release of your friends. I'm calling you without the cartel's knowledge to make you an offer that I hope you'll take seriously. Trust me when I tell you my boss has no intention of releasing your friends in one piece."

Steve switched gears. "A letter was delivered to our three missing persons before they were kidnapped. What were the initials on the back of the envelope the letter came in?"

"I must say you guys have been busy. The script letters were **WSB**. They stand for Wilson, Simpson, and Baker."

Steve looked at the Chief, who held up his hand and signaled to Steve he wanted to speak. He said, "Very clever, Mr. Marks. Now tell us what you want."

"Before I do that, there's one more thing you need to hear that you know nothing about. My cartel friend, who has been with your three missing friends since they were taken, is the personal assistant of the Camino cartel's boss of the Miami operation."

"What's his name?"

"The boss or my cartel friend?" asked Mark.

"Both."

"Tell you what. I'll give you both names after I tell you one more true story."

Hartman was losing his patience. "It's your show, Mr. Marks."

Mark began telling them the Cliff Notes version of Harrison and Charlotte Walters' disappearance. "My cartel friend's father used to run Walters International, a large logistics company based in Miami. Through his company, he also did some work for the Camino cartel, who have controlling interest in the company. Two years ago, while his son was about to start his senior year at Yale, his father's luxury sailboat was sabotaged and exploded while he was sailing from Miami to the Bahamas on a pleasure trip with his wife."

"Were his parents killed?"

"That was the plan on orders from my boss, which I can prove. I only found out last week that they survived. My friend also had no idea his parents were still alive until recently. Since the explosion, his parents have been secretly moving around the Caribbean islands every few months."

"A fascinating story, Mr. Marks. Now one more time, tell us what you want," demanded Steve.

"I assume you're recording all of this. If not, listen carefully. I want full immunity from any prosecution, in writing from a U.S. Attorney, for me, my friend and both his parents. I also want federal witness protection available for all four us. In exchange, I will work with you to arrange the safe return of our three captives unharmed." Mark then spelled out his encrypted email address.

Hartman asked, "Anything else? What do we get besides the return of your kidnap victims?"

"My friend and I will testify in court that the head of the Camino cartel in Miami ordered the kidnapping, including the initial draft of the letter you somehow managed to find. My friend's father will also testify in court that same man was responsible for the attempted murder of him and his wife."

"And just how do you propose to accomplish all that?"

"Before we go any further, I'll need the immunity agreements by six p.m. today. Sorry for the rush, but time is of the essence. My boss is planning to visit your friends next week on Tuesday, and it will not end well for them if they're still where we have them hidden. If the boss or his three-man armed security team get wind of this conversation, my friend and I will also be in jeopardy. Just so you understand the risk we're both taking and the urgent need for absolute compliance with our demands."

"You said you'd give us some names so we can check out your story. What are they?" asked Hartman.

"My friend's parents are Harrison and Charlotte Walters. There was plenty of news coverage when they went missing in 2016. Their son's name is my friend Jamison Walters. He graduated from Yale in 2017."

"What's your name?"

"Mark Davis. I have a criminal record for computer hacking and attempted fraud prior to being hired by the boss of the Camino cartel in Miami the day I was released from Miami Dade Correctional in 2011. That should give you enough information to discreetly check out what I've told you."

"OK Mark, you said we could talk to Emily. How do we reach her?" asked Steve.

"I'll have her call your cell phone in one hour. That will give you time to start checking out what I've told you. As soon as I have the signed immunity agreements later today, I'll tell you what happens next. The sooner the better, the clock is ticking. And if you screw with me, you'll never see Emily Baker, Chuck Wilson, or John Simpson again. Do we have a deal?"

"If what you told us checks out *and* we hear from Emily, we have a deal. Why are you doing this?"

"When I learned a few days ago that our boss ordered the sabotage of Harrison and Charlotte's sailboat in an attempt to have them killed, I told Jamison. He agreed with me it was time to get out. The boss told us the three captives would not be harmed, but we've still not been told how, when, or even if, they'll be released unharmed, which we now doubt. Jamison and I both decided to roll the dice with you before putting the lives of three innocent people we now believe are at serious risk when the boss gets here on Tuesday."

"One last question. How can we find your boss?"

"Not to worry, Detective. I expect him to be in court very soon."

"What's his name?"

"Joseph Camino."

Chapter 52

Immediately after the call ended, Steve was jacked and got things moving.

"Chief, we'll need an MP3 audio file attachment of that entire phone call as soon as possible. I want to email it right away to Dale. He and his DEA team should be able to verify most of the information Mark gave us faster from his end. If the information checks out and we get a call from Emily, we need to find out how fast we can get those immunity agreements. And we need Hank, Robby, and Billy in here pronto."

The Chief said, "I'll get the MP3 recording from Harry, who set up the recording equipment. Shouldn't take him very long. I'll also call Hank, Robby, and Billy. While we're waiting for the audio file of the call, see if you can reach Jill Carrington on her cell and tell her what's going on. Send her the recording and tell her we may have found Emily Baker."

"Chief. I'll be in my office. Ask Billy to see me as soon as he gets here."

Steve called the County Prosecutor and filled her in on what was happening. "Jill, I'm expecting a call from Emily shortly. I'll explain everything later. In the meantime, listen to the recording of a phone call we just had with a Mark Davis. I'm emailing it to you in a few minutes, and I'd like to get your take on it. I'll call you back as soon as I can. And please don't discuss any of this with anyone. Emily's life is on the line. We need to keep the circle tight."

"I understand Steve, no problem. Thanks for the heads up."

Ten minutes later, Steve emailed the phone call recording from Harry to Dale and Jill, then called Dale. He cut to the chase. "Dale, sorry to interrupt your Saturday. We have a situation and need your help."

"Sounds urgent, what's up?"

"I've just emailed you a recording of a phone call the Chief and I had a few minutes ago with a man who says his name is Mark Davis and knows where our three kidnap victims are being held. He also claims to be working for the head of the Camino cartel's Miami boss, who he named as Joseph Camino. Davis told us he and a guy named Jamison Walters, a close friend of his who also works for Camino, can help us get our people back, and also help us take down their boss. Davis said his friend Jamison is Joseph Camino's personal assistant. I'm hoping you can verify what Davis told us on the call."

Dale pulled over and practically shouted into the phone. "Did you just say this guy Davis works for Joseph Camino and his friend is Camino's personal assistant? Did I hear that right?"

"That's what he claims. We just need to verify his info and play this out very carefully. Use only guys you can trust one hundred percent. We need to keep this in-house until we sort it out. Davis told me he'd have Emily call me within the hour. I'll call you back after I talk to her."

Dale pulled back onto the street and said in a rush, "I was driving to meet an informant on another case, but that can wait. I'm about thirty minutes from the office. I'm turning around and heading there now. I'll get a couple of my best guys to meet me. We'll start checking out the information in the recording as soon as we listen to your audio file of the call."

"The recording will be in your email when you get there. I'll call you back as soon as I can, hopefully after I've talked to Emily. We're going to have to move fast if the information is solid. Camino is scheduled to meet with our kidnap victims on Tuesday."

Steve checked his watch. It had been forty-five minutes since the call with Mark Davis ended. He returned to Hartman's office and put his cell on speaker for a call he hoped would be from Emily. Just as he got there, he saw Billy coming down the hall.

"Billy, thanks for coming in. Follow me, I'm expecting a call from Emily in a few minutes."

Billy was momentarily speechless. "Did you say Emily?" Before he could get an answer, he followed Steve into the Chief's office, and they both sat down in front of his desk.

"Billy, thanks for coming in," said Hartman, looking a little anxious. "Steve, Hank is on his way and should be here shortly. Robby was in North Charleston with his wife watching their son's soccer tournament. He'll get here as soon as he arranges a ride home for them."

"What the hell's going on?" asked Billy, still trying to catch up.

Steve looked at his friend and smiled, "Less than an hour ago, the Chief and I may have talked to one of the kidnappers. We recorded the call, and I need you to listen to it. But first, the caller told us he would have Emily call me on my cell in one hour, which is any minute now. I'll get you up to speed after the call."

The three men sat anxiously in silence waiting for Steve's cell phone to ring. Five minutes later, at ten-fifteen, it did. Steve answered it on speaker and put his cell on the Chief's desk. "This is Detective Steve Harris."

"Detective Harris, my name is Jamison Walters. I'm sitting here with Emily Baker. Before I put her on, a few ground rules please. Mark filled me in on your call with him this morning. As promised, I'm going to put Miss Baker on the phone. Before I do that, let me assure you that Emily and her new friends, Chuck Wilson and John Simpson, are all in good health and have been well taken care of since I arrived here with them last Tuesday, along with three cartel armed guards."

"Where's here?" interrupted Steve.

"Detective, when Mark receives the immunity and WITSEC documents he requested, we'll review our plans with you for their safe return."

"Please put Emily on the phone."

There was a pause before Emily said in a strong voice, "This is Emily Baker. Chuck Wilson, John Simpson and I are all fine. Mr. Jamison has ordered me not to tell you where we are, but we have been treated well and hope to see our family and friends soon. Please tell my Aunt Marie I love her and promise to take her to the beach when I get home. Chuck asks that you let his friend George Cooper know he's OK, and John wants you to tell his wife Mandy that he loves her very much."

Before Steve could say anything, Jamison was back on the line, "Detective Harris, if you agree to work closely with Mark and me, we have a way to get your friends home safely. Just as long as the three cartel guards with us don't find out about it. If they do, all bets are off."

The line went dead. Steve spoke first. "I met with Emily twice in May when she identified both Rodriguez and Francisco. It sounded like her. We need to get the recording of that call to Dale and Jill right away. I'll also get Hank to bring Marie Parker in here to see if she recognizes Emily's voice. We need to be as sure as we can before we call in the FBI. Before we do that, we've got to get a solid handle on all of this and take Jamison's warning seriously."

Billy said, "Where can I listen to the call you got this morning?"

"In my office," said Steve. "I'm going to call Dale and Jill back and see what they make of the recording I emailed them earlier. If Mark Davis and Jamison Walters are who they say they are, we need to be ready to move very fast."

The chef jumped in. "Steve, as soon as you get Mark's information confirmed by Dale and Hank gets back with Miss Parker, let me know. I agree we shouldn't get the FBI involved until we're sure we know what we're dealing with."

Billy followed Steve to his office to listen to the Mark Davis call. On the way, Steve found Hank in his office. "Hank, call Marie Parker and tell her you're on your way to pick her up and bring her here. Tell her something urgent has come up, and we need her help right away. Just tell her we may have some good news about Emily so she doesn't panic, but no details. Bring her to my office when she gets here."

"What do we need her for?"

"We just spoke to someone who claims to be Emily. We need Miss Parker to listen to the voice on the call and tell us if it sounds like her."

Hank grabbed his cell and called Marie. When she answered, he was already headed to the parking lot on the run.

Chapter 53

Saturday, September 8, 2018

After her phone call with Steve, Emily remained in Jamison's locked office on the first floor.

He said to her, "You did well. My friend Mark will remain in contact with Detective Harris to finalize our plan to get the three of you out of here safely. Meantime, I can't stress enough the importance of not tipping off any of my three security guards."

"Understood," replied Emily, hoping against hope they finally had a way out.

"I've already warned Chuck and John, but it wouldn't hurt for you to quietly reinforce this with them. If one of my guards overhears any of you and gets wind of any escape attempt, your lives and mine will be in serious danger."

Before leaving his office, Emily fought to stay calm despite the emotional rollercoaster ride she was on. With as much confidence as she could muster, she turned around and smiled. "I still don't understand what's going on but thank you for helping us."

As she walked down the hall from Jamison's office, she passed Sarge before he went in. Towering over Jamison in front of his desk, the large black man said with an extra edge in his voice, "What the hell was that all about?"

Jamison already had his explanation ready. "She wanted to know when they would be going home and asked if she could at least call her aunt to tell her she was OK. I told her the boss is planning to be here next week, and it will all be over soon."

Sarge said with a menacing grin, "It certainly will."

***

After talking to Emily, Steve called Dale back. "I just talked to a woman who says she's Emily Baker. Hank Reed, one of our detectives, is going to bring her aunt here to listen to the call and tell us if it sounds like her. What did you make of our call with Mark Davis?"

"So far, all his information checks out. Mark Davis did do time for computer fraud and was released in 2011 like he said. There was a lot of news coverage when Harrison and Charlotte Walters went missing two years ago. And they do have a son. Jamison did graduate from Yale in 2017. And Davis also knew about Jorge Rodriguez and Teddy Francisco."

"You think this guy intends to actually help us?"

"I do. He could have gotten some of his information on the internet and elsewhere, especially if he's an accomplished hacker. But the clincher for me was the mention of Joseph Camino. The man's been a mirage."

"If Marie Parker confirms Emily's voice when she gets here, we need to get those immunity agreements and WITSEC details emailed to Davis as soon as possible today. I also sent the recording to our County Prosecutor Jill Carrington and want to get her take. Meantime, I'm going to email you and Jill the recording of the call we just had with who we think was Emily. I'll be in touch."

When Steve got Jill on the phone, she sounded excited. "Steve, I just finished listening to the call you emailed me. Assuming the information from Mr. Davis checks out, I think it's likely he has them or knows where they are. I'm just about to listen to your call with Emily. Were you able to verify it was her on the phone?"

"Marie Parker is on her way back here right now with one of our detectives to listen to that call. If her aunt confirms it was her niece on the phone, we're going to play it out with Davis and find out how he plans to get all three of them back to us safely. How long will take to get those four immunity agreements and the WITSEC option if we decide to proceed?"

"Steve, I have a friend in the U.S. Attorney's office. I'll brief him and see what he suggests. As you know, the U.S. Marshals Service runs the Federal Witness Security Program. I'll ask my U.S. Attorney friend to help us with that as well. Judge Templeton, who has the Francisco trial, may also be willing to at least give me some guidance when I explain the situation and tell him we may have found our missing witness."

Steve hustled back into his office to update Billy and get his take on the Davis phone call before Marie got back to the station with Hank. "Billy, is this guy on the level or are we still chasing rainbows?"

Billy said, "There's no way he would have a photo of all three of them unless it was a clever photoshop. And unless there's a leak in this department, how could Davis also know about Chuck Wilson and John Simpson being kidnapped by the cartel? Or about the three initials on the back of the envelope found in John Simpson's garage.

If Dale confirms Mark's information, and Miss Parker confirms Emily's voice, there's not much doubt he knows where they are. And you already know our chances of finding them on our own before Teddy's trial are slim and none."

Steve nodded. "I can't disagree, Billy. I'd like you to be here when I play the call for Miss Parker. I'll meet her in the lobby and bring her back here as soon as she arrives with Hank."

***

When Hank got to Marie's townhome, she was waiting for him. She saw Hank coming up the walkway and opened the front door before he got there. "Detective, what's going on? Have you found Emily?"

"Good morning, Miss Parker, sorry for interrupting your Saturday, but we need your help with something. Detective Harris will brief you as soon as we get back to the station. There's nothing to be alarmed about. We may have a lead and need your assistance."

"Of course, anything I can do to help. I'm ready to go."

Thirty minutes later, Steve met Hank and Marie as soon as they came through the front door of the police headquarters building. "Miss Parker, thanks for coming in. We're going to meet in my office. There's something I need you to listen to."

"What is it?" she asked anxiously.

"We got a call from someone this morning claiming to be Emily, and we want you to listen to the call and tell us if it sounds like her."

Marie was momentarily speechless, and Steve offered her his arm. "Let's go to my office and find out if it was your niece we talked to. If it was, we're going to get her home. For now, it's critical that you discuss any this with absolutely no one, not even Richard. I'll explain everything after you listen to the call."

In Steve's office with Billy and Hank, Marie started crying as she listened to the call. "It's her, it's Emily. I'm sure of it. Is she safe? Where is she?"

Steve spent the next few minutes calmly explaining what was going on, leaving out most of the specifics. "We believe she's safe, and we're working with someone who has offered to help us get her back home safely. I can't go into all the details, but Hank will keep you updated as we move forward. I know this has been an ordeal for you, but we're doing everything possible to bring her back home safe and sound. We just need you to stay strong a little while longer."

Marie's hands were still shaking when Steve finished telling her what was happening. "Thank you, Detective Harris. Please bring my niece back to me." Then, for a brief moment, she smiled and said, "Funny she would promise to take me to the beach when she gets home. She knows I never go to the beach."

Steve glanced over at Billy and Hank before he said to her in a reassuring voice, "Emily was probably just trying to let us know she's OK and looking forward to seeing you."

As soon as Hank left to take Marie back home, Steve said to Billy, "What do you make of Emily's mention of the beach?"

"She's a smart young woman," answered Billy. "I think she was trying to give us a clue about where she's being held. I'm going to look at our short list of potential small airports along the coastline again and see if any are especially close to the ocean."

"Good idea. While you do that, I'm going to let the Chief know Marie confirmed the voice on the call was Emily's. We need to get those immunity agreements and WITSEC paperwork from Jill to Mark Davis pronto. I'm convinced he wants to help us, and we don't have a lot of time before Mr. Camino shows up to interrogate them. When Davis has what he asked for, I want you and the Chief with me when I call him. We need to find out exactly how he plans to get everyone out of harm's way."

Chapter 54

Saturday, September 8, 2018

Just after five p.m. on Saturday, thanks to some help from Dale, Steve finally got the email from Jill he was waiting for. Attached were Federal Immunity Agreements for Mark Davis, Jamison Walters, Harrison Walters and Charlotte Walters, all subject to the safe release of Emily Baker, John Simpson, and Charles Wilson. Both the Immunity Agreements and an offer of entry into the Federal WITSEC program were subject to their sworn testimony against Joseph Camino for the kidnapping, as well as Mark getting Jake Thomas to testify about Camino's attempted murder of Jamison's parents.

The agreements were signed by Walker Higgins, Assistant US Attorney for the Southern District of Florida, and Charleston County Prosecutor Jill Carrington.

After printing two copies, one for himself and one for the Chief, Steve scanned and emailed them in an attachment to Mark and asked him to call back as soon as he reviewed them. He dropped off a set of the agreements to Hartman and headed for Robby's office, where he and Billy were still reviewing the short list of small airports near the beach.

Over Robby's shoulder, Steve asked, "What's the closest airport to coastline?"

Robby looked up from his computer screen. "The Pinewood Airport on the Outer Banks is definitely the closest. It's a small, private airstrip that runs along Highway 12, the main north and south road along the ocean. Take a look at this aerial."

Steve moved in for a closer view of the computer screen, and Robby pointed as he zoomed in. "Look at this area just north of the airstrip on the ocean side of Highway 12. There are a few large homes not very close to each other in this stretch of woods along the beach. Each home looks very secluded and probably can't be seen from the road. Not a bad spot to hide three people."

"Good work, Robby. What do you think, Billy?" asked Steve.

"It's still a needle in a haystack, but that certainly fits our criteria. If Emily was trying to give us a clue by mentioning the beach, looks like she has a great view of it if that's where she is. What do you want to do?"

"For now, nothing. Let's see what Mark Davis tells us. I've asked him to call me after he reviews the immunity agreements I just sent him from Jill. Let's go to the Chief's office. Robby, grab Hank and meet us there. I spoke to him briefly after he dropped Miss Parker back home on Daniel Island. I'd like all of us to hear what Mark has to say."

Twenty minutes later, Steve answered his cell and put it in speaker mode. The number was blocked. "Steve Harris here."

"Detective Harris, thank you for the agreements I requested. Everything looks in order. I've signed them and emailed them back to you. It's too risky and time-consuming to get Jamison's and his parent's signatures, you'll just have to trust us. Of course, I can't *guarantee* the safe return of your three friends, but I'm confident our plan will work with your help."

"Where are they being held?"

"On the Outer Banks in a private home. Other than not being able to leave, they've all been well taken care of, just as I assume Miss Baker told you. Sort of like a forced beach vacation."

Steve looked at Billy and Robby and gave them a thumbs up. "Where are you calling from?"

"Florida. My address isn't important right now. Here's what I have in mind."

***

Jamison was locked in his office when Mark called him on his burner at five-thirty p.m. "I just explained our escape plan to the detectives in Mt. Pleasant. We got the signed immunity agreements for you and me and your parents, and witness protection offers for all of us, as long as we agree to help them get our guests back to them safely and testify against the boss."

Before Mark could continue, Jamison interrupted him. "Mark, have you seen the news?"

"Been a little busy lately, did someone take out the boss?"

"You wish. There's a big storm in the Atlantic headed our way. It's forecasted to strengthen into a major hurricane by the time it gets here. If that happens, there may be an evacuation order for the Outer Banks. We need to be on the move sooner than later."

There was silence on the other end before Mark finally said, "Damn, that's not what we need right now. Stay loose, and I'll check it out. I need to get back to Detective Harris and figure out if we need a Plan B. We may be forced to move the timetable up to Monday."

***

Saturday afternoon on the Outer Banks was sunny and warm with a light afternoon sea breeze. At six p.m., all three of them were sitting in the library room for their daily thirty-minute TV allowance of the evening news before dinner. None of the guards or Jamison joined them.

Ten minutes before the newscast ended, the news anchor reported that a powerful storm in the Atlantic was rapidly intensifying. Based on the current tracking models, Hurricane Florence was currently heading directly for the North and South Carolina coastline. Storm surge and high surf watches were already issued, and a state of emergency had been declared in five states and Washington D.C.

When the hurricane news segment ended, Emily said quietly, "We've gotta get out of here. If that storm stays on its current track, the governor will probably issue an evacuation order very soon, at least for the Outer Banks. We definitely won't be able to stay here."

Chuck looked over at her and said, "I had to evacuate from McClellanville to escape what turned out to be a twenty-foot storm surge from Hurricane Hugo back in '89. I never want to go through something like that ever again. If a strong hurricane makes landfall anywhere near the Outer Banks, the property damage and loss of life could be a major disaster."

John lowered his voice to almost a whisper. "We need to talk to Jamison. The timetable for the plan he reviewed with us may need to get moved up."

Emily said, "I'll try to get him alone and talk to him."

Just as they were about to head to the dining room, Jamison walked into the library. "There's a strong hurricane headed our way. For now, sit tight until I figure out what we're going to do."

Emily said, "We just saw it on the news. If there's a mandatory evacuation, the police will be out in force to make sure the residents comply."

Before returning to his office, Jamison said, "I'm going to leave the TV on so you can watch the Weather Channel until dinner is served at seven."

***

On Sunday morning, Jamison had his routine daily meeting with the security team at six a.m. He was back in his office at eight a.m. for his regular morning call to update the boss. But for the first time since he arrived at the beach house, there was no answer.

Two hours later, the boss called Jamison back with some unexpected news.

Chapter 55

Sunday, September 9, 2018

Less often now than the first few weeks after it happened, Steve still had the same recurring nightmare from his rookie cop days, mostly when he was under stress. He always woke up with a start at the same moment he always did, just as the crackhead in the pharmacy was about to squeeze the trigger again before Buddy Evans fired two shots into the man's face.

His nightshirt was damp as he glanced at the clock on his nightstand. Five a.m. He lay still for a few minutes until his heart stopped racing. Hoping not to wake Janet, he carefully slipped out of bed and headed for the bathroom. Before padding downstairs, he quietly closed the bedroom door.

He started the coffee machine and turned on the TV in the den to the Weather Channel to get the latest five a.m. advisory on the storm from the National Hurricane Center. Hurricane Florence was slowly becoming a dangerous storm, still well out in the Atlantic and moving westward at six mph. The tracking models that showed the storm's likely path, commonly referred to as the 'cone of uncertainty', predicted a landfalling major hurricane someplace along the North and South Carolina coastline later in the week.

When the coffee was ready, he poured a cup and headed back upstairs for a quick shower before getting dressed and driving into the office. When he returned to the bedroom, Janet was awake and leaning up on her elbow. "Same nightmare?"

"Yeah, sorry babe, didn't mean to wake you. I'm fine. I talked to Mark Davis again last night before our team meeting broke up and told him about our decision to set up the extraction plan for some time tomorrow instead of early Tuesday night. The storm is getting stronger and still heading toward us. We're in for some rough weather, and this one looks like it could get nasty."

"You think we're going to have to evacuate?"

"Looks that way. I'm guessing Governor McMaster will be ordering an evacuation sooner than later for everyone along our coast, including the Charleston area. And when he does, the I-26 lane reversal plan will be put in motion, and all lanes will be switched to westbound only from Charleston all the way to Columbia."

"What are you going to do?"

"The timing couldn't be worse, but we have no choice. The team is meeting at eight this morning to get all of our assets coordinated and in place. Since North Carolina Governor Cooper may order an evacuation of the Outer Banks, which is likely, we've got to get up there today."

Janet said, "If we need to evacuate, Molly has invited me to drive to Greenville with her and their girls to stay with one of her old friends from Savannah who now lives there. School will probably be canceled tomorrow. I'll make sure our boys stay at Clemson. You and Billy can catch up with us later in Greenville if you need to. Just be safe, hon. I know you want to rescue Emily and the others, but don't risk your life with this storm. You know what Hugo was like."

"Don't worry, babe, we'll be smart. Good idea for you guys to head west and get off the immediate coast as soon as you can. And make sure the boys know what's going on. Also make sure you fill up with gas today."

"Yes sir, Detective Harris, understood sir," she laughed before turning serious. "Just be careful. I love you."

"Love you more. Billy and I will be riding up to the Outer Banks together. We'll be fine."

When he finished getting dressed, he kissed Janet goodbye and told her again to be careful on the road. From the closet, he grabbed some rain gear and the go-bag he'd repacked from his Hilton Head trip last week and locked the front door behind him.

By six-thirty a.m., Steve was in his office at police headquarters and got the coffee going. In the conference room, he turned on the TV to catch the local news. While the storm was still a few days away, today would be crucial to get his team and everyone else briefed and ready to execute the rescue plan sometime on Monday. He texted Dale and asked him to call when he could.

At seven-thirty, Billy was the first member of Steve's small team to arrive in the conference room carrying a take-out coffee cup and a box of donuts. By eight a.m., Chief Hartman, Hank, and Robby had joined them.

As they were getting settled, Steve said, "Morning everybody, thanks for coming in on this beautiful Sunday morning. We've got a big day in front of us, so let's get started. Coffee is on the table with donuts compliments of Billy. I know you all want a result you can be proud of as much as I do. It's been a long road, and it's time to end this thing and get our people back."

Steve then began his briefing. "As you guys know from our meeting yesterday afternoon, we've moved up our timetable due to the potential hurricane headed this way. We may be able to use it to our advantage if we move quickly. Governor Cooper is expected to order an evacuation later today or sometime tomorrow morning, at least for the coastline of North Carolina, including the Outer Banks. Governor McMaster will likely do the same for our coast if the current storm track holds."

He opened a file folder and continued, "Early last evening, the Chief and I made several phone calls to our emergency contacts for the South Carolina and North Carolina FBI and Highway Patrol in both states. We discussed our current situation, including what we learned yesterday from Mark Davis and Jamison Walters about the whereabouts of our three kidnap victims and their armed guards, as well as our phone call with Emily. We also reviewed our plan to get them back and asked for their help."

Hartman said, "Our first call was to Bill Jackson, FBI Special Agent in Charge in the Columbia Field Office. Bill was aware Emily was missing from the statewide missing persons alert Hank put out this past week, but he had no clue about two other people being kidnapped at the same time. At first, he was pissed that we didn't get him involved earlier. He calmed down when Steve explained the link between the three kidnap victims and the Camino drug cartel that started with the port murder last August."

Steve added, "We gave Agent Jackson the highlights of our investigation and why we decided to keep it in-house. I told him our concern that if all three kidnap victims were together and being held by the cartel, a major FBI manhunt could spook the cartel and force their hand before we at least tried to verify their location, assuming they were even still alive. I also told Jackson we didn't expect to be contacted by someone from the cartel, but the call from Mark Davis yesterday changed everything."

"How did he react to our rescue plan?" asked Billy.

"Bill Jackson is an FBI veteran of over twenty-five years and a no-nonsense guy," said Hartman. "Once he got a handle on the situation and what we needed, he was all in. He still wasn't happy we kept him in the dark, but he understood our decision to keep a light footprint in our investigation. The last thing any of us wants now, including the FBI, is a shootout at the OK Corral."

Steve said, "Bottom line, after also briefing Jane Fielding, the FBI Special Agent in Charge of the North Carolina Field Office, along with both the South Carolina and North Carolina Highway Patrol Commanders, everyone is on board."

"I also called Harland Zimmer, Chief of Police for the Town of Duck on the Outer Banks," added Hartman. "Harland is an old friend I met several years ago at an annual Chiefs of Police Conference in New Orleans. He's got a small department of four officers and expects to have all hands-on deck if the Governor orders an evacuation of the Outer Banks. Harland told me he's going to have his hands full but offered to do what he could if we needed any local assistance."

Steve looked over his notes. "Our assets will include eight armed FBI agents and two FBI snipers, plus Bill Jackson. They'll all be arriving in unmarked cars, plus a SWAT van from North Carolina. Everyone expects to be in Duck by late this afternoon. Bill Jackson will finalize the extraction plan, and everyone will be briefed shortly after we all arrive."

Hank asked, "What's the plan for our team, Steve?"

"You, Robby, Billy, and I will drive to the Outer Banks at ten a.m. this morning. We'll take two cars and should get to Duck around four p.m. this afternoon. I'll drive Billy and Hank will travel in his car with Robby. We've all got room reservations at the Duck Inn for tonight. We'll hook up with Jackson when we get there for a final planning session and briefing for the FBI teams and Highway Patrol officers. Bill will arrange clearance for all of us to get onto the island in the event the bridges are closed to traffic onto the Outer Banks if there's an evacuation order today."

The meeting ended at nine a.m. Everyone said they'd be ready to hit the road in an hour. Steve and Billy headed to McDonald's for a quick bite before returning to meet up with Hank and Robby for the drive to the Outer Banks.

A few minutes after ten a.m., both cars pulled out of the police parking lot together and headed for I-95. Five minutes later, Steve got an unexpected cell call from an unknown number. When he answered, the caller identified himself. He put his phone in speaker mode and glanced over at Billy. "What's up, Jamison?"

"Detective, I just got off the phone with my boss. We've got a big problem."

Chapter 56

Sunday, September 9, 2018

Steve remained calm and said, "Jamison, we just got on the road headed your way, tell me what's going on."

"The boss decided to move up his visit to keep ahead of the storm and told me to get everyone ready to leave this afternoon. He said he'd be landing at the Pinewood Airport around four p.m. today to fly us back to Miami immediately. He wants everybody there when he lands and be ready to board the plane."

Steve took a moment to let the news sink in. Jamison was nervous and blurted, "Did you hear what I said?"

"Who else knows he's coming?"

"Just me, and I assume Mark may also know, but I wanted to talk to you first before the boss calls again. If your friends fly out of here with him, you'll probably never see them again."

"OK, thanks for the heads up. Stay cool and let me work the problem from this end. I'll call you when we figure something out. Stay put and don't mention anything to anyone there, especially your security guys. We've still got some time. Just don't do anything stupid and stay off the road."

The stress in Jamison's voice was quickly turning into panic. "OK, OK. The latest news is that the Governor may issue an evacuation order for the Outer Banks sometime tomorrow. One way or the other, if that happens, the local cops will probably be doing house to house checks to make sure everyone gets off the island."

Steve said as evenly as he could, "Jamison, you've got to chill. If your security guys sense something's going on, the entire plan will be in jeopardy. Trust me, we'll find a solution."

After ending the call, Steve called Mark. "I just got off the phone with Jamison. He told me your boss is landing at the Pinewood Airport this afternoon to fly everyone back to Florida. I'm working on it, but I need you to keep Jamison steady, he's nervous as a cat. If your security guards get suspicious and go on high alert, we're going to be in trouble."

Mark said, "Understand. Jamison is trying to call me right now, probably to ask me what he should do. I'll tell him to sit tight and act normal until we hear back from you. Keep in touch."

"Good, thanks Mark. I'll let you both know when we figure something out. Our FBI guys are all heading for the Outer Banks and should be in Duck by late this afternoon. We just need to stop that plane from landing there today."

After ending the call, Steve said to Billy, "I thought we planned for the worst, but not this. Any bright ideas?"

"Actually, I do have one if we can get some help from the Duck Police Chief. I forgot his name."

"Harland Zimmer."

"Right, Chief Zimmer. Anyway, the best way to stop Mr. Camino from landing this afternoon is to block the runway. It's a private airport so we should be OK."

Steve thought about it for a few seconds before he said, "That's actually a good idea, assuming we can pull it off without Camino suspecting anything. Whatever we do needs to look like some kind of routine preparation ahead of the storm."

Bully suggested, "See if you can reach Zimmer and ask him if he can help us."

When Steve got the Duck Chief of Police on the phone, he explained the problem and the urgency of keeping Camino's plane from landing. "Chief, we don't have time to get permission from the owner of the airport to close it. Lives are at stake. Would it be possible block the runway with some heavy equipment, dump trucks, anything that would look like emergency staging ahead of the storm?"

Chief Zimmer paused for a moment before he replied, "The good news is that airport is unattended. Pilots just call the owner for permission to land and pay him a landing fee in advance. I'll issue an emergency order to temporarily shut down the airport and ask forgiveness later."

After another pause, Zimmer floated another suggestion. "What if we could get two or three power company trucks parked on the runway. They're going to be needed anyway if that storm makes landfall near the Outer Banks.

We can also probably get a couple dump trucks from one of the larger towns out here and use them as well."

"Chief, I think that would do it. What can we do to help? Bill Jackson from our FBI Field Office is on his way and will be here later this afternoon. FBI Agent Jane Fielding from your North Carolina Field Office has also been briefed and is on call if we need anything. Maybe she could make some calls and pull some strings. Time is not on our side to make this happen."

"OK, I'll call around for the dump trucks, but it might go faster if you call Agent Fielding and see what she can do on her end about the power trucks. Impacts from the storm, starting with the outer rain bands as it approaches the coast, won't be felt for another two or three days or so. There will still be plenty of time to get all the trucks returned on Tuesday, assuming your rescue operation goes well."

"Thanks Chief, that works for me. See how fast you can get those dump trucks to the airport. I'll talk to Jane and Bill about helping us borrow some power company trucks. We owe you one."

Steve next got Bill Jackson on his cell. Before he could explain why he was calling, Jackson said, "I just got on I-95 and should be in Duck around four-thirty or so this afternoon. The rest of my team will also be arriving on the Outer Banks late this afternoon. Where are you?"

"We just left Mt. Pleasant and won't get there until around five. But we've got a situation."

When Steve finished telling him about his call with Jamison and the plan to block the airport runway, Jackson said, "Hell of a problem. If that plane lands, we're in deep shit. Let me talk to Jane Fielding. She and I have worked together on a couple FBI joint task forces. We'll figure something out. I'll get back to you when we've got a plan in motion. Bottom line, we need to make that airstrip unusable one way or the other by three p.m., if at all possible, in case Camino shows up early. That gives us less than five hours. I like the power truck idea, and I think we can make that happen."

***

Jane answered Jackson's call with her usual brisk greeting. "FBI Special Agent Jane Fielding."

"Bill Jackson here. I'm on the road to Duck to meet with the guys from Mt. Pleasant for an early dinner tonight to make sure everybody's on the same page. But something's just come up that can't wait, and we need your help."

When he finished briefing her on the problem and a possible solution, Jane said, "Bill, you're right, Joseph Camino cannot be allowed to land on the Outer Banks today. I agree your idea might keep him from suspecting someone has tipped off the cops about his arrival if it looks like the airport is being used for storm prep."

"Anything you can do from there will be very welcome."

"Let me make some calls. If I can arrange for two or three power trucks from Raleigh in the next half-hour or so, they could be at the airport by your three p.m. time frame. I'd rather not tie up any power trucks from the Outer Banks if we can avoid it."

"I agree, thanks Jane. Tell whoever you talk to that we'll guarantee the return of the trucks, no later than Tuesday."

"I'll call you when I have some news."

Thirty minutes later, she called back. "We're all set. Before noon, three power trucks from Raleigh will be on the road toward Duck with a police escort. With no stops, the drive will take about three and a half hours, which will put them at the airport around three-thirty. I know you'd like to have the trucks in position earlier, but that's the best we can do."

"Excellent! We're cutting it close, but it is what it is. Steve told me the Duck Chief of Police is also getting us three local dump trucks. He plans to park them across the middle of the runway in the next hour or two. Might be a little too obvious to fool Camino, but at least it would be enough to keep his plane from landing. When the power trucks arrive, they can be staged along with the dump trucks to make it look like normal emergency staging ahead of the storm."

Bill said, "I'll brief Steve and he can relay the info to the Chief in Duck. Have your agents call me as soon as they arrive today for our final briefing. We need to stay fluid. No telling Camino's next move if he can't land."

***

After talking to Chief Zimmer, Steve called Hartman and briefed him on what was happening. "Chief, we owe your buddy Chief Zimmer a case of beer.

The man has his hands full but didn't hesitate to jump in and help us out. I'll keep you updated at this end."

"Thanks Steve, you guys be safe up there. And start thinking about where you plan to drive after you secure Emily, Chuck, and John. If Governor McMaster orders an evacuation of Charleston, you know I-26 will be full of traffic after the lane reversal."

As Steve and Billy continued driving north on I-95 in front of Hank and Robby, they passed the exit ramp for Florence, South Carolina. Billy couldn't help himself and quipped, "Florence is one popular lady around these parts."

***

By Sunday afternoon, Florence was a Category 1 hurricane and still ramping up. Sustained winds near the center were fast approaching 100 mph as of the two p.m. advisory from the National Hurricane Center based on the latest pass through the eye of the storm by one of their special hurricane hunter airplanes. A damaging Category 3 hurricane, or possibly a Category 4, was now predicted to make landfall someplace along the North or South Carolina coastline later in the week. The center of the latest projected storm track was the Outer Banks.

Chapter 57

Sunday, September 9, 2018

At two-thirty p.m. on Sunday, Joseph Camino called Jamison. "We're still on schedule to arrive at the airport around four p.m. Make sure our three friends and the security team are all at the airport with their luggage and ready to board. I don't want to be on the ground any longer than necessary."

"What about the two Suburbans?"

"Tell Frankie he needs to stay behind to handle a few chores. When everyone gets to the airport, have him park one of the Suburbans close by but off the road and out of sight. Make sure he wipes it clean and removes the plates. Tell him to return to the beach house in the other Suburban and wipe everything down in the house. I want no traces anyone was there. When he's finished, he needs to drive to the Raleigh airport and leave the second Suburban in long-term parking, same drill. Wipe it down and remove the plates. He can then book the next available commercial flight to Miami with his fake creds. Tell him to call Antonio when he gets there."

Jamison was furiously scribbling notes. "Yes sir. Anything else you need us to do?"

Before he abruptly hung up, Camino ordered, "Just make sure everyone's personal stuff is out of the house before you leave. If the cops come snooping around, it needs to be completely empty like you were never there."

Jamison found his three guests sitting in the living room. He told Frankie to get the security guards to the living room right away. When everyone was together, he gave them their marching orders. "Change of plans. Everybody get packed and be ready to leave in an hour. Willy, you, Sam, and Frankie load the bags into the Suburbans. Tex, you stand watch by the front door." At least Emily now knew their real first names, but she still liked hers better.

Sarge, aka Willy, spoke up and said, "What's the big rush, and where are we going?"

Jamison replied, "The boss wants everybody at the airport when his plane lands in less than two hours. All of us except Frankie will board the plane and fly back to Miami. Frankie, I'll give you your instructions from the boss on the way. You'll be coming back here after we take off."

As soon as everyone started packing up, Jamison went to his office and locked the door. When Steve answered his phone, Jamison was talking fast. "Just heard from the boss. He's still scheduled to land around four p.m. and wants all of us there to immediately board his plane."

"OK Jamison, listen carefully. He's not going to land because the airport runway will be blocked with some dump trucks and maybe some power trucks. Get everyone ready to leave for the airport anyway, but don't get there before three-fifty at the earliest. The power trucks won't get to the airstrip until around three-thirty, and I don't want you there until the power trucks are positioned and the drivers are gone."

"Got it. I'm sure the boss will be calling me as soon as he realizes he can't land. He's going to be mighty pissed off. Should I call him when we get to the airport and tell him the runway has some trucks parked on it and the airport is closed?"

Steve said, "Good idea, call him when you get there so he doesn't suspect anything, but don't arrive too early. Just act normal and call me back when he tells you what to do next."

***

They all stared in confusion at the trucks parked on the runway when the two SUVs pulled into the airport at three-fifty. Jamison got out by himself and told everyone else to stay put. The plane was less than ten minutes out on its final approach when Jamison made the call.

Camino was already in a bad mood for having to fly in the small turboprop instead of his luxury jet so they could land on the short runway. He barked, "Any problems Jamison?"

"Sorry sir, we just got to the airport. Three power trucks and some dump trucks are sitting on the runway. Looks like the airport has been closed to park some emergency vehicles ahead of the hurricane."

"What the hell are you talking about?"

"Boss, it's a small airstrip and there's no room to land the plane. The runway is blocked."

"Stay where you are, we're almost there," he shouted back.

Camino moved from the cabin up to the cockpit and sat next to his pilot to see for himself. When the airstrip came into view, he roared, "Son of a bitch! Johnny, is there enough room to land this thing?"

The veteran pilot scanned the blocked airstrip. "Boss, we need all that runway, and those trucks are in the way."

When he got closer, he pulled up and banked the plane over the ocean. Camino was now in a full-blown rage and yelled, "Circle back and take another pass. I want to see it again."

On the next flyover, Camino saw the two black SUVs parked on the side of the runway with Jamison standing next to one of them before the plane rose and headed back over the ocean. Camino asked his pilot, "Where's another small airport near the coast? I don't want to fly inland."

Johnny punched in a search for North Carolina airports into his phone. "Boss, there's a small airport south of us down the coast, fairly close to Wilmington."

"How long a drive from here?"

The pilot pulled up a map of the airport location and studied it. "Looks like the Cape Fear Jetport is about two hundred and eighty miles from here, about a five-hour drive by car."

"Dammit! OK, call that airport and see if we can land there."

Camino called Jamison back. "Stay there and I'll get back to you. We're trying to see if we can land at a small airport near Wilmington. If we get that confirmed, you and one of your guys will need to drive everyone there in the SUVs to meet us. We'll all fly out from there tonight. It's about a five-hour trip, depending on traffic."

"Yes sir, standing by. What about Frankie?"

"If we're cleared to land, drop him back at the house to finish cleaning up. Tell him to find his own ride to the Raleigh airport. Cab, limo, Uber, I don't give a shit. Tell him to figure it out."

A few minutes later, Steve called Jamison and asked, "What happened?"

Jamison answered Steve in a raised voice, hoping to be overheard, "Hi Mark, thought you were the boss. We're all here at the airport, but it's closed. The boss is now trying to get clearance to land at a small airport south of us near

Wilmington. He's calling me back in a few minutes. If he gets clearance to land, he wants us to start driving toward Wilmington and meet his plane there."

"OK, that was fast thinking. After he calls you back, no matter what he says, tell everyone the boss just told you to go back to the house and wait for further instructions. When it's safe and you're alone, call me with an update after you hear back from Camino. You can do this, Jamison. The cavalry is on the way. Just stay cool, we've got your back."

Ten minutes later, Camino called Jamison again, "OK, we finally got clearance to land at the Cape Fear Jetport. We'll meet you there. I'll text you the location, just start driving south toward Wilmington after you drop Frankie back at the house."

"Yes sir, understood."

Jamison got in the driver's seat next to Emily and turned back onto Highway 12 toward the beach house. Behind them were John and Frankie in the middle row. From the third row, Sarge yelled up to Jamison in his usual menacing voice and demanded, "Who was that on the phone?"

Jamison answered, "That was the boss."

With his trusty Glock at his side, the big man said, "You got two calls, who was the other one from?"

Jamison didn't hesitate to take control, stared into in the rearview mirror back at Sarge, and snapped, "What's with all the bullshit questions? You nervous or something? The first call was from Mark Davis to tell me he'll have our transportation ready when we land in Miami tonight. I told him what was going on at the airport, and we're waiting to hear back from the boss to see if he can land at a small airport near Wilmington. The second call was from the man himself."

"What did he want, or is that also none of my business?"

Jamison took a chance. He knew he had to sell the lie hard. He raised his voice in the best angry impression he could muster and snapped, "You got a problem? The boss told me to get everyone back to the house for the night. He decided to fly back to Miami and will let me know as soon as he decides where and when he wants us to meet him tomorrow. You got any more questions, I'll be glad to pass them along. You know how much the boss worries about keeping the hired help personally informed."

Sarge growled back to Jamison, "Just forget it, college boy."

Emily closed her eyes and was finally able to breathe a sigh of relief.

Chapter 58

Sunday, September 9, 2018

Steve made three more calls from his car when he reached Highway 12 on the Outer Banks, still several miles from Duck. The first was to Jane Fielding to update her on the current situation and ask her for another favor. DEA Agent Dale Hawkins needed some FBI assistance to get Joseph Camino into custody before he flew out of Cape Fear in the next few hours.

Dale was watching the Miami Dolphins season opener when he took a call. Steve said, "Hate to disrupt your Sunday afternoon, but I knew you'd want to hear this. Joseph Camino just tried to land at a private airstrip on the Outer Banks to pick up our three kidnap victims and fly them to Miami. We blocked the runway with some trucks so he couldn't land. Camino is now headed to a small airport near Wilmington, North Carolina."

Dale turned off the game and said, "Did you say Joseph Camino is going to be at an airport in North Carolina tonight?"

"He told Jamison to immediately drive everyone, including the security guards, to meet his plane at the Cape Fear Jetport, about thirty miles from Wilmington International. It's about a five-hour drive from the Outer Banks. I just told Jamison to ignore the order and return everyone back to the beach house."

"When will Camino be there?"

"Actually, he should be landing shortly. I just talked to Jane Fielding, the Special Agent in charge of the FBI North Carolina Field Office in Charlotte. She's been in the loop all day and sent us four of her best agents and two FBI snipers to help us with our rescue plan. My team will be meeting them, along with more FBI agents from our South Carolina Field Office, at the Duck police headquarters in the next hour or so. We're planning to get our kidnap victims out of harm's way some time after midnight tonight."

"Steve, we've also gotta grab Camino before he leaves that airport."

"Way ahead of you, Dale. Jane told me she's flying two of her agents from the FBI Raleigh office to Wilmington International as fast as they can get there. Figured you'd also want to be there. I told her I'd be briefing you, and she's expecting your call."

Steve was still on Highway 12 when he made his third call, this one to Bill Jackson. "Bill, where are you?"

"I just got to the Duck Inn. My agents are all here with me. You still on the road?"

"We're almost there and heading to see Chief Zimmer at the Duck Police Station as soon as we get into town. You and I need to meet with the entire team at his station. I already talked to Jane and her North Carolina team will meet us as soon as they can get there. She told me they should all be in Duck around five-thirty."

"Sounds urgent, has something happened?"

"I just talked to Jamison, and we're going to need a new game plan."

After Steve finished reviewing his latest call with Jamison, Bill said, "We definitely need to move up our timetable and go in sometime tonight. See you shortly."

***

By six p.m., the small conference room in the Duck Police Station was standing room only when the last of the FBI agents, including two snipers, joined Steve, Billy, Hank, Robby, Chief Zimmer, and two of his patrol officers. Bill and Steve stood in the front of the room to handle the briefing.

Bill spoke first and said, "For those of you who don't know this man, Detective Steve Harris was a decorated Army Ranger, including a tour in Iraq, before joining the Mt. Pleasant police force when he got out." He looked over at Steve and added, "Hopefully, we won't need your combat skills tonight."

Steve looked over the room and said, "Looks to me like we already have plenty of skills in front of me. Thanks to all of you for coming on short notice. You FBI guys have already been briefed by Special Agent Bill Jackson here, as well as North Carolina Special Agent Jane Fielding. Bill will be running the op, and everyone will take their orders from him. I've also been updating Agent Fielding back in Charlotte by phone all afternoon on our current situation, which has changed in the last couple hours."

Steve continued by recounting how they prevented Joseph Camino from landing his plane at the nearby Pinewood Airport. He also reviewed his latest phone call with Jamison and added, "Only our inside man Jamison Walters knows Mr. Camino is expecting everyone to show up at the Cape Fear Jetport in a few hours. I told Jamison to ignore Camino's order and drive everyone back to the beach house, which is just north of us. He'll tell everybody there that the boss man will be calling him with new instructions in the morning."

Fred, one of the North Carolina FBI agents, said, "Pretty gutsy move. Who's this Jamison guy?"

"Jamison Walters happens to be Miami cartel boss Joseph Camino's personal assistant and has decided to help us. It's a long and complicated story we don't have time to get into right now. What you need to know is that we had no idea where our three kidnapped South Carolina residents were being held until we were contacted yesterday morning by Mark Davis, a cartel associate of Jamison."

Everyone in the room was now riveted on what Steve was telling them. "Davis is based in Florida and has been handling surveillance operations for the Camino cartel for the past several years. He and Jamison were involved in executing Camino's plan for the entire kidnapping operation from the start."

Another agent asked, "How do we know this isn't a setup?"

"Good question, Charlie. Davis explained to us what motivated him and Jamison to help us. He also told us some things that only someone inside the cartel could've known. We believe him. We also confirmed his information with Dale Hawkins, a Miami DEA agent we've been working closely with for the past year on a related murder case of a Camino drug runner at the Port of Charleston in my neck of the woods.

Hawkins has been on the hunt for the cartel's senior leadership for a long time. The man about to go on trial in my port murder case is a Camino enforcer. Joseph Camino suspects at least one of his three kidnap victims is a key witness for the prosecution in that trial, which is scheduled to start later this month in Charleston."

Steve looked around the room and added, "Gentlemen, the reason we're all here now was a text Davis sent us yesterday with a recent photo of all three captives together at the beach house up the road. Davis also arranged with Jamison to allow us to talk to one of the kidnap victims, a young schoolteacher named Emily Baker. That's why we decided to initiate this rescue mission on such short notice."

"Why has Camino waited so long to interrogate them in person?"

Steve paused a moment before answering, "Frankly, we're not absolutely certain, but Agent Hawkins shared a theory with us that makes sense. Bottom line, what matters right now is rescuing three innocents who are in serious danger. And the clock is ticking. We need to get them out of that house before morning."

Bill took over and said, "Steve's right, and I know you were all briefed that this rescue operation would happen tomorrow night. But since Camino is now expecting to meet everyone this evening in Wilmington, we need to get those people safely out of that house tonight."

If any of the men in the room were concerned by the sudden change in plans, they didn't show it. Steve walked over to a bulletin board sitting in a corner and placed it in front of the conference room. On it was a grainy aerial photo of the beach house that Chief Zimmer had scanned from Google Maps.

He pointed to the photo and said, "Here's the house where they're all staying. It's very secluded and can't be seen from the road. The good news is that the house is surrounded by woods on three sides. The back of the house is on the beach overlooking the ocean. Jamison warned me there are high-tech motion-sensor floodlights around the entire perimeter. Video cameras inside and out are monitored around the clock."

Two hours later, a new extraction plan was ready, and everyone in the room was on board.

Chapter 59

Sunday, September 9, 2018

Jane Fielding answered Dale's call immediately. After introducing themselves to each other, she said, "Steve gave me a heads up, here's what I have in mind. I can arrange for two of my agents to helicopter to Wilmington International. They can be ready to leave within the hour. I can also ask the Wilmington Chief of Police, a good friend of mine, to send a couple of his best detectives to meet them. My people will wait for you if you're planning to be there."

"I wouldn't miss a surprise party for Camino for anything. I'll be there as fast as I can. We have a DEA private plane available on standby for emergencies, and this definitely qualifies."

"One more thing, Dale. For his ears only, how about if I call whoever's in charge at the Cape Fear Jetport where Camino is landing and brief him on what's going down. If you agree, I can tell him not to clear Camino's plane for takeoff under any circumstances before you get there."

"Perfect, do it! We've been trying to haul Joseph Camino's ass into custody for a very long time. I'll fly into Wilmington International with one of my guys. I'll let you know our ETA in Wilmington and hook up with everyone as soon as we get there. Text me the name and cell numbers of the lead Wilmington detective and whoever you talk to at the Jetport. I'll touch base with both of them as soon as I'm airborne."

"Good luck and happy hunting."

"Thanks Jane. After we get this bastard in cuffs, dinner on me anywhere you say."

***

Thirty minutes later, Dale was on his way to a local airport where the DEA Gulfstream was parked in a private hanger. With him was Gus Hilton, a

258

member of Dale's elite DEA team. Both men were trained in advanced strategies and tactics to conduct major drug busts and arrests of high-level drug dealers. Joseph Camino was at the top of Dale's list.

At the hanger, they were greeted by a seasoned Air Force combat veteran who flew reconnaissance missions in Iraq. Dale said, "Hi Gil, thanks for getting here so fast. Hope I didn't ruin your Sunday dinner."

"Nah, when I'm on call, Margaret is used to last minute orders. The office told me you need a quick flight to the Wilmington International Airport, and the flight plan has already been filed. They also faxed over a copy of an outstanding arrest warrant for Joseph Camino. We're ready to roll."

"Let's do it," said Dale and the two DEA agents climbed aboard. They were quickly cleared for takeoff and headed for Wilmington. On his sat phone, Dale called Wick James, the senior detective from the Wilmington Police Department. Jane's text said he would be meeting them at the airport.

"Detective James, Agent Dale Hawkins here from the DEA office in Miami. What's your status?"

"Been expecting your call, Dale. Call me Wick. Right now, I'm in the security office at Wilmington International with two of our senior detectives. The two FBI agents from Raleigh haven't arrived yet. We've been briefed by Special Agent Fielding and are standing by to meet your plane and assist however we can."

"I'm in the air headed to you with Gus Hilton, a member of my team."

Wick said. "Our transportation will be a commercial van with decals plastered on both sides from a local commercial cleaning service, including their popular slogan *Your dirt is our bread and butter*. I also have overalls for all of us with the cleaning company's logo. Best we could do on short notice in case we need them."

Dale laughed and cracked, "Good thinking, I just hope you guys didn't get taken to the cleaners for the cost of van rental. As soon as we arrive, we need to load everyone up and drive to the Cape Fear Jetport. That's where our bad guy is waiting for some guests to meet him before they all take off in his King Air by around nine-thirty or ten tonight. I'll fill everyone in when I get there. How far is that Jetport from Wilmington International?"

"It's south of us, about a forty-five-minute drive."

"Perfect. We should be landing by seven-thirty." Dale gave Wick the tail number of the DEA Gulfstream.

"We'll be ready to go as soon as you get here," said Wick. "Agent Fielding told me the two Raleigh agents will be here ahead of you. She's already pulled some strings with airport security, and everyone is cleared to leave in the van immediately."

"Nice work, Wick. See you shortly."

Dale then called Scott Singer, the manager on duty in the Cape Fear Jetport operations office. "Mr. Singer, my name is Dale Hawkins with the DEA in Miami. FBI Special Agent Jane Fielding said she would try to reach you and expect a call from me."

"Yes sir, I already spoke to Agent Fielding. She said you'd be calling to brief me on what you need. All she told me was that you're planning to arrest someone at our airport before their plane takes off. How can I help you?"

"Mr. Singer, we believe a high-level drug dealer arrived there late this afternoon in a King Air to pick up some people who will be meeting him later this evening. As soon as those people arrive, our target is planning to fly everyone to Miami. We need to arrest this man before he takes off."

"Understood, Agent Hawkins. We did have a King Air land about an hour ago with one pilot and one passenger. That plane is parked near our hanger area."

"Mr. Singer, please don't discuss this conversation with any of your staff. Our target is likely armed and will not hesitate to shoot anyone who tries to detain him. All I need you to do is keep an eye on that plane. If the pilot calls for clearance to take off before we get there, call me right away on this number. My team and I should be there before eight-thirty. Do not, I repeat, do not attempt to interfere with this man. His guests aren't scheduled to arrive until sometime after nine-thirty. He'll probably be waiting for them in your lounge."

Singer said, "Do you want me to have someone in the lounge to keep an eye out for him? I don't even know what he looks like."

"No sir, absolutely not. We don't want to spook him. Just go about your normal business, and I'll call you when we arrive at the airport. We'll be in a Cleanup Masters company van and wearing the company's standard overalls. We'll be there for your routine weekly cleaning service in case someone asks or he spots us. When we get there and I call you, make sure none of your people are anywhere near the lounge or in the lobby. We'll take it from there. All we want you to do is keep an eye on his plane."

"Got it. What do I do if another plane lands and the passengers go into the lounge to wait for their transportation?"

"Not a thing. We'll make sure no one is put in harm's way. We've done this before and won't jeopardize any civilians. Thanks for your cooperation. I'll speak to you when we get there."

Dale hoped Singer was smart enough to follow his instructions. If he didn't, his arrest of Camino could easily go sideways.

Chapter 60

Sunday, September 9, 2018

When Joseph Camino landed in Cape Fear, he said to Johnny, "Let's grab some dinner. If Jamison got on the road right after he dropped Frankie at the house, everyone should be here around nine-thirty tonight, ten at the latest. We OK to leave the plane parked on the tarmac until they get here?"

"Sure boss, no problem. I'll let the ground agent know we're expecting some guests, and we'll be flying out around ten p.m. or so. I'll get someone to fuel the plane and call us a cab."

On the way to a local Italian restaurant recommended by the cabbie, an old-timer who was born in Cape Fear and never left, Camino called Jamison's cell for an update. When he didn't answer, Camino figured he was probably driving through a stretch with no cell service. He left Jamison a voice mail to call him back as soon as he got his message.

When they got to the restaurant, he called Jamison again. No answer again. His anger rising, he said to his pilot, "Something's off, Jamison's not answering my calls."

"Probably just spotty cell service, boss. I'm sure he'll call as soon as he gets your message."

Camino wasn't convinced, but there wasn't much he could do about it. They ordered a bottle of wine with linguine and clam sauce and waited for Jamison to call back. When they finished eating and waiting for their coffee, Camino made a final call to Jamison's cell. Still no answer. He called Mark. "Mr. Davis, when was the last time you heard from Jamison?"

Mark knew the boss would eventually be calling him and was ready. "He called me shortly after he left the Pinewood Airport. He told me they were all driving to Wilmington to meet your plane after they dropped Frankie back at the house. I assume he's on his way."

"Have you talked to him since then?"

"No sir, is something wrong?"

Camino was now seething and ordered, "He's not answering his phone, find out where the hell he is and call me back." Before Mark could respond, the boss had already hung up.

He waved the waiter over with the universal hand gesture for the check. Camino left cash on the table with a generous tip, and he and Johnny quickly left the restaurant. When they got outside, the boss told his pilot to call a cab. "Tell them to step on it. We need to leave right now. I'm taking the cab to the Wilmington Airport."

Surprised, Johnny asked, "What about our plane, boss?"

"I still haven't heard from Jamison. Something's going on, and the cops may have been tipped off we're here. I'm not waiting around the airport to find out. I've got plenty of creds with me and will book a round trip flight to Miami. You take a cab back to the plane and immediately fly home."

"What if the cops are there?"

"What if they are? You're just a pilot waiting to fly some friends back to Miami, and there's been a change in plans. They'll be looking for me, not you. If there's no cops, go straight to the plane and take off."

"What about all our passengers from the Outer Banks?"

"We'll deal with that later, nothing we can do about it right now. Since Jamison isn't answering my calls, I'm not even sure he left. If I find out Jamison is setting me up, I'll kill that asshole myself."

When the cab arrived, Camino got in by himself and ordered the cabbie, "Wilmington International Airport and step on it."

***

On the way to Cape Fear in the cleaning van, Dale and his team were finalizing the details of their plan to get Camino into custody. Less than twenty minutes away, Dale got a call from Scott Singer.

"What's up, Mr. Singer? Anything wrong?"

"That King Air you asked me to keep an eye on just took off. He didn't even ask for clearance."

"That son of a bitch! Did anyone see who boarded the plane?"

"Yes sir. One of our maintenance guys who fueled that plane earlier told me only the pilot got on after he showed up and paid for his fuel."

"Is he sure only the pilot got on that plane?"

"My maintenance guy was servicing another plane in the hanger near where the King Air was parked. He was positive the pilot took off by himself."

"Thank you, Mr. Singer. Not what I wanted to hear, but we appreciate your help."

After the call, Dale said to everyone in the van, "We missed him. Camino's in the wind."

***

Sunday, September 9—National Hurricane Center 8 P.M. Advisory: *Hurricane Florence has strengthened over the past two days and has reached the warm and deep water in the Atlantic. Florence will continue to strengthen rapidly and is predicted to become a major hurricane by late Monday. The storm is forecasted to reach Category 4 hurricane status by Tuesday with wind speeds in excess of 130 mph. The storm is expected to cause extremely high coastal storm surge and flooding, with the potential of major structural damage and loss of life when it comes ashore. The current storm track shows Hurricane Florence making landfall along the North Carolina coastline by Friday morning.*

Chapter 61

When the new rescue plan was finished and everyone agreed, Steve suggested they all return to their rooms and get some rest. He asked them to be back in the conference room, geared up and ready to go, no later than one a.m.

Steve was on his way back to the Duck Inn from the police station with Billy, Hank, and Robby following the briefing when he got a call from Dale. He put his phone on speaker, and Dale replayed the events in Wilmington and the bad news about Camino.

Steve said, "Sorry to hear that, Dale. Missing Camino was my bad. I told Jamison not to answer any calls from him, and Camino probably got suspicious when he couldn't reach him. Just a guess, Camino may have decided to take a cab to the Wilmington Airport and book a commercial flight back to Miami. That's what I'd do. You may have even passed him going in the opposite direction on your way to the Cape Fear Jetport."

"We definitely could have passed each other. Nothing surprises me anymore with this guy. Not your fault, Steve. I'd have told Jamison the same thing. Better to keep Camino waiting for everyone in Cape Fear and not risk Jamison making a mistake while talking to him. What if Camino asked Jamison to hand his phone to one of the security guards? Could've been game over. It was smarter to keep Camino in the dark. Getting those people out of that beach house is your first priority."

"Where do you think he's headed?" Steve asked.

"It's a needle in the haystack at this point. Even with fake IDs, Camino's too smart to take a one-way flight. If I was him, I'd book a round-trip flight to Miami with an intermediate stop in another city, then book another round-trip flight from that city to Miami using a different set of bogus creds. The man didn't stay off our radar this long without watching his back and being prepared for anything. He's long gone."

"One of these days, he'll make a big mistake," said Steve.

Before he ended the call, Steve gave Dale a quick summary of their new rescue plan and promised to get back to him after it was over.

***

Just after midnight, Steve drove his team back to the station. When he got to the conference room, he wasn't surprised to find several FBI agents already there, including Bill Jackson. Steve said, "Guess it's now good morning, Bill."

"Hey Steve, just going over a few details with my South Carolina guys. Fred and the other agents from North Carolina will be here shortly. Their motel rooms are up the road in Corolla."

Chief Zimmer had two coffee pots on, and everybody helped themselves as they arrived. Bill stood in the front of the room to start his final briefing when everyone was in the conference room a few minutes before one a.m.

After they were all seated, Bill said, "Gentlemen, make sure your comms and night vision goggles are working before we leave here. Anybody in this room needs a vest, see me. We can't afford any mistakes tonight, so make damn sure the plan is crystal clear in your mind. We're dealing with three, maybe four, armed professionals and three unarmed civilians. Our cartel inside man Jamison is also unarmed. There's no room for error. The last thing we want is a shit show with guns blazing."

Steve added, "We know from Jamison that the security guards are under orders to stop any of the three kidnap victims from escaping by whatever means necessary, including terminal action."

Bill stood next to a blackboard with a diagram of the outside of the house to review the details of the rescue plan one more time, starting with the deployment of each team member.

Bill said, "Steve, you'll be with Charlie's team in the rear of the house. Billy, park Steve's car off the road and position yourself inside the tree line a hundred yards or so south of the driveway entrance. Hank and Robby will hunker down in the trees at the same distance north of the driveway. There shouldn't be much traffic this early in the morning, but some of the locals may decide to leave early ahead of a likely evacuation order tomorrow. Stay out of sight so you don't attract any looky-loos. If any of the security guards decide to make a run for it when we breach the house, take them down."

Speaking to his South Carolina agents, Bill said, "Charlie, you, Steve, and your team will initially deploy a quarter mile or so down the beach and out of sight. Three men north and two men south. At two fifty-five, move closer to the house and keep out of sight. Wait for my go command to move on the house.

Fred, you and your North Carolina guys will deploy in the woods, two along each side of the front of the house. There should be one of the security guards patrolling around the outside of the house, so make damn sure your team stays silent and out of sight until we're ready."

Bill then addressed the two FBI snipers. "Buck, you'll need to very quietly find a spot in the trees with a clear view of the rear and north side of the house. Marty, you'll do the same and cover the front and south side. When each of you are in position, Buck will give one click on his comms and Marty will make two clicks."

"As soon as you're both set, the rest of us will take our final positions. I'll be in the woods along the front right corner of the house. At two fifty-nine, take the outside guard down as soon as either of you has a clear shot. Those darts will put him on the ground quick and keep him there for several minutes. Alert me when he's been neutralized."

Bill then looked over at Harland Zimmer. "Chief, you'll park as far as possible off the road, a couple hundred yards south of the driveway entrance. Your other two officers will park the same distance north of the driveway. Keep your lights off. If all goes well, you guys will transport Jamison and the three hostages back to the police station after all three security guards and the chef are in custody, one way or the other. If there happens to be any gunfire, stay where you are until I tell you to move."

Bill then asked Steve to review his intel from Jamison on the interior of the house. Steve referred to another rough blackboard diagram and said, "According to Jamison, each of the three captives will be in these three bedrooms on the second floor. Every night they must be in their rooms by ten p.m. until seven a.m. the next morning. Their doors will be locked, and they've been told by Jamison to keep them locked until someone knocks twice and says the two code words."

He then pointed back to the diagram and said, "There are three more bedrooms on the third floor where the security guards and the chef sleep. There are also these two bedrooms on the north side of the house along this hallway on the first floor. This bedroom closest to the rear of the house is used for Jamison's office, where he also sleeps. The first bedroom off the hallway from the front door is where the surveillance equipment is located, including several video monitors. The monitors are manned twenty-four hours a day by one of the security guards, or sometimes Jamison. He won't be watching the monitors tonight."

Steve looked around the room and said, "Everybody with me so far?"

All heads nodded affirmative, and he continued, "Jamison told me the three security guards rotate every four hours. During the day, one of them guards the front of the house and one watches the back. The third guard handles the surveillance monitors. At night, one guard patrols around the house, front and back, one is on the monitors, while the third man and the chef sleep in two of the rooms on the third floor. At night, the three guards rotate at nine p.m., one a.m., and five a.m. Jamison will be in his bedroom office on the first floor with the door locked."

When Steve finished, Bill recapped the timetable and said, "At precisely three a.m., the power for the entire house will be cut off. One minute or so before that happens, the outside guard will be taken off the board by one of the snipers with his tranquilizer rifle. That sniper will then alert everyone the man is down, including his location. One of Fred's team will cuff him, gag him, and stay with him until the operation is over. If he starts to come around too soon, he'll be given another nap with a rifle butt."

"Immediately after the guard is down, Fred and Charlie's teams will quietly deploy to the front and back doors. When the power goes out, both teams will breech the house. Fred's team in front will rush to the bedroom with the monitors. Keep in mind the guard will be on high alert when his monitors go down. Charlie's team will double-time it to the third floor and isolate the third security guard and the chef, who may or may not be armed, in their bedrooms. Steve, you trail Charlie's team through the back door and take up a position on the second floor to protect the three kidnap victims if something goes south."

Steve looked at his watch and wrapped up the briefing. "When Bill gives the all-clear signal after all three security guards and the chef have been secured, I'll bring our three friends out to the driveway and get them into the Chief's patrol car. Bill will get Jamison from his room downstairs. Fred's team will transport the four prisoners back to the station in the SWAT van, where they'll remain under guard until the North Carolina team hits the road and returns them to Charlotte later this morning."

Bill raised his voice and barked, "Gentlemen, let's do this."

Chapter 62

Monday, September 10, 2018

By two forty-five a.m. Monday morning, everybody was in position. Bill noticed there was only one SUV in the driveway and assumed the second Suburban must be in the garage under the house. It was time to get Emily and her two friends to safety.

When the large black security guard Emily called Sarge came into Marty's view from the trees along the south side of the house at two fifty-eight a.m., the big man was hit in the chest with a well-placed tranquilizer dart and dropped in his tracks. Marty quietly said on his comms, "Outside guard down, south side of house."

At precisely three a.m., the power was cut, and Bill called into his mic, "Go! Go!"

Fred and his team charged through the front door wearing their night vision goggles and rushed to the first-floor bedroom where the monitors were located. Shorty was momentarily startled when he heard the front and back doors smash open. Before he had time to find his weapon in the pitch-black darkness, the bedroom door crashed inward, and he was quickly greeted by the barrel of a gun in his face.

Tonto and Frankie were asleep in their rooms on the third floor when they heard the racket downstairs. Tonto immediately got to his feet and turned on the lamp next to his bed. He instantly realized the power was out and the house was under attack. When he heard intruders pounding up the stairs, he pointed his automatic weapon at the bedroom door.

In one of the other third-floor bedrooms, Frankie sat up and tried to identify the noise he heard coming from downstairs. He turned on his lamp. Nothing. By the time he heard footsteps running up the stairs, he slowly felt his way in the dark to a corner of the room, crouched down and waited.

Seconds later, both men heard someone shouting. There were three bedrooms on the third floor, and Charlie and his team didn't know which two the bad guys were using. Well clear of the hallway and all three bedroom doors, Charlie yelled, "FBI, remain on your bed. Do not approach the door. Do not fire your weapon. Failure to comply will be met with lethal force."

He didn't have to wait long for a response. Frankie was no hero and stayed where he was. But Tonto decided to open fire and emptied his weapon, spraying bullets into his bedroom door and the walls on both sides of it. As soon as his initial volley ended, Charlie and his team unleashed a deafening barrage of return fire, blowing the bedroom door off its hinges.

Just before Tonto had time to slam another magazine into his weapon, Charlie low-crawled through the doorway and fired his assault weapon on full auto from right to left and left to right. Through his goggles, he saw Tonto's bullet-riddled body hit the floor face down and blood begin to puddle on the dark hardwood floors.

From one of the other bedrooms, Frankie began yelling, "Don't shoot. Don't shoot."

Charlie's number two man, Les Walker, shouted back, "Stay away from the door and lie flat on the floor." Frankie wisely complied as another loud boom blew a hole in the door latch. Walker crouched down next to the door and cautiously pushed it open with the barrel of his gun. He then took a quick peek into the room and saw the chef on his back with his hands raised.

When the gunfire stopped, Steve yelled up from the second floor, "Charlie, everybody OK?"

Charlie called back, "All good. No one hurt, except the asshole who went all Machine Gun Kelley on us. He's dead on the floor, no rush with his transport. The other guy's in cuffs. We'll bring him down with us."

By three-thirty a.m., the operation was over. One dead bad guy and no friendly casualties. On the downside, the third floor would need a few repairs before the next rental.

Into his mic, Bill said, "Well done, everybody. The house is clear, power will be back on in a minute. Steve, bring down Emily, John, and Chuck. I'm sure they'll be very glad to see you. I'll get Jamison. Chief, bring your car to the front of the house to transfer some happy people back to the station. Billy, Hank and Robby, take your cars to the Duck Police Station. Everybody meet back in the Chief's conference room."

After the lights went back on, Emily heard two knocks and the words "Finish Line." She slowly opened her bedroom door a crack and peeked out. Steve was smiling and said, "Hi Emily. Ready to go home?" She was still shaking from the gunfire and began sobbing when she recognized him. The nightmare was finally over. She hugged him tight and held on like her life depended on it. In more ways than she could imagine, it had.

As their luggage and personal belongings from the house were loaded into the trunks of the police cars by some of the FBI team, the three former captives had a heartfelt group hug at the bottom of the porch stairs. With tears in his eyes, Chuck looked directly into Emily's and said, "You're the bravest young woman I've ever met. You helped all of us keep it together and stay focused. Thank you, Emily."

Before they broke their embrace, John seconded Chuck's sentiments and said quietly, "You're one tough lady, Emily Baker. Next time I run into the bad guys, I want you on my team."

Still too emotional to speak, Emily just nodded at both of them through tears of relief before they were all escorted to the police cars and got in.

Chapter 63

Monday, September 10, 2018

When they were back at the station, Steve escorted Emily, Chuck, John, and Jamison into the Chief's office. "I know this has been a very stressful time for all of you," he said in a reassuring voice. "As soon as I have my final briefing with the entire team and make a couple of phone calls, I'll be back to discuss where we go from here. Billy Jones, a private investigator and member of my team from South Carolina, will stay here with you until I get back."

Before he left the room, he shook Jamison's hand and said, "Son, without the help of you and your friend Mark Davis, we'd still be searching. All of us, especially the three people sitting next to you, appreciate it. Feel free to tell them why you decided to help them."

Emily asked, "Detective Harris, can I call Aunt Marie and tell her I'm OK?"

Steve explained to all of them, "Before any phone calls, Bill Jackson, the Special Agent in Charge of the South Carolina FBI Field Office, along with Billy and me, will brief all of you on the plan we have in mind to keep you safe. We're still not out of the woods. Special Agent Jackson, the man who led the raid on the house this morning, is looking forward to talking to each of you."

Steve left the four of them with Billy and walked into the conference room. The chatter among the FBI teams stopped when Steve reached the front of the room and stood next to Jackson. "My hat's off to all of you for a precision operation. We didn't have a lot of time to plan for many contingencies, and fortunately we didn't need any. Bill and Jane Fielding both told me you guys are good, and you just made me a true believer. Thank you."

Steve looked over at Harland Zimmer. "Chief, we all owe a special debt of gratitude to you and your officers for your help yesterday and this morning. The outcome might have been very different without you guys, especially helping us get the airstrip blocked. This community is lucky to have you and your men here for them through some difficult days ahead with Florence bearing down."

Bill took over and said, "Gentlemen, before you head back to your rooms, there are a few important details that Steve and I need to go over with you. As Steve just mentioned, there's a serious hurricane headed our way. Governor Cooper is expected to evacuate the Outer Banks and surrounding coastal communities sometime later this morning. I know you're all anxious to get on the road, so please pay careful attention to what we're about to tell you. Steve, why don't you brief everyone on what you learned last evening."

Steve took a sip of coffee and began, "As you already know from our briefing earlier, Joseph Camino, the boss of the Camino cartel in Miami, planned to land at the local airstrip just up the road to pick up his three captives and security guards, along with Jamison. When we stopped him from landing, he ordered Jamison, now his former inside man at the house, to drive everyone to meet his plane at the Cape Fear Jetport near Wilmington. From there, Camino planned to fly everyone back to Miami.

As I mentioned earlier, Jamison and his cartel associate Mark Davis are now working for us. We've given both of them an immunity agreement in exchange for their help. Jamison returned everyone from the airport back to the beach house yesterday afternoon and stayed there instead of driving to Cape Fear. He then ignored all phone calls from Camino for routine updates about when he expected to arrive in Cape Fear."

Everyone's eyes were now laser-focused on Steve as he finished the story. "Last evening, a team of two DEA agents from Miami, along with two FBI agents from Raleigh, plus two Wilmington detectives, all met at the Wilmington International Airport. Their plan was to drive to the Cape Fear Jetport, where Camino's plane was waiting, and arrest him. That small airport is only a forty-five-minute drive from Wilmington International.

Halfway there, they got word from the Cape Fear Jetport manager helping them that Camino and his pilot must have separated, and the pilot flew their plane out alone. We suspect Camino got nervous when Jamison didn't answer his calls. The good guys missed Camino by about twenty minutes."

At this revelation, murmurs throughout the room broke the silence. When everyone settled down, Steve added, "One of the three captives you rescued this morning is a key witness in the murder trial of a Camino hitman. The

274

Camino cartel will do everything it can to keep this witness from testifying. That trial starts in Charleston in two weeks."

Steve paused for effect and looked around the room. "Gentlemen, it is absolutely imperative that no one, especially the media, finds out what went down here tonight. My team from South Carolina will be transporting the three people you rescued this morning, along with Jamison, to a safe house as soon as we leave here. We all need to keep an airtight lid on this entire operation. As far as anyone on the outside knows, it never happened. We're still searching for three missing people from South Carolina."

Bill took over. "Any questions?" There were none. "It's been a long night, try to grab a couple hours' sleep before you FBI guys hit the road. I suggest you get an early start to beat the traffic over the bridge before an evacuation is ordered."

To the North Carolina team leader, Bill said, "Fred, keep the three live prisoners secured in the SWAT van and under guard until you get to Charlotte. I'll make arrangements with Chief Zimmer to get the dead guy transported to the County Coroner. When I talk to a federal prosecutor later this morning, I'll let you know how he wants us to proceed. Call me when you're on the road, and I'll stay in touch. I'll also brief your boss as soon as I can reach her. I'm sure Agent Fielding will want to meet the van when you arrive in Charlotte."

Charlie, the South Carolina team leader, said, "Boss, we're going to start back around eight this morning. When do you want to meet with us back in Columbia to go over our post-op report?"

Bill smiled and said, "Charlie, let's meet with your team in my office at nine a.m. on Wednesday morning. I'll handle the official report." With a big grin, he added, "I just hope it doesn't get misplaced in the office paperwork shuffle."

When everyone except Steve and Bill left the conference room, Steve said, "Before we talk to our four new guests, I just wanted to personally thank you on behalf of Chief Hartman and the entire Mt. Pleasant Police Department for leading the op this morning. You helped us save some lives. Wait here and I'll bring them in."

Bill dropped his normal command tone and quietly replied, "Steve, this could have ended in a dozen different ways and many of them bad. I'm just glad the good guys won this round."

Chapter 64

Monday, September 10, 2018

Steve and Billy led all of them into the conference room. Watching Emily, Chuck, and John sitting together in front of the room next to Jamison, Steve was struck by how the constantly shifting events of the past two weeks had so dramatically turned the lives of these strangers with such different backgrounds into an improbable band of survivors.

Bill shook each of their hands, including Jamison's. He said to the three former captives, "Your courage and cool under pressure in the face of extreme danger from a ruthless drug cartel is nothing short of heroic."

When he got to Jamison, he looked directly at him. "Your decision to help us at significant risk to yourself is appreciated by all of us. Despite your involvement in the events that led us to the Outer Banks in the first place, we couldn't have found them in time without you and Mr. Davis."

Steve had been thinking about how to explain what would happen next. He and Bill sat down in front of the group. Steve said, "I know each of you wants to contact your families and friends to let them know you're OK. We want that for you as well. You also need to know that the Camino drug cartel was responsible for the kidnapping. And while it doesn't excuse his involvement, in the end Jamison did the right thing. The cartel's plan was to pick all of you up at the local airstrip yesterday afternoon and fly you to Miami. Fortunately, Jamison tipped us off, and we kept them from landing. Jamison then agreed to ignore the orders from his boss to drive you to Cape Fear yesterday afternoon and meet his plane there."

The three of them looked over at Jamison, and Emily mouthed a silent "thank you." Jamison said, "Nothing I say can make up for my involvement in bringing the three of you to the Outer Banks. But when I learned a few days ago that my boss had tried to murder my parents two years ago, I wanted to get back at him. I thought my mom and dad had died in a boating accident until I talked to them last week."

Emily was surprised at this revelation and asked him, "Where are they now?"

Jamison looked at her and said, "They've been hiding in the Caribbean since their sailboat was sabotaged. My friend Mark and I have been working with Detective Harris and the FBI for the past couple days to assist them with your rescue in exchange for their help to get my parents safely back to the United States. We've also agreed to testify against the cartel, including Joseph Camino, the mastermind of the plan to kidnap you."

Steve said, "The problem right now is that the Camino cartel will keep looking for you to stop any of you from testifying about what you might have seen at the Port of Charleston last year in the murder trial of a senior cartel man named Teddy Francisco. I assume you've already discussed this possibility among yourselves and figured out this was the most likely reason you were all kidnapped and held captive in the first place."

He looked directly at Emily to underscore his point. "Mr. Francisco's trial is scheduled to start in Charleston in two weeks. We don't think the cartel knows for sure which one of you is the key eyewitness for the prosecution. Once the trial ends, the cartel will no longer need to find you. Except for Jamison. They will still want to make an example of him for betraying them and disrupting their entire scheme. We also have a plan to keep him safe."

Chuck asked, "What are we supposed to do until then?"

"We're going to keep all of you safe, but right now we can't let anyone know where you are. Two of your three security guards and your friendly chef are now in our custody and will be detained with no outside contact until after the trial. The third guard was killed in the shootout at the house. Everyone involved in this rescue operation understands the situation, and the details will be kept under wraps until we're able to guarantee your safety."

Emily interrupted and asked, "Which guard is dead?"

Steve was surprised by the question. "All I was told by the FBI team was that he was a Native American."

Almost to herself, Emily said flatly, "Tonto."

Everyone looked at her and Steve asked, "Who's Tonto?"

Emily explained, "I gave each of the security guards my own names and his was Tonto. The other two were Sarge and Shorty."

Before Steve had a chance to follow-up with her, John jumped in with another question. "What about my wife?"

Steve answered, "We've been in regular contact with Mandy and Emily's aunt since we learned you were missing. Billy and I will be personally calling them tomorrow, and we'll also meet with them when we return home to let them know you're all safe and will be rejoining them soon. Chuck, we've also been in touch with George Cooper. He's been very worried about you. I met with George when we searched your cabin for any clues about where you might be. You're lucky to have such a good friend."

Steve reinforced the decision to keep them protected at an undisclosed location. "Until Mr. Francisco's murder trial is over, we cannot reveal your location to any of your families and friends. The cartel will stop at nothing to try to find you before the trial starts."

He paused to let the news sink in. Nobody spoke until Bill said, "We know this is not what you want to hear right now, but we can't risk your safety under any circumstances. You three kidnap victims have made it this far, we just need you to hold on for a few more days."

Emily was the first to respond. "Detective Harris and Agent Jackson, thank you for not only rescuing us, but also being upfront and honest explaining the situation we're in. I can't speak for the others, but whatever you need me to do, including testifying at the trial, I'm in. Just please make sure Aunt Marie and my boyfriend Richard understand what's going on and that I'm OK."

She looked over at Chuck and John, waiting for them to say something. Chuck looked at Steve and said, "Thanks for letting my friend George know I'm safe. Since we have no choice, we all need to stick together. John, you with us?"

John grinned and said, "I can't leave you guys by yourselves. Who's gonna make sure you don't do or say something stupid? Detective, thanks for letting my wife Mandy know I'm fine."

Steve said, "Mandy actually hired my friend Billy here to find you. In fact, that's how we eventually put two and two together and figured out all three of you were probably being held together by the cartel. You were all seen on some port surveillance tapes stolen by the cartel. They wanted to keep each of you from testifying about what you might have seen the morning of the murder that cartel operative Teddy Francisco is on trial for."

Jamison spoke up next. "Guess you can't get rid of me yet, just don't expect me to keep you entertained any longer." The tension finally broke when everyone laughed.

Steve wrapped up the briefing. "We've reserved a room at the Duck Inn for each of you to clean up and get a little rest. Your bags will be in your rooms. We'll all have breakfast together at the Duck Diner. Let's meet in the lobby at eight a.m. Billy and I will be on guard until we leave for breakfast. The two Mt. Pleasant detectives who worked on your case with me will join us. Agent Jackson will also meet us for breakfast before heading back to South Carolina. And remember, no phone calls."

"Where will we be going?" asked Emily.

Steve smiled and said, "As far away from the Outer Banks as we can before Florence arrives."

Chapter 65

Monday, September 10–Tuesday, September 11, 2018

When everybody got to the motel and checked into their rooms, Steve and Billy stayed in the lobby. Billy said, "Just like old times, partner. Haven't pulled an all-nighter with you since we got stuck with overnight KP duty on our first day of basic training. I know you have several people to talk to. Let me touch base with Molly, then I'll take the first shift while you make your calls."

Steve grinned and said, "I almost forgot about that first day at Leonard Wood when we met each other."

"Yeah, and we'd have been fine if you hadn't decided to go all gung-ho and stand next to me in the front row of the formation with the other newbies. We were the tallest guys in the platoon and easy volunteer targets for Drill Sergeant Ballbuster."

Steve laughed and shot back, "He already had your sorry ass picked out. I was just along for the ride."

It was almost six a.m. on Tuesday morning when Steve called Janet. Groggy from being awakened out of a sound sleep, she mumbled, "Hello, is that you, Steve?"

"Hi hon, sorry to call so early. We just finished up. We got them all out, and they're safe."

"Thank God! I've been worried sick about all of you."

"We're all good, babe. The past day was one for the books, but our rescue plan went off without a hitch early this morning, thanks to the FBI teams that were with us. I'll tell you all about it when I see you. We've still got some work to do. Are you and Molly all set to head to Greenville if the Governor orders an evacuation?"

"His office has scheduled a press conference for nine a.m. this morning. He's expected to announce his evacuation order then. Where will you be going?"

"Billy and my team still need to escort the people we rescued to a safe house far enough inland to avoid the brunt of Florence. South Carolina FBI Agent Bill Jackson, who led the rescue operation, will confirm the location to us shortly. We're all having breakfast in a couple hours before we head out. I'll call you when I have more details. Billy just talked to Molly to let her know what's going on."

"I'm just glad you're all safe. I'll call Molly and get ready to go. Before I went to bed last night, the hurricane was blowing up and still headed for the coast. I'm sure we'll need to leave. Try to get some sleep in the car and let someone else drive."

"Hank and Robby are getting a couple hours of sleep now and will take the first driving shift for both cars. Stay safe and I'll call back when I know more. Love you."

"Love you too, hon."

Steve's next call was to Chief Hartman. He was already up and recognized the caller ID. "Everything alright, Steve?"

"We got them, and everyone's safe."

"Outstanding, never a doubt. Great news, Steve! Congratulations to the whole team."

"The four of us are driving out of here in a couple hours to take our friends to a safe house. Dale almost caught up with Joseph Camino himself last night, but just missed him. We're now worried the cartel will be gunning hard to find Emily and the others before the trial starts. Right now, Camino doesn't know we have them, but he'll figure it out soon enough."

Steve reviewed the events since they left Mt. Pleasant yesterday for the Outer Banks. "Chief, please have Jill Carrington call me as soon as you can reach her. I need to brief her on what went down and coordinate our next moves before Teddy's trial. I also plan to touch base with Dale and tell him how things played out here this morning."

"Congrats again to everyone involved up there. I'm proud of all of you."

"It was definitely a team effort, Chief. We also couldn't have done it without a major assist from Chief Zimmer. The man came through for us big time to help us stop Camino from landing at the local airport up here. Camino was planning to fly his captives back to Miami. With Chief Zimmer's help, we blocked the runway and kept Camino's plane from landing."

"I'll give Harland a call later today. He's going to need some help up there if the hurricane makes landfall on top of them. We'll do what we can to lend him a hand."

"He'll appreciate that. We definitely owe him one."

Steve then called Dale and told him about the hectic morning's events. He added, "I'm going to call Mark Davis and see if he's heard from Camino. Mark may still be in play to help us if Camino doesn't think he was involved in Jamison's decision to ignore his orders. Mark told us Camino would end up in court, but he never explained what he meant."

"Thanks for the update, Steve, excellent news! Keep me in the loop. I'm still pissed we missed Camino. I just hope Mark meant what he said."

Mark had been up most of the night waiting for some news of the rescue attempt. When Steve called and told him the details, he was ecstatic and said, "Camino called me early last evening and asked me if I'd heard from Jamison. I told him I hadn't, and he was not a happy camper. He just ordered me to find Jamison, whatever it takes. I'm not sure if he still trusts me or not."

Steve said, "Mark, when we first spoke to you last Saturday, you said Camino would end up in court. You still haven't told us how and when you thought that would happen."

When Mark told him, Steve's jaw dropped.

***

Joseph Camino was waiting in the New Orleans airport for his flight to Miami after arriving in the Big Easy from Wilmington through Cincinnati on Tuesday morning. He called Jake Thomas, who he had always considered a trusted advisor, and briefed him on the events of Monday. He wanted to know if Jake thought Mark Davis could have been involved in the failed attempt to bring the captives to Miami.

Camino had no idea Jake had betrayed him by telling Mark about Camino's order to sabotage the Walters' sailboat, which ultimately led Jamison and Mark to alter the outcome of events on the Outer Banks. Jake just smiled to himself and said to Camino, "I talked to Mark yesterday, and there's no way he was involved."

Camino then made another call, this one to his pilot. "Johnny, I want you to fly to Raleigh right away and rent a car. Take Sal with you and get your asses over to the Outer Banks. I want to know if anyone is still in that beach house."

"Boss, there's been an evacuation order for the entire coastline. I'm not sure we'll even be allowed on the island."

"I don't give a shit. If you get stopped, tell them you're picking up your mother who lives alone and doesn't drive. Figure something out and just do it. Call me when you get there."

Johnny and Sal took US 64 from the Raleigh-Durham Airport to the Virginia Dare Bridge, which was still open both ways to and from the Outer Banks. From the bridge, they arrived at the beach house fifty minutes later. It was empty. Before calling the boss, they drove over to the Pinewood Airport. The trucks that had kept them from landing yesterday afternoon were gone.

The airstrip was clear.

Chapter 66

Tuesday, September 11, 2018

Steve and Billy were sound asleep in the back of their car before they even reached the Wright Memorial Bridge to take them off the island. Hank took the first driving shift with Emily in the passenger seat next to him. Robby was driving the other car right behind them with Chuck, John, and Jamison. Chuck was happy to make himself useful as Robby's backup relief.

An hour later, Steve was instantly alert when his cell buzzed with a call from Bill Jackson. "What's up, Bill? You find us a location?"

"We've got you a safe house, but I don't want to discuss the location over an unsecure line. Give me Billy's cell number and I'll text him the address. Two of my agents are already on their way to the house and will be waiting for your arrival. Your guests will be safe there, and I'll keep the house under twenty-four-seven surveillance until the trial, just to make sure. There will be an encrypted cell phone for you when you get there. Call me on that cell when you arrive."

When Billy got the text from Bill, he jotted down the address and handed it to Hank. Emily asked, "Where are we going?"

"Someplace safe," Billy said to her before switching off his phone and falling back to sleep. Jill Carrington called Steve thirty minutes later. He was still asleep, and she left a voice message.

A little after five p.m., both cars pulled into the driveway of a large farmhouse on the outskirts of Asheville, North Carolina. They'd all been on the road over seven hours since leaving the Duck Diner for the 450-mile drive to the western side of the state. An unmarked car driven there by one of Bill Jackson's FBI agents was already parked in front of the house.

The old two-story stone house had six bedrooms and was situated on the edge of an open three-acre plot of land about five miles from downtown Asheville. The retired owners of the house now spent most of their time in

France and rented the house while they were away. Jackson had a friend rent it for him for the next month.

Before Steve got to the front door, an FBI agent came out to meet them and said, "FBI Special Agent Brad Milton. Bill sends his greetings. Agent Brian Murray came with me and is inside. How was the trip?"

Steve said, "Hi Brad, all good. Thanks for getting the house ready for us. I'll introduce everyone after they get settled."

"Steve, the place hasn't been occupied for a couple months, and our cleaning crew just left. We stocked enough food for the first couple days. We'll take care of getting more tomorrow. Brian and I will be staying in one of the upstairs bedrooms as long as we're needed."

"Perfect, all of us are pretty beat, so I anticipate an early night. We stopped to eat about two hours ago. If you have anything for sandwiches in case anyone gets hungry before they hit the sack, that would be great. My colleagues and I will bunk here tonight and head out tomorrow morning. We'll put our guests in the four empty bedrooms, and our two detectives can take the other empty room. Me and Billy Jones, a Charleston PI with my team, will find a spot to curl up. About all I need is a couch."

"What are your travel plans?" asked Brad.

"With the evacuation of the coast, Billy and I will probably stay with some friends in Greenville before we head back to Mt. Pleasant when the coast is clear. Billy is also a personal friend. Hank and Robby, two of our Mt. Pleasant detectives, are meeting their families in Spartanburg tomorrow. From the last weather report we heard on the radio; sounds like we got off the Outer Banks just in time."

"You definitely did. Bill filled us in on your situation. Whatever you need, just holler. Here's our cards and your new cell phone from Bill. I've got the number if we need to reach you after you leave."

Everyone was still standing around in the driveway while Steve finished his conversation with Brad. When he rejoined the group, Steve said, "Welcome to Asheville. Make yourselves at home. FBI agents Brad Milton and Brian Murray will be staying in the house with you. My team will stay here tonight and leave early in the morning. There are plenty of empty bedrooms, the lady gets first choice. There's also some sandwich stuff and drinks in the fridge, just help yourselves. Let's all meet in the living room in one hour, and I'll brief you on our plans for the next few days."

After meeting Brian Murray and turning on his new burner phone, Steve checked in with Bill and returned Jill's call. "Hi Jill, sorry it took so long to get back to you, but I wanted to get everyone to the safe house that Bill found for us before calling you."

Steve told her where they were and briefly summarized the events of the past twenty-four hours.

"We're going to keep Emily and the others here until the trial. No calls in or out. Two of Bill Jackson's agents will be staying in the house and setting up twenty-four-hour watches in twelve-hour shifts. The cartel is going to be turning over boulders searching for them."

"Wonderful news, Steve. I will need to meet with Emily to go over her testimony before the trial. Right now, I'm driving to Atlanta to stay with my brother. Sometime next week, I can drive up there to see Emily. I'll also need to go over your testimony whenever it's convenient."

"That works. I'll be back in Mt. Pleasant as soon as the coast is clear."

Jill added, "By the way, I called Judge Templeton this morning before the mandatory evacuation was announced. He told me he plans to delay the start of the trial for only one day based on the current storm track. The latest forecast has Florence making landfall someplace on the North Carolina coast this Thursday or Friday. Still too early to tell, but it looks like Charleston will escape the worst of it. If that turns out to be accurate, jury selection will begin on Tuesday, the 25th."

Steve gave her his new cell number and said, "Call me on this number when we need to talk, it's an encrypted cell from Bill. I talked to Mark Davis this morning, and he's also willing to testify at the trial if needed. There's one other surprise from Mark you need to know."

When he told her, Jill was speechless.

Chapter 67

By Tuesday, the governors of Virginia, North Carolina, and South Carolina had ordered evacuations of their coastlines. The monster storm was forecasted to slow down and stall after making landfall later in the week as a possible Category 4 hurricane with life-threating impacts, including dangerous storm surge, catastrophic flooding, and damaging winds. Hurricane warnings were posted up and down the southeast coast. Tropical force winds above 39 mph were expected to arrive onshore sometime on Thursday.

Early Friday morning, September 14, Hurricane Florence finally made landfall just south of Wrightsville Beach, North Carolina, some one hundred and seventy miles south of Duck. Three days earlier, the storm had reached its peak intensity with strong Category 4 hurricane wind speeds clocked at 150 mph. An eyewall replacement cycle and less favorable conditions near the coastline reduced the wind speed to 90 mph when Florence came ashore as a strong Category 1 hurricane.

Although the wind speed had lessened, the slow movement of the storm when it reached the coast caused widespread heavy rain throughout North and South Carolina. A powerful storm surge and record amounts of rainfall resulted in massive flooding along the North Carolina coast from New Bern to Wilmington, swamping most major roads and highways well inland.

The city of Wilmington was temporarily cut off entirely due to severe flooding. Many North Carolina towns recorded record rainfall, including over 33 inches in Swansboro and 36 inches in Elizabethtown.

When the deadly storm system had finally dissipated by Monday, September 18, Hurricane Florence left in its wake over twenty-four billion dollars in damage, lingering power outages, and fifty-four deaths from Virginia to Florida, forty of them in North Carolina.

Fortunately for Charleston, Florence was downgraded to a tropical storm with maximum sustained winds of 50 mph as it slowly passed by well north of the city. Damage from the storm was limited to some minor local flooding, downed trees, and power outages. By Saturday, most of the local power had been restored.

Charleston Mayor John Tecklenburg met with reporters after the storm had passed. "The National Weather Service told us this would be a very dangerous storm, and unfortunately that turned out to be true for many along the North Carolina coast and just to the north of us. Here in Charleston, we were blessed to be spared a direct hit."

Amanda Knight, Mt. Pleasant Emergency Management Director, commented, "We were lucky. There were no reports of serious damage, other than the power outage Friday night and a few trees down."

As soon as the storm moved through, the lane reversal of I-26 from Charleston to Columbia was discontinued, and the eastbound lanes from Columbia to Charleston were reopened to normal traffic. On Saturday afternoon, Steve, Billy, and their families all returned to Mt. Pleasant.

***

The following Tuesday, a week before the scheduled start of Teddy's murder trial, Joseph Camino called Teddy's defense attorney. "Mr. Franklin, has the storm caused the judge to reschedule the trial?"

"The judge has delayed the start by only a day. He advised the prosecution and defense to be ready to begin jury selection next Tuesday instead of Monday."

"Have you received the final witness list from the prosecution yet?"

"Yes, I finally have it."

"Are any of our friends on the list?"

"Yes sir, all three of them are on it."

"How's Teddy holding up?" asked Camino.

"Your son is fine."

Chapter 68

Tuesday, September 25–Tuesday, October 2, 2018

The historic Charleston County Courthouse is on the corner of Broad and Meeting Streets in downtown Charleston. The intersection is dubbed 'the four corners of the law' since Federal, State, County, and City buildings stand on each corner. The Neoclassical courthouse was designed by famous Irish architect James Hoban, who also designed the White House. The three-year courthouse construction project began in 1790.

Steve sat in the back of courtroom number two on the second floor as the first set of prospective jurors from the Charleston County jury pool filed into the jury box. It had been over a year since he started a routine murder investigation of a man found murdered with one bullet in the back and two more in the head just outside the back gate of the Port of Charleston. The past year had turned out to be anything but routine.

In some ways, Jill Carrington believed the jury selection dance was almost as important as the trial itself. She was sitting at the prosecution table on one side of the middle aisle. Seated next to her was her number two, Carly Davidson, a seasoned prosecutor in her own right who had ambitions to run for Charleston County Prosecutor whenever Jill decided to step down. Louis Franklin for the defense was at the table on the other side of the aisle. Next to Franklin was the defendant, Teddy Francisco, and Franklin's second chair, Attorney Blake Martinelli.

After some opening remarks to the first set of potential jurors by Judge Templeton, the tedious process of jury selection began. The goal for both sides was to seat twelve honest and unbiased citizens of Charleston County, committed to listening to all of the evidence before rendering a verdict, as long as it was in their favor. Jill knew she would need to convince all twelve to convict Teddy for the murder of Jorge Rodriguez. Louis only needed one to disagree.

Judge Templeton kept the process moving along, and by late Tuesday afternoon, after a hard-fought day of hand-to-hand verbal combat over almost every juror, both sides were satisfied when the final jury of seven men and five women was seated, along with two alternates. Court was recessed for the day. Opening statements from the prosecution and defense would begin at nine a.m. on Wednesday morning.

Despite the best efforts of the cartel to find them, Emily, Chuck, John, and Jamison remained hidden in the Asheville safe house. Mark was still in the clear after being ordered by Camino to keep looking for Jamison and everyone else who had disappeared from the beach house, which sustained extensive damage from the hurricane. Steve stayed in touch with Mark, who in turn kept Jamison's parents updated while they remained off the grid in the Caribbean.

The trial began with Jill's opening statement to the jury. After welcoming them and introducing herself, she outlined the bones of the prosecution's case, including what she characterized as 'overwhelming evidence' that would prove beyond any reasonable doubt Teddy Francisco murdered Jorge Rodriguez in cold blood on the morning of August 7, 2017. She told the jury she would show Teddy was in the Charleston area on the day of the murder. She also promised to link him to the Camino drug cartel and a cocaine seizure at the Port of Charleston shortly before the murder.

Saving the best for last, Jill closed with her intention to produce an eyewitness who would put Teddy and his murder victim, Jorge Rodriguez, together minutes before Rodriguez was murdered. She further told the jury that a timeline of the events at the Port of Charleston that morning would be corroborated by a time-stamped port surveillance video of the murder.

Teddy's lead defense attorney, Louis Franklin, predictably tried to shoot holes in the prosecution's case in his opening statement. He ended his fiery rebuttal with a full-throated charge that the prosecution's so-called evidence to convict Teddy of murder was purely circumstantial and proved nothing. His client was unequivocally not guilty.

After the lunch break, Jill stood up and began to methodically present the case against Teddy. Buddy Evans testified about the discovery of the body, and Bob Jenkins handled the forensics and his discovery of the shell casing found at the murder scene under the victim's body. New York and Miami DEA agents, including Dale Hawkins, testified about Teddy's links to organized crime and the Camino drug cartel.

Unfortunately for the prosecution, Jerry Reardon, the port mole confirmed by Mark, was unavailable to testify due to his untimely death when his car ran off the road into a grove of trees on I-26 in South Carolina, one week after his sudden disappearance from the port. An inspection of the car by the accident investigation team determined the primary cause of the crash was brake failure due to a punctured brake line.

The start of court on Thursday was delayed for an hour, which Judge Templeton apologized was due to an unavoidable matter on another case. Jill spent the rest of Thursday and all day Friday building her case against Teddy, before Templeton adjourned court for the weekend.

Steve testified the entire morning on Monday about his ongoing murder investigation that eventually led to Teddy's arrest outside a nightclub in Miami. He also testified about his two interviews in May with an eyewitness who identified the defendant and the murder victim arguing along the security fence at the Port of Charleston a few minutes before the murder.

As expected, Franklin objected on the grounds of hearsay and demanded the name of the alleged eyewitness. Jill stood and asked the judge if she could approach the bench. Judge Templeton waved her and Franklin forward.

Templeton said, "Miss Carrington?"

"Your honor, due to the security concerns I continue to have, I ask the court's indulgence to hold the identity of our eyewitness until tomorrow morning when the witness will take the stand."

Louis jumped in. "Your honor, the prosecution has insisted on keeping the name of this witness a secret since you granted Miss Carrington an extra week to find this mystery person. The defense again demands to know who this witness is without any further delay."

"Mr. Franklin, you will have ample time to cross-examine the witness tomorrow. Miss Carrington, is the name of this witness on your witness list?"

"Yes, your honor."

Franklin protested, "I haven't been able to locate three of the prosecution's witnesses since we received the prosecution's witness list."

Jill smiled and said, "If Mr. Franklin will provide their names, I'll be happy to have my investigator look into their whereabouts this afternoon."

Templeton said, "Very well, since Miss Carrington has promised her witness will be available to testify tomorrow morning, I see no reason to disclose the name of this witness until then. Mr. Franklin, you will have ample time to question the witness in your cross. Step back and take your seats."

Franklin stormed back to the defense table, and Jill slowly returned to her chair after giving Steve a quick nod. Franklin continued his aggressive cross of Steve after the lunch break for the rest of the afternoon. When he was finished, Templeton gaveled the court in recess until Tuesday morning.

Emily had been driven back to Charleston from the Asheville safe house on Monday by FBI Agent Milton and booked into a small motel in West Ashley under Milton's name. Chuck, John, and Jamison remained at the safe house with FBI Agent Murray.

Early on Tuesday morning, Emily was taken by police escort to the courthouse, where extra security had been added inside and outside the famous landmark. She was led through a side entrance and remained in a heavily guarded office until she was called to testify.

Courtroom number two was packed with reporters and spectators. By now, the trial had gained national attention given the alleged link between the defendant and the Camino drug cartel. Four heavily armed DEA agents in street clothes were seated apart in the back of the courtroom, along with four plain clothes detectives, including Robby and Hank. Billy was also with them. Outside the courtroom were several more security officers in the lobby and on the second floor.

Chapter 69

Tuesday, October 2, 2018

The arrival of Joseph Camino and his bodyguards at the courthouse was expected by Steve. When Mark found out from Jake Thomas what had happened to Jamison's parents, Jake also confided to Mark that Teddy was Joseph Camino's son. Before Teddy went to work for the Bruno crime family in New York, Happy Bruno and Camino had both agreed Teddy needed to change his last name to keep the link between the Bruno and Camino crime families hidden from law enforcement.

Camino entered the courthouse dressed casually in tan slacks and a blue blazer. He made no attempt to hide his identity since he was confident no one would expect him to show up at the trial. Especially since the only two people he ever told that Teddy was his son were Jake Thomas and Louis Franklin.

The cartel boss had told both Thomas and Franklin the previous Saturday that he planned to see Teddy at the trial on Tuesday. He said he also wanted to find out for himself the name of the eyewitness his people had failed to keep under lock and key. He was now convinced it was Jamison, not Mark, who had betrayed him. He told them he would bury the traitor as soon as he popped his head up.

When Jake had told Mark that Camino would be at the trial on Tuesday, Mark immediately gave Steve a heads up and reminded him of his promise that Camino would end up in court.

Camino walked through the metal detector just beyond the courthouse front doors and was followed into the lobby by two muscle-bound bodyguards. The three of them headed for the stairs to the second floor and courtroom two. Teddy was already at the defense table, looking back at the people entering the room. Franklin had told him his father would be there today.

Dale was dressed in a security guard uniform and recognized Camino as soon as he entered the lobby. He said quietly into his lapel mic, "He's here and heading for the stairs with two bodyguards and several other courtroom spectators. He's wearing a blue blazer and tan slacks, and his goons look like WWE rejects. You can't miss them. Everybody wait to move on my command."

Dale then climbed the stairs and reached the second-floor landing just as Camino opened the door to courtroom two. In the hallway outside the courtroom, Dale looked over at Steve, who was also dressed as a security guard. He motioned Steve over, and both men entered the courtroom together behind Camino and stood in the back near the door.

Camino found an empty seat three rows behind Teddy. His two bodyguards sat two rows further back, four seats apart from each other. When Teddy saw his father coming down the aisle toward the defense table, he smiled and nodded to him.

Twenty minutes later, the courtroom went quiet as Judge Templeton slowly approached the bench, and the bailiff said, "All rise."

Dale stood up and said into his comms, "Now!"

In a simultaneous rapid deployment, Dale and the four DEA agents in the back of the courtroom ran up the aisle and surrounded Camino. Steve and the other armed detectives also moved quickly up the aisle directly behind the DEA agents and neutralized the two confused bodyguards. At the exact same time, two armed SWAT officers entered the courtroom through the side door to the judge's chambers and stood in front of the bench.

Before the stunned courtroom even had time to react, Judge Templeton stood up and banged his gavel three times. In a loud voice, he said, "Everyone please sit down, the situation is under control. Do not interfere with the law enforcement officers."

Joseph Camino was handcuffed by Dale. "Nice to finally meet you in person, Mr. Camino. I'm arresting you for the kidnapping of Emily Baker, Chuck Wilson, and John Simpson, and the attempted murder of Harrison and Charlotte Walters. We'll add a few more goodies later."

Dale read him his rights, then whispered in his ear, "Your sorry ass is mine, hotshot." Camino gave him a menacing tight smile but said nothing.

As soon as Camino and his two bodyguards were led out of the courtroom, Templeton banged his gavel again and asked everyone to please be silent and remain seated. When the buzz of voices finally stopped, he sat back down and calmly addressed the courtroom.

"Ladies and gentlemen, this court apologizes for the disruption. The man who was arrested was a senior member of a major drug cartel in Miami. Unfortunately, he and his two friends decided to pay the City of Charleston a friendly visit this morning, but we were unable to show them the Southern hospitality they were expecting. Please remain in your seats until the jury has left the courtroom before you exit in an orderly manner. This court is adjourned until nine a.m. tomorrow."

Templeton banged his gavel once more and returned to his chambers. During the entire episode, Teddy remained frozen in place, too shaken to move, until he was cuffed and escorted back to his holding cell.

Chapter 70

Wednesday, October 3–Thursday, October 4, 2018

After the explosive courtroom arrest of Joseph Camino on Tuesday, Emily was escorted by two members of the SWAT team from the courthouse back to her motel room in West Ashley. Two FBI agents were posted at the motel until they returned her to testify the next day.

Emily finally took the stand on Wednesday morning. Before she testified, Jill played the time-stamped surveillance video of the argument at the port between two men shortly before Emily could also be seen on the video running past the port entrance gates and the security fence at the same time. A second time-stamped video showed Rodriguez being shot twice in the head a few minutes later. The shooter had his back to the camera and couldn't be identified on the video.

Jill approached Emily and established her identity for the jury. She then asked, "Miss Baker, was that you on the video I just played running around the main entrance to the Port of Charleston last year on Monday, August 7?"

"Yes, ma'am," replied Emily.

Jill held up the same photo of Jorge Rodriguez that Steve had shown her back in May. "Miss Baker, do you recognize the man in this photo?"

In a strong voice with convincing determination, Emily replied. "Yes ma'am, that's one of the men I saw arguing with a taller man near the Port of Charleston entrance that morning."

Jill showed the photo to the jury and identified the man in the photo as the murder victim, Jorge Rodriguez. She returned to the prosecution table to retrieve a second photo and approached Emily again. She held up the photo and went through the same drill with Emily before showing it to the jury.

"Miss Baker, do you recognize the man in this photo?"

"Yes ma'am, that's the taller man I saw arguing with the other man that morning."

"How did you know who these two men were?"

"I didn't. Detective Harris showed me six photos this past May and asked me if I could identify any of the men I saw at the port on August 7. I pointed to one of the men I saw that morning. That was the first photo you showed me. A couple weeks later, Detective Harris brought me a different set of six photos and asked me if I could identify any of them. I recognized the man in the second photo you just showed me."

"You testified you didn't know who they were, so you didn't know their names?"

"Yes ma'am, that's correct."

"Wasn't it dark that early in the morning? How were you able to identify them?"

"Both men were standing under a light pole above the port security fence. At the time, I thought it was strange for two men to be having an argument there that early in the morning, and I was curious so I slowed down on my morning run. The taller man turned to watch me until I was past them, and I got a clear look at both their faces as I ran by. Then I just kept running back to my apartment."

"How far away from them were you when you ran past them?"

"About ten strides."

Some laughter broke out in the courtroom before Judge Templeton gently banged his gavel and said, "Order please."

Jill paused and smiled at Emily. "And for any non-runners on the jury, how far would you estimate ten strides to be?"

More laughter and Emily's face reddened in embarrassment. She sheepishly replied, "Sorry, that would be around twenty-five or thirty feet."

Jill then retrieved a large blowup of a photo mounted on foamboard from behind the prosecution table and entered it into evidence. The photo showed the light pole and security fence area where Emily said she saw the two men arguing, as well as the portion of the port entrance where she was running as she passed by them. Both areas were marked with an 'X' on the photo.

She hoped Louis Franklin would object and he didn't disappoint her. He jumped to his feet and said in a loud voice, "Objection, relevance."

Jill looked at Judge Templeton and said, "Your honor, County Coroner Bob Jenkins will be recalled to testify that this photo was taken by his forensic tech. Mr. Jenkins will also confirm the distance between the two men Miss

Baker identified along the security fence and her own location when she ran by them is twenty-seven feet."

"Objection overruled," said Templeton.

Jill showed the photo to Emily, then held it up in front of the jury box before putting it on an easel in front of them. She turned back to the witness box. "Miss Baker, will you please tell the jury what this photo shows."

"The two 'X' marks on this photo show where two men were arguing along the fence and where I was when I ran past them."

"Miss Baker, do you see one of the men you saw that morning in this courtroom?"

Emily pointed to Teddy and said, "Yes ma'am, that's him sitting right there."

Jill looked at the jury and said, "Let the record show Miss Baker pointed to the defendant, Teddy Francisco."

Turning back to Emily, Jill asked, "Are you positive that man is one of the two men you saw arguing that morning?"

"Yes ma'am, that's him. I'm certain he was there."

Louis Franklin did his best to discredit and challenge Emily's testimony during his cross examination in an attempt to plant some doubt. But Emily held firm and insisted she clearly saw both men together that morning. By the end of his cross, Emily had won over the jury.

Jill's final witness was County Coroner Bob Jenkins. He explained the origin of the photo Jill presented earlier showing the positions of Emily, Jorge and Teddy. He also testified the actual distance between them, based on his own measurement, matched Emily's estimate.

With no further questions from Franklin, Jenkins was excused from the witness box. Jill stood up and said, "Your honor, the prosecution rests."

When they returned from the lunch break, Judge Templeton called the defense. Louis was out of options. The damage was already done, and he knew it. After Emily's convincing testimony, he couldn't put Teddy on the stand now, even if he wanted to. Without any credible witnesses to testify on Teddy's behalf, Louis was only left with his closing argument.

The defense rested and court was adjourned for the day.

In her closing on Thursday morning, Jill highlighted the evidence against Teddy and hammered home Emily's eyewitness testimony that identified Teddy and linked him to the port surveillance video. She ended by telling the jury, based on all the evidence presented to them, Teddy Francisco was guilty of the brutal murder of Jorge Rodriguez beyond any reasonable doubt.

Before the trial started, Louis tried to get the first-degree murder charge reduced to second-degree. But there was no way any lawyer, even the great Louis Franklin, could credibly explain away the surveillance video of a double-tap execution to the head of Jorge Rodriguez after he was already face-down on the concrete entrance lanes to the port's back security gates.

Louis knew he was beaten before he started his closing argument, but did his best one last time. He insisted the prosecution's evidence against Teddy was totally circumstantial and dismissed Emily's testimony as suspect and simply not credible. He finished by giving the jury a classroom tutorial on reasonable doubt and told them they must find his client not guilty.

The jury was given the case after lunch to begin their deliberations in the jury room. By the end of the day, the quick verdict was unanimous.

Teddy Francisco was found guilty of the first-degree murder of Jorge Rodriguez.

Epilogue

January 2019

In the three months since the end of Teddy's trial and the arrest of Joseph Camino, Emily's life had begun to get back to normal. She returned to her classroom and was welcomed with open arms by the students and teachers at Mt. Pleasant Elementary. Chuck was back on the road in the *Chucktown Special* hauling containers from the port, and John returned to his job on the docks.

The news media frenzy over their safe return had finally died down, and Emily began running again. She still planned to run her first marathon in Charleston at the end of January. She and Richard were engaged on New Year's Eve, and Steve agreed to walk her down the aisle.

It was Emily's idea to get together as many of the people who took part in their rescue as possible to personally thank them. Chuck asked Marge Mason, his friend and waitress at T.W. Graham, to ask the owner of the popular McClellanville restaurant if he would be willing to open for a private party. When Marge told the owner what was being planned, he not only agreed, but told Marge there would be no charge for hosting the party. Since the restaurant was normally closed on Mondays, the date was set for Monday evening, January 17.

Emily had already confirmed the date with Chuck and John. All three of them had vowed to stay in touch with each other after their ordeal had formed an unbreakable bond that would last a lifetime. To help with the cost of food and drinks, she suggested they each kick in the $1,000 that was in the safety deposit boxes they had retrieved at the Bank of Charleston. Chuck and John quickly agreed it was the perfect way to use the money.

Chuck even offered to drive Emily to the party in the *Chucktown Special.* After they both had a laugh, she told him she'd already promised to ride with Richard and Aunt Marie.

Emily had earlier written a heartfelt letter to Steve, thanking him for his persistence in finding her and her two new friends, especially when she began to lose hope on the Outer Banks with no way out. Steve loved the idea of the party, and she emailed him a list of the people she wanted to invite. She also asked him for suggestions and contact information for others who were involved in his year-long murder investigation and the search and rescue operation on the Outer Banks.

When Emily arrived at the restaurant with Richard and Marie an hour before the party was scheduled, Chuck was already there and introduced them to Marge and Chuck's best friend, George Cooper. Each table on the side porch was topped with place tags and fresh flowers.

Aunt Marie and Richard sat on both sides of Emily at one end. Steve and Janet, Dale, Chief Hartman, Chief Zimmer, and Hilton Head Chief Calhoun, were at the other end. Billy and Molly sat across from John and Mandy, Billy's now former client. George sat next to Chuck, and Marge insisted on helping to serve everybody some of the best seafood in the Lowcountry.

Emily and Steve personally greeted all twenty-five guests as they arrived. Emily hugged her school principal, Mary McCarthy, when she came through the door. Behind her was Janice Peterson, the office manager of her apartment complex who was with Steve when he discovered Emily's copy of the letter in her mailbox that jump-started the search for her.

Peterson asked Emily, "What made you think of mailing that letter to yourself?"

Emily explained, "I knew I was in trouble and believed someone was watching my every move. I figured out a way to secretly copy the letter at my school and mail the copy to myself in hopes someone would eventually get around to opening my mailbox. Detective Harris told me he guessed what I was up to as soon as he saw the hand-written envelope addressed to myself, even before he opened it. He told me you were a big help."

Peterson said, "Well, I didn't exactly agree to open it on the spot, but Steve quickly got the search warrant I asked for before he opened it and found the letter and your note. Without that letter, I'm not sure what would've happened. Steve told me that was the lead he needed to eventually find you. You were very brave."

When Dale arrived, he gave Emily a bear hug and said, "You had us going there for a while, young lady. Lucky for you, you also had a bulldog detective in your corner who refused to give up until he found you. Steve has told me all about you, and I'm glad to finally thank you in person for your role in helping to convict Mr. Francisco and arrest the man responsible for your abduction."

Emily moved closer so no one could overhear them and said very quietly, "Thank you, Agent Hawkins. Could you do me a favor?"

"Sure, if I can. Just name it."

She moved outside, away from the restaurant door, and Dale followed her. "I don't know whether this is even allowed or if it can be done." She took a plain envelope from her purse. Inside was a personal note to Jamison. "I just wanted to let Jamison and his parents know I've been thinking about them and praying they're well and will remain safe until Mr. Camino's trial."

Keeping his voice down, Dale replied, "I'm not sure, but I know someone who works in the department that handles the witness protection program. I'll see what's possible, no promises, but I don't think it will be a problem."

She nodded and shook his hand. "Thank you very much. Detective Harris told us without Jamison's help in the end, we might not have made it."

Port security managers Joe Cartwright, Rob Campbell, and Fred Waters arrived together, followed by Jill Carrington, who once more thanked Emily for her crucial testimony that helped convict Teddy. Mt. Pleasant Police Sergeant Buddy Evans and Charleston County Coroner Bob Jenkins, who were both at the Rodriguez murder scene with Steve at the start of it all, came in behind Jill.

The drinks were flowing, and the lively conversations continued among old and new friends throughout the restaurant before everyone began taking their seats on the porch. After the key lime pie was served, Emily stood up and the room became silent.

"Chuck, John, and I have a lot of people to thank tonight, and I just wanted to say how grateful we are to all of you for your prayers and never giving up on us." After wiping away a tear as her emotions were getting the best of her, she looked over at Steve. "Detective Harris saved our lives. If it wasn't for his optimism, his experience, his determination, and friends like all of you, the three of us might not be here to thank each of you from the bottom of our hearts."

Steve stood up and began clapping loudly, and everyone rose to join him. Emily Baker, Chuck Wilson, and John Simpson were finally back home and among friends, exactly where they belonged.

Two weeks later, Emily finished the Charleston Marathon.

***

On Monday, September 16, 2019, nearly a year after Joseph Camino's arrest in Charleston, his trial began in the Wilkie D. Ferguson Jr., United States Courthouse on 1st Avenue in Miami. A dozen federal drug charges, including conspiracy, obstruction of justice, and a list of related organized crime felonies, were added to the government's charges of the attempted murder of Harrison and Charlotte Walters and the kidnapping of Emily, Chuck, and John.

The prosecution witness list included Jamison, Harrison and Charlotte Walters, Jake Thomas, Mark Davis, Dale Hawkins and Steve Harris. Mark and Jake had both accepted the FBI's request to remain in the Camino organization and continued to feed Dale whatever new information they could gather about the cartel until Camino's trial.

In exchange for his damaging testimony against Camino, including his attempted murder of Jamison's parents, Jake was given the same immunity agreement and WITSEC protection as Jamison and his parents. Art Winston, who had cut a similar deal with the FBI for his involvement in the illegal drug operation at Auto Warehouse, also testified against Camino.

Emily, Chuck and John each took the stand to recount their abduction and confinement on the Outer Banks that started with the anonymous letter.

Ellis Gordon, named by Mark as the cartel inside man at the Bank of Charleston where Camino's kidnapping scheme began, had still not been found. Speculation by the DEA and FBI was that Gordon had either been taken out by the cartel or fled the country under an assumed name and was hiding off the grid.

The origin of the now infamous letter was traced back to Camino in an encrypted email he had sent to Mark with an attachment of his original draft of the letter. The prosecution's case on the kidnapping charge was sealed when the jury heard Mark's secret recording of a phone call Camino made to him with detailed verbal instructions for the entire scheme. On the stand, Mark told the court he made the recording to protect himself and Jamison if Camino's plan went south.

Steve also testified about the discovery of the letter that Emily had covertly mailed to herself, which ultimately led to the rescue mission on the Outer Banks.

The trial judge granted the federal prosecution team a request by the FBI and the Marshal Service to honor Jamison's witness protection status during the trial. Jamison's explosive testimony as Camino's personal assistant, as well as a vigorous cross examination by Camino's lead defense attorney Louis Franklin, were conducted via a live video conference set up in the courtroom.

The sensational trial was in its fifth week, with wall-to-wall news coverage on every cable news channel, when the jury finally began to deliberate Camino's fate. Dale attended as much of the trial as he could in person, before and after his own testimony, and Steve flew back to Miami the day before the verdict was announced to be there with Dale.

A year after Hurricane Florence made landfall along the North Carolina coast, another Florence came calling two thousand miles to the west. When the trial was over, Joseph Camino was found guilty on all counts and sentenced to life at the Federal Supermax ADX Prison in Florence, Colorado.

Acknowledgments

Fortunately for me, my wife Kathy is an avid fiction reader. After kicking around the central idea for the book with her to make sure it had enough legs to drive the story, Kathy proofread each chapter after it was written. Her comments and suggestions throughout the writing process were invaluable to help me keep the multiple story threads and timelines on track. Her positive reinforcement and encouragement also kept me going throughout the entire journey to the finish line.

The moment of truth came when I made a big ask of some people whose opinions I value, to read the manuscript and give me their honest feedback. They responded with some excellent comments and suggestions to improve the book.

Special thanks to the initial readers and good friends Carly David, Tom Iafrate, and my sister Patty McFadden. Carly's enthusiastic response to the manuscript confirmed for me that the ambitious storyline worked. Tom's initial editing suggestions were extremely helpful, and Patty's diligent proofreading of every sentence was welcome and much appreciated.

During a visit to Kathy's sister Maureen Simpson and her husband Paul in Colorado when the manuscript was in still in its early stages, Paul read the first 40 pages and offered some valuable insight. His positive comments after reading the final manuscript were icing on the cake.

Family friend Steve Biel, an excellent writer in his own right, gave me some important advice that helped improve the narrative and enhance the backstory of one of the important characters.

After my own self-editing of the initial manuscript, Winnie Van Meir and Jane Ellen Herron, both fellow members of Stella Maris Church, offered to read the manuscript. Their comments improved the final draft.

Sincere thanks also to Austin Macauley Publishers for offering a first-time novelist an opportunity to turn his manuscript into this book. My compliments to their entire staff who made it happen.

A final thanks to the rest of my family and friends for their interest as I worked on this project. Your support meant a lot. I love you all!

Art Zimmerman 2024

Art Zimmerman was born in Chester, Pennsylvania, and grew up in the nearby rural town of Aston as the oldest of seven children. After graduating with a B.A. in Journalism from Penn State University, he began a lifelong career in the advertising agency business in Pittsburgh and later New York City, before moving to Charleston, South Carolina, and starting his own ad agency. An avid runner, he has finished 40 marathons, which are featured in his book *One Runner's Personal Journey* published in 2020. Art and his wife, Kathy, currently reside in Mount Pleasant, South Carolina.

Made in United States
North Haven, CT
02 May 2025

68514911R00167